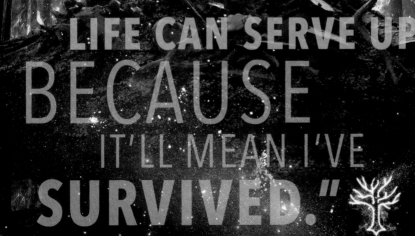

TO **FEEL** EVERY OF PAIN AND HAPPINESS

LIFE CAN SERVE UP, BECAUSE IT'LL MEAN I'VE **"SURVIVED."**

A DARKEST MINDS COLLECTION

THROUGH THE DARK

ALEXANDRA BRACKEN

HYPERION

Los Angeles   New York

First Hardcover Edition, October 2015
First Paperback Edition, January 2018
10 9 8 7 6 5 4 3 2 1
FAC-025438-18166

Printed in the United States of America

This book is set in Avenir Next Condensed, Edlund,
Minister Std/Monotype
Designed by Marci Senders

Library of Congress Control Number for Hardcover Edition: 2015023543
ISBN 978-1-368-04215-4

Visit www.hyperionteens.com

For the dreamers, believers, fighters, and readers who have been part of this journey from the beginning, with all my love

CONTENTS

PREFACE

I HAD JUST FINISHED A FIRST DRAFT OF *NEVER FADE*, book two in the Darkest Minds series, and was settling in for a bit of a writing break when my editor, Emily, e-mailed to ask if I'd have any interest in working on a novella for the series. Truthfully, I was a little daunted by the idea of stepping outside of Ruby's point of view; after all, so much of my understanding of her world was tied up in *her* and how she saw it. But I quickly realized that this was an incredible opportunity for me to really explore what was happening in this world, and to do so outside of the filter of her fears and limited knowledge. Even better, I finally had a way to show readers what was happening in the United States outside of the main story line, and give insight into the struggles others—not just the kids—were facing. And so, the idea for *In Time*, the story of a young man fighting to start off as a skip tracer, was born. This was followed a year later by *Sparks Rise*, meant to give readers a glimpse of what life at Thurmond was like after Ruby escaped, and now, exclusive to this bind-up, *Beyond the Night*, the story of the chaos and confusion in the weeks after the original trilogy ends.

For best reading, I recommend this order: *The Darkest Minds*, *In Time*, *Never Fade*, *Sparks Rise*, *In the Afterlight*, *Beyond the Night*. Or you could simply read all of the novellas after you've finished the novels—these side stories have never been required reading to understand what's happening in the novels, but they do weave themselves into the main story lines in unexpected, and, I hope, exciting ways.

After years of being asked by readers for a bind-up of the novellas, I'm so pleased that *Through the Dark* is finally here. To me, the title perfectly encapsulates the message of these novellas, and I think the series overall: that no matter how terrifying or dangerous the world may seem, there is still a place for hope in it, and the way through it is by protecting and loving one another.

In
Time

PROLOGUE

SOMETIMES, EVEN WHEN THE ROADS ARE QUIET AND the others are asleep, she lets herself worry she made the wrong choice.

It's not that she doesn't like the group—she does. Really. They stick together and they play it smart, driving on side streets as much as they can instead of the highways, with the open, endless fear those offer. They're never mean unless they've gone without food or sleep or both for too long, or when they're scared. When they camp for the night, they sleep in a great big circle, and the girls like telling stories about the kids they knew in Virginia, at East River. They all laugh, but she has trouble putting the faces to the names. She can't remember where the lake was in relation to the fire pit, and she wasn't there that one time they all put on a play for one another. She wasn't there because she was with her friends. She was in a different car, a better one, a happier one. Because when the girls stop telling these stories, the same ones over and over again, there's only silence. And she misses the warmth of her friends' voices, even if they were just whispering, lying and saying it would all be okay.

5

Maybe it's bad—she doesn't know—but secretly she's glad no one expects her to tell stories of her own. That way she gets to keep them to herself, tucked tight against her heart. She presses her hand there when she's scared, when she wants to pretend it's them teasing and laughing and shouting around her, and not the others. When she wants to feel safe.

She keeps her hand there all the time. Now.

The mountains around her are flying by and the girls are screaming that they need to go faster, faster, faster. She sees the car through the back windshield of the SUV. The man hanging out the passenger-side window looks like he is aiming the gun directly at her. The driver has a face like he'd be willing to drive through a firestorm to get to them, and she hates him for it.

She wants her voice to join with the others' screaming and crying. The words are lodged in her throat. The boy behind the wheel needs to stop the SUV, slam on the brakes, let the monsters chasing them get out of their own car and think they've won. We are five to their two, she thinks, and if we can catch them by surprise—

But their SUV is suddenly flying like it's gone up a ramp. The seat belt locks over her chest hard enough to steal her breath in that one second they're in the air—then they're spinning, the glass is smashing, the car's frame is twisting, and not even she can hold in her screams.

ONE

LISTEN, NO MATTER WHAT ANYONE TELLS YOU, NO ONE really wants this job.

The hours are endless and the pay is crap. No, I take that back. It's not the pay that's crap. There's a sweet little penny in it for you if you can hook yourself a decent-sized fish. The only thing is, of course, that everybody's gone and overfished the damn rivers. You can drop in as many hooks as you want, buy yourself the shiniest bait, but there just aren't enough of them still in the wild to fatten up your skeletal wallet.

That's the first thing Paul Hutch told me when I met him at the bar this afternoon. We're here to do business, but Hutch decides that it's a teaching moment, too. Why do people constantly feel like they have to lecture me on life? I'm twenty-five, but it's like the minute you take actual kids out of the picture, anyone under the age of thirty suddenly becomes "son," or "kid," or "boy," because these people, the "real adults," they have to have someone to make small. I'm not interested in playing to someone's imagination, or propping up their sense of self-worth. It makes me sick—like I'm trying to digest my own stomach. I'm no one's *boy*, and I don't respond to *son*, either. I'm not your damn dead kid.

Someone's smoking a cigarette in one of the dark booths behind us. I hate coming here almost as much as I hate the usual suspects who haunt the place. Everything in the Evergreen is that tacky emerald vinyl and dark wood. I think they want it to look like a ski lodge, but the result is something closer to a poor man's Oktoberfest, only with more sad, drunk geezers and fewer busty chicks holding frothy mugs of beer.

There are pictures of white-capped mountains all around, posters that are about as old as I am. I know, because our mountain hasn't had a good snow in fifteen years, or enough demand to open in five. I used to run the ski lifts up all the different courses after school, even during the summer, when people from the valley just wanted to come up and do some hiking in temperatures below 115 degrees. I tell myself, *At least you don't have to deal with the snotty tourists anymore*—the ones who acted like they'd never seen a real tree before, and rode their brakes all the way down Humphreys' winding road. I don't miss them at all.

What I miss is the paycheck.

Hutch looks like he crawled out of a horse's ass—smells like it, too. For a while he was working at one of those tour group companies that let you ride the donkeys down into the Grand Canyon. They closed the national parks, though, and the owner had to move all the animals back to Flagstaff, before ultimately selling them off. There's no work for Hutch to do there anymore, but I'm pretty sure the woman lets him sleep out in the stables.

He's been here for hours already; he's looking soggy around the edges, and when I walked into the dark bar, he glanced up all bleary and confused, like a newborn chick sticking its head out of an egg. His hair is somehow receding and too long at once, the wisps halfheartedly tied back with a strip of leather.

Trying to speed things up, I slide a crumpled wad of money his way. The stack looks a lot more impressive than it actually is. I've been living off tens and twenties for so long I'm convinced they stopped printing the bigger bills.

"It's not that I don't think you can do it, son," Hutch says, studying the bottom of his pint. "It just sounds easier than it is."

I should be listening harder than I am. If anyone knows what the job's really like, it's him. Old Hutch tried for six months to be a skip tracer, and the prize he won for that misadventure was a burnt-up, mutilated, four-fingered hand. He likes to tell everyone some kid got to him, but seeing as he's managed to burn down two trailers by falling asleep with a cigarette in his hand, I'm inclined to doubt it. Still, he milks it for all he can. The sight of the gimp hand gets him sympathy drinks from out-of-towners stopping in the Evergreen. Some extra nickels and dimes, too, when he's holding a cup at the corner of Route 66 and Leroux Street, pretending his white ass is a military vet from the Navajo Nation. Somehow he thinks that combination elevates him over the rest of us bums.

"Can I have the keys?" I ask. "Where'd you park it?"

He ignores me, humming along to the Eagles' "Take It Easy," which this bar has on loop apparently for no reason other than the fact that Arizona is mentioned once in it.

I shouldn't be buying this truck from him. I know there's going to be something wrong with it; it's older than I am. But this is the only one I can afford, and I have to get out of here. I have to get out of this town.

"Another one," he says stubbornly, trying to flag down Amy,

the bartender, who is doing her absolute best to deny his miserable existence. She and I have talked about this before—it's hard to look at him. His teeth got bad over the years, and his cheeks sag so low they're practically hanging like wattles against his neck. He's only forty-five, but he already looks like the after photo of a meth addict—the mug shot of the killer on one of those crime TV shows they're always rerunning. His breath alone is like a punch to the face.

I used to like Hutch a lot. He got to know my dad when he dropped off fresh produce at the restaurant. Now it's like . . . I don't know how to explain it so it makes sense. It's like he's a cautionary tale, only one you know you're speeding toward without brakes. A glimpse of the future, or whatever. I just look at him and I know that if I don't get out of this place, I'm going to be this old man who's not even old, but smells like he pisses himself on a regular basis. The guy who spins and spins and spins on his barstool, like he's riding the old carousel at the fairgrounds.

Hutch slides the key out of his pocket but slams his hand down over it when I reach for it. His other hand traps mine, and then he's looking at me with these wet, feverish eyes. "I loved your daddy so much, Gabe, and I know he wouldn't want this for you."

"He tapped out, which means he doesn't get a vote," I say, ripping my hand free. "I paid you. Now tell me where you parked it."

For a second, I'm sure he's going to tell me he parked it at the mall, and I'm going to have to walk my ass up the highway for an hour to get there. Instead, he shrugs and says finally, "On the north end of Wheeler Park. On Birch."

I slide down from my stool, finishing off the pint I just paid fifteen bucks for. Hutch is still watching me with these eyes like I can't describe. He pauses, then says, "But I'm telling you now, you ever find someone who likes the job, you better goddamn run the other way because you're looking at the real monster. You're looking right at him."

I take my time walking to downtown—excuse me, "Historic Downtown," they call it, like it needs that distinction because there's another, more important downtown in Flagstaff, with skyscrapers. I take my time because the sun is out and it's a beautiful blue-sky morning—the kind that usually makes everything beneath the sky seem that much shittier in comparison, but not today.

Out of the corner of my eye, I see the old train station where my dad and I used to lay pennies to be mauled on the tracks. For the first time in years, I consider crossing the street to sit on one of the benches, just because I know I'll never do it again. I don't know how I'd pass the time besides sit, though—what few trains are still running don't take this route anymore. I've been doing a lot of that lately. Sitting around, doing nothing, thinking about work but not finding it. I think that's the problem, all that sitting; it leads to thinking about all this bullshit, about the parks they had to turn into graveyards, about Dad's restaurant's still being empty after all these years, about the fact that we had to move to a new trailer because we couldn't get the blood off the walls of the old one.

Damn Hutch, I think. The only thing Dad wanted was an out.

I head past the boarded-up shops. When I was a kid—I use that phrase a lot, *when I was a kid*. That was, what? Fifteen years ago? Are you still a kid when you're ten? I guess it doesn't matter, but it was right around then that this part of town was done up nice for the tourists. The buildings are practically ancient by Arizona standards. Dad told me most of them, including the red brick one with the white turrets, used to be old hotels. Now they're bead shops, or they sell mystic crystal bullshit from Sedona or fake petrified wood. *Those* are the shops that survived the economy's face-plant.

There's no one out wandering around this morning, and little traffic. That's the only reason I can hear the chanting three blocks from where the "protest" is taking place. I think about cutting up a block and going the long way, but the city commissioned this horrible memorial wall mural there that makes my skin crawl every time I pass it. In it, there are these five kids all running around this flower field. One of them is on a swing hanging from a cloud. It's called *Their Playground Is Heaven*, if you ever make the trek up to Flagstaff and are in the mood to hate humanity that much more.

The mom squad is out in full force in front of City Hall. Of course. It's a day that ends with *y*. Back a few years ago, I thought they might accomplish something just by the sheer number of bake sale goods they were producing and selling to raise money for the BRING THEM HOME fund. Now it's obvious that was never the point.

I keep my head down and my hat pulled low, ignoring the squatty woman who rushes up in her too-tight mom jeans and bright yellow MOTHERS AGAINST CAMPS shirt, shoving her clipboard in my path.

"Have you signed the petition to *Bring Them Home*?"
Not really, lady.
"Would you like to sign the petition?"
As much as I'd like to swallow a bowl of broken glass.
"Why not?"

Because I'm not super into the idea of having a couple thousand little freaks running around the country blowing shit up.

I take the clipboard and squiggle on one of the empty boxes, hoping it's enough to get her to leave me alone. What's really amazing to me is that despite the fact that they managed to grow their numbers, it seems like they're doing less. Even with the addition of the spin-off group, Dads Against Camps, I know for a fact they haven't gotten any information out of the government.

They have to know how pathetic they all look, right? They stubbornly gather here like cat hair to a black sweater, but there aren't any politicians in City Hall these days—they just bus folks up from Phoenix every once in a while to make sure the town hasn't dissolved into chaos or to barricade it off if it has. The parents just can't bring themselves to break the pattern. Every day it's the same scene of them standing around and talking to each other, hugging and crying and cupping ragged-edged photos of their freaks between their hands. These people—the "real adults," my mom calls them—they sit around looking for forgiveness from the guilty. But if they really wanted to accomplish something, they'd be down in Phoenix. They'd be in D.C. or New York, trying to find whatever hole President Gray dug for himself, to make him answer for what he's done.

They don't even seem to notice every last bit of their freedom has been stripped from them, from *all* of us; they just care about *the kids, the kids, the kids.*

I want to tell Mrs. Roberts to stop being such a damn hypocrite—to tell Mr. Monroe, and Mrs. Gonzalez, and Mrs. Hart that they did this to themselves. They sent their "babies" to school that day and then stood around the playground fence with the rest of us, watching as the black uniforms ushered the freaks onto the buses. They regret it; now they see what most of us suspected all along. Those buses were only going one direction: away from them.

Here's the thing I don't understand: The government tells you over and over again, through the news, through the papers, on the radio, that the only way these freaks are going to survive is if they receive this rehabilitation treatment in these camps. They even roll out the president's kid to prove that it "works," parading him around the country in some kind of celebration tour that's clearly designed to soften people's attitudes about sending their freaks away. Okay, sure, fine.

But after a year or two passes, more and more freaks are affected. More are sent to these rehab camps by desperate parents. But in the meantime, we're not seeing any "cured" freaks coming out of them. Not in year three, or year four, or year five. If these parents had been paying attention from the beginning, not running around like a band of panicked chickens, all of them scrambling for the last scrap of hope, none of them willing to be the one to stand up and question it, they would have seen the lie a mile away. They would never have registered their freaks in that online database, the one the government basically just turned into a network to help skip tracers and PSFs later collect the freaks that weren't sent willingly.

It's been six years. They're not coming back, and even if they were, look at what these "real adults" have let this country become. Why would they want to bring a kid back into a place like this? Where the newspaper they'll read is filled with lies, and every step they take and word they speak will be monitored. The kind of world where they can work their whole lives, only to be slowly smothered by knowing they'll never amount to anything and things will never get better for them.

I just want them to admit that they did this to themselves, that they let Gray take their kids, but they also let him steal hope for the future. I'm so sick of having to feel sorry for these people when the rest of us are suffering, too.

I just want them to admit to themselves we've lost more than a few freaks.

I just want us all to stop lying.

There's no gas in the old blue truck. Of course. I have to hike all over town begging people for a quarter of a liter here and another quarter there, and all the while these people are looking at me like I've asked them to set themselves on fire. I know the right people to talk to, though. They were the smart ones who saved up each gas ration the National Guard doled out by the old Sinclair gas station. I remember waiting under the sign—the big green dinosaur—shivering because it was five below, and the entire city was lined up down the highway, waiting their turn. About two years ago, the National Guard just stopped coming, and when they disappeared, so did the gas.

So did a lot of things.

They've turned the old fairgrounds into a trailer park and campground. Ten years ago if you had asked me to imagine a world where thousands of people were crammed into a few miles of space while thousands of houses sat empty and locked up by banks . . . I don't know what I would have thought. Probably that you were talking about a bad movie.

Hutch says each kid can bring in around ten thousand dollars.

Ten thousand dollars. One or two aren't going to be enough to buy myself a real house or anything like that, but it might be enough to do one of those two-year university degree programs. With a certificate, I might be able to find a steady job in another town, and maybe that'll mean an opportunity to own some kind of home, even if it's in the far future. Staying here, I wouldn't have a choice.

I triple-check to make sure the truck is locked before I start trudging through the muddy grass toward home. Already I sense the curious eyes following me, taking a second look at my truck. Considering. I've been there. We've all been there. It's always easier to take something than work for it—but I don't know how many people want a thirty-year-old gas-guzzler with paint rusting off in huge clumps.

And anyway, I'm not going to be here long enough for them to swipe it. In and out. I told myself that the whole drive over. In and out.

The door to our trailer creaks as I open it and rattles as it slams behind me. It was a gift from the United States of America, but everywhere there are parts stamped with MADE IN CHINA. The aluminum sides are so thin they pop in and out depending on which way the wind is blowing.

There's not much room beyond the space for the bunk beds at the back and a small kitchenette, but Mom's figured out a way to hook up a fist-sized TV on the fold-down table where we're supposed to eat. No one's got the cash or time to create any- thing new anymore, so it's either news or reruns all the time. Right now, it looks like an episode of *Wheel of Fortune* from the 1990s. Sometimes I think I like the days we have no power better, because that's the only thing that breaks her out of her trance long enough for her to remember to eat and wash her hair.

She doesn't even look up as I come in—but I see it right away. She's taken my original draft notice and taped it back up on the small fridge. I keep ripping it and she keeps taping it, and I keep explaining and she keeps ignoring me.

"The PSF recruiters were by again," she says, not breaking her gaze on the TV. "I told them about your problem and they said you should come in and be double-checked. You know, just to be sure."

I close my eyes and count to twenty, then stop when I remember that's what Dad used to do. Mom's brittle blond hair looks like it hasn't been brushed in weeks, and she's wearing a pale pink robe over a Mickey Mouse shirt and jeans. Otherwise known as what she slept in last night and the night before. I open the fridge just to be sure I'm right—and there it is. The endless, gaping nothing. We ate the last can of soup last night for dinner, so if she didn't go out to get her boxed rations this morning—

"Why do you smell like smoke?" she asks suddenly. "You been at the bar? Your daddy's old bar?"

I walk toward the bunk at the back, lift my small backpack off it, and sling it over my shoulder. "I'm heading out."

"Did you hear what I said about the PSFs, kid?" she asks, her gaze drifting back down to the TV. Her voice getting real, real small.

"Did you hear what I told you the last ten thousand times you brought it up?" I say, hating that anger is winning again. "They won't take me. The National Guard, either."

I think she's hoping they'll get desperate enough eventually to want me. But the past five times I've met with the recruiter, they've told me the knee I blew out playing soccer, and the screws that the doctors put in to reconstruct it, disqualify me. I've tried everything—forging paperwork, trying to apply in another county. It doesn't work. They know that people want in—it's the only guaranteed paycheck left in this country. You serve your four years in hell and you get a check each and every month.

"All your friends, though," she says, "can't they help you get in?"

I haven't heard from them in four years, since they went into service. Apparently you put on the uniform and you get sucked into some kind of black hole. The only reason any of us know they're alive is that the government keeps cutting these checks and sending them home to their families, keeps sending a few extra cans in each of their ration boxes.

"I'm leaving," I say, tightening my grip on my backpack. My keys jangle in my pocket as I move, loud enough for her to look up again.

"What did you do?" she demands, like she has any right to. "You took that college money? You bought that truck?"

I laugh. Really, truly laugh. Eight hundred bucks isn't enough even to think about college, never mind apply. It was expensive before; now it's just stupidly expensive. Not to mention there're only a few universities left. Northern Arizona shut down, the University of Arizona shut down, most of the New Mexico and Utah schools, too. There are some state schools still open in California, I think, and one of the University of Texas campuses. I'd be okay in Texas. I'm not delusional enough to think I could afford one of the few fancy private schools back east, like Harvard.

Two freaks are really all I need. If it turns out I'm good at this, then great. I'll save what I get from freaks three, four, and five. The real problem is Mom and the rest of the people in this town don't think big. They're the kind of folks who are too satisfied with the small hand life's dealt to think that a bigger pot might be out there.

They can't see I'm investing in my future. They've already invested too much in this town.

"You're a damn fool," she whispers as I kick the door open. "You'll be back. You have no idea how to take care of yourself, kid. When this blows up in your face, don't come dragging your ass back here!" And when that doesn't work, she gets mean. "You're a goddamn fool, and you'll end up just like your daddy."

She trails me the entire way back to my truck, shouting whatever nasty word her mind can drum up fast enough. She knows the truth as well as I do: that I've been taking care of her all this time, and without me, she's not going to last.

And I don't care. I really don't. I haven't had a parent since Dad blew out the back of his skull.

All that spewing draws eyes and interest from the sea of dirty silver trailers around us. Good. I want them to see I'm leaving. I want them to know I did what no one else could. They can tell the story to their neighbors, spread it around town in whispers of awe. The last sight of me they'll have is the back of my head as I'm driving away. When they talk about me years from now, only one thing they say will really matter.

I got out.

TWO

AFTER TWO WEEKS OF HUSTLING UP AND DOWN THE I-17, busting my ass to get my first score, I'm forced to admit that at least one thing Hutch said was true: the other skip tracers have overhunted these freaks to the point of extinction.

Don't get me wrong, I didn't expect to walk up to a tree, shake it, and have a few freaks come tumbling out. I got the sense years ago that the ones who dodged the rehab camp pickups were few and far between. It's just simple statistics. When you lose 98 percent of a population and then that remaining 2 percent is divided 75 percent in camps to 25 percent on the run, you're . . . working with a smaller number.

A real small number.

I slam the door to my room behind me, ignoring the dirty look I get from the old lady who runs the place. She's outside monitoring the water meters, making sure none of us are going over our allotted amount, which isn't that much given that we're only paying fifty bucks a week to stay in this place. Her two middle-aged sons help her manage the riffraff that's always blowing into and out of her joint; they collect the rent and make sure nobody's trying to turn tricks or sell something they shouldn't be selling at a proper business establishment. The sign outside says this place is a motel, but they've been running it like short-stay apartments ever since the economy crashed.

The motel was built in the 1960s and clearly hasn't been renovated since then. It's a two-story dirt-brown complex stripped down to the bare necessities, with a few pots of dying flowers scattered around to freshen the place up. But it's so damn hot and dry this summer, even up in Cottonwood, these violets never stood a chance.

"You coming back to pay for your two weeks?" the old lady calls as I unlock the truck. Her name is Beverly, but she wears her dead husband's old bowling shirt day in and day out, and his name, according to the embroidery, was Phil. So naturally my brain calls her Phyllis.

"I'll be back tonight," I tell her. I'll have to be. Cottonwood is on the safer side and pretty rural, but Phyllis is so damn cutthroat about her profit that I wouldn't put it past her to throw me out and bring another person in if she doesn't have the cash in hand by sundown. Every once in a while I see her eyeing me, and I worry that she has some kind of freak ability of her own to tell that my wallet is getting down to nothing.

I give her a friendly wave as I pull away, then drop all but one finger as she turns back to her work.

Nice. Sticking it to the old lady.

I'm not stupid. I saved enough money to survive until I got through the first score, provided that first score came within a month or two. The thing I didn't exactly think through was how I was going to start looking. Hutch gave me his worn FUGITIVE PSI RECOVERY AGENT manual to use, but he sold all the tech that came with it for beer money when he got back to Flagstaff. That's the shittiest part of trying to get started: you have to find a kid and turn it in before you're officially registered in the skip tracer system. *Then* they give you that tablet that's hooked into their profile network. *Then* you can start earning points and moving up in the rankings. I read in the book that the more points you earn by adding sightings and good tips to the skip tracer network, the more access the government gives you to things like the Internet.

The Internet would make this about two thousand times easier, I think, turning onto the highway. My gas light is blinking, has been for days. I've worked out a system, though. I think I can stretch the tank at least another two outings.

I call it a system to make myself feel better about the fact that I'm hunting for clues in the most ass-backwards way imaginable. I drive to one of the nearby small towns, like Wickenburg or Sedona or Payson, and get out, leaving the truck somewhere I think people won't be tempted to try to steal it or jack the gas from my tank. I walk through the neighborhoods, making sure to swing by the local schools. People always seem to leave the MISSING posters there, tacked up along the rattling metal fences. Maybe they think the kids are hanging around the places they used to haunt and they'll see the flyers and think, *Man, I really should go home—Mom must really miss me.* I take them down one by one, collecting them so I can check them against the skip tracer system later. Once I have access to the network. Once I actually find a kid and bring it in.

One more day, I think, finish out the week. Then I'll suck it up and use whatever money I have left to buy gas and drive down to Phoenix. More neighborhoods, more abandoned buildings, millions of families—I should have better luck there. It just stings a little, you know? I don't like that I'm already having to compromise on my plan.

The only thing that ever seems to come easy these days is my shit luck.

I decide to take the I-17 south to Camp Verde today, for no other reason than I haven't hit it in a week. One of the gas stations there is still in business, though the place's real value is the steady stream of truck drivers flowing in and out of there, bringing gossip with them.

I switch off the AC to try to preserve gas, rolling down the window to let in some fresh air and sunshine. Dad used to say that it took effort to think good, positive thoughts, but it was easy to let your mind spiral to all the terrible outcomes, to worry about things that hadn't even come to pass yet. I see it now more than ever, because all I need to do is think about him, and I feel myself slipping. I start heading down that road of understanding why he did it. He was humiliated by losing the restaurant, I know he was, but it was more than that—it was that he knew that restaurant was the only life for him. And when the world took it from him, suddenly Dad was out of choices. He had us, and he couldn't afford to move himself somewhere else, let alone the three of us. We trapped him there, and he took the only out he thought was left for him.

I've taught myself the trick that when it starts to feel that way for me, too, I need to go outside and walk it off. I need to roll down a window and let the green, earthy scent come wash out the warm stink of blood that seems to be seared into my nose forever.

A red SUV flashes in my rearview mirror, pulling me off that black, ugly road and back onto the one in front of me. I do a double take, because the bastard behind the wheel is really, truly gunning it, almost like he's trying to escape the shadowed mountains behind him. A second later, it's flying by me, swerving to cut in front of me. The whole truck rocks as a beige sedan blows past me, following the first car at a speed that makes me instinctively pull my car onto the shoulder, even after both other cars have long since passed. My heart is slamming against my ribs, and I'm so pissed off about the asshole drivers, I'm still so stuck on that last image of Dad facedown in the old trailer, it takes me a second to recover.

Lame. I rub a hand across my forehead. Lame, lame, lame. If those assholes wanted to race, they could have picked a side road, where there was no chance of hitting anyone. Granted, the three of us are the only cars I've seen since I left Cottonwood, but still. Dying as collateral damage in a high-speed car accident is definitely not part of the plan.

"Move your ass," I mutter. "Jesus, you pansy . . ."

I turn on my blinker to merge back over before realizing how stupid that precaution is. I could drive down the center of the highway if I wanted to—so I do. Just to see what it feels like. And you know what? It actually feels pretty damn awesome, like I own the whole open stretch of valley in front of me, like I could—

I slam on my brakes, and my truck stops about five feet later.

The red SUV is flipped over, literally upside down, in the grassy median that separates the northbound and southbound lanes. It's smoking and two of the wheels are still treading against the air. Parked diagonally across the lanes is the beige sedan. Two men jump out, both of them wearing those tacky-looking hunter camo jackets, rifles out in front of them. One is the taller version of the other. Both have long, stringy dark hair that's gathered in clouds of frizz under their hats. They're fully bearded, and full bellied, and for a second I want to laugh. But that's when the girl appears.

She has a head of dark curls and is wearing a tank top and jeans. To her right is a short blonde, bundled up in an oversized black hoodie. Cowering behind them is an even younger girl, Asian, with long, flowing black hair. That one keeps trying to turn back to the SUV, but the blonde keeps grabbing her and pulling her in close to her side.

The guns are suddenly up and level with the men's, and one of them fires at the SUV's back window, shattering the glass. I can hear the girls scream and suddenly I'm out of the car, and all five of them are staring at me.

"Get the hell out of here!" one of the men shouts, his gun turned back toward me. I throw up my hands, because what the hell else am I supposed to do? None of this feels real. I'm seeing a kid and a teenager for the first time in six years, and it's like my brain can't understand it.

The girls bolt. Out of the corner of my eye, I see them go, cutting across the highway. The older one touches the hood of one of the cars that has been abandoned there, and its headlights flare to life—its engine roars. She makes this motion like she's sweeping the dust off it, and without any other warning, the car is shooting across the median toward the men—the skip tracers.

Holy shit.

You hear about the things these freaks can do, but you sort of figure that some of it has to be exaggerated. There's no way someone can blink and set a house on fire, right? And that girl, she just . . . she just . . .

The skip tracers have to dive out of the way to avoid getting hit, but whatever crazy power resuscitated the car suddenly blinks out, and it rolls to a slow stop on the opposite shoulder. I don't think it was ever meant to hit them, only pack enough of a punch to serve as a distraction. I'm half horrified, half amazed that it works.

"They're running," I yell at the men, throwing my arm out in their direction. The girls are trying for the shelter of the Tonto National Forest.

The men chase after them on foot, shooting me these looks like it's *my* fault. I don't know, maybe it is. Maybe I should be running after the freaks, too, see if I can swipe one of them for myself. There's nothing in the handbook that says you can't, or that you get docked points. It seems like it could be dangerous business to find yourself suddenly being hunted by the same people you just stole from.

But they could have other stuff I need.

I'm not proud of it, okay? But I go and look anyway, peering through the sun's glare on the driver-side window to see if they left anything valuable lying out. There's a small wad of money in one of the drink holders, but I don't see any of their tech. Figures.

The door is unlocked, which pretty much makes the decision for me. I slide the money into my back pocket, giving a salute in their direction. They won't miss it, I tell myself. They're going to have thirty grand coming their way if they nab those girls. Those *things*.

The handbook tells you not to think of them like they're actual humans. That's easier after watching the psychic ninja jump-start that car and send it flying, but I still don't know that I can follow the advice. One of the skip tracers they quoted said that he likes to think of them as dogs—puppies, really. Living creatures that aren't like us but still have needs. I'll start there. Puppies—no, puppies are too cute. I'll stick with freaks.

And it's the strangest thing, because as I walk by the flipped SUV, I swear I can hear a dog whimpering nearby. I tell myself to keep walking, to get the hell out of here before the beards make it back and notice what's missing, but my eyes slide toward the dark figure in the SUV's driver's seat. With the glass blown out of the windshield, I can see the unnatural angle of the kid's neck. His long dreads fall around the place where his head is jammed against the car's roof, but they don't cover the jagged shards of glass embedded in his throat. Blood is still spilling down over his chin, gliding over his dark skin, into his open, unblinking eyes.

Not even cold yet.

The body. The kid . . . the thing.

I remember being ten, bumming around behind Dad's restaurant after school with two of my friends. One afternoon we pushed all the garbage cans onto their sides because one of us had the genius idea of jumping over them with our bikes like the guys we'd seen on MTV—one of those stupid shows. Only, when we turned the first one over, there was a dead cat behind it. I will never in my life forget that damn cat. The way its gray fur was matted, coated with blood, the back half of its body broken by what I'd guess was a car. The three of us, we just sat there staring at it, taking turns trying to get close to it without puking. For hours.

And that cat was the first thing I thought of later that night when I found Dad's body.

What is it about horrible, violent things that capture us? I'd never seen a dead thing before that moment, but years later, it would be one funeral after another and everyone would want to know every detail about each one. The twenty-four-hour news stream would stop pretending like there were other stories to report. And all of us, we were hooked to the coverage of the hundreds, thousands, millions of deaths like junkies, waiting to see how bad it would get, drowning in it. And when the D.C. bombings happened, forget it. I stayed home from work for two weeks, overdosing on CNN.

There's a second of silence before the pounding starts and a small, pale hand begins slamming against the back passenger window. I feel my legs moving, running, bringing me around to the other side of the SUV, where the doors are hanging open.

There's a girl, maybe eleven years old at most, in the seat directly behind the driver, peering at me through the wreckage, her face streaked with blood. She's hanging upside down, struggling with her seat belt. The driver's seat looks almost broken in half, bowing back so that the small kid is pinned in place. For a second, I doubt my first impression and I think I'm looking at a boy. Her black hair is spiked out around her head like a pixie's, and it takes me a moment longer than it probably should to realize she—it—is wearing a bright pink dress.

The seat belt's jammed, I think. I'm dimly aware of my hand's reaching toward her—it, dammit—and all of a sudden I'm gripping the strap myself, trying to rip out the buckle by force. I climb inside to go at it from a better angle, and her look of relief turns to one of irritation—like, *Hey, asshole, if that was ever going to work, would I still be sitting here?*

Her face is pink with the blood rushing to it, but she managed to get her right leg free. She strains, stretching it out as far as it'll go, using her toe to point at the dead kid in the front seat. At the knife strapped to his hip. Damn, I think. Why don't I have a knife? And because she clearly thinks I'm an idiot, she makes a sawing motion with her hands against the part of the seat belt over her hips.

"Yeah, yeah, I get it," I mutter. I'm trying to ignore that voice in the back of my head, the one that sounds suspiciously like my dad. He's asking, *What are you doing?* He's pointing out, *Stealing money is one thing, but if you think those are the kind of guys to let you get away with this* . . .

Isn't three enough for them, though? They have to be greedy and take four freaks in? I just need one. Just one to get this operation going. Aren't they stupid for not checking to see if this freak was alive before they ran after the other ones? It seems like I was supposed to find her—*it*—like this one was meant for me. Somewhere deep inside, I know I'm right. I know I'm never going to have it this easy again. It's a gift, and it's meant for me, and I'm going to take it.

Those guys wouldn't hesitate to take her from me. Of course, I can't know either way, but who's to say they wouldn't just shoot me in the back and step over my corpse to get to her? Yeah.

I need this freak. I need food and gas and money to pay Phyllis so she can start hounding some other poor schmuck for his rent.

I'm going at the seat belt with everything I've got, and I still haven't cut through it. The strap did a number on the girl; I can see the red welt forming where it locked across her neck as she was thrown forward.

"Stay still!" I snap, because she's twisting and squirming like a fish in hand trying to get back to the water. Finally, the fabric frays and snaps altogether. The girl is slight enough to slide down from under the strap across her chest, falling onto the SUV's crushed roof. She has to crawl through the broken section of the driver's seat. I see her eyes start to drift toward the body there, and I don't know, I don't know why, but I don't want her to see it.

"Come on, come on!" I hold both hands out to her and she practically slides right into them. She weighs next to nothing; she's all fine, delicate bones and sweat and blood-slicked skin. I haul her out of the SUV, trying to crane my neck away from where she has her arms locked around it, almost like she's going in for a big hug.

"Jesus, kid, stop—I'm not rescuing you!" I say. "Are you that stupid? Stop it!"

I try to force the image of her face out of my mind, to kill the corner of my heart where sympathy comes home to roost. *Think of them like stray dogs,* the handbook said. *They have to be brought in, or put down if they exhibit too much fight.*

The first kick to my crotch makes me see stars. The little feet in those stupid-ass pink tennis shoes are all of a sudden flying, beating against my chest and legs. I stumble forward, throwing both of us down onto the warm asphalt. She's up and on her feet while I'm rolling around on the ground, holding my crotch, trying not to cry.

Shit—I need to get up, I need to get up, I need to—

I push myself onto my knees and try to lunge for her, but the freak is so damn pint-sized all she has to do is duck and my arms are cutting through air. I go lurching after her, thinking she's going to try to lose me down the road, disappearing into the low, dry brush that dots the green valley.

Instead, she crashes into the skip tracers' beige sedan, throwing both hands out against the hood. The whole car makes this low, whining sound, the way my middle school violin used to sound when it wasn't tuned and I tried to drag the bow across it. I snag her around the waist, swinging her away. This time, I don't make the same mistake. I throw her over my shoulder and she knows better than to fight back.

"*Hey!*" A shout slices through the silence, echoing down the open road. I spin around, searching for the source. One of the beards is running for us. There's a flash of silver, like the light is giving me a wink. That's where my brain goes. Not that it's a gun, not that I should drop that kid and book it for my car, but *Oh, look! A sparkle!*

"Drop it!" he hollers.

The bullet slams into the warped frame of the SUV, making me jump. I've seen them—guns, I mean—before on TV, and in movies, and in games. But real guns, they're loud. Angrier.

I can't move. Physically cannot put one foot in front of the other. I can feel my brain racing in circles around the realization of what's going to happen if I don't get my ass in gear. Why don't I have a gun? Why didn't I save enough to buy one before I left?

It makes me feel stupid, like I'm some elementary school kid who shows up for varsity tryouts.

A sharp pain shoots through my lower back. The little girl jams her bony elbow against my kidney again. It hurts like a bitch, but I stumble forward, and once I'm moving, I don't stop, not for anything. I can't. The beard is right there. As I reach the truck, I see him stop and brace himself, and I know what that means even before he raises his arms and aims. I practically throw the girl into the truck's cab and dive in after her. *One-two-three* bangs— Jesus, this guy is trying to kill me.

I'm trying to keep myself from shaking. I'm trying to keep from thinking about the freak thing buckling herself into the seat next to me. I'm trying to remember which pedal is gas and which is the brake, and all of a sudden we're flying backward instead of forward. Bullets ping against the tailgate. In the rearview mirror, the beard has to dive to avoid being crushed under my wheels. Reality comes back like a blow to the head, and suddenly, I'm whipping the car around, shifting the gears. The truck squeals and moans at the pressure I'm putting on the gas, but it gets the job done. I watch the other beard run out of the charred trees, waving his arms through the air. The first one snags the rifle off his shoulder and brings it up to eye level, but we're too far away. I finally let my eyes drop from the mirror and realize I'm driving down the middle of the road again.

We're out of there.

I don't know why the relief comes out as a laugh. This is zero percent funny. Zero percent. The gas light is glowing like a red demon and those guys have a car that's about twenty years younger than mine, but as the minutes tick on, I realize they're not following. They would have caught me by now.

Then I remember.

I glance to my right, at the kid—the freak sitting next to me staring out the window. There's something almost . . . I don't want to say that she looks broken, because I know she is. They all are; otherwise we wouldn't be in this situation in the first place. It's more that her face has gone completely blank, and she's staring at the passing forest but not seeing it. The reflection I see in her window, with the blood caked beneath her nose and across her forehead, makes me feel like she's kicking me all over again.

It is kicking me all over again. I can't even get that part right. *It* is not human. *It* is a living creature with needs, but *it* is not one of us.

"Did you do something to their car?" I ask, surprised at how rough my voice sounds. I worry for a second I was somehow screaming without hearing or feeling it.

She nods.

"That makes you what?" I almost don't want to know, because I know the answer is not going to be Green. My luck is never, ever that good. I can barely keep the stupid color system straight. They tried to model it after the old terrorist warning scale. That whole *threat level is orange, so you should feel above-average levels of fear that someone is going to blow up your plane.* That system. I think Red is when the kid can explode things or start fires, Blue means they can move shit around, Yellow is . . .

Shit. Yellow is messing with electricity. Like frying cars. Holy shit.

"You're Yellow?" I ask.

It's only when she nods that I realize I haven't heard a single word out of her.

"What? You too good to talk to me?"

She looks at me like, *Give me a break,* her dark eyebrows drawing sharply down.

"You can't?" I press. "Won't?"

She doesn't answer and I have to tell myself to stop. This whole not-talking thing works for me. It's easier to think of her as a freak if she can't or won't whine about being hungry or start screaming until her lungs burst. And anyway, I don't care. I definitely do not care. *Ten grand, sitting next to me.*

"Any chance those guys can come after us?" I ask, because, in the end, that's really all that matters.

Nope. I see the answer in her face. There's a bit of pride there, too.

It takes five full miles for me to realize that whatever she did to the skip tracers' car, she can just as easily do to mine. If I'm remembering right, the handbook says that they can manipulate electricity only through touch, so I just need to keep her hands in one place and her mind convinced she won't be able to escape. I jerk the car onto the shoulder and throw the parking brake on. My "supplies kit" is nothing more than an NAU duffel bag full of whatever crap I could buy off the policemen who got let go in the economic crash. Handcuffs. Some zip ties. A Taser that doesn't work but I feel could be a pretty good threat.

My hands are still shaking, and it's embarrassing and awful, and it makes the fact that I can't figure out how to use the zip ties that much worse when the girl has to do it herself. I feel her silently judging me as she slides the flat end through the end with the nub. She puts her hands through and then tightens the loop by taking the flat end between her tiny pearls of teeth and pulling. When she finishes, the kid puts her hands delicately back in her lap and looks at me, all expectant. Like, *What's next?*

"I'm not saving you," I remind her. But something makes me wonder if she even wants me to.

THREE

I'M ACTUALLY STUCK.

I need gas to make it up to the PSF station in Prescott—the only one in northern Arizona—but the gas is in Camp Verde, south of here. And to get to Camp Verde, I'd need to backtrack, risk running into the skip tracers I just screwed over. Chances are if the kid fried their car, they're still sitting there. Or they're walking down the freeway to get help.

So I find myself back in Cottonwood at Phyllis's joint. I don't really remember driving there, or the sun starting to go down, or how I managed to park, but the dashboard clock tells me it's six o'clock. And somehow, I've managed to sit here next to this kid for a silent two hours, running through every possible plan.

Tomorrow. By tomorrow they'll be out of Camp Verde and the PSF station will be open. After I fill the truck's tank, I can backtrack to Prescott to drop her off and pick up my new tech and her bounty. Tonight we can stay here. She may be a freak, but I'm bigger than her and I think I can lock her in the bathroom from the outside. I can watch her for one night.

We have to wait another twenty minutes before the men and

women loitering on the sidewalk, enjoying the cool twilight, are finished with their conversations and cigarettes. Then I take the girl's arm and force her to slide across the bench, out my door.

I worry, just for a second, that I might be pulling on her arm too hard as I run the length of the parking lot, but I have to hand it to her. Little Miss looks like she got herself into a cage fight, and she still more than keeps up with me.

I fumble with the key to the room, sliding the cheap plastic card in and out, getting a red light every time. I glance around, convinced Phyllis or one of her sons is going to pop out of thin air, hand extended, waiting for the rent money before they reactivate my key. Before I can hash that particular conundrum out, the little girl reaches up and touches the reader, and the light goes out altogether. I hear the lock pop, and suddenly, she's the one dragging us inside the dark, musty room.

Compared to my old trailer, the motel room might as well be Buckingham Palace. But there's this tiny, nagging ache in my stomach as the girl glances around. The longer she stands there looking, assessing with those dark eyes, the more ashamed I feel. I didn't make the queen-sized bed before I left. The abysmal mauve country chic quilt is a rumpled pile on the ground. Both nightstands bookending the bed are littered with food wrappers, soda cans, and a few stray beer bottles.

The kid sucks in a deep breath of stale air, and the way her mouth twists into a painful grimace makes me wonder if she's caught in some kind of bad memory. The desk behind her is piled with dirty clothes awaiting the five dollars I need to wash them. I don't smoke, never have, never will, but both neighbors do and I swear the stench is somehow bleeding through the paper-thin walls.

I push the girl forward, toward the bathroom.

"Clean yourself up," I tell her just as there's a knock on the door.

I feel about ten times more panicked than the girl looks as she walks to the bathroom and shuts the door. I stand there, just to make sure she doesn't have ideas about causing trouble, but the knocking turns into pounding.

I look through the door's peephole and one of Phyllis's boys glares back at me. He's got a good twenty years on me but also is carrying about a hundred extra pounds tucked into his bright yellow polo shirt. I keep the chain on as I crack the door open, more to make a point than to stop him.

"Yeah?" My brain is scrambling to remember the guy's name. He's the one who's actively balding. The other one just looks like he lets his mother cut his gray hair. I know this one is trying to figure out how I managed to get back in.

"You need to be outta here tonight if you aren't going to pay," he says. "I *thought* we made that perfectly clear."

"I'll have the money for you—" I start, but then I remember the lump of bills in my back pocket. I didn't get a chance to count it before I stole it, so I start to thumb through them, making a show. That's when the bathroom's crappy faucet sputters to life. What's-his-name looks up sharply, trying to wedge himself farther between the door and the frame.

"You know it's extra if you have another person sleeping here," he snaps.

"Oh, she's not spending the night," I say, wagging my brows. "You know how it is." Except, clearly, this guy does not know how it is. And also, given the age of my "guest," that was one of creepiest things that's ever come out of my mouth.

"Here—here's the hundred," I say. And two hundred slides back into my pocket. Nice. "Tomorrow I'll be out of your hair."

The guy stares at the twenties in my hand like it's Monopoly money.

"Where'd you get this?" he demands, snatching it up and recounting the five bills himself. "You doing something sketchy in here? Something we need to know about?"

"Just finished some freelance mechanic work," I say, holding up three fingers. "Scout's honor."

"You wouldn't know honor if it was spitting in your face," the man mutters, still staring at the bathroom door at the other side of the room, the shadow of her feet moving beneath it. He's looking at it like he's thinking, like he's finally realized what I meant earlier, and suddenly, he's interested.

"She done with you?"

Well, at least I'm not the biggest scumbag here.

"Already booked." The words taste like vomit in my mouth. So all of a sudden it doesn't matter to him that hookers definitely fall under the category of *something sketchy*? "Sorry, dude."

His meaty hand swallows the money. "Out by noon tomorrow. Not a second later."

"Sure," I say, worrying that he's waiting to get an eyeful of my "guest," waiting to follow her out to the parking lot. Jesus. "That it? Okay, great."

I slam the door in his face before he can get another word out, and flip the dead bolt over. I watch the guy stand out there for a few more minutes, and don't turn away until he finally sucks it up and leaves.

Leaning back against the door, I survey what's left of the groceries I bought two weeks ago. I have a bag of chips, a cup of ramen, a loaf of bread and peanut butter. I don't realize how hungry I am until I see how little I have to eat. I could try to order something in, but that's the kind of luxury I know would draw unwanted attention from the other residents of Phyllis's motel. I can't go pick something up without leaving the girl alone to potentially escape. She can live with a sandwich. All kids like peanut butter sandwiches.

Unless they're allergic to peanut butter.

Okay. She gets the ramen. I just have to remember to sit far away while she eats it so she can't throw the hot broth in my face.

I bend down, pouring the last of the water from the gallon jug into a chipped mug to zap in the microwave. I pour the hot water straight into the Styrofoam container, my stomach gargling at the first whiff of the roast chicken flavoring.

What if she's a vegetarian?

Shit—no, stop it. She doesn't get to be a vegetarian.

It is a living thing with needs, but it is not human.

It is a living thing with needs, but it is not human.

It is a living thing with needs, but it is a freak.

It has also been in the bathroom with the water running for the past fifteen minutes. I let my brain get as far as wondering if it's possible to drown yourself in a sink full of water before I cross the room in two long strides. The door's lock has been broken since I got here and she has nothing to block the door with.

The first thing I see is the trail of bloodied puffs of toilet paper on the counter. She's left the water running at full blast, and the drain, which functions at half capacity on a good day, can't handle this load. The water has breached the shallow basin and is spilling out onto my feet. The vanity lights cast everything in a sour glow.

The kid is sitting on the ground in that little bit of space between the toilet and the shower, her face stubbornly turned away from the door. Her shoulders are still shaking, but the only noise that escapes her is pathetic sniffling. As she scrubs at her face, I realize I never cut the zip tie around her wrists, and I start to get a fluttering panic low in my stomach.

When she does turn to face me, the only trace she was ever crying is in her eyes, which are still a raw pink. The cut across her forehead is finally scabbing over, but she's managed to reopen the one on her chin.

"Stay here," I say. "Right there." I have a tiny first aid kit I bought off the old high school nurse. I don't know that she was really supposed to be selling her supplies, but we were the last class to graduate before they shut the schools down, so I guess there was no point in pretending she'd need it one day.

The only bandages I have seem absurdly large, but they'll do as good of a job as any. I tell myself it's worth it to use them because otherwise the PSFs could dock some of my reward money for "medical costs," but really, it's just hard to look at her face like that.

I peel the first one out of the package as the vanity lights begin to buzz and flicker. I glance up at her under my dark bangs. "Don't zap me. I'll kick your ass."

She finally loses that terrible forced blank look and snorts, rolling her eyes.

It's a quick job that's not especially gentle, but she sits there and takes it. She doesn't say a thing. I have to swallow the irritation that comes with it; if the freak would just act out, try something, it would make this whole process that much easier on me. I feel like she's waiting for me to screw up and make a break for it, or she's just laughing at how terrible I am at this gig. Laughing like I'm sure the rest of them are back home.

"I made dinner," I say, mostly to fill the silence. The freak just watches me, her mouth twitching like she might smile, and I know I'm right. She thinks I'm a joke.

Maybe I'm doing this all wrong—I shouldn't just give her the food. Maybe she should have to earn it through good behavior? I don't think she's scared of me. But she should be—she needs to be. She has to know what's coming.

While she sits and carefully eats the ramen I left for her on the cleared desk to avoid spilling, I take out the knife I swiped from the dead kid and kind of . . . make a show of twirling it around. But eating with her hands tied like that takes up so much of her concentration, I'm ignored.

By the time she finishes, I can feel the frustration and embarrassment burning just under my skin. I grab her arm and pull her off the chair, working a plan out as I lead her to the bed. I force her down onto the floor, trying not to echo her wince as she sits.

"Don't move," I bark, leaving her only long enough to get one pair of handcuffs out of my duffel. The bones of her ankle are tiny enough that I can tighten one end around it and latch the other over the metal bedpost hiding beneath the bed's ruffled skirt.

And again, she just stares at me the entire time, and I feel my face flush with heat, the way it always used to when I was flustered and on the verge of crying as a dumb kid. The bandage covering her chin exaggerates its point as she tilts her head up.

"Stop it," I warn her, feeling anger rise like a swarm of hornets in my skull. "Same thing that happened to your friends is gonna happen to you, so you can wipe that stupid look off your face—*stop it!*"

Jesus, I can't stand criers. I turn my back as her face crumples, just for a second. And I wonder, in a way that pisses me off all over again, if she was crying in the bathroom because of what I was going to do or what happened to her friends. Not knowing for sure what happened to them, really.

Why were they all traveling together like that, anyway? I swipe the handbook off the nightstand and bend the soft cover between my hands. That other Asian girl—was that her sister? Did her sister really just leave her there to save her own ass? Cold, man. Is that what these abilities do to them? Turn them into animals that know it's all about survival of the fittest—

STOP. IT.

Because the situation already isn't uncomfortable enough, 2A, the neighbor to my right, apparently has a guest of his own for the evening. I can feel the bedpost knocking against mine through the wall and scramble to grab the TV remote before the moaning starts. Static, static, static, news, game show rerun . . . I settle on *The Price Is Right* and turn the volume way up. This damn freak—I should have just left her, hoped to find one closer to Phoenix. She's pricked every last one of my nerves with this act of hers, trying to pretend she's all innocent and sweet to work me over, to put me in this exact place where I feel like I have to make sure she doesn't have to deal with an ugly thing like that.

There has to be something in the handbook about PSFs being willing to pick up a kid instead of me having to drive to Prescott to drop her off. I don't like the way my brain keeps circling back to wondering if I should give her one of the pillows or a blanket or if she can send an electric charge through the bed frame and kill me while I'm sleeping.

There's a brief description in the book about what each color represents, but nothing about the theories of what caused the "mutation," as they so eloquently put it. *Abilities fluctuate in strength and precision depending on the individual Psi.* Great. Of course life hands me the one that's *strong* and *precise* enough to KO a car.

It's sort of amazing to think that for as long as this has been going on, they're still not any closer to figuring out what caused it or how to fix it. The rest of us would love if Gray would remember he's supposed to be fixing the economy, too, not just pouring money into research for this supposed virus. What does it matter if we save the "next generation of Americans" when we can barely keep the current one going on what little we have? Nobody wants to have kids these days, not when it means potentially losing them a few years later. Birth rates are way down; there's no immigration into or emigration out of the country because they're terrified of the virus's spreading. The future is all they want to talk about these days, not the present. Not how we fix things *now*. *How will America move forward after losing an entire generation?* the radio broadcasters want to know. *If the Psi can be rehabilitated, how will they handle being reintroduced to society?* asks the *New York Times. Is this the end of days?* cries the televangelist.

Maybe we all die out and the freaks inherit the world. No one seems to want to suggest that possibility, though.

There's nothing about a PSF pickup in the handbook, of course, though there's this: *If you feel like you are in imminent danger and the Psi you are pursuing is classified as Red, Orange, or*

Yellow you can request backup from nearby skip tracers through the network. The Psi Special Forces unit and the United States government are not responsible for any reward disputes that may follow.

So . . . that's ruled out, seeing as I still have zero access to the skip tracer network.

I roll off the bed, walking the long way around the freak to get to my food hoard and mini-fridge. As I slather peanut butter on the stale bread, I tell myself, *Tomorrow you'll be eating steak. Pizza. Whatever you want.* Right now, though, I just feel exhausted at the thought of having to deal with all this again tomorrow. I can't even psych myself up with the mental image of throwing the bills in the air as I jump on Phyllis's crappy-ass bed, letting them shower down around me.

The beer might as well have been NyQuil. Gone are the glory days of high school, when I could down bottle after bottle after the Friday-night football games and then stay up late enough to watch the sun rise from the roof of my buddy Ryan's house. One and done.

I don't want to think about Ryan, though, or any of them. They left me behind, vanished into a world of black uniforms and secrets. It's fine. I swear it is. Sometimes, though, I just wish one of them had fought to take me with them. It's hard to be the person who gets left behind, and never the person who gets to do the leaving.

I'm just starting to drift off to sleep, the handbook open across my chest, when the game show ends. At some point, I must have dozed off, because the next things I'm aware of are Judy Garland's unmistakable crooning and her big brown eyes meeting mine as I squint at the screen. It's that famous song about the rainbow— lemon drops, birds, all those nice things. She's flanked by her little dog and a sepia-toned Midwest sky. The next time my eyelids flutter open, the house is in the tornado, crashing down.

I pat around the bed, searching for the remote just as Dorothy opens the door of her house to the Technicolor world of Oz.

It's . . . somehow nicer than I remembered. My dad forced me to watch it with him when I was a little kid, maybe seven or eight, and all I remember thinking was how stupid the special effects were compared to those in the action movie I'd just seen in the theater the night before. I hated everything, even the way Dorothy's voice seemed to wobble when she talked.

And I swear, the minute that big pink bubble appears and the good witch, whatever her name is, appears in that froufrou dress, I feel the bed jerk as the freak handcuffed to it twists to get closer to the screen.

I prop myself up on my elbows, peering down at her in the dark. She's rearranged herself so she's sitting awkwardly on her knees. I know the handcuff must be digging into her skin, but she doesn't seem bothered by it. Her face is reflected in the TV's glass face, and even before the Munchkins start singing and parading around, I see her eyes go wide and her lips part in a silent gasp. She's riveted, like she's never seen anything like it before. That seems impossible. Who hasn't watched *The Wizard of Oz*?

It keeps her quiet and occupied—and to be honest, I'm too lazy to get the remote from where it's fallen on the floor. So I leave it on and switch off the light on the nightstand. I try to sleep, but I can't. And it's not that the TV is on too loud, or that it's too bright—I actually want to watch this. My brain wants to puzzle out why my dad was so hell-bent on getting me to sit through the whole thing. Like with everything he else loved, I'm searching for him in it. A line he borrowed, some kind of philosophy he gleaned from it . . . and really, all I can see is how this candy-colored world must have made him happy on the days he could barely bring himself to get out of bed.

I don't want to think about this—to bring Dad into it now, when I'm already feeling this low. The virus-disease-whatever hit these kids at a young age, but my dad carried his sickness with him his whole sixty years of life, through the good years and the bad ones, and the terrible ones after he lost his restaurant. Until the weight of it finally sank him.

I want to laugh when all the characters start delivering the moral of the story, that all these things they're looking for have been inside them all along—that that's where goodness and strength naturally reside. They want you to think that hopelessness and sadness are like infections from the outside, and that you're supposed to be strong enough to fight them off. But I know better, and I think the freak does, too. Those feelings are also born inside you, only they're colder, sharper, heavier. If you don't get the help you need, it starts taking more and more of you to push them away. Until finally, like Dad, you've got nothing left to give.

In the end it's not about winning or losing—the fight's never fair to begin with.

"Now I know I've got a heart," the Tin Man says as I shut my eyes and roll away from the screen, "because it's breaking."

The girl has nightmares. It's the only time I hear her talking, and it scares the shit out of me. I sit straight up in bed, fumbling in the dark for the knife I left on the nightstand. I think a wild dog's broken in, or one of those feral cats I always see lurking around the motel's Dumpsters. My brain is still half asleep—well, three-quarters asleep. I don't remember about the kid sleeping on the floor until I'm basically stepping on her. I don't even assume the noise is human, because it can't be. No way. The words that come crawling out of her mouth aren't words at all, but these gut-wrenching, god-awful moans.

"Nooooo, pleasssssse . . . nooooooo . . ."

I stand over her, and stand there and stand there and stand there, and I think, *Wake her up, Gabe, just do it,* but that feels like a line that shouldn't be crossed. That means I care.

I don't. No matter what she does or doesn't do, no matter how hard she makes this for me, I won't ever care.

The bed creaks as my weight sinks back down into it. I half hope the noise will wake her and get me out of having to make the decision. One hour drives into the next, and I lie there, as still as I can force myself to be. I listen to her cry all night, and it feels like a punishment I deserve.

FOUR

Morning comes in a blinding burst of white light as the thick motel curtains are thrown aside, their metal rings screeching in protest. The flood of sun into the dark, musty room is so sudden that my body reacts before my brain does. I drop off the side of the bed and stagger onto my feet, throwing up a hand to shield my eyes.

Shit—*shit*! I slept too long, what time is it, where's the—

A few things come into focus quickly. First the pile of clean laundry sitting on top of my duffel bag, just to the left of the door. I can smell the fresh scent from here and take a step toward it, confused. Out of the corner of my eye, I see a small form at the desk, sitting in front of two plates of food—powdered doughnuts, some fruit snacks, and pretzels—with my jar of peanut butter open between them. Clear plastic wrappers are dangling over the edge of the room's small trash can, caught on the lip. I know exactly where they came from: the vending machines in the laundry room.

Carefully coating each pretzel on her plate with a delicate

dab of peanut butter, she keeps her back to me as I walk to the table. The zip tie is gone, and so are the handcuffs. She's changed, too, out of her dirty, bloodied clothes into a baggy pink Route 66 T-shirt and jeans she's had to roll up a few times at the ankles. I stare at them until I remember there's a donation box in the laundry room that no one's ever done anything with, filled mostly with kid stuff.

With the exception of the bed I just fell out of, the room is impeccably tidy. The trash is gone, and she's even cracked the window open slightly to get fresh, cool air flowing in. I storm to the window and throw the curtains shut. The room is pitched into darkness, but I don't care. It makes it easier somehow.

"Are you *stupid*?" I yell. "You think this is going to work on me? That if you play nice with me, I'll be nice right back? Are you really that big of an idiot that you think I want to *help* you?"

She shrinks a tiny bit in her chair, but she doesn't look away. She doesn't even blink, and I can't help it—I know she's a freak, I know that I shouldn't be talking to her at all, or acknowledging this, or letting her get me this worked up, but it all explodes inside me until I feel anger making a mess of every other thought in my head.

Even if she wasn't trying to play that game, she obviously thought I couldn't take care of myself, let alone her. And this was her way of throwing it back in my face, wasn't it? Mocking me. Why else wouldn't she have run when she had the chance? Clearly I don't know how to latch the handcuffs, I don't know how to restrain her, and I can't even keep myself alert enough to know when she's left the goddamn room.

Why did I think I could do this? The freak won't say a word, but I just look at her and I know the dialogue running through her head. *He sucks, he's dumb as roadkill, he's better off scrubbing trailers.* Same script as everybody else.

But I'm not. I'm not. I swear I'm not.

I can be better than this. I know I can be. These freaks, they all know the right way to mess with your thoughts, make you doubt yourself, but I won't let her. Not anymore. The clock says that it's only eight in the morning. They'll be open. I can get rid of her now and be done with this. Get the ten-ton weight off where it's caving my chest in.

"This isn't Kansas, Dorothy," I snap at her. "People here aren't nice. They aren't your friends. *I'm* not your friend."

She ignores me, swinging her legs back and forth on the desk chair as she chows down on her breakfast. I get the look—the one I'm starting to think of as *that look*—in return. One eyebrow raised, lips pursed, eyes blazing with *Give me a break, buddy.*

I leave the food there and take her arm, ignoring her wince as I yank her up from her seat. I fasten two zip ties around her wrists this time, not caring when she makes a small noise of surprised pain. We're leaving. Right now. I'm going to show her how serious I am. She'll finally see she should have run when she had a chance.

She's wrong about me.

I decide to risk driving up to Prescott without doubling back down to Camp Verde for gas. Now that they've started drilling in Alaska, tankers have been showing up on the highway again, but the station in Camp Verde is the only one that gets reliable shipments. It's not that I'm afraid those skip tracers will still be there waiting for me on the highway; I just want to get this done and over with so I can start hunting kids for real.

I'm going to think of this as a trial run for the real thing. Practice.

My gamble pays off. I find a gas station, though I'm out almost two hundred dollars with still almost half a tank left to fill. I'll get the rest on the way back, I tell myself, waving to the station attendant. I keep my eye on the highway and the ever-green forest cupping the station in its earthy palm as I make my way back over to the truck. I've heard stories about people getting mugged for gas. It sets me on edge every time I have to stop.

I open the passenger-side door, angling my body to block the view of the kid sitting knees-to-chest on the floor. I don't let her protest; I don't let her move. I was banking on her false sense of security by leaving her in the car and expecting her not to tamper with it or run, but I won't do it anymore.

The handbook recommends employing the use of rubber gloves to restrict Yellow freaks' abilities; if they can't form a connection with the electricity, they can't control it. The best I could find in the station were the gloves my mom used to use when she still washed dishes. I know they're not thick enough, but I'm going to double up and hope that's enough.

I use the knife to cut the zip ties off, and she slumps forward, rubbing her wrists with a faint, grateful smile. For someone who says nothing, her face is incredibly expressive. It's how I know she's so repulsed when I pull the gloves out of my back pocket and try to jam them over her hands. It's the first time she fights me on anything, really fights—hitting and kicking until I have bruises up and down both arms. For once she's acting like a real kid having a meltdown, and it throws me that much further off my game. I don't even bother aligning them on each finger; she can wear them like mittens for all I care. Another zip tie over her wrists will be more than enough to hold them in place.

The kid never once loses the defiant set of her shoulders, but her dark eyes practically burn with the betrayal. I can see the plan forming behind them, and I cut it off before it can take root. "You scream or run or try to draw attention to yourself, I'll knock you out. I have a Taser, and since you seem to like electricity so much, I'm more than happy to introduce you to it."

Then I slam the door in her face. But each step I take around the truck has me feeling a foot smaller, until I finally reach the nozzle and get to pumping the gas. I think, Maybe this is what Hutch meant when he said the ones who like doing this are the real monsters. You have to be a bully. You have to teach them to behave, or they'll walk all over you.

I keep trying to tell myself none of us would be in this situation if it weren't for them. If they hadn't gone freak on us, if those other ones hadn't died, things would have gone on as usual. Mom would be at home taking care of her garden, and Dad would be alive, working himself to the bone keeping his restaurant running and his customers happy. I just wonder, you know, what kind of person the Gabe in that world would have been.

According to the handbook, all PSF recruitment centers and bases are forced to take in Psi refugees when you have them in your custody and honor their bounty. This is only a recruitment center and administrative offices; the real base is down in Phoenix, with most of the state's population.

Maybe I'm reading too much into this, but it just seems a little cruel they had to set up shop in the old elementary school.

No one's coming in or leaving, though the parking lot is filled with cars ranging from old junkers like mine to military Humvees and vans. I loop a pair of handcuffs through the girl's zip tie and lock them on the metal bar beneath the passenger front seat. She doesn't beg or plead or cry—not that I expect her to. But she doesn't look resigned to her fate, either, which—given her Houdini act this morning—makes me feel a little nervous as I lock the door behind me.

I want to scope things out myself before I take her inside. Take things slow. It seems like the smart thing to do. They need to be able to register me in the network and outfit me with all the tech I'll need. Hutch says sometimes they'll try giving you the runaround in the hope that you'll just give up on ever being treated fairly. Make things as frustrating and difficult as possible. That's why he gave up after his first score, at least.

Ten thousand dollars, I remind myself. A future. Or at least the start of one.

Lincoln Elementary is a stately kind of brick building. Classic in a way that a lot of the newer buildings from the second half of the twentieth century aren't. A fully uniformed PSF meets me at the door with his rifle resting against one shoulder. I've seen pictures and shots on TV, but man, in person, it's a whole new level of intimidation. Whoever decided to jack Darth Vader's red-and-black color scheme knew what they were doing.

"What's your business?"

Not getting my ass shot.

"I'm here about . . ." The words trail off. The school's entry hallway has been converted to look a great deal like a police station. There are desks with uniformed PSFs behind them around the perimeter, and a rainbow of men and women hanging around the waiting area in hunter camo and caps, biding their time until it's their turn to be seen.

I don't see any kids, but maybe they have us bring them in through the back?

"How many times do we have to tell you to check your damn *applications*?" a man shouts from the far end of the hall. The man sitting next to him stands and slams his hands down on the desk, prompting the PSF next to him to stir. "We already searched the plate numbers in the system! He's not registered—yet!"

The hall carries exactly two words from the man sitting next to him. "Stolen" and "score." And even before they start to turn to go, I know I'm standing less than a hundred feet away from the beards.

Holy shit.

I back through the door, but I have no idea what excuses I'm mumbling to the soldier. I burst back out into the parking lot at a full run.

Because this isn't suspicious at all! Good job, Gabe!

Shit, shit, *shitshitshit*—even if I were to wait for them to leave, the officers in this station will recognize the plate number when I give it to them on my application. Not to mention they probably have me on camera acting like a sketchball at the door.

Phoenix. I can do Phoenix. I'll change my clothes, wear a hat and sunglasses, swap out my license plate with one from one of the abandoned cars I find along the I-17. It's less than a two-hour drive. If the gas situation starts to get touchy, well, I'll figure it out.

I feel better now that I have a plan. It's probably what I should have done in the first place, but it's okay. Lesson learned.

The kid is still sitting on the floor when I jump back into the driver's seat. There's a rumpled piece of notebook paper smoothed out over her knees that she immediately tries to stuff back into her jean pocket. From my vantage point above her, though, I can read at least the first half of it: *We love you. If you need help, look for*

Look for who?

"Well, Dorothy," I say as I turn the key in the ignition. My mind scrambles to come up with some excuse that won't make me look pathetic. "They're not accepting freaks at this location. Looks like you've got two more hours of freedom."

I swear, she can see right through the lie and she looks . . . unimpressed, to say the least. I put the car in reverse and she climbs up into the passenger seat, dropping the handcuffs into the drink holder between us.

Okay. Seriously. What the hell?

The girl sighs, but deigns to show me her trick. With the cuffs in one hand, she slides what looks like a warped bobby pin out of her pocket. I glance between her and the highway as she wiggles the bent end of the pin in a small hole on the handcuffs I've never noticed before. The metal arm springs open.

"Kid, you have the worst sense of self-preservation I've ever seen," I tell her, because now I know not to use the handcuffs on her. I'll stick to zip ties. She's trying to teach me how to do my job, and while a tiny part of me is impressed she knows how to do this, a bigger part of me wants to stretch out across the highway and wait for someone to just run me over. All my anger from the morning has drained me to the point where I can only feel humiliated and tired about all this.

"I didn't rescue you," I remind her, but she reaches over—gloves and zip tie and all—and turns the radio on. I listen to hip-hop or I listen to silence, so naturally she finds the one station blasting out Fleetwood Mac and sits back.

"I don't think so," I say, switching it off.

She reaches over and turns it back on, this time cranking the volume up just as the song changes to something that sounds like it could be Led Zeppelin. And the look she gives me as I start to turn the dial again probably should have caused me to spontaneously combust.

"Okay, okay. Geez." I'm going to think of it like her last meal before death row. She gets this. Only this.

Thirty miles later, the truck's back right tire blows out just outside Black Canyon City. Who fixes it?

Guess.

Guess.

I'm not an idiot, I know I'm not. I've watched my dad change out his tire for a spare before, but I never had the experience of doing it myself. I barely get the car onto the shoulder of the highway without losing my shit. Meanwhile, Dorothy hops out of the car, her hands bound, and goes around to the back, looking for a spare I know old Hutch is too cheap to have supplied. The look I get when I meet her around back can be summed up in one word: *Seriously?*

Traffic is light enough on the I-17 today that we can walk along the outer edge of the nearby string of abandoned cars without fear of being spotted.

Jesus. Is this what it feels like for these freaks—these kids? Constantly having to look over their shoulders, jumping whenever a car buzzes by, because in those two seconds, one wrong glance means the jig is up? I only have to be worried about another skip tracer spotting us and swiping my score; she has to be worried about everyone from skip tracers to grannies with access to phones.

We stop next to an SUV, and she crouches down, inspecting the tire. Her eyebrows draw together, and her forehead wrinkles, like she's trying to mentally measure if this tire is the same dimensions as the others.

Dorothy holds her hands out to me, and I stare at them, confused. She nods toward them, giving them a small jerk, and I realize what she wants.

"You gonna run?"

She rolls her eyes.

"Nice. Real nice."

I only cut the zip tie, expecting her to take the gloves off herself. Instead, she carefully adjusts them so they align with the right fingers. They're laughably oversized on her, reaching up past her elbows—almost like the way a superhero would wear them.

I crouch down next to her as she uses the small tool kit and lift to remove the hubcap, then each nut holding the tire in place. She works quickly, methodically, but slow enough for me to keep track of what she's doing.

"Who taught you how to do this?" I have no idea why the words escape. Maybe it's because it's such a nice day out; the sun is warm, not sweltering, and there's a nice, cool breeze stroking down the sides of the nearby mountains and cutting across the valley. We ditched the evergreens a while back and have hit the full-fledged desert, but I swear the air still has that fresh flowery smell. This is the kind of landscape everyone sees when they think of Arizona. The part I grew up in might as well be Colorado in comparison.

"Your dad?" I ask. She shakes her head. "Brother? Yeah, your brother?"

Dorothy takes a break from what she's doing and holds up two fingers. I'm surprised I know exactly what she's trying to say. "Two brothers? Where the hell are they?"

Wrong thing to ask. A shadow passes over her face, and I get a stiff shoulder turned toward me in response.

"Was that other Asian chick your sister? The one who ran?" I ask, waiting for her answer. "No? Really? But you have one?"

Okay, two brothers and a sister. Interesting. If they aren't with her, they must be too old to be affected by the Psi virus, in camps, or dead. Somehow, judging by the way her face lights up when she "talks" about them, I don't think the latter is the case.

But where the hell are they? If I had a little sister, I'd be taking care of her. I would have clawed my nails down to broken stubs trying to keep her safe, not let her go running with a group of other kids. Where were they even going? Just bouncing around the country, from one place to another?

I think about the way she cried in the bathroom when she thought I couldn't hear her, and I hate the way my heart seems to lurch down to the pit of my stomach. I shouldn't have asked her those questions, no matter how curious I was. Because you take these freaks and you stop thinking about what they can do and instead focus on the people in their lives, where they come from, what games they liked playing with their friends, and you find yourself on unsteady ground all of a sudden. You start to let all those things seep in, and suddenly they're kids again with bony skinned knees, grass-stained clothes, and hands always in something they shouldn't be. They're just . . . little kids.

And they have even fewer choices than I do.

Dorothy shoos me away, motioning with her hands that I should take the SUV's license plate and get on with switching it out with mine. I don't know how she knows I'm supposed to do this, other than from experience. Maybe that's how those kids went undetected: any time they thought they'd been spotted, they'd switch cars, and when they couldn't, they'd switch plates.

Smart. How many other tricks does she know?

Not only does that tire fit, it inspires us to replace the other three. Might as well—they were looking worn and low on air. I doubt Hutch ever thought to get them rotated or had the funds to buy new tires every few years like I know you're supposed to. Stuff like that becomes a luxury rather than a necessity when you get down to the bare bones of life.

It's not until later, when we're sitting a few blocks from the diner I've just bought us sandwiches from, with the windows rolled down and the Rolling Stones screaming out of the stereo, that I remember I never put a new zip tie around her wrists. I remember she took the gloves off to eat and never put them back on.

I remember, and I don't really care.

"What's your name, Dorothy?" I ask. "Your real one?"

She dips her finger into the ketchup that's dripped onto the paper her sandwich was wrapped in and writes, in even, delicate strokes, *ZU*.

"Zu?" I say, testing it out. "What the hell kind of name is that?"

She reaches over and punches me in the arm—*hard*. I manage to wince only a little, but it's an all-out inner war not to reach up and rub the throbbing muscle. Meanwhile, she's looking at me, motioning like I need to exchange my name for hers.

But man, I don't know. I don't know what the point is, or what I'm even doing. It's starting to feel hard again, all of it. It was nice to forget, for ten whole minutes, the reason we are sitting here together in the first place. The kinds of thoughts my brain starts turning over feel dangerous. Like: How can they be so bad? How can anyone not human like sandwiches and Mick Jagger and know how to change a tire? I start to wonder if maybe the things we're so afraid they'll do to us are the things they have to do to survive the tidal wave of hatred and fear we send coasting toward them.

"Sorry," I say, just because I know it will annoy her, "you're still Dorothy."

I feel like I've been swept up and dropped on my head in a world that looks like mine but is slightly different. Brighter, more vibrant—or at least missing some of the dust and grime that's collected over our lives after years of neglect. I can't tell which direction is right or wrong anymore, but I know I want to stay.

FIVE

OUR NEXT STOP IS A LONELY LITTLE GAS STATION IN Deer Valley, just south of Anthem and Cave Creek. I doubt Zu is familiar enough with Arizona to know how close we are to Scottsdale, and that from there, it's spitting distance to Phoenix. But with no warning other than a sharp intake of breath, she seizes the steering wheel and nearly gets us into an accident as she jerks it toward the exit.

"Jesus—! What the hell?"

One hand points to the gas light and the other points to the gas station next to the off-ramp.

"With what money, Dorothy?" I ask. "I barely have enough for a gallon, since I still haven't been able to turn your ass in."

Trust me. I narrow my eyes, but she meets my gaze head-on. *Trust me.*

Unsurprisingly, we're the only ones here. I navigate the truck around, picking the pump farthest from the small convenience store and the worker peering out his window at us. The gas tank is on the driver's side, which means that Zu, when she follows me out, jumping down from the door, is blocked by the body of the truck.

"Now what's your plan?"

She mimes putting a credit card into the slot, but I could have told her before that the pumps don't take card payments anymore. You have to pay up front in cash.

Zu doesn't look fazed. Instead, she jerks a thumb back toward the store and the man still watching me and then does that jibber-jabber motion with her hands, pressing her four fingers against her thumb repeatedly.

Distract him!

I shake my head, stuffing my hands into the back pockets of my jeans, but I do like she asks. Because there's no chance *that* could go horribly wrong.

It's already about thirty degrees warmer than it was in northern Arizona. I come down here so rarely that the hundred-degree heat always feels like opening an oven door and leaning in. The station attendant at least has the fans cranked up behind him, even if the owner is too cheap to shell out for real AC.

The bells above the door jangle. I glance back over my shoulder, surprised to see the formerly blank-screened pump suddenly light up with numbers. I don't know what the attendant can tell from watching his register's screen, and I don't know what the hell the girl is doing, but a quick plan comes together in my head. It's as dumb as it is simple.

I feign a big trip, crashing headlong into the shelves of candy. I thrash my arms out, knocking most of it to the ground in mess of epic proportions. The attendant must think I'm having some kind of a seizure, because all of a sudden, he's at my side where I'm sprawled out on the floor, checking my pulse, shoving a thick candy bar between my teeth, like he's afraid I'm going to bite my tongue off.

"Sir? Sir? Sir?" I don't know that anyone has ever called me *sir* before, much less three times in fewer seconds. "Are you all right? Can you hear me? Sir?"

I make a big show of moaning, clutching my head as I turn onto my side. Just past the attendant's hip, I can barely see the pump Zu is working, the way the numbers are spinning and ticking up, like she's somehow pumping gas without paying for a cent of it.

"I'm going to call for an ambulance—"

The poor guy is so old and so genuine that I do feel a little sorry about all this, until he has the nerve to say, "It'll be okay. You're okay, kid."

"I'm just . . . It must be the heat," I say, grabbing his arm as he starts to pull away. "I'll be okay. Do you have . . . Can I buy a bottle of water from you?"

Please say I have enough left to buy a water bottle.

"No, no, no," the man says, rubbing what little white hair he has left off his sweaty forehead. "You wait here. I'll get you a cup of water from the cooler in the back."

I know it takes more than a few minutes to fill the truck's tank, but whatever Zu's managed to pump is going to have to be enough. I wait until the old man staggers onto his feet, straightens his ugly polyester blue uniform, and disappears into the back before I jump up and go running for the truck.

The timing is just right. She sees me coming around and jams the nozzle back onto its resting place. I give her a boost up into the cab, glancing at the pump's screen. She's somehow just stolen over three hundred dollars' worth of gas.

The tires squeal as we go tearing out of there. I'm whipping around corners, looking for the on-ramp back to the I-17, laughing, laughing, laughing because I can't seem to get rid of the adrenaline any other way. Zu reaches over and buckles me in, then does the same for herself. Her round face is flushed, but I think she looks pretty smug. I would be, too.

"Your brother teach you how to hijack a pump like that?" I ask when I can breathe normally again.

She shakes her head. No—it's a new trick. I want to think about all the thousand ways that could have gone wrong, how there's a good chance if the store has cameras, my face and the car is likely on them. I don't know how this works, though—if that old man is going to shuffle back over to his register and see that someone's been pumping gas without paying. And who's going to smack the law down on me? Would the police really have time to follow up on this when they already have enough trouble to deal with in Phoenix?

Who cares? If they come after us, they come after us. They can try.

I'm not thinking straight—I know I'm not because the next words that come out of my mouth are so batshit crazy I almost don't recognize my own voice. "If you help me find another kid, I won't have to turn you in."

But really, is it *that* crazy? She's already proven herself to be a hell of a lot more resourceful than I am. She's handy and basically means an unlimited supply of gasoline whenever and wherever I need it. And who knows? Maybe they have some kind of psychic link to one another. They can move cars and start fires and move a grown man across the length of a field. How is that any crazier? It doesn't have to be her.

The smile slides down her cheeks bit by bit, and the disappointment I see in her eyes tells me the answer is no, long before the shake of her head.

It doesn't make sense to me. I'm giving her a way out—I'm saving her life, and she doesn't even pretend to act grateful? Maybe I was right before and she really *does* want to be taken in. She's tired of running, tired of being hunted, and she just wants to walk back into the arms of the nearest black uniform and be done with it. That would at least explain why she didn't run all of the times she could have. She wasn't staying with me because she liked the company, obviously.

Look, I'm not a proud guy. I'm nobody's favorite. I'm just getting by and have been for pretty much all my life. I'm not interested in college because I want to go on and be a doctor or a lawyer or one of those assholes who sit around with their heads in their hands on the stock market floor. On the scale of winners to losers, I know I fall somewhere in the middle.

I'm just trying to get myself to the point where I at least have *options*. I don't understand why little Zu doesn't feel that need, too, why she'd throw her freedom away like this. I don't know anything about these camps, but I know if nobody is allowed to whisper a word about them, they can't be good. If she can't see that, she's too trusting—she's that man in the gas station offering to give me water while we're robbing him blind. People like them, they can't see the world for the wreck it is.

I mean, okay, I will admit it stings a *little* bit to know she'd rather be locked up than with me. Maybe— It could be she just doesn't understand what she's throwing away here. Maybe I need to explain it to her?

We've been sitting in the parking lot in front of the PSF station for almost ten minutes now. Unlike the one in Prescott, there's a steady flow of people milling in and out. This includes the clusters of PSFs and the National Guardsmen they brought in to help smother the food riots that started the last time they tried to pass out rations to the growing population of homeless. Because, hey, guess what? When your average summer temperatures are over 105 degrees, people are going to do whatever they possibly can to get bottles of water, including trying to knife one another.

The generic-looking building is in the shadow of a number of empty skyscrapers, including the silky blue glass column of Chase Bank's former hub. The baseball field named after the company was closed even before all the professional sports drizzled from a few games a season to none. I've heard rumors that a number of homeless have overrun the field; it's constantly being fought over by gangs looking to expand their territory. At least, those are the rumors. Heaven forbid any of these government clowns ever give us real information about what's going on, outside instructions to "avoid central Phoenix whenever possible."

Three beige stories of tiny windows—it looks so harmless. You'd never know it was a military base from a distance, and I know it probably wasn't built to be, but it just adds to the feeling that I'm about to go in and make a business transaction.

"Ten thousand dollars," I tell her. "That's all these people think you're worth."

She doesn't say anything. The afternoon sun is low and gives her ivory skin a warm glow. The bandages I applied yesterday are starting to peel. Every now and then she has to reach over and smooth the edges back down. I can tell that Zu is thinking hard about something. Her throat is bobbing, like she has to swallow the words one by one.

"You did this to yourself," I say, my voice going hoarse. Jesus—I can feel my stomach turning as I look back out across the cracked asphalt. A car pulls into the space to the right of us, one of those white, windowless vans that serial killers seem always to use.

Out comes this woman with this head of bleach-blond hair that's been so fried by chemicals there are these horrible kinks in it. She's wearing acid-wash jeans and a leer as she catches sight of Zu in the passenger seat. When she spots me, her smile falters a little, but she recovers and bends down to Zu's eye level. The little condescending wave she gives the kid makes my stomach twist and turn over.

And then Zu shoves the door open as hard as she can, right in the lady's smug face.

"Holy *shit!*"

The skip tracer goes down in a limp, unmoving heap. Zu, meanwhile, is all action. She shoves the door open the rest of the way and steps over the woman to get to the van. By the time she wrenches the sliding door open, I have enough sense to start crawling after her.

The woman is out cold—you'd have to be to stay on the burning asphalt that long willingly. I glance around, horrified that someone's witnessed this, but Zu only has eyes for the small figure that's curled up in a little ball of leather straps and chains in the middle of the van. She waves me over impatiently, like, *Can you catch up with the rest of the class, please,* and I jump from our car to the other, only bending down to pluck the keys from the unconscious woman's hands.

The kid—this boy who's twelve, maybe thirteen at the most—stops struggling the minute Zu takes the blindfold off his eyes. I'm not really believing what I'm seeing. The van smells terrible, and it's clear from the stain that the boy's gone and wet himself like the baby he really is. He's shaking, screaming something at her around his gag. I let Zu take the keys and undo the handcuffs around his wrists and ankles herself.

I see it out of the corner of my eye, resting on the front passenger seat next to a small handgun—a shiny black tablet, the kind they only give to registered skip tracers.

"Oh my God," the boy cries when she's able to untie the gag. His chest is heaving with every breath he takes, and he's crying the way I used to when I was a kid and I came home with a bad grade or after a lost soccer match and my mom would tell me not to be so goddamn pathetic about such stupid things. He's sobbing the way I did the night I found my dad's body.

"Thank you, thankyouthankyou," he sobs, clinging to me.

The boy's legs don't seem to be working, so I lift him into my arms and carry him to my truck. I already know it's not going to be this one, either.

I don't know what the hell I'm doing anymore.

I hit the I-10 and all of a sudden I'm just driving, going as fast as I can without catching any attention I don't want. Every time I look up into the rearview mirror, I expect to see some kind of military SUV gaining on me, streaking down the freeway with guns blazing. Or at least a white van with a frizzy-haired woman sporting a new shiner leaning out her window to fire at me mid-chase.

I've seen too many action movies.

Zu calmly holds the boy's hand, and he actually lets her. I guess that's the difference between kids these days and the kinds of kids I grew up with. They don't have much pride—at least not enough pride to act like a punk and be rude because he's secretly humiliated about having pissed himself and cried in front of a girl. I guess they can overlook these things, given their circumstances. It's kind of sweet, in a way . . . like normal puppy love, only with the addition of freak superpowers and hormones.

I have to hand it to him, too. Now that he's calmed down, I think he might be trying to flirt with her. He keeps asking her questions, but she only nods or shakes her head.

"She doesn't talk," I explain finally. "But she understands what you're saying."

"Oh."

I look at him out of the corner of my eye—ginger, an explosion of freckles across his face, dressed in nice enough clothes to tell me someone out there cares enough to know he's missing. He fidgets and shrinks back against the torn leather seat.

"What's your name?"

"Are you like the woman?" he asks instead of answering. "A skip tracer?"

At this point, I am the exact opposite of whatever a skip tracer is supposed to be. Zu points at me and gives a big thumbs-up, and I feel like she's just singlehandedly elected me the next president of the United States.

"Oh," he says again. "Okay. My name's Bryson."

"Nice," I say. "I'm Gabe. This is Dorothy."

She reaches around Bryson and punches me in the arm again. "Ow. Fine. Zu."

"Zu?" Bryson grins. "That's cool."

69

Okay. It is a little cool. Better than, like, Pauline, I guess.

"How'd you get picked up?" I ask. After two days of talking to myself, it feels weird to be having a conversation.

He sighs, banging his head back against the seat again. "It was really stupid. Della's gonna kill me."

"Della being your mom?" I didn't start calling my mother by her first name until I turned twenty and was embarrassed to have the word associated with her.

"No, she's . . . she's watching me and my brother and a couple other kids. She and her husband are really nice and they're taking care of us until things get better."

"She's hiding you?" I ask. Wow. The lady must have balls of steel. I should know. Terror's got mine in a viselike grip. "Then yeah, I'd say Della is probably going to kill you."

The whole setup is really fascinating. This woman, Della, and her husband, Jim, had recently moved to a quiet neighborhood in Glendale—one that was still hanging in there while the streets and cities around it started vacating with foreclosures. They didn't have children of their own but were the friendly kind and, more importantly, were open enough with their views on Gray to be immediately trusted by the others. It started with one kid in Bryson's neighborhood disappearing the night of his tenth birthday. Then, a few months later, another kid vanished. Finally, when it was Bryson's birthday, his mother woke both him and his brother up in the middle of the night and brought them over to Jim and Della's house, telling them only that they needed to be good and stay hidden until she came back for them.

"You didn't like it there?" I ask.

"No—no, Jim and Della are the best. She's a really good cook and Jim's been teaching us how to fix cars in the garage. It just sucks to have to stay in the attic a lot of the time. We don't really get to go outside, either."

"And you got caught because you got sick of it?"

Another sigh. "Because they said they were going to take us to California, to a place there that was safe, and my brother, he's such a baby—he didn't want to go without this stuffed bear he used to sleep with. I just thought . . . it's not so far between our houses, and if I snuck out during the night I could be real quick, you know?"

Zu nods, all sympathy, but there's something about her expression that makes me think she wants to ask him a question.

"I'm guessing the skip tracer was lurking around the neighborhood, waiting for one of you missing kids to turn back up?"

"I guess."

This is the part where I'm supposed to say something to make him feel better. I know it is, because Zu is giving me this look like *That's your cue, buddy.*

"Well . . . it was nice of you to try. I'm sure, um, your brother appreciated it."

"If I were smart, I would have taken Marty with me. He's a Blue—he could have, like, thrown her down the street to help us get away, or something."

"What are you?" Do not say Red, please, God, do not say Red. . . . The Yellow was scary enough at first. I'm not really sure I could handle that.

"Green."

"Which means what?" I press. Jesus, where am I even going? I need to pull off eventually, but I just want to get as far away from Phoenix as possible. "You have a good memory?"

He shakes his head. "I'm just good at math—puzzles. Sooo dangerous. Too bad you can't throw puzzles at a gun."

I let out a low whistle, more at the bitterness in his tone than the mental image.

"I'm really . . . I'm really scared I messed it up for everybody. That somehow the skip tracer figured out where I was hiding and got Della and Jim in trouble and the others—"

"Nah, man, I doubt it, not unless you said something," I say, cutting him off. If I'm not allowed to panic and freak out about this situation, no one else can. "Do you have a way to contact them?"

He has a phone number I can call; it's just a matter of finding a working, unoccupied pay phone. They basically went extinct once cell phones came around, and then, when no one could afford cell phones or their service, suddenly there were lines around the block to use the precious few pay phones remaining.

I find one, finally, at one of those outdoor strip malls that have one nail salon and one Chinese food restaurant still open. I have no idea what they're doing that the rest of us aren't, but whatever. Good for them.

Just to make sure no one's going to stumble across us, I decide to wait it out a few minutes. Make sure it's safe to leave them here alone. When I'm convinced it's safe, I turn to interrupt their conversation.

"But I'm sure Della would let you stay, if you wanted to," Bryson is saying from where he and Zu are huddled in that little bit of space between the dash and the seat. "The attic is big and we have video games!"

I snort, but a second later, a sharp pang cuts through me. I look down at Zu for her reaction as she scribbles out her response on the back of the same worn scrap of notebook paper I saw her looking at earlier.

I lean over his shoulder to see her response. It's weird, because her handwriting looks the way I'd expect her voice to sound—big, girly, light. *I'm going to my uncle's ranch in San Bernardino.*

Which is . . . where, exactly? California, I think. If she expects me to drive her all the way out to Southern California, she has another think coming.

"I'll be right back," I tell them. "Lock the doors, okay? And stay down."

I pick up the receiver gingerly, wiping down the mouthpiece against my shirt, like that's going to help. I pop in the dollar in change and dial the number Bryson wrote out on the back of my hand. It takes a moment for the call to click through to the tone; I glance back over my shoulder, making sure they aren't peeking over the dashboard to watch when I specifically told them not to.

It rings three times, and just when I'm sure I'm going to be kicked to voice mail, a breathless voice answers.

"Um, yeah, hi, I think I . . ." Oh, shit. Does Gray still have his cronies listen in on calls? I mean, would they have any reason to listen in on this particular house's calls? "I think I found your, um, stray . . . ra-dog."

Shit, I almost said rabbit. Be cool, Gabe.

The woman—Della, I'm assuming—is silent.

"I'm happy to drop him off, but maybe it would be, um, better for you to come get him? He is a big dog. Nice . . . uh, reddish fur? Do you know which one I'm talking about?"

"Yes," she says, her voice soft. She's Southern—unexpected. "Can you tell me where you are? I'd be happy to meet you."

I lean back out of the booth, trying to see the nearest street name. Sweat is pouring down my back, and not just because of the heat. "I'm grabbing dinner at Mr. Foo's on Baseline and Priest Drive."

"All right." I can hear her keys rattle as she grabs them. "Okay, I'll be there in less than a half hour. Do . . . do I need to bring anything with me? To thank you?"

"What do . . ." Oh. *Oh.* She's asking if I need some kind of reward, I think. Crap. I mean . . . I guess I just assumed the only financial gain was in turning the kids in, not, you know, returning them. I'm so stunned I can't think of a thing to say.

"Hello?"

"Some gas money would be great, I guess," I manage to get out, "if that's okay?"

I can't really sort out my thoughts, even as I hang the phone up and make my way toward the car. The kids both turn and look at me, these little faces with big eyes, as I slide in and slam the door behind me. My forehead falls against the steering wheel as I lean into it, closing my eyes.

"Did you get Della?"

There's a rustle of paper and faint scratching. I open one eye just in time to see Zu pass a note back to Bryson. It's such a natural, typical thing for these kids to be doing in such a bizarre setting under such horrible circumstances that I have to smile, just a little bit.

"Zu wants to know if you need her to find us something to eat," Bryson says, reading the paper.

I sit back, giving her an exasperated look of my own. "Della's coming in a half hour. If you're hungry, I can get whatever fifteen bucks will buy at Mr. Foo's."

They both shake their heads, and I realize, my exasperation blooming to a whole new level, that they're worried about me being hungry. "I'm fine. We'll wait until Della gets here."

It's my job to keep a lookout in the parking lot for her car or anyone or anything that could be suspicious—which in this day and age is pretty much everything, but this part of town is as dead as we could hope for. Out of boredom, I start fussing with the skip tracer's tablet I swiped.

The home screen is a map of the United States that quickly zooms in on Arizona and then drops a red pin on the location of the PSF base in downtown Phoenix. A window pops up, letting me know it can't connect to a local wireless network, but would I like to engage the satellite service for a small fee?

No. Hell no. That means someone on the other end can use that same connection to trace the location of the tablet.

What's surprising, though, is that I can still use it without letting it hook up to the Internet. Maybe all the information is preloaded into the tablet, and you only need the Internet to download updates? That seems reasonable; the only thing spottier than the Internet these days is President Gray's resume as leader of the free world.

The main menu is a series of buttons that range from GPS services, to a digital version of the handbook, to something called "Recovery Network."

So *this* is what Hutch was going on about. After I tap the button with my finger, the screen changes, switching over to a list of names and pictures of kids. Most of the photos are kind of heartbreaking—they look terrified in them. The ones that are in camps have the red word RECOVERED across their photos. None of them list where the camps are, but in each profile is a kid's basic information—approximate height and weight, hometown, parents' names, whether or not the kid was turned in or "recovered."

It's curiosity, I'll admit it. There's a search bar at the top of the screen, so I type in *Zu*. I try not to glance down at her as the tablet loads the results. And, great, over three hundred names come up. It went through and picked out any kid who had *zu* in any part of their name, including a surprising number of Zuzanas and Zuriels.

But her name is Suzume. I know it the minute I see it, even though her doll-like face is framed by thick, glossy long hair. The tears hadn't finished drying on her face when they'd taken the photo. She looked at the camera like the lens was the end of a gun waiting to fire.

Twelve years old, from Virginia. An only child.

At large, her listing says. *Yellow. $30,000 reward for recovery. Highly dangerous, approach with caution.* Then, because it's all not horrible enough, it lists the date she escaped her "rehabilitation program" as being only four months ago. The number they gave her is 42245.

Below that is the field the skip tracers use to leave tips. There are two sightings reported in Ohio and one dated a few months ago, in late March, in Virginia.

A pounding between my ears starts at a low, uneven beat and races to a shattering pulse. Suddenly, I'm seeing two screens instead of one, and then they're both blurring and I can feel my blood start to fizz beneath my skin, pounding at my temples. My whole body heats, like it's being taken by a fever. I can't breathe, I can't breathe, I'm going to be sick.

They cut her hair short, I think.

She can't talk, because of what they did to her, I think.

It was so bad there she had to escape, and every day she has to deal with assholes like me trying to send her back, I think.

Why did I never think this was a possibility? Not even once. I was so focused on turning her in I hadn't even considered she'd already been inside, and what she'd found there had been horrible enough that she had to escape. And she did it. She got out. We both got out and we found each other, and maybe it wasn't an accident after all. Maybe this is really what I was supposed to have been doing all along.

I want to ask her about it. I want to know the truth, even if I can't hear her form the words. She can write it out for me, I don't care. I want to hear what they did to her there—who did it to her—and I want to kill every single one of them. My mind is flashing with images of my friends. In their black uniforms, marching the kids up and down the halls. The crushed look she gave me when I forced her hands into those gloves and tied them together, like she was some kind of animal. More than anything I can't stop thinking about the expression on her face watching that stupid movie in my motel room—the way it visibly lifted when Dorothy stepped out of that house and into the sweet dream of Oz.

Because she knows what it's like to live in a world of black, and black, and the tiny bit of white, but when she escaped it, she didn't find the rainbow of colors, the dresses, the singing, the dancing. She only found ugliness.

She only found me.

SIX

DELLA IS YOUNGER THAN I EXPECTED, SOMEHOW. I GUESS I heard the words *no kids* and assumed that meant she was elderly, not someone who looks like she's in her late forties. Her white sedan is the only car that pulls into the parking lot the whole time we're sitting there, so it's impossible to miss her, even before she drives straight for us.

Bryson pops his head up just as she parks right beside the passenger door. We're set as far back away from the storefronts as the parking lot will let us be, but I know we're going to have to make this quick. At best, someone will see us and hopefully think we're exchanging drugs or some other illegal substance, not kids.

She's wearing blue jeans and a brown T-shirt and all it takes is seeing that head of fire-red hair for her guarded expression to fall. The lady still has her looks—a nice smile, a warm, open face. She doesn't look wrung-out the way my mom did. She's standing there, her aviator sunglasses on, her sunny blond hair curling around her shoulders, and she has her hands on her hips.

"I'm sorry, Miss Della" are the first words that come out of Bryson's mouth when he opens the door. "I'm so, so sorry."

She doesn't look like the lecturing type, but I have a feeling if he were her flesh and blood, he'd be on the receiving end of some serious ass-whopping. Instead, she just cocks her head to the side, gives a faint smile, and opens her arms to him. Bryson goes willingly, burying his face in her shoulder. He basically collapses against her. I only relax when I realize the open door is blocking him from view.

"Y'all had some day, huh?" She lifts her sunglasses as she looks from Zu to me. "You're younger than I expected!"

I laugh.

"I have a son about your age," she continues, blue eyes inspecting me. "This feels like a stunt he'd pull, so you'll have to excuse me—I'm trying to fight the urge to lecture you about taking big risks like this."

Weird. Bryson said she didn't have any kids.

I shrug. "No risk, no reward, right?"

Her smile falls just that tiny bit.

"Oh—*no*, I mean, no I don't mean it like that," I say quickly. "It's just, the world, you know? Nothing changes if you don't take a risk."

"That also sounds like him," she says dryly. "Do me a favor and save your mama the heartbreak of joining up with the Children's League to see that particular thought through."

Della is illegally harboring kids in her own home. Of course her kid joins an underground group that seems hell-bent on making Gray's life miserable. It lights a fire at the back of my mind, burning through all the other vague possibilities I'd been slowly working through. I want to ask her more about it—more about her son—but she turns her attention to Zu, who, I swear, has not blinked once the entire time she's been watching her.

"Hi, hon, how are you doing?"

She manages a shy smile that Della returns twice over.

"I have that gas money," she starts, shifting her gaze back to me. "Where are y'all headed? Do you need a place to stay for the night?"

"We're going to California," I tell her, ignoring Zu's surprised expression as she whips her head around. Of course we're going now. "Her uncle has a ranch out there I'm bringing her to. Then I'm going to see if I can find some work."

"You got your papers all in order? A plan to cross the border?"

And just like that, my heart's in the pit of my stomach. "What do you mean?"

Della's expression softens, but there's something sharp working behind her eyes. "It's the whole mess with the Federal Coalition and the League—they're based out of Los Angeles, so Gray's been tightening border security in the hope he can starve them out by not letting imports or exports through. You need special permission from the government to cross state lines."

Well . . . shit. I press my lips together, trying to fight back the sting of disappointment. I'm sure there's another way in that doesn't involve driving. Or walking a couple of hundred miles through the desert in the summer.

"Do you need to get there soon? Would you have any way of getting the paperwork for it?"

"I mean . . . I guess we could . . ." My mind is fumbling for a way we could possibly sneak into California. On the back of a semi-truck? Could I bribe someone?

"Well." Della drags the word out, running a hand back through her hair. "I guess you're in luck, hon. A little bit in luck, at least. I have papers you can use, but they might be more of a hindrance—and you're going to have to figure out a way to hide her as you cross."

"Wait—wait—what?"

Della smiles. "My husband, he's a special kind of mechanic. He works for one of the companies that maintains the canals and aqueducts that bring water out of the state, so he has paperwork to cross state lines. I think they're just in the dash. . . ."

Such is the force of Della that I don't even remember getting out of the truck and walking around to meet her in front of the sedan. She points out the two special foil stickers affixed to the window. "I can't give you these, unfortunately, but if you hit the border around midnight, they have fewer soldiers posted and they're far more likely to be lazy and just wave you through. If not, show them these papers. . . ." She leans in through the open window, pops the glove box, and hands me a neat bundle of papers. "The company is on the auto-approvals list. If they ask for an ID to match against the name on the paperwork . . . well, you'll have to get a little creative or say a little prayer and floor it."

I swallow hard and nod.

Della puts a hand on my shoulder, smoothing out the front of my shirt like it's the most natural thing in the world—but she catches herself and gives a rueful little laugh. "Force of habit, sorry. Two boys will do that to you."

I didn't mind it all that much. Honestly, it was kind of nice.

"Are you sure?" I ask quietly. "I mean . . . your husband, doesn't he need the papers?"

She waves it off. "He'll understand. Honestly. I want you to take this car and I want you to get that little girl someplace safe, okay? You understand that's your job?"

I feel a little lightheaded at the weight that comes thundering down on my shoulders, but I nod. It is my job. I'm doing this.

"You're up for it, aren't you?" Della lifts her sunglasses again. "I know you are. I do. And you know how? Because you've made it this far. You called me, not the PSFs, not any of the skip tracers. There's so much evil in this world, and you brought just that tiny bit of light back into it—not for the money or the credit or anything other than to help another human being out. And that's rare, real rare. You're a good man, and you should be proud of yourself."

And it's like when she says it, I do feel good. Genuinely good. I can't remember the last time I felt so light. All the blood rushes to my face, but I'm not embarrassed. It's just that my chest gets tight, and I have to hold my breath or else I'm going to burst out crying all over this stranger. I feel like if she touches me in that caring, simple way again, I'm going to explode into stardust.

And that's when I realize it: not since Dad. No one's told me something I've done is great or right or even worthy—and maybe it hasn't been up until this moment. Before he took his life, he used to tell me that sometimes we don't know what we're looking for until we find it. I've been so angry, at him and at everyone else, that I don't know how to handle the way I feel now. Because I think I might be happy. I think I might know what I'm supposed to be doing.

Bryson and Zu share a quick hug and he gives me this little fist bump before he climbs into the sedan, settling there like he belongs. I reach over to buckle my passenger in when she seems preoccupied with shaking the last bit of ink out of the dying pen I provided.

As Della gives me her directions for the fastest way to find the freeway and get to Southern California, I can see Zu frantically scribbling something down on that same sheet of notebook paper she and Bryson wrote their notes on the back of. I see the same handwritten message I caught a glimpse of before, only now I know Zu wasn't the one to write it. The penmanship is too neat, too careful to be hers. When her arm moves, I can finally read the whole thing:

We love you. If you need help, look for my parents—they're using the names Della and Jim Goodkind—and tell them I sent you.

I startle when Della reaches in to squeeze my shoulder and say good-bye. Zu looks up, panicked, and quickly folds the notebook paper up and leans over me to give it to her.

"Stay safe, honey," Della says, blowing her a kiss, "the both of you, please."

"I'll do my best," I tell her, shifting out of park. She steps back so I can roll the window up.

I don't really know why I look in the rearview mirror as we drive away. I still feel a little bit like I'm walking through somebody else's good dream, like none of this is real. And I know I won't get the story out of Zu, not the full one, anyway. That's okay. We're allowed to have our secrets. Starting now, I'm leaving the past alone in the past.

Growing smaller and smaller in the reflection, Della unfolds the sheet of paper. But I see her when she presses her hand against her mouth, when she slumps against the side of the sedan—overcome, in relief, I don't know. Zu's message is only three words, but they nearly bring the lady with a spine like steel to her knees.

Liam is safe.

I think about stopping for the night—finding some cheap motel room along the way to California and trying to get a little bit of shut-eye to recharge, but I can't bring myself to. After using Della's money to fill the gas tank as much as I could, I'm left with the same fifteen dollars I had before. Any place charging that little for a room is the kind of place where we'll wake up and find our car gone in the morning.

Zu keeps her eyes on the green freeway signs as we zoom past. By the way she keeps tapping her fingers against her leg, I think she's counting them. We can't keep a steady radio signal this far out in the desert, and I think the silence is starting to unravel some of her confidence. The lightness I felt earlier talking to Della is slowly bleeding away, too, into the dark, barren landscape around us. For the first time in my life, I miss the trees up north. I miss being surrounded by the known and familiar, and having it tucked in around me like a blanket.

I can't keep ignoring the fact that after I drop off Zu, that's it. That's the end of my current plan unless she and the other kids desperately need me to stay and help them. And while it's a great plan, I need a little more than that, especially since I don't have the money for any of the state schools in California that might be open. I could see if there are any jobs there as a fieldworker, or in construction. Maybe their police force would take me. If not, I guess there's always the Children's League. I doubt they'd be picky, and at least I know I'd be doing something real to help the kids. Something to think about.

I like that. There are choices now. Possibilities.

"This place you're going," I say, "is it nice?"

She already wrote the address down for me. Smart thing had it memorized, and realized, even before I did, that we could roughly navigate our way there by zooming in on the skip tracer tablet's map until it showed the surface streets around San Bernardino. I'd only been to California a few times, enough to start feeling a bit nervous once we hit Quartzsite, one of the last few Arizona towns along the I-10 before the border.

Zu shrugs.

"You've never been there before?" I press. "Even though it's your uncle's place?"

She weaves her fingers together, then rips them apart.

"Ohhh," I say, "he doesn't get along with the rest of your family?"

I get a thumbs-up for that. "Are you sure he's . . . I mean, I know it's your uncle, but he'll be okay taking you in?"

Zu wraps her arms around herself, miming a big embrace.

"I hope so, kid, 'cause I don't think you can stick with me if I go looking for, like, the Children's League."

It's like I've slapped her in the face—the moment the shock passes, she looks visibly upset. At first I think it's because what I've said was a little mean, but she's freaking out, shaking her head, waving her hands. *No*—her mouth forms the words in the dark—*not them.*

"Why not?" I haven't heard, you know, pretty things about their methods, but they do get their point and demands across in a way the parents sitting around on the steps of Flagstaff's city hall never did.

She's frantically looking around the different compartments of the car, pulling out sheets of paper, then putting them back when she sees there's something important written on them.

"Dorothy, Dorothy—it's okay, calm down." I can tell she's getting more and more frustrated—and just when I think she's going to pull the Band-Aids off her face and write on the backs of those, she finally just settles on using the last of the ink to write the message on her palm.

NO!!! THEY ARE TERRIBLE! SCARY! YOU ARE BETTER THAN THAT!

I snort, drumming my fingers on the steering wheel. For a few minutes, I can't say anything at all. There's a stone in my throat and I can't swallow it. A few minutes ago, all I could taste in my mouth was the McDonald's hamburger I scarfed down for dinner. Now it's so dry my tongue sticks to the roof of it.

"All right," I tell her. "All right. I'll figure something else out."

Because even if it's not true, I want it to be.

You can see the border station from a good three miles away. The floodlights are cranked up so high they look like they form a solid white wall. It's only when you get closer that you start seeing the lengths of barbed wire and the enormous military tanks and trucks they have haloed out around the freeway, and the small, old building where the border agents used to sit and wave you through.

We pulled over a while back to get Zu situated, but I still feel sick about it—really, genuinely sick with fear. I've got her folded down in the gully of space where the dashboard curves out, but she's only covered with a blanket and a large duffel bag of clothes we picked up at one of those Goodwill drop-off sites. I wonder if she can even breathe under there, and I wonder what's going to happen if they demand to search the truck, and I wonder if she's somehow going to have to save me from this, too.

"Don't say anything or move no matter what, okay?" I tell her.

There are bright orange signs everywhere telling me to reduce my speed, but they seem a little redundant. The floodlights are so damn bright it's hard to see anything and you have to take your foot off the gas to avoid crashing into the barrel barriers or any one of the uniformed National Guardsmen and -women.

Shit, shit, shit. I grip the steering wheel. I have the AC going at full blast, so high it's practically deafening, but my back is sticking to the faux leather seat. *You're fine, Gabe—Jim! You are Jim! You are Jim Goodkind and you have every right to be driving through here—*

A soldier steps out of the little station building, lifting her hand against the glare of my headlights. I'm waved forward, but not through, like I was stupidly hoping.

She raps her knuckles against my window and I roll it down, trying to remember how to breathe. In out in out in out in outinoutinout . . .

"Can I ask what business you have in California?"

Say something. Say anything. There is a little girl right next to you and she needs you to act like the twenty-five-year-old you are, not the three-year-old your wimpy-ass guts are telling you to be.

"The aqueduct . . ." I swallow, forcing what I hope is not a demented smile onto my face. "My boss thinks someone on the California side might have tampered with it. Water levels are suspiciously low. I have to check it tonight before they come in tomorrow morning."

I have no idea what words are coming out of my mouth. I have no idea if there's a canal that flows from California into Arizona. I always thought it was the opposite—that California was hogging the Colorado River and leaving us with nothing—but maybe

I just spent too much time with drunk, bitter Grand Canyon tour guides growing up. I'm smiling so hard, though, I've lost all feeling in my face.

Shit. Why didn't I practice this? Why can't I ever think far enough ahead?

"I have all of my paperwork—passes," I add weakly, fumbling with the glove compartment latch.

The soldier glances down at her clipboard, then back up at my face. "I don't have any notes about this maintenance trip. . . ."

I lean closer to the window and let my voice drop to a whisper so she also has to lean in to hear me. "They think the Children's League might be involved. No one's supposed to know I'm coming."

Great. Now in addition to looking sketchy, I also look like a conspiracy theory whack job. Great way to inspire confidence in my sanity.

Dammit, this isn't going to work. Why did I think this would work?

The other soldier in the booth, who planted himself in front of the TV, sticks his head out to see what's going on. The soldier I was talking to turns around, about to explain it to him, but he cuts her off. "Heron Hydraulics is on the auto-approvals list—I'll give you a copy tonight to study for tomorrow." He turns back to me. "Sorry, sir. Go ahead."

I stare back at him dumbly. The other soldier has to give me a wave to get me moving.

But no more than a hundred feet later, there's a whole other border station set up—one Della neglected to mention. It's not nearly as impressive as the first one, but I can see a small dark figure moving inside the tiny booth as I approach. Hanging from the metal levers blocking the path is a sign telling me to HAVE FEDERAL COALITION–ISSUED PASSES READY.

Shit. Do I have those? I turn the overhead light on again, letting the car coast forward through that small sliver of free land between the two competing governments. I can't find anything labeled with the Federal Coalition's name in the variety of rainbow-colored official documents. By the time the car comes up to the metal bar standing between me and the velvet black of California's stretch of desert, I'm fighting not to start hyperventilating.

What can I tell them—how can I spin my story so I seem sympathetic to them, not Gray? Does it matter? Are they looking for me to be sympathetic toward them? Does that make me seem more suspicious?

But by the time I get there, the police officer—highway patrolman, I realize, rare breed they are—just reaches over and presses something on his desk, and the metal bar rises. He doesn't even turn around in his seat, from which he's watching the same program the National Guardsmen were.

I let myself speed up, waiting for him to try to stop me. To show half as much initiative to do something as the first soldier did. But he just sits there, and it's like all the lights are on, but no one's home. No one cares. Given how long it's been since the Federal Coalition was formed and how little they've done to help anyone, it seems appropriate.

Zu's face is flushed, but she's beaming when I lift the bag and blanket off her. When I don't return her smile, her dark brows draw together in a silent question, but I don't want to tell her. I don't want her to know that all of a sudden I'm not sure this is a safe place, either.

SEVEN

SAN BERNARDINO DOESN'T LOOK ALL THAT DIFFERENT from the part of Arizona I found Zu in. It's not covered in a thick coat of evergreens like Flagstaff, though I'm convinced I see a few mixed in with the shapes of other kinds of trees. It's a valley, a nice one, surrounded by black-faced mountains that seem to lean in more over us the farther I drive from the lights of the city at the heart of it.

I heard rumors that California wasn't hit as hard as the rest of us, but driving through these streets makes me feel like I've stepped back ten years in time. There are none of the scabs I got used to seeing back home: no sea of silver-backed trailers, no abandoned cars, no tent cities. The gas prices are still astronomical, judging by the price boards, but none of the stations have been shuttered with signs like NO GAS HERE or TRY CAMP VERDE.

The address Zu gave me is a good twenty miles outside the city's reach. It starts getting quieter, colder as the hours pass by. Eventually I have to roll up my windows and turn down the radio.

"Hey, Dorothy," I say, shaking her out of sleep. "Is this the place?"

It's pitch-black out here, but there are lights strung up along the wooden fence leading up to the large one-story home. It's done in the typical southwestern ranch style—every detail, from the obligatory cacti in pots around the entryway to the bleach-white cattle skull that hangs on the door. I let the truck's headlights wash over the building once before I switch them off and park the car on the dirt driveway.

"What do you think?" I ask her. "I don't see any lights on. . . ."

She unbuckles her seat belt, her mouth pressed together in a tight line.

"You want to wait here while I see if anyone's home?"

I'm not going to lie. A big part of me was hoping that someone would be up, waiting for us. That her friends those skip tracers were chasing would be here to greet Zu and tell her all about how they gave the beards the slip. It wasn't so crazy—I never saw them take those girls away. They weren't in the PSF station in Prescott as far as I could tell.

They're probably asleep, I think, smoothing my hair back. Yeah. It was just shy of midnight, an hour when nothing good can happen. We all should be in bed before then, I think.

Of course she doesn't want to be left in the car, but she lets me carefully maneuver her behind me, at least. I feel her small hands gripping the back of my shirt to keep track of me, and the thought that she's depending on me is steadying.

I ring the bell and knock, but no one comes to the door. We even walk the perimeter of the house, peering through the windows, but nobody's there—only furniture covered in white sheets.

Maybe her uncle up and abandoned the place. Given how long it took me to drive the length of the driveway through the sprawling property, it seems like this place would take a monumental amount of work to maintain and keep thriving, even in a great economy. I thought I saw a few cows or horses in the far ends of the grassy field behind the house, but I think exhaustion tricked my brain. All I see now are rocks.

I reach around to take Zu's arm, wondering how to explain this to her. It seems unfair that I have to be the one to break her heart over this—to point out that she fought so hard to get here for nothing. But just as the words start to form in my mind, we hear a muffled bang from the smaller building set off from the main house. Some kind of stable or garage, probably.

The doors are shut, but I see the line of warm, milky light under them—and I see it switch off as we carefully, quietly come up on it. Zu stays behind me the whole time, her hands clenching fistfuls of my shirt.

I take the metal handle in my hand and slide the door open slowly, feeling my pulse jump as it scrapes across the rocky dirt. And for a second, I'm confused, because the face that appears in the darkness is Zu's—Zu the way I'd seen her in the skip tracer network, with long, silky hair. Her eyes go wide, and her mouth opens in a scream.

And then I see the blond hair behind her, the girl with the gun in her hand who doesn't even hesitate before she fires it straight at my chest.

It feels . . .

I feel . . .

It's like . . .

My mind blanks with the fiery burst of pain that tears through me, ripping me up from the inside out. I can't—what's— I don't understand, the girls are yelling, the three of them from the valley, but the last thing I feel before my legs go is Zu at my back trying to hold me up.

Move—I don't want to hurt her, but I can't feel anything below my waist. I'm going to collapse back on her, I'm . . .

When my eyes open again, I'm on the ground and warm rain is spilling down on me from the clear river of stars overhead.

"—the man from the road, I thought he—!"

Zu flashes in and out of my vision. She shoves the girl with the gun, beats her hands against the teen's chest. I hear "call," "can't," "hospital," and then nothing but the sound of my own heartbeat. I want to lift my hands, to apply pressure to the place in my chest she's just cracked open, but I can't breathe—I can't—I can't—I'm choking on air and the metallic bitterness coating my tongue.

One of them disappears into the dark of the stables. I can smell the place's old musky animal scent, the sharp, fresh hay, but even that begins to fade. Zu's face appears over mine, and her mouth is moving, her lips are moving, with a message for me and only me, but there are no pens here, no paper. I can read the desperation and fear in her face. I see her hands come down against my chest, but I can't feel them.

"D-Dorothy—" My throat burns. It's the only way I know the words are leaving it. "Guess we . . . shouldn't have left Oz. . . ."

I feel myself drift back. Her whole body is heaving with sobs, snot and tears dripping down her face, and I want to say so much to her, and I want to tell her—Her face begins to dissolve into gray, and it takes my breath with it. My voice.

Stop it, you stupid kid. Jesus, stop crying.

Don't you know I hate it?

Dorothy, it's so stupid. Don't be so stupid about this.

Don't.

Don't—

SPARKS
RISE

ONE

SAM

I DON'T FORGET FACES.

I don't forget anything my eyes have landed on—not the smallest detail of the white flowering wallpaper in our neighbors' house, not the cursive letters written on my classroom's whiteboard, not the numbers that flashed on the screen as the man in the white coat adjusted my position under the machine's metal halo, the signs on the towering fence as our bus pulled in for the first time. DANGER! HIGH VOLTAGE, AUTHORIZED PERSONNEL ONLY, NOT A LOADING ZONE, STAY ALERT.

Its smells and sounds have gone hazy; I think, sometimes, that I can remember what it was like to lay out in the freshly mown grass in our backyard. I think it smelled sweet. I think I can just about remember how silky Scout, our golden retriever, was, lying in a patch of sunshine. There was laughter, too, from the Orfeo kids trying to climb over the wall between our houses, half tumbling into the bushes. What I remember most is the cloudless powder-blue sky. I couldn't take my eyes off it. I haven't seen one like it since.

This place has reduced my world to gray, black, brown.

Everything gets filed away inside my head, neat and tidy, until I need it. Somehow, without trying, I pull the right card out of the deck each time. I test myself all the time; that same white coat, the one who'd been all freezing fingers and sneered words, told me not to—that using my freak catchall of a memory would somehow overload it, and I'd be as dead and stiff as the kids already buried. They tried that lie on all of us, I'm sure.

For the first two years, I'd catch myself doing it, drawing out those memories, and close my eyes, throat swelling with thick panic. *Stop it, you'll die, you'll die, Sam—*

For the next three, it was like a dare. Each success was a small pop of bright exhilaration to pepper forever sunless days. Every time I did it and nothing happened, I'd get that same feeling I had each time I snuck over to the Orfeos' house on the Fourth of July, and they'd secretly save me one of their sparklers to run around with before my parents could even realize I was gone. I'd think of Dad preaching from Job, *Yet man is born unto trouble, as the sparks fly upward.*

Now . . . I just don't care. A few months turned into years and now those years are morphing into forever, and there's no getting out. It used to be enough to live inside the gray, to accept the things I couldn't change even if that meant everything. They've been holding these warnings about a possible second wave of deaths, like an axe over our heads, as long as I've been here. Using our abilities will trigger it. Acting out will trigger it. Speaking or reading or thinking too hard about anything will trigger it. Only, they've done such a good job of making this place hell that I wouldn't be surprised if the real one turned out to be a much nicer place.

Salvation will be found in obedience. Dad's parting piece of advice when he walked me to the school bus that morning. I've dismantled the phrase a thousand times in my head and tried to reassemble it into something I read in the Bible. He spoke in parables and proverbs, and when he realized what I was, he barely spoke at all. Some part of me still thinks he would have loved me more if I'd died, because it'd mean I was saved.

Mom only wanted whatever Dad wanted.

I thought that was what I wanted, too, until I saw my bunkmate actually die in front of me. In this cabin, almost a year ago, as hard as it is to believe now. And it was nothing like those men in suits with the dead-eyed smiles promised—that it'd be as simple as going to sleep and never waking up. But that night, I'd stood over her and watched death come and electrify her from the inside out—I remember thinking, stupid and stunned and exhausted, *This can't be right,* because IAAN wasn't supposed to make your body thrash, wasn't supposed to make you scream loud enough that not even clenched teeth could contain the sound. I thought it would be quiet, and authoritative—like a steady, warm hand reaching through the darkness to lift you out of this world.

Dad always spoke of God with more fear than reverence—always conscious of how angry He was with us, always disappointed as we fell short of His plan. In Sunday school, every lesson and teaching had been softened for us. He wasn't an angry God, but a loving God. He was there for us when no one else was. We could lean on Him for strength.

Now I think that Dad was right all along. There's no mercy, not in life, not even in death.

I'm already awake when the morning alarm starts clanging through the speaker in the far corner of the room. I stay on my back a moment longer, rubbing my hands over my face, before sitting up and sliding over the side of the bunk bed. My bare toes land on the edge of the wooden frame beneath me, and I use it to stretch over my mattress and straighten out my sheets. My shoes and sweatshirt are under the bottom bunk, but the space next to them is empty and has been since they took Ruby away.

No one is talking this morning, but the cabin is filled with small sounds of life. The old bunks creak and groan as the girls sleeping up top jump to the ground. Yawns stretch tired faces wide open. Joints crack as stiffness is worked out. I slip my shoes on, running my fingers along the fading number scrawled there in black permanent marker, 3284, to brush the dirt away. I can't bring myself to look at the empty bed again, the bare mattress where she used to sleep.

I need to stop obsessing over this, but I can't help it. Climbing up, climbing down, I can't avoid the empty space; it sucks the air out of my chest, makes my head ache. I don't understand how someone I barely knew can bring tears to the surface faster than thinking about my parents, my cousins, the other girls I've lived with for the last seven years. It's like sitting in front of a nearly complete puzzle that's missing only one piece—but that piece, the one that completes the image, is just . . . gone. Not in the box.

Somehow, I lost it.

I know I must have, because Vanessa, Ashley, all of them gave me these looks when the dark-haired girl first showed up a few years ago.

"Whatever you fought about, it's not worth it," Ashley had whispered to me. The older girls were braver about talking in the morning. "I hate to see you guys like this. She doesn't even talk now."

This swell of hurt and fear and something that felt too close to panic had tackled me from behind. The air was coming in and out of me in sharp bursts. There was no explanation for it, other than I was . . . something was wrong with me. My head. I didn't forget faces. I didn't forget anything. And yet everyone was acting like she'd been with us from the beginning. They were making me dizzy with these looks of confusion and pity and curiosity. I broke into a cold sweat at Ashley's words. The pieces of me that were already barely holding together after the punishment I'd taken a few days before began to drift apart.

Is this the second wave? I remember thinking. *Do we slowly lose what we can do?* Were our minds just going to one day blink out?

But all the other cards were in place. I tested it every morning, every night. Address numbers on my block. Mia Orfeo's bookshelves. Pages of the Bible. Patterns of Christmas tree ornaments. No Ruby, never any Ruby before that moment. She'd come right over to me, small and pale—face smeared with grime like she'd been working in the Factory all day with us. And she'd gripped me like I was going to be able to drag her out from whatever she was drowning under. Green eyes, shining with pain. The PSF that day had pounded me into the ground with his baton before locking me in the cage for hours. I must have said something to him to make him punish me. A wrong look, something I muttered. But that was hazy, too. They must have brought Ruby in while I was gone.

That was the only word she ever said to me: *Ruby.* I asked when she'd come in, what her name was, and the only thing she'd managed to choke out was her own name.

The truth is, she lived like a shadow. Silent, always trying to make herself as small and quick as she possibly could. The PSFs, they never picked on her, they never noticed her, and it was hard not to be resentful when I could barely make it one day without—

I shook my head, smoothing my hair back into a ponytail.

How can I remember each day from the moment they brought me through the damn gate until that evening, but she's just not there? She's dissolved like smoke.

How can you miss something, feel so awful about it, when you're not sure you had it in the first place?

From the next bunk over, Vanessa clucks her tongue in warning—a *hurry the heck up*. I can tell we have a day of rain ahead of us by the way the mildew stench seems particularly strong. If we're getting rain, it means it's too warm for snow, and that is always, always, always a blessing.

The winter uniforms are nothing more than forest-green sweats. There are no coats, unless you're working in the Garden. The Laundry, Factory, and Kitchen are all, in theory, heated. At the end of each Garden shift, you pass the woolen gray monstrosities back in; I can't tell if it's because they just aren't willing to pony up and pay for coats for the whole camp, or if they're afraid we'd try to stash something inside of them. Hiding sharp-tipped trowels and hand pruners, smuggling strawberries, I don't know.

I take another deep breath and hold it in my chest until I can't resist the burn. Falling into my spot in line, the earthy dampness of the cabin finally fades under the familiar smells of plain detergent, shampoo, and sleep-warmed skin. The overhead lights that snapped on at the alarm wash everyone's skin out to a chalky ash.

The electronic door locks click one, two, and three before the heavy metal swings open and a PSF steps inside, her eyes sweeping over our lopsided lines. With Ruby gone at my right, Vanessa has had to step up into her space, leaving Elizabeth alone at the back to walk with the stare of the PSF burning into her neck.

The steel-gray light from the overcast sky creeps into the cabin like a delicate fog. I blink my eyes against it, fighting the urge to hold up a hand to shield them as the PSF inspects first our uniforms and, next, the general state of the cabin.

Rather than say a word, the woman, blond hair twisted into a tight, low bun beneath her black cap, whistles and waves us forward, the way she would call a dog to her side. It sets my teeth on edge and spun my exhaustion into annoyance. There's something about her smirk today I don't like. Her eyes keep darting back and forth between whatever is standing out along the soggy trail and us.

I square my shoulders as Vanessa and I pass by her, a half-hearted attempt to brace myself for the freezing January air; the sting of it turns our skin pink and our breath white. I was wrong about it not being cold enough to snow; in a West Virginia winter, what's rain one moment turns to icy sleet in the next, and then, just as you settle into that misery, suddenly there are large, fluffy snowflakes drifting down around you like feathers.

I'm so distracted by the effort it takes to not give in to the clench of my shoulders and arms, to concentrate on not showing them how badly my body wants to shiver, I don't even see them until the lines have filed out behind me. Cabins are opened and emptied by number, a careful sequence that involves stopping, going, stopping again as everyone is led out onto their right trail, wherever it is they're supposed to be going—wash houses, Mess

Hall, or straight to work until lunch. It's timed down to the second, and half of the time I think it only works because everyone's too tired and cold to try to resist being dragged into the pattern. What's the point, anyway?

But because every day is exactly the same, it should have been the first thing I noticed—the very first, given the bright red vests they're wearing. The uniforms beneath them are dark, smoky gray—not the black of the PSFs. The pads of my fingers sting just looking at them—it'd been so hard to get the plastic needle through the thick fabric, I'd pricked myself enough times to draw blood. Three months ago, we'd sewn buttons on them, as well as patches of numbers across the breast pockets. I'd thought nothing of it at the time. We'd dyed and stenciled any number of prison uniforms, so I'd just assumed . . . I just thought we'd never see them again.

Beside me, Vanessa manages to cut off her gasp but can't get her body's instinctive response under control. To our PSF's satisfaction, she flinches and looks away quickly, like the sight of the Red alone could burn her.

I don't need to look around me to know that at least half of our cabin has already figured out what's happening. Those same girls have already moved on to drawing further conclusions that will take me another week to puzzle out. For all our differences, our Green minds really only function in two ways—my way, the storage locker, or their way—the ability to connect multiple dots of a situation or problem as easily and quickly as breathing. I get the impression we bore them every time we try to talk to them, like they always know what we're about to say next. In a fraction of a second, they can look at Vanessa's reaction, see how young the new people are, assess the color of the vest, recognize the uniforms we helped stitch together, and recognize now, in context, that the frustrating number patches were really Psi identification numbers. I can practically feel their minds churning behind me, whipping up a frenzied series of thoughts. *Reds.*

If I know them, those girls will be thinking ahead, their conclusions slanting toward the future. *Why are they here? How will it affect me? When will they leave?* But I'm trapped in the past. Do the other girls remember, the way I do, the faces under the caps they wear? They're blank, so completely vacant that it looks like their features have been painted on their skin.

My stomach begins to turn over itself, the burning taste of sick rising in my throat like acid. How? How did they do this to these kids? I know the first face that we pass along the way to the Mess Hall; I know that girl because she was at this camp. She was here for almost two years before they took the Reds and Oranges out that night. I don't forget faces, and even though I'd tried cutting the memories up and storing them in a dark, locked place, I can feel them bubbling back up, trying to merge together again. Fires in the cabins. Fires in the Mess Hall. Fires in the wash houses. The sky stained black with smoke. The boy who tried running from the Garden, who fried himself against the fence when his fire couldn't melt the metal fast enough. That winter, that whole winter, we'd gone without real vegetables and fruit because the only things he'd set on fire that day were our food and himself.

The thing about the Reds was this: no matter how still they were, watching them was like having eyes on a pot of water set to simmer. A small uptick in temperature could set them to boil—it could happen that fast, in a second of carelessness. They were the monsters of our stories, ones who couldn't bring themselves to lurk in the shadows. And as terrifying as they were, as little as they cared about the rest of us, I never felt so defeated as I did when the camp controllers removed them. Because even if the rest of us were pathetic and too scared to even make eye contact, they were always pushing back, they were always fighting, they never fell into the pattern.

I thought they'd killed them. We all did.

My feet get sucked down into Thurmond's dark mud; I can't even feel the cold anymore; panic heats my blood and makes my hands jitter at my side uselessly.

They hold no weapons that I can see—no guns, or knives, or even the handheld White Noise machines. I guess that makes sense. They're the weapons themselves.

What have they done to them? How easy would it be for them to do it to the rest of us?

I count twenty along the way to the Mess Hall, spaced out evenly, filling in the gaps where there used to be PSFs. Where there are black uniforms, they're hanging back off the trails, watching us pass by in clusters, talking to each other and smiling, actually *smiling* about it, the sickos.

It feels like a challenge—like they want to see us shrivel up just that little bit more when we see how helpless we really are. Just when you become numb to the cold running bony fingers up and down your bare skin, when your muscles become too used to the punishing schedule of go, go, go, go, work, work, work, when you realize it's possible to turn a deaf ear on hateful words—that's when the men up in their Tower know they need to change the rules of whatever game they're playing with us.

Vanessa keeps trying to catch my attention; I see her nodding toward each Red we pass, as if I could somehow miss that they're there. The sleet has turned back into rain, and before we get within a hundred feet of the Mess, we're all drenched, the icy water slicing through our clothes and skin, down to our bones. I can't give the PSFs the pleasure of seeing me look at each of the Reds. I try to watch them out of the corner of my eye, assessing each face. I recognize about half of them; that makes sense. There just weren't that many Reds at Thurmond to begin with, and even back then, they tried to keep boys and girls separate at meals and the different work rotations. It was harder to cross paths with them, and it takes me a little longer to dig around for the right memories, but I have them. My eyes shift again, assessing what's ahead as we come up on the Mess Hall. And then—

I think I've been shot.

It happens that fast; the pain slices clean through me, and I imagine the bullet hits my heart at an angle. There are snipers on the roof of the Control Tower. They are always watching, always adjusting their aim. It's intolerable. The hurt takes away my breath. Sinks my feet in place.

But I'm not bleeding. I touch a hand to my chest, just to be sure.

Sammy. I can hear him say it even now. I've fought so hard to keep the sound of his voice from disappearing. *Sammy Sunshine.*

I'm not dying. Hallucinating, maybe. Because I think I just—I think I just saw—

Vanessa is the one that ultimately moves me forward again, driving her knee into the back of mine. The sting of it eases as I convince myself I imagined it. My fingers curl and uncurl into and out of fists and I feel like I'm somehow running inside of my own skin. I can't settle myself. I'm going to scream. The only way I can keep it from escaping is to press a fist against my mouth.

By the time we're inside the cloud of warm air drifting out from the open Mess Hall doors, the urge to look again is like a rubber band snapping and snapping and snapping against my skin. I wish I had resisted, not looked up at the boy posted at the door, his hands clasped in front of him, his stance steady and strong. Our eyes meet and dart away, and I hear his stiff black gloves creak as his fingers tighten around each other. The Mess is heated, yes, but it feels only lukewarm compared to the heat that's coming off him. A twinge of dread-stained recognition creeps down my spine, bone by bone, until I think my legs will dissolve under me. I recognize him the way you know the feel of sun on your skin after spending too long in the shade.

My mind doesn't let me forget faces. Sometimes it feels like a tiny miracle. A blessing. Others, a curse, some kind of punishment for all those times I disobeyed my parents and ran wild around the neighborhood. Good kids go to heaven; bad kids need to be rehabilitated. Now I know that must be true; I know that someone, whether they're up in paradise or down here in this little slice of hell, is trying to break me. I am being tested.

The years between us have thinned out his round face, made good on the promise of inheriting his father's chiseled features. Dark eyes sit below dark brows, thick dark hair. The rest of us are so drained of life after a sunless winter, we may as well blend into the snow, but he is lit from within. He is the best thing I have ever seen in my life. The worst thing.

I can't—I swallow the bile, try to shove away the last image my mind's preserved of him. Ten years old, calling up the singsong password to get into our imaginary castle in Greenwood—that secret kingdom he invented in the thick cluster of trees behind our houses. His hair shines like a raven's wing as he climbs up the rope to the tree platform his father had helped us build, takes his seat on the pillow we stole from one of their couches, and starts to read the story of the lost prince of Greenwood and a young knight—me—setting out to find him. He'd spent all day in school writing it; it made my chest tight to picture it, one arm wrapped around the notebook, protecting it from the cruel eyes of the boys sitting around us.

If I could, I'd spend my days locked inside the fantasy of our stolen time there, but I've never been able to disappear so completely into my imagination the way he could. It's stupid to be so hung up on it now. Even then, we should have been too old for play like that, or at least old and clever enough to name our magic land after something other than our neighborhood street. But it hadn't mattered then, and it doesn't matter now, and what surprises me, more than almost anything, is how badly it hurts to realize by our own rules I would be denied access to Greenwood, anyway—the requirements were kindness and goodness in your heart, and I barely know what those words mean anymore. I think of them and I see *him.* So how did they do this—to the boy who'd struggled not to cry when we found the overturned nest of eggs in Greenwood? *They didn't even have a chance,* he'd said.

I want to cry, I want to cry so badly, but the helpless fury that's been threatening to choke me for years has finally burnt through the last soft part of me. I want to give up.

Even in another life—another world—where everything was good and sweetly normal, seven years would never have been enough time to forget the face that belonged to Lucas Orfeo.

We won't be fed again until dinner, but I couldn't bring myself to eat a bite of the soggy mashed potatoes or the vegetable stew.

We've been eating the same tasteless crap for weeks, so it wasn't like I was missing much. I just didn't trust my stomach not to send it sailing right back up as soon as I managed to swallow it down.

Fear followed us into the Mess Hall, coating the silence, expanding until I thought it would eventually push the walls out of alignment. It multiplied faster than the weeds in the Garden. This is what makes it so hard—well, one of the many things that puts this place at the corner of bleak and misery. There's never an explanation. Not for the way we're supposed to behave, not for why they do the things they do. When they first began work on the Factory, Ruby said—

No. That wasn't right. Ruby wasn't here when they began turning the dark dirt over, burrowing down into earth. She hadn't been the one to wager the guess that the camp controllers were finally going to take care of the problem of us—permanently. Put us where no one would ever be able to find us.

I braced my forehead against my hands, trying to rub away the throb of pain behind my temples. I blinked again, and the image of a little dark-haired girl was gone, replaced by a panicked kind of anger. It grated on my nerves. Sent my heart galloping for no reason at all.

I was thankful for it, though, because the anger was the only thing strong enough to distract me from watching Lucas. The Reds, the five we'd seen before, had entered the Mess Hall and had made steady passes up and down the rows of silent wooden tables and benches. I wondered if they'd sensed as clearly as the rest of us had that they were still being watched, even as they'd been clearly elevated to watch us. The PSFs clustered in the corners of the large room, heads bending toward each other as they picked and tore apart the firestarters' every stiff movement. Part of me wondered if they were more afraid of the Reds than we were.

Lucas passed by our table twice, once behind me, once in front of me. Each time I looked away before he could catch me watching him, taking in every inch of his appearance, searching for my friend in him. Trying to convince myself I wasn't drowning myself in some kind of desperate delusion. It was like not realizing you were starving until a feast was laid out in front of you.

Older, taller, harder Lucas. Lucas with the dimple in his chin. *Red.*

The word ran circles around my mind as we walked over to the Factory, a single word that somehow encompassed a whole dark cloud of thoughts. *Red, Red, Red, Red.*

I'd thought about it, you know, wondered if the two of them were still alive, if they were in a camp like mine. My first few weeks here, I'd daydream about seeing them from across the Mess Hall or Garden, get hit with the false high of warm recognition despite it all being in my head. I clung to the possibility of it, even as the years marched on. Lucas would be Green, like me. I just wouldn't see him because they kept the boys and girls separate. Mia would be Blue, which would also explain why I hadn't seen her. They didn't let the colors mix unless we were in the Garden. I nursed that little hope for years, shielding it, keeping it close to me like a candle in a rainstorm.

And maybe some part of me remembered that story—Sir Sammy, fair knight, off to find and rescue Prince Lucas from the outcropping of rocks that doubled as a dungeon and fortress depending on the day. I'd sing, and he'd answer with a shout, I'd sing and he'd answer again, over and over until we were tired of the game or were called in for dinner. I always found him where I knew he'd be. It was the searching that was the important part.

Eventually, you grow up and you stop pretending. This place beats every last dream out of you. It clears your head of such stupid things. The truth is simple, not a glossy fairy tale. Lucas was a year older than me and three years older than his sister, Mia, but neither had been hit with IAAN in the time I'd known them. They moved away a few months before I realized I'd already been affected by . . . the virus, the disease, whatever it was. Their parents had both lost their jobs and headed a ways north to try to find work in a bigger city.

Bedford was a small town made even smaller by the economic crash and the bottomed-out markets that the people on TV couldn't shut up about. My parents hadn't let me say good-bye to the Orfeos—they'd never liked their "influence." They'd whisper that word like it was the devil's own name. *Influence.* They didn't like how I acted when I finally came home, zipping through the rooms, trying to recreate the carefree way we'd run around their house and outside in Greenwood, smacking each other with plastic swords. They didn't like it when I told them about Mrs. Orfeo giving us snacks, or when I repeated something she had said. It took me a while to understand that when you don't like someone, nothing they can say or do will ever seem right. Something as harmless as giving a kid a cookie becomes something aggressive, a challenge to their authority.

So I'd watched them drive off from my bedroom window, crying my stupid eyes out, hating everyone and everything. I didn't stop until I found the bundle of sparklers he'd left for me in the tree fort. The notebook of stories he'd spent three years writing. I kept them there so my parents wouldn't find them and take them away. I wonder all the time if they're still there. If Greenwood exists anywhere outside of my head.

My family only got to stay because we lived off the charity of the Church. I don't know if my parents are in the old house, or if they picked up and moved as far from the memories of their unblessed freak child as they could. I wish I didn't care.

Lucas and one other Red, a girl with cropped blond hair, served as our escorts. I had to force myself to stare at the back of Ashley's head to keep from looking at him when he suddenly matched my pace. I swear, he was warm enough that the snow melted before it touched him—that he kept me warm that whole miserable trek through the mud and sleet. But that would have been crazy.

Where was he sent, if not to Thurmond? Where is Mia? Is she like him, or me, or is she one of the other colors?

The metal Factory doors always sound like they are belching as they are dragged open by the PSFs waiting inside. My hands are useless, cramped and stiff from the cold, but I try squeezing the water from my hair and sweatshirt anyway. We leave a trail of smeared mud and water behind us that the Green cabins on cleanup rotation are going to have to mop up after last meal.

Ice still clouds the skylights—not that there's any real sun to filter through the clouds of dirt this morning. Winters stretch on forever in this place, dragging out each dark hour until it becomes almost unbearable. There's one thing I can't remember: what it feels like to be truly warm.

The building is large enough to swallow several hundred kids whole. The main level is nothing but stretches of work tables and plastic bins. The metal rafters above are usually crowded with figures in black uniforms clutching their large guns, but today there's only a dozen, maybe less. About that many on the ground, too. A thought begins to solidify at the back of my mind, but I push it away before it can take shape. I need to focus. I need to get through today, and maybe tomorrow will feel easier. It always gets easier as you get used to it.

I see one of the PSFs throw an arm out, pointing to where Lucas needs to stand against the far wall. When he stares at him blankly, the black uniform lets out an explosive cuss and maneuvers him there by force. We see, at the same exact moment the PSFs do, that the Reds need to be shown exactly what to do. And somehow, this scares me more than thinking that these kids have been turned against us, that they might want to voluntarily hurt us. It means that they are nothing more than weapons. Guns. Point, ready. Point, aim. Point, *fire*. They are like the old metal toy soldiers Lucas was given by his grandpa. Unable to act on their own, but shaped with edges sharp enough to cut your fingers if you're not careful.

I don't care what he is. I don't care what he could do to me—I care about what they've done to my Lucas. I've seen enough Red kids to know what the ability does to them, how hot they burn inside their own heads. We thought that they took these kids out to kill them, and now I see they've done something much worse. They've taken the soul out of the body.

Is this the cure? Is this what they've been working on?

After all these years, this is what we have to look forward to? Blank faces, blank minds. And their eyes . . . My stomach clenched. The Reds hadn't particularly cared who got in the way of their abilities, but when another kid got hurt, it was more often than not an accident. With each escape attempt, each fight they sparked, we knew that when it came down to it, they would be on our side.

I move stiffly into place, fitting into my usual spot at our table. It's only when they shut the doors that I begin to feel sensation coming back into me, and even then, it's only because Vanessa and Ava are crammed next to me, shoulder to shoulder. Can't talk, but at least we can share the heat that comes off our skin as we start moving.

A plastic bin on the table is filled with what looks like an assortment of old cell phones. There are no instructions given, only three separate bins in front of that one, each a different color. In the Factory, you assemble, sort, or disassemble. They want each phone broken down into three parts—I watch Vanessa take apart the first one to see if her suspicions match mine. Battery in one bin, the storage card in another one, the plastic casing in the third.

The work we do here isn't important. They can't give us anything sharp, or anything we may be tempted to take and use later as a weapon—against our soft skin, or theirs. No scissors, even. It's all just work to tire us out. Make us easier to shuffle around and be prodded into our places. After standing on your feet for six hours each day for weeks on end, there's not enough fight left in you to resist the pull of sleep at night. Not enough thoughts left in your head to wonder where the uniforms you've sewn or phones you've dismantled are going.

My fingers seem to be as jumbled and clumsy as my mind today. I can't get it together—keep it together. I drop the phone case in my hand before I can even pop the battery out, sending it crashing against the concrete floor. Ava stiffens beside me, shrinking away so that any PSF who may be watching will know that it wasn't her. I drop down onto my knees, quickly patting around blindly under the table until my fingers close around it.

Get it together, Sam. My head feels light enough to drift away from my neck like a balloon. I try to stand up, and my vision flashes white black white. When Vanessa takes my arm, I let her help me back onto my feet. But the grip doesn't ease up, even after I'm steady.

I feel the approach from behind like a cold wind blowing up the back of my shirt, exposing me. *This is what a bird feels like,* I think, *when they feel a storm coming in the distance.* I know my breath is coming out in light gasps, and I hate myself for it. I hate the way I want to crawl under the table and fold myself smaller and smaller until I disappear completely.

I do not know what, in the end, makes a person who they are. If we're all born one way, or if we only arrive there after a series of choices. The Bible claims that the wicked act on their own desires and impulses, because God is good, only good, and He would never compel a soul to wickedness. That I'm supposed to count on justice in the next life, even if I can't have it in this one. My father would say that the Devil works us all to his own ends and that we must constantly be on guard to protect ourselves from him. It helps, sometimes, to think of the man behind me as the Devil himself; it's easier to become the lion I need to be. I can pretend I know his tricks, that he's not an unpredictable human with a temper he carefully cultivates like a rose with razor thorns.

It helps. Sometimes.

He doesn't say anything at first, but his breath is hot on the back of my neck, and his smell—oil, cigarette smoke, vinegar, and sweat—wraps around me like an embrace, trapping me where I am. My movements become painfully careful. The sweat that comes to my palm makes holding on to each case a challenge, but I won't let my hands shake. I refuse to give him the pleasure of knowing that he affects me any more than the other PSFs.

He's one of the few that still wears a full PSF uniform; all black and menace, with the embroidered red Psi symbol over his heart under the stitched name *Tildon*.

I keep my eyes on the bins in front of me, but I wonder, I wonder all the time, if he or any of them would do these things if we were allowed to meet them eye to eye. Would they feel as free to hurt someone as human as they are? Maybe they just wouldn't care.

I should know better; he's not someone who likes to be ignored. The PSF lets out a disgruntled sound that seems to rip through my eardrums. He takes a step back and I'm just about to release the breath I'd held when I feel a hand slip under my sweatshirt. Under my shirt. A thumb rubs down my spine.

It's me.

I see the thought reflected in the relieved faces of the girls around me. This is the third day in a row since the rotation began that he's zeroed in on me, come sauntering over like a hunter picking up a bird he's shot out of the sky. I can't believe it. I don't want to believe that it's *me*.

My muscles lock first. My head buzzes, emptied of every thought. The sudden shift from badgering bully to—to *this* actually tilts my world. It's a soft, delicate touch, and so vile I think my skin is actually crawling to get away from it. I don't know what to do—I know what I *want* to do. Scream, shove him away, give in to the burn of bile in my throat. I've been hit so many times it's never occurred to me that this kind of touch could be that much worse than the pain. The hand slides around my hip, down—

I straighten, turning my head to the side. Vanessa's face disappears as she turns away, letting a cloud of curling dark hair protect her. What does she have to be afraid of? It has taken years for us to see the pattern of his interest, the careful process of his selection. Last month, when we overlapped cleaning duty with another Green cabin, a girl whispered to us about what happened to her bunkmate. While I am in the room, there will be no one else to him. Only, the attention from the past two days has focused, sharpened from mocking cruelty to something . . . something like *this*.

"Work faster." His voice makes me think of the way condensation collected on walls of my parents' unfinished basement. The stones are so dark and the lighting is so bad, you don't feel the cold drip until it's already on your skin. You can't avoid it.

I see his reflection in the screen of the next phone I pick up. His body is hot and damp and it repulses me more than even the sight of his face. How can someone who looks so normal, like the man who'd delivered our mail each afternoon, be this way? I want to know what hole he crawled out of, and how I can send him straight back into it.

There are others watching this happen, from above, from around me. I feel their eyes, can sense the attention in the room shifting the longer he stands there, smelling my hair, pressing against me. Even as the hatred boils over in me, shame is right on its heels. It's the stupidest thing in the world, I know it is, but I am ashamed of what he is doing to me and that others are seeing it.

When I still don't react, he grabs my wrist, wrenching it back up into the air. "Search!" he calls out, clearly delighting in the word. "Assistance!"

It was quiet in the Factory before, but now I can actually hear the rain bleeding through the cracks in the ceiling. Rain and sleet slash against the walls and glass overhead, washing against them like waves. I think I am drowning; I am actually choking trying to get air to my chest. Before today, I would have stood there and just taken it, but I know now that there's something he's looking for. Something he wants to see.

He'd lie about me stealing something from the bin just to strip off every last layer of clothing and shred of defense I have left in front of everyone. When we were kids, this was nothing. A female PSF would lead us to the far corner of the room and stand over us as we took off our uniform to prove that we weren't hiding anything. I'm not a kid anymore, and none of the women seem to be coming forward. I see one in the rafters, older, thick at the waist, and she's watching this all play out with a pinched look on her face. She isn't walking toward the stairs. None of them are.

But they don't look surprised.

So he starts the process for them, tugging my shirt the rest of the way out of my shorts. I hear Vanessa let out a startled gasp, swinging around and bumping the table.

I push my elbow back, trying to dislodge him.

"Careful," he warns.

Hot shame washes through me. I'm furious at myself for showing these other girls I won't fight back. Ava is watching me with eyes that are pools of helpless horror, and I realize, with sudden clarity, that if it were any one of them, *any* of the girls in my cabin, I would have done something immediately, said anything to have made it stop. I need to do the same for myself.

Because I know where this is heading. Before the Green girl told us, we'd heard whispers in the wash houses and out in the Garden. I know what language his touch is trying to speak, and I feel old Sam, the lion, roaring through my blood again. No one gets to believe that I won't fight.

I know that pride is a sin, but I would rather be dead than let him—*any* of them—think for one more second he's allowed to do this to me.

When I feel him lean forward again, I don't hesitate. I drive both elbows back into his gut, catching him off guard. I know it doesn't hurt him—that's why I throw my head back and make sure to nail him in the face, too.

And I feel like I'm spinning, spinning, spinning, reckless with delight in the small power I've managed to take back.

Vanessa and Ava both scream. Out of the corner of my vision, I see a blur of red coming toward us and I realize that my vision is hazy because my eyes are watering from the blow. My blood is thrumming in my skull, but I can't feel any pain. I barely hear Tildon when he starts cussing and spitting out one vile word after another. A PSF stands a short distance away with bugged-out eyes, looking between us and a soldier talking into his radio, saying, *No*, and, *Calm Control*, and *Handled*—

I swing around to face Tildon as he gasps out, "Little . . . *bitch!*"

He's clutching his nose, the words muffled by fingers and blood. He fumbles for the small White Noise machine at his side and I lash out with my foot, kicking it away. I feel a thousand feet high, like I could land another hit on him before the soldiers in black reach me. So, I do. I haul my hand back and slap him as hard as I can across his face, curling my fingers at the last second.

The nails I've broken working day after day in this Factory cut into the slick, fleshy part of his cheek. The breath goes out of him like a blown-out tire; the blood dribbling down his lips sprays out, sending a fine mist of it onto my sweatshirt.

He is scarlet with rage as he stumbles toward me, swinging his free arm to try to club me with his meaty fist. The girls around me have crawled under the tables; I'm dimly aware of the voices and wait for the White Noise, the gunshot, the end to my story. It's been so long since any of us tried this that I wonder if they've forgotten what they're supposed to do.

They come out of the stunned haze soon enough. The swing of a nearby baton registers as a change in the flow of the air around me. It whistles as it swings down. By the time it's there to connect with my skull, I'm already falling forward. The weight that's slammed into me from behind drops me to the floor. My chin connects with the concrete and I taste blood. There is not a single part of me that isn't throbbing in pain, but somehow I'm not done yet. The figure on top of me is feeding the fire. I kick back, trying to catch him—he can't have me, I won't let Tildon do this.

My hands are wrenched from under me and pinned with difficulty against my back. The hand that closes around them is large enough to capture both wrists at once and secure them with plastic binding. I toss my head back, rearing up like a bucking horse, and the warmth at my back shifts, leaning closer to my ear. He breathes out one word.

"Sammy."

TWO

LUCAS

HE IS GOING TO KILL HER.

You spend time living inside anger, you start recognizing its varying violent shades. He huffs and puffs like the Big Bad Wolf, and he's so slow to recover from that first blow to his chest, he can't avoid the back of her skull as she sends it sailing straight into his face. Between the blood that's rushed to his face, and the blood that's come rushing out of his crooked nose, the PSF's skin looks blistered by his own rage. This is the kind of anger that cracks bones. Crushes windpipes.

It's not until she turns around and claws him across the face that the realization sinks my heart like a stone. The trickle of recognition turns into a roar as the girl turns back in my direction, breathing hard, harsh lines turning a beautiful face defiant. She looks like some kind of warrior with her thick, honey-blond hair falling out of its tie, her face flushed with grim satisfaction. This is the face of a girl who once jumped out of our tree and broke her arm, just to prove to me she wasn't scared like I was.

This is Samantha Dahl.

You fucking idiot, I think savagely, my hands pressing tight against my legs to keep from curling into fists. *Shit, shit, shit.* I've seen her before as she was walking toward the Factory—well. Before that. I saw her this morning going into the Mess. I saw her inside the Mess. I saw her every step of the walk over here, feeling every bit as creepy as I must have looked hovering nearby. My eyes kept skipping back to her, drawn to her face like a lone candle flame in the dark. I'm so damn stupid that even when I saw the faint scar above her lip, curved toward her nose, I thought, *She must have had a cleft lip like Sammy.* I was so damn busy looking around, searching for one particular face, that I missed the one right here.

He touched her. I watched him do it. Draping himself over her like that—I thought he wanted to intimidate her, push her around like they do with all the kids here. But the look on his face was like a snake's—eyes glassy, mouth in a permanent, smug smirk, skin gleaming under the milky lights. He looked drunk on the feeling, turning his face toward her ear. I had to concentrate on controlling my breathing. Up in the rafters, the PSFs hovered like hawks, unsure whether or not to intervene with the hunt happening below. I don't know what they thought when they looked at each other, but I do know they didn't do one damn thing to stop it when he got a hell of a lot bolder. Useless pricks. I know what "search" means. He was going to strip her right here, in front of everyone. Use it as an excuse to demean her. Control her totally.

And Sammy—she was never going to let that fly. I see it in her face. She knows exactly what's going to happen to her, and she just doesn't care. She is a fighter against the ropes, ready to go down swinging.

I can't do a damn thing.

They haven't given me the order to move. To restrain her. To do anything other than stand here like a scarecrow, trying to keep the fluttering kids at bay with nothing other than their own fear. To the camp controllers and PSFs, our minds have been drained of will, of impulse, of that fluid connection between the head and the heart that lets you make decisions. The Trainers know the fire in us is bottomless. They took care to beat the flames out early into the program, leaving us little piles of embers that respond only to their hands adding fuel to turn sparks into a blaze.

The PSFs need to think I don't feel a thing as I watch the scene play out like a car crash in front of me. I've survived this long under the government's "care" because I have followed the only rule I have: *Don't react.* I must stand as blank-faced as the others even as the temperature spikes to a thousand degrees in the center of my chest, and I sweat with the effort it takes to control myself to be *still.* I can't throw years of work away in an instant, let them drag me out back and put me down like a dog—the way they did to the other kids who didn't take to their training methods. The ones who burnt themselves out, too hot, too volatile for even the most skilled Trainers to approach. Some resisted the training for weeks—months. I could see the light moving in their eyes when everyone else was checked out, vacant, scratching at their lives like dull pencils until the Trainers handed them a sharpener. I am the last one. I know it. The others are standing right in front of me, but they're gone.

I protect my fire the only way I know how.

There's a place deep inside of me that no one can reach. I keep the things there I won't let the Trainers take, locked up tight where no knife can cut them out, no lash can slice them, and no shock of electricity can void them. When I was a kid, a little one, it was a place where stories took shape—where Greenwood really existed. In class, I'd be listening to the drone of our teacher one minute and, the next, fighting giants with Sammy, running from wizards, defending our tree from monster rats. If Mrs. Brown called on me, forget it. I was gone. When I snapped out of it, either because someone kicked my chair, the other kids were laughing at me, or the bell went off, I still left the room smelling the damp dirt in the forest, feeling scratchy bark on my palms. My heart would still be slamming against my ribs.

There's that phrase: getting lost in your own thoughts. Well, I disappeared. Mom gave me the dumb, horrible nickname Turtle because of it. She'd catch me sitting at the kitchen table staring at my notebook, not moving, just playing some crazy idea through, watching a full-on film of imagination play behind my eyes, and have to physically shake me back into reality. Same with reading. I lost so many hours to books with the world blanked out around me. Maybe different parents would have tried to break the habit, but mine let me slide into my shell when I needed to. I was the one that stopped letting myself go. When things got . . . when they got bad, I had to grow up. Stop dreaming.

But damn if the first time the Trainers had me down, hands tied, feet tied, I was scared so shitless I just instinctively went to that headspace. It was like jumping into the deep end of the pool, letting myself sink to the bottom as they hammered away the surface of the water. I was deaf to their voices, even as they screamed in my ear. I felt the echo of the pain they gave me later, when my skin stained itself with bruises and I tried to knit the open pieces back together. They pulverized us early on, turned us to raw meat. Easier to shape that way. It was a cycle. Show fear, get pain. Show anger, get pain. Show humor, pain. Happy, pain.

Sadness, pain. Want, pain. In the spaces between eating and pain, they drugged us. Sweet, black nothing.

That's what's left in the others. Nothing. Their armor wasn't as strong as mine. They couldn't get lost in a maze of memory the way I could. I write myself different pasts. I write myself different futures. The scenes feel real enough that I let myself stay locked inside my head for hours as the Trainers drill me with threats, rake poison words down my back.

Whenever they eased off, gave me food, water, medicine for the hurt, I didn't think *thank you, thank you, thank you, I will listen to you now I will never let you down again I need you thank you thank you* the way I heard the other kids sobbing until they were silenced with more pain. I didn't even notice. I was safe inside memories of Mom and Dad dancing as they cooked dinner together, forcing us to sing with them. Mia making me watch her perform a play she'd written about unicorns and fairies. Sammy. Sammy in the sunlight, laughing. Sammy racing me to the top of the tree, then again to let me win once. Sammy insisting I press my lips against hers just once as we sat up in our tree. Ten and eleven, three days before the move, my heart beating so hard, so fast I thought she could hear it, too. She wanted to know what was so great about kissing, and I couldn't ever say no to her when she turned those determined dark eyes on me.

Seven years I've been coaching myself for a moment exactly like this. I knew that I would find Mia in a place like this, and I'd need to be able to keep a lid on my anger until I figured out how to get us out. Lying on my cot at our facility, I imagined her shivering, pale, starving. I imagined them hitting her for one of her signature comebacks. I practiced the mask of apathy that came to the others so easily, killed my heart just enough to play the game.

It was pointless. I should have known my weak-ass heart better than that. Right now, I feel like I'm about to detonate. The heat under my skin is hot enough to melt my bones. My left arm gives a sharp jerk, and the humiliation of losing control over my body's horrible tic only makes the burn worse. I can't make it seem like I'm helping her, I can't lose this chance to find Mia and be sent back to the facility. But he can't do this to Sammy.

He called for assistance, I think, mind scrambling to put together the logic. I hear the camp controllers' voices chirping in my ear, asking for a status. And even though I can hear one of the PSFs, a woman, reply, no one up in the rafters is moving to give the man any sort of assistance. The command hangs in the air, waiting for someone to accept it. The Trainers told us our primary purpose here was to keep the other kids from acting out. Save fire, we were allowed to use force when necessary to meet that goal.

Good enough.

My body lurches forward. I jump over the tables between us, sending the girls working there flying back like a startled flock of pigeons. By the time I reach her, the PSF has the baton in the air, swinging down toward her, and the others are finally moving, taking aim. I slam into her from behind, too hard for her to really brace herself for the impact of hitting the ground, but I try to maneuver one of my arms beneath her. The PSF's baton catches the side of my skull and pain explodes behind my eyes.

Sam's body goes limp with shock and then, even after everything, she starts to fight again. It's the last gasp of energy from an animal that knows it's pointless, but still won't surrender. Not easily, not willingly. I admire the hell out of her for it.

"Restrain her!" I hear one of the PSFs shout.

Glad to, asshole. She's trying to buck me off, and the movement is enough to hide how bad my hands are shaking. I manage to get her arms behind her and reach for one of the zip ties in the pouch of my belt. Even the rain outside disappears under the PSF's hollering to the others, his wild gesturing, as the woman I saw before, her stance and face rigid, listens with one hand on his shoulder. The girls, the poor kids, are braced on the ground with their hands over their ears, like they're waiting for a bomb to drop. If they weren't scared of the Reds invading their hellhole, they are now.

I know it's a risk, but I have to try—if she keeps thrashing and struggling to knock me off of her, someone will take my place. And that someone won't care whether she walks out of this building in one piece.

I lean down, pressing a hand harder against her bound wrists. When did Sammy get to be so much smaller than me? Her wrists are like flower stems. I feel how easy it would be to break them.

Damn. I don't know if God still listens to me when I try talking to him. I don't know if he really knows the thoughts inside our heads or hears silent prayers. But please—please let this work. Let me get Sam out of here.

"Sammy." It's one word, spoken so quickly, so quietly near her ear, I don't know that you could count it as a whisper.

But she hears me. Her long body relaxes under where I've straddled her, and I pull back just as the woman PSF comes forward. Psi Special Forces Officer Olsen. Her dark skin is taut against the bones of her face as she cuts off Tildon's path toward us and looks between my carefully arranged face and where Sam's is pressed against the filthy floor. There are two horns that come over the speakers, one long, one short, and the two girls next to us each suck in a shuddering breath.

My head jerks up. I scan the room for the other Reds and see them reaching into the pouches on their belts—earplugs. *Dammit.* I was right. I release my grip on Sam long enough to pull mine out, jam them into my ears as far as they can go, and brace myself for impact.

A hit of Calm Control is like taking an icy cold bath where the water's been spiked with razors. The Trainers used it on us in the beginning, on and off and on and off for hours, but stopped a year in, when they realized daily use was making too many kids crack. And, let me tell you, you can reset broken bones and stitch up too-deep cuts, but you can't piece a mind back together after it shatters into a thousand flaming, furious pieces.

I remember those first days, though. They'd keep the flood-lights in our white cells on all day and all night, watch for the moments it seemed like you were about to finally pass out and sleep and then . . . the explosion of blinding hurt. No matter how deep I was in my own head, I could hear it muffled, the way I do now—growling static broken up by piercing screams that knock the breath out of you.

I hurt all over, a dull ache that turns into a chill rippling up and down my spine, but Sam—she's convulsing. Her breath rips in and out of her in sobs. It's the same for the other girls. The Factory fills with these horrible, breathy moans of pain; some of them sound like they're being eaten alive by it.

Olsen nods at me, signaling that I need to get up and move. I can't. For a second, it feels like my knees and feet have been cemented to the ground; it feels like if I don't keep a hold on Sam's wrists, her fingers, she's going to blow apart.

Get up, I command myself. *Don't look at her.* They would know—that I wasn't in their grip, that there was something between me and this girl. I keep my eyes focused on the PSF as I return to my full, stiff-backed height. For a moment, she studies the letter and numbers stitched over my uniform's pocket: M27.

"Situation under control." Olsen speaks into her comm unit; I can hear it in the one in my ear with a half-second delay. "Disable Calm Control."

Don't look at her. It is almost impossible. Panic sends my pulse through the roof. The PSFs swarm where Sam is on the ground, locking her inside a ring of black. I yank out my earplugs as the kids around me start to stir.

"You *know* what's supposed to happen, goddammit!" Tildon is shouting. "She *assaulted me!* It's my job—"

Olsen's gaze is so cold, it freezes the words in his throat. *She knows,* I think. She saw what happened, and for the first time I wonder if all of this has happened before, if the resignation in her eyes means she knows it'll happen again. And again. And again. But what can she do? There are tiers of punishments in this place—the Trainers made us memorize them. Additional work, missed meals, exposure, isolation, corporal punishment. They could pick and choose from the list, combine them, if that's what gets them off. What Sam has done is so far beyond being forced to skip dinner, I'm actually terrified I did the wrong thing in saving her.

Four minutes pass. No one moves. I breathe in. I breathe out. I try to dispel the heat trapped inside of my head. I'm afraid if I take a single step, I'm going to borrow the heat from the electricity powering the lights and send showers of sparks down over everyone's heads. *Control. Nothing. Numb. Control. Nothing. Numb.* I can't get a grip on my heart. It just wants to gallop. I have to slip inside my head, just to get away from this moment. But even my brain doesn't cut me any slack—the first memory that stirs up, meeting me, is Sammy, age eight, informing me she doesn't want to be a princess of Greenwood, she wants to be a knight, thank you very much. I laughed. She cracked a wooden sword against my head.

My fingers relax, as do the muscles in my shoulder and arm. Sam always quiets me; she finds me and leads me out of these dark places. The tic is still there, but less noticeable if I slide my hand into the pocket of my uniform trousers. The Trainers would have told the PSFs and camp controllers the tic—that involuntary spasm of muscle and joints—is a Red's calling card, and when it comes around, it means we're heating up. We're thinking, dreaming, tasting fire. Fine if it comes hand in hand with an order to attack, not so fine if it appears out of the blue. Mine has always been less pronounced than some of the others'. Disappears completely as long as I'm mostly calm. Thank God. I'd seen too many other kids get "treated" by a month's worth of daily, repeated ice-water submersions if they so much as flinched at the wrong moment.

Finally, the doors to the Factory are dragged open, and a dripping, dark figure jogs inside. He brings the frigid air in with him, cooling my temper, freezing me at my core. He's in what almost looks like civilian clothes—a black poncho, black slacks, boots. Under the heavy, rain-slick fabric, I see the lumps and bumps of a utility belt with a holstered gun. The man wipes the rain off his face as he pushes his hood back. The dark, graying stubble on his face gives it shadows that aren't really there. He strides toward us, every movement strong, brisk, efficient. He isn't military, but like the Trainers, he probably used to be.

I remember him. This is O'Ryan. He's the one that gave us our "orientation" the night before, when we were brought in. He assessed us as we passed by, the way my mom used to examine the cuts of meat in the grocery store, then waved us on to collect our uniforms and our red vests.

Camp controller. Shit. *The* camp controller. Something sticks inside my throat, sealing it off from the air I need to think.

Tildon shoots to his side, his face covered in grime and blood. Next to O'Ryan, who is as steady and silent as a mountain, he looks like an idiot as he flails and moves into the next phase of his tantrum. O'Ryan crosses his arms over his chest, listening but not listening, his eyes glancing between Sam and the PSF. Olsen speaks up toward the end, explaining how I was the one to finally restrain her, that I acted quickly and behaved exactly as I should have.

O'Ryan's pleased expression turns my stomach. I hide my clenched fist behind me and give him a salute when he says, "Well done, M27." And every second his eyes are on me, I have to wrestle with the anger all over again. I have to think of Mia's face when my fingers rub against each other, ready to snap a flame into the air. *Hurting him helps no one.* It wouldn't get me closer to finding my sister, it wouldn't do a single thing to help Sam—but I have a feeling it would be pretty gratifying to set the asshole on fire. I want so badly for all of them to experience the kind of hurt they've inflicted on us.

But more than that, I want to cover Sam. I want to cover her so none of these people can see her like this, too weak to even lift her head. The other kids are only just coming out of their daze, waking back up to this nightmare. They stay in the positions they've been taught to assume, though—face down on the floor, hands on the back of their heads. *Drip, drip, drip* goes the rain through the holes in the roof, splattering over them, into their plastic bins. The room smells like damp animal and urine and cigarette smoke. The lights flicker as the wind picks up.

"Fine, then put her in isolation. Two weeks," O'Ryan finally interrupts.

"Isolation," Tildon sneers. "She *attacked* me! The little bitch deserves at least twenty-five strikes! And I want her in the cages, not the Infirmary."

It's the first time Sam shows any reaction since the Calm Control. Her hands claw at the ground at that word, *cages*. Where the hell is that? The blood is draining out of my head. They said they sometimes tie them to the fences outside of the Garden, but isolation is the upper level of the Infirmary. Little padded, lightless cells. The kids there are broken, or need to be broken. Every hair on my body seems to prick and stand at attention.

"Fine. A night in the cages and ten strikes." I don't know if he saw Tildon's face light up, but O'Ryan quickly adds, "Delivered by Olsen."

Her posture relaxes as she swings around, away from Tildon's sputtering.

One last look from O'Ryan silences him for good. "Go clean yourself up," he says quietly, layering his voice with just enough of a threat to make Tildon straighten, "and report to my office immediately after."

He let a kid get the best of him—there'll be some kind of disciplinary action, at least. He deserves to be smeared against the ground like the shit stain he is. It won't be enough to balance out what he did to Sam, but it'll be something.

Olsen flicks her hand toward Sam, staring at me. These PSFs are all the same, aren't they? They resent the fact they brought us in to fill in the gaps in their security, but they love the power they wield in outranking us. We aren't human to them, even now that we're supposedly on the same side. We don't get eye contact or words. It makes me feel like a damn dog, staring at a master shouting a command in a language I don't understand.

It takes me a moment to translate what she wants, and, just as quickly, the horror slams right back into me. They're going to do it right here—they're going to hit her right here, and they want me to hold her up while they do it.

Fuck.

Them.

Olsen stares at me expectantly. The moment crashes down around me, and I feel something inside of me strain to its ultimate limit. I want to cry—I want to sob like a baby, *Don't make me do this, not to her, not to Sammy.* Why did I have to volunteer for this place? Why did I have to come here and find her? I wanted Thurmond because that's where they were supposed to take Mia. All I want is to find her. Mom and Dad are gone now. I'm all Mia has left. I'm her only chance to get out. I can't blow this and show them I'm not what I'm supposed to be. But I can't do this to Sammy. I would rather cut out my own heart.

My left arm twitches so hard, it's actually painful. I grab Sam under the armpits like she's one of Mia's dolls and try to prop her onto her feet, turning her around to face me when Olsen gives a little twirl of a finger. Her knees won't lock, and with her hands tied behind her, I can't hold her up as gently as I would have liked. I can't turn my back on the black uniforms and shield her from this, take the hits meant for her. There's a voice at the back of my head telling me to take her and run, to set the building on fire and just *go*, but I can't—I *can't*—my need to live, to find Mia, is a rope around my neck. I'm hanging us both with it.

Her lashes flutter and I know she's coming back to herself, which makes it that much more horrifying. *She's going to think I want this. She's going to hate me.* The thoughts are there, even as the more rational part of me thinks, *She doesn't even recognize you.* I feel sick enough supporting her full weight, watching her head loll to the side. I don't know how it's possible to feel worse when Olsen shakes her head and motions for me to clear the bins and lay her over her work table.

The girl with dark curling hair is openly crying beside my right foot. She gets a kick from one of the PSFs, who, apparently, is offended by the small whimpering sounds. I give up Sam's soft weight to the table, arranging her carefully so the hard wood supports her chest. I've barely stepped back when Olsen pushes forward, her baton in the air. In the space of one heartbeat to the next, she's already hit Sam twice, once across her shoulder blades, the other across her bottom, she alternates with each strike, and I know they're getting harder because Sam starts grunting at the impact of each one. Her eyes are open, devoid of light. I think she's looking at my empty, shaking hand, but then I realize she's not looking at anything at all. The pain and anger and hatred play out over her features, and I think, *She's got a fire in her,* I think, *I can't let it go out,* I think, *Please, God, please make this stop, I'll do anything*—

And then it does. Olsen is finished and looks back at Tildon, who is faintly smiling as he tries to smear the rest of the blood off his chin with the back of his hand. "The cages," he reminds her.

I don't know what they are, or where they are, but when Olsen says, "Follow me and bring her," I know that I'll at least be able to follow her into their hell. There's that, at least.

There's that.

I have to carry her over my shoulder, pinning her legs against me with one arm. Several times, I completely lose track of Olsen as she stomps through the rain and mud, arms swinging under her poncho. There's no way to shield us from the downpour, and I remind myself that I am supposed to be an unfeeling drone. I can't be cold or furious or even snap back at the PSF when she turns back to shout over the wind, "Keep *up!*"

Instead, I focus on Sammy's breathing. Feeling it go in and out in its light, but steady rhythm, calms the pounding pain in my head and the dizzying wave of nausea. I try to think of us in our tree fort, using slingshots and pebbles to defend our turf from those jackasses down the street, the Strider boys, but I send the memory sailing back to the farthest corner of my mind. Those thoughts are like grains of sugar in the salt of my life, and I don't want any part of them to be polluted by this moment.

I can't even give myself the pleasure of what I'd like to do to Tildon—I'd give my anger away in a heartbeat. So I focus on Sam's soft weight the whole walk over to a small wooden shack attached to the back of the Mess. It wasn't included in our debriefing. When they walked us through the camp this morning, I'd assumed it was storage for the Mess's kitchen.

Olsen stops outside of the metal door and taps her ID card against it, shielding the black pad from the rain. Sam is silent, but her teeth chatter as she shivers. My grip on her tightens as the door swings open, and I realize the shaking might be a mixture of terror and cold.

The room is small, the walls lined with stacked individual metal crates. The air in here is damp and frigid. There's a dark, wet crack in the ceiling. The moisture collected there is dripping down, catching the rust coating the cages' thin bars and falling to the ground like drops of blood. I know they must have kept dogs here at one point; the smell doesn't reach my nose so much as assault it. There are still sacks of unused dog food stacked beside the door. Collars and leashes hang useless and forgotten on hooks.

There are windows lining the top of the back wall, but only a faint gray-blue light manages to escape in. Olsen fusses with the light switch. Almost as if they'd been watching the struggle from the monitors in the Control Tower, a voice filters through our comm units: *"All units—we've lost the primary generator, backup is at 50 percent. Visuals are down. Return all Psi to their cabins and engage the locks manually. Status update in five."*

"Shit," I hear her grumble, swiping at her face in irritation. "Falling apart—"

Falling apart is one way to describe what's happening to this place. Falling to fucking shambles is probably more accurate. The last inspection deemed it unlivable, which also feels like a massive understatement. "You will participate in the relocation of the Psi at Thurmond to nearby rehabilitation facilities," the Trainers had told us on the flight over. "You will assist them in monitoring the Psi as the Psi Special Forces officers and camp controllers make the arrangements, remove the materials held there, and disassemble the structures."

When I first got here, I panicked at how little time there was to find Mia and get her out, but the swift guilt that came with the thought of having to leave the others boiled the contents of my stomach. But, now that I'm here, I am so damn elated that these kids are getting out, no matter the circumstances. Nowhere in the world is worse than this camp. No place as damp, cold, and filthy. I think the sun has forgotten this place exists.

"Put her down," Olsen says sharply. I can't drop her, but I can't set her down with the care I want to. Sam slumps forward on her hands and knees at the center of the old kennel. Olsen cuts the restraints on her wrists. I'm actually stupid enough to think, *This could be worse.*

"You know where to go." It takes a second to realize that she's talking to Sammy, not me. She tries to get up onto her feet, but pitches forward, off-balance. My body instinctively moves toward her. Olsen holds out an arm, blocking me—she watches, her face void of anything resembling emotion as Sam crawls toward the cage at the center of the bottom row. I don't want her so close to it—the pile looks unstable, one small knock away from crashing down. The movements are stiff and agonizingly slow as she struggles forward. She doesn't stop.

She hesitates a moment, then pulls the door open.

She crawls inside.

I am in shock.

I am . . .

Fire is calling my name. It is whispering words of encouragement, sweet things. It wants out, for me to fan the heat until it's a vortex that can't and won't be stopped. Olsen's back is to me, and there's no power feeding the camera in the upper corner of the room. It becomes an option, a real one, to turn her, this place, to ash. I think I can overpower even the storm outside.

"You deserve this for provoking him. He—" Olsen catches herself before another word can slip out. She hooks a padlock through the crate's door. Sam inches back, along the metal interior. The crate is just big enough for her to sit up with her back hunched over her knees. It's as far as she can get from this woman, her dirty lies and accusations. "Don't come into the Factory with your face clean. I will find you a larger uniform. Don't look at him, don't act like you want it. He will leave you alone if you stop tempting him."

This has happened before. Maybe not to Sam—maybe to a different girl. Many different girls? I'm surprised I'm not glowing in the dark. The pain in my head, in my chest, makes me sway.

"He likes your hair, I think," Olsen says, almost more to herself than to Sam. "That's easy enough to take care of."

Sam doesn't look up. Just nods. What choice does she have? This is a place that turns beautiful things into shadows. They'll cut off her hair and the traces of sunshine in it. They'll rough her up, make her harder, uglier, skinnier, instead of solving the real problem.

Olsen stands up, kicks at the door one last time to test it, and then turns back to me and inclines her head toward the exit. I set my jaw and follow, pressing my arms against my sides to hide the involuntary jerk my left shoulder gives. Shit. Twice in a single day. I need to cool it.

Just as I think she's going to force me to leave with her, she turns her back toward the crates and murmurs, "Stay here until notified by Control that surveillance is operational, then return to your assigned posting."

I don't have to leave her here alone. I don't know who to thank for tossing me this life ring of mercy, so I settle on God. Olsen waits for my curt nod before opening the door and ducking out into the storm, letting the door slam shut behind her.

For the first time in seven years, there is no one watching me. There is a camera in the corner of the room, but if the power is out in this craphole, what are the chances it's feeding out to Control Tower? The weight bearing down on me from all sides pulls back, and I feel boneless as I lean forward against the door and press my hands against my face. I don't want her to see me on the verge of losing it.

Minutes pass before a soft sound reaches my ears. I spin on my heel, mistaking it for moans of pain. But it's . . . there's a melody. It's raw, carried out on uneven breaths, but she's humming. The words come to me, rising up through bleak memories. I know this. *He's got the whole world in His hands, He's got the whole world in his hands, He's got the whole world in his hands.* How many times did we sing this in Sunday school while kicking each other under our table?

I step closer and see her shaking, her whole body. From the cold, from exhaustion, from pain, it doesn't matter. She tries to smother it by curling up tight, but her breath hitches and I know she's trying as hard as she can not to cry. She's fighting fear itself with both hands tied behind her back.

I know it's not actually meant for me when I shuffle forward again, and the song dies on her lips. She looks up just as I crouch down, dark eyes flashing uncertainly. I brace myself for this. If she doesn't remember, then—I shake my head.

"*This little light of mine,*" I sing softly into the silence. "*I'm gonna let it shine . . .*"

Her breath catches again, but the look on her face hardens and her words come out in a snarl. "If you're making fun of me, you can go to hell with the rest of them."

She doesn't remember. It's pathetic how my heart gives a painful jerk. I force a small smile on my face, which only deepens her scowl. "The last time I made fun of Sammy Dahl, she beaned me with a sword and almost knocked me out of a tree."

It takes her a moment to process what I've said. I can actually see the light come back into her brown eyes. The air leaves her chest in a shuddering, disbelieving laugh. "You remember. You remember me."

My relief is mirrored on her face as she crawls toward me. A laugh or sob bubbles up in my chest at the irony of both of us afraid of the same impossible thing. It takes a sharp blade, a huge effort to separate one half of a coin from the other. It would take something a hell of a lot stronger and sharper to separate me from her.

"Lucas," she whispers.

It feels so damn good to hear my name and not a number. To hear it from her. My mom and dad used to tease me so much about her—puppy love, they called it. I guess I must have been leashed, because I followed her around like one. I would have followed Sammy anywhere, led her out of any trouble she got herself tangled in. She made my little eleven-year-old heart actually flutter. She turned me dumb and shy with a single smile.

Even this morning, before I made the connection, she had my full attention. Whatever it had been before, the feeling solidified, took root, blossomed. Having her on the other side of the metal bars, only inches away, suddenly feels too far. I didn't appreciate it enough when I was holding her before. I didn't recognize the miracle of it. *She's real, she's here.*

It's a mess inside me. She has cracked me, left me open and exposed. I'm suddenly terrified of how fast it can and will all disappear. I can't stop trembling. The feelings that come roaring out are trying to wash me away from the moment. It's been so long since I've let myself really—*really*—feel something other than anger that I'm not sure I can even remember the names of half of these emotions, only that they eat me up, they devour me whole, and I have never been so grateful as I am in this moment that I am capable of the simple act of *feeling*. I understand now, maybe in a way I didn't before, what the other Reds have lost to the Trainers. They will never have this, will they? They might not ever know the feeling of cozying up to a lightning bolt, what it feels like to look at someone's face and see your heart there.

The peace inside my head, the murmurs of happy memories, they're pale compared to how it feels to live inside a real moment like this. I let my heart tune itself like a radio jumping between stations; I can't move, but it feels like I'm careening around the room. I am bursting with that same breathless excitement I had whenever Sam and me would run through Greenwood. When I'd get myself lost and wait for her to come. She is singing a song that only I can understand, and I call back, I call back. She finds me where I've been hiding all along.

You are the biggest sap in the universe, Orfeo.

We're not supposed to care about others. The Trainers want

to leave nothing in our hearts but them. I focus on her face again, tired, pale, bruised, and think of sunlight, grass, golden hair, the feel of rough bark on my palms as we climbed up and up and up into the tree fort. The singe of sparks on the Fourth of July as they rose and showered down around us. I don't speak until the bad feelings clear and my mind is blue skies again.

"Hey, Sunshine," I whisper. My parents' nickname for her, Sammy Sunshine. The word stuck in my throat, left it raw. "I'm sorry. God, I'm so sorry—I wanted to kill them, all of them—"

"You couldn't," she says, resting her forehead against the bars. I want to melt the hinges off the door, pry it open and scoop her out. Sam must read it in my face because she adds, quickly, "You *can't.*"

Her soft breath fans across my face. I breathe in the smell of soap and detergent and rainwater.

"Are you in pain?" I ask, though I already know the answer.

"I'm okay," she says, bravely. "I've had worse." I shudder, because of course she has.

Her hands are small enough that she can slide one through the gap in the crate's bars. She reaches for me and I seize it like I'm drowning and she is the only thing that can pull me clear. My other hand hooks on the door and, within an instant, she's covered my fingers with her own. It's not enough.

"You're warm," she whispers, a strange note in her voice.

"Red," I say, trying to hide the flush of shame. "Comes with the territory. Megafreak."

Sam pulls her face back, her eyes hard. "Who called you that?"

"No one. Everyone." I smile, recognizing her indignation all too well. "What are you gonna do about it, Sammy?"

She looks down, her own small smile touched with sadness. "Let the air out of their bike tires. Set off fireworks under their window. Hit them with snowballs walking home from school."

"My champion," I say. "My hero." I'd seen her do all that and more when some of the guys at school picked on me for no reason other than my best friend was a girl. Kids can be real dicks, even without the freak abilities.

Sam seems to remember where we are suddenly, breaking from her own daze. She tries to pull her hand back through the bars, but I won't let her.

"The power is out," I remind her, "the camera isn't on. It's just you and me."

Her face is so flustered that I know it's more than that. Sam has her pride. She doesn't want me to see her like this, despite everything. This may be the one chance I have to talk to her; she has to know that the only thing I care about is that she's safe and alive and that I hate that I can't hold her and touch her and . . .

I almost can't believe it, that it's the first reaction I have, that it's still there after everything that's happened this morning.

It's because you've been alone, it's because everyone is gone and you can't admit to yourself you're scared, and because it feels like home, it'll feel like nothing ever changed. I know all of it is true, but I also know, on a very basic, human level, hers is the most beautiful face I've ever seen. They must have created art specifically for people like her, to try and fail forever to capture these small looks, all her various angles and the colors of her moods.

The urge is overwhelming, and I wonder . . . I wonder if she's thinking about the same thing, because her eyes keep flicking down to my lips before finding my eyes again. It doesn't make sense. She's in pain, we are in actual hell, and none of it seems to matter.

But isn't this how it always was with us? When we were together, the world shrank around us. Nothing else existed outside of that space between us. We took Greenwood with us wherever the two of us were together.

"Lucas," she says again, "it's . . . this isn't . . . were you here? Before?"

I shake my head. "No—I don't know where the Facility is, but I was never here. Mia, though—I overheard the PSFs say they'd bring her here." I almost can't ask. "Have you seen her?"

"No. What color is she? Do you know?"

For a moment, I can't speak at all. I want to look at Sam's face, the curve of her cheek, her eyes, until the blistering pain leaves. Sometimes I am suffocated by the memory of how helpless I was then, when I tried to get her away from the PSFs. I had fire, but they had Calm Control trapped in a little device. "I don't know. They took her before she . . . before she changed. I had already gone through it, but they wanted to take her as a *precaution*. They kept saying that. *Precaution*. I overheard one of them say she would be taken here, but—" It's the first time I've admitted this out loud, and it feels just as horrible and bitter as I knew it would. "I don't know if she lived through the change. When it happened. What she is."

Sam gives me a sharp look. "No. She survived. She would have. Mia was strong."

"Strong doesn't have anything to do with it."

Still, she continues on, undaunted, and I love her for it. "She's not Green. I would have seen her by now. There's a chance she could be Blue. There are so many of them, and unless we have the same shift in the Garden. If she was Yellow—"

I don't like the catch in her voice. "If she's Yellow, *what*? There aren't any Yellows here."

"They took them out a little bit after the Orange and Red kids," she says. "She might have been here and then taken out— moved. I don't think they would have killed them. If they didn't do it to the Reds—"

"Right. If the Red monsters get to live, then everyone else should be fine."

"Stop it," Sam says, and this time succeeds in pulling away from me. "Lucas, look at me. Look at me." As helpless against her as always, I do. "The Reds who were here were . . . very broken. I don't think it was their fault. But they were the only ones brave enough to try to do something. Fight back. I didn't hate them then, and I don't hate them now. I'm not afraid."

"You aren't afraid of anything," I say.

"She could be here. I'll help you look. We'll find her," she says. "Is that why you came here? Did you have a choice?"

I nod. They gave us the illusion we were choosing our assignments, thinking, I guess, that it would help us commit if we felt like we were making the choice of our own volition. All they did was open a door for me I'd been waiting to look through for seven years.

The rain and wind beat against the building, filling the silence. I finally see why the concrete under me is so wet—there's a gap between the wall and foundation in the back corner of the room. I look back at the bags of wasted dog food and start to rise, thinking I can at least stop the hole up.

"No—" Sam says sharply. "Wait—Lucas, don't—" Her voice falters. "Don't go."

I lower myself back to the ground. "I wasn't leaving. I won't leave you."

She's shaking again, watching me out of the corner of her eye. My heart gives a painful lurch.

"When—?"

"The change? A few weeks after we left Bedford—"

"That soon? Are you—"

"The same old Lucas?" I have to joke about this, I'm that desperate for one small part of this to feel normal. Normal-ish. Not soul-crushingly awful. "Unfortunately. Only now, I'm slightly more flammable."

She doesn't look amused, but my smile encourages hers, just a little bit. Her frantic plea fades from the room as if the rain were carrying it away. *"Fortunately."*

I try not to beam.

She studies me as openly as I study her. I feel caught somewhere between a memory and a dream, because everything about her is the same but just that tiny bit different. The roundness to her face has thinned out, and damn if what my mom said wasn't true all those years ago—she looks a lot like her own mother. The difference is, Mrs. Dahl had this . . . frigid quality to her, like a doll whose sole purpose was to have her hair brushed and her clothes changed before being placed on the shelf again to be admired. Never played with. Sammy seems almost feral in comparison, adapted to her situation here the way a lost dog has to relearn how to live outside in the wild. She's never, ever going to be trained; she's always going to bite and bark and run away.

He knows that, too, I think. Tildon knows that she's a challenge and he won't be satisfied until he's broken her. Pulled out all of her teeth and claws.

Finally, Sam asks the question she's been hovering around, unsure if she can approach it. "You're . . . not like the others, are you?"

As if on cue, a voice in my ear buzzes, *"Still on auxiliary power. All PSF units, report in."* I listen as twenty voices chirp in alphabetical order. *"Cabin one secure." "Cabin two secure."* Mess Hall, Infirmary, all of it, locked down. I sag against the crate. I have more time. It might not seem like much, but, to me, it's everything.

"Lucas?"

I glance at her concerned face, remembering her question. "I'm different. I didn't break."

She starts to slide her fingers through the bars again, but catches herself before she can reach me. I bow my head toward her, heaving in a deep, tired sigh. I don't know what to say. My mind is bending itself into knots of knots, trying to figure a way out of this, how I can help her, how the two of us can leave and find Mia together. It doesn't stop, the ache in my skull doesn't disappear, not until Sam tries again—reaching out to brush the dark, wet hair off my face. Her fingers are like ice, but I'm overheating, I'm burning.

"Don't go near the others, Sam," I whisper. "Don't look at them. Don't try to talk to them. There's nothing . . . human left inside. They'll hurt you. It's what they were trained to do."

"But not you?"

"I'm not . . . I'm not totally right inside," I try to clarify. "I've felt what they want me to feel." The sweet nothing that comes from pushing through the pain, leaving your mind empty. "But I have . . . ways of dealing."

I see her digesting this, the moment her eyes light with understanding. There's a faint smile on her face. "Turtle."

I squeeze my eyes shut and nod. Mom's nickname scorches my heart.

"It helps me cope. If I'm lost in my head, I can't hear them. I don't feel them. They can't break me, but they can't know they haven't. So I have to . . . I have to do the things they ask. Bend. Follow orders."

"Sometimes we have to bend," she says, "to survive."

"Is that what you call this morning?" I ask. "Bending? Looked more like snapping to me."

Sam lets her hand fall away, turning her gaze away from mine. Her jaw sets stubbornly, jutting out slightly. It's so Sammy, I have the irrational urge to laugh, but I'm not sure I really remember how. This is the girl who never wanted to play princess.

"Was that the first time he did that?" I say. "How long has he . . ."

"How long have I been *tempting* him?" She spits the word out. I see the lion coming back into her. Her nails curl against the floor like claws. "Since the rotation started a few days ago. He was just assigned to our cabin block. Some of the girls in another cabin . . . Look, it'll be okay. I'll figure out a way for him to lose interest."

God. It's exactly what I thought, isn't it? He's fixated on her. He's fixated on other girls in the past. And instead of dealing with the actual issue, the camp controllers keep moving him around. Not even moving him to a block of *boy* cabins.

Unless they already tried that, too, and it didn't matter to the piece of shit. I feel like I'm going to be sick. There's smoke in my lungs, filling my chest.

"It's him, not you." I say the words fiercely. "You've done nothing wrong. If he tries it again, I'll—"

"Do *nothing*," she says. "You can't. No, *listen* to me. You have to find Mia and figure out . . . You have to get out of here. Promise me."

"I won't promise," I say. "If he touches you again, he's ashes."

"You can't do *anything*, Lucas. You can't. That's the point of this place."

And that's just it, isn't it? They've taken everything away from us, including the right we have to protect ourselves. This is what it means to be powerless—we are dependent on them for everything, even common decency. We have to trust that they'll behave like actual humans.

"Run. As soon as you get a chance. Get out of here and find your parents and—" Sam leans forward again, cutting herself off. Her brows draw together. I can't hide my expression from her, and I know how it must look. I don't want to have to hide the pain anymore. I can't hide anything from her, anyway.

"Oh . . . oh, Lucas, *no*," she whispers. The missing years stretch out between us, and I hate that I have to fill them, that I have to tell her this. I hate all of the what-ifs. What if we'd just stayed where we were and tried to fight through it? What if I'd come to Thurmond with Sam and Mia and I'd known, at least, where I could find them? "What happened?"

I try to shrug off the ache that pierces my chest. "We—we went up to Pennsylvania, to live with Grammy and Pops. You remember?"

"Of course."

"We couldn't stay with them after they started making those announcements about Collections. I'd already changed. It was too dangerous and people knew where we were. So we left and went a few towns over." We lived out of our car in an abandoned parking garage, but I couldn't tell her that, not when her face was already so shattered. It wasn't even that bad, you know? We put up sheets in the window during the day, when Dad went out to look for work, and Mom and Mia would try to outdo each other with their stories. Sometimes I think about being small enough to lie across the backseat, my cheek against the fabric, just listening to Mom as she voiced each of her characters. Dad would come back with food and a smile, lean across the way and kiss her. I miss the days that were boring, hot, and long, because those were the days when I felt safe.

"It was just . . . it started as a carjacking. The two guys were out of their heads on something. It turned into something else when they realized me and Mia were there. My parents weren't going to let us go. Mom reached for the money we'd been keeping in the glove box. They panicked, thinking she had a gun, too. Dad tried to cover her. It was over so fast."

"Are you sure they're dead?"

The stench of blood and smoke fills my senses, and the rumbling of pain starts at the back of my head, carrying forward like a rattling drum. I focus on the rain's pattering so I don't have to hear Mia's screaming.

"God," she says, "of course you are. I'm sorry. You can't . . . you . . ." She's blinking hard, trying to clear her throat until she gives up, and I see the first tears collecting on her lashes.

"Your folks?" I ask.

I didn't like the Dahls. At all. Sammy was the best thing

about them, and they never once recognized it. I don't know how someone like her could survive in a house that's just so . . . stiff. Stiff words, stiff hugs, stiff dinners. Mom felt so sorry for her, liked to tease out Sam's devious, wicked streak with her own. Anything she lacked at home, we would have given her. We were always overflowing with the good stuff. My house in Bedford was loud and messy and so sweet, so bright the memories almost hurt to look at.

Sam shrugs. "Dad walked me to school. That was the last I saw or heard from them."

I don't know what to say to that that wouldn't be horrible and offensive to the people who raised her. I can't do anything but lean against the crate. Sam does the same, and I try to imagine what it would be like if there wasn't that barrier between us, if we'd lived our lives the way they were supposed to pan out. The missed things—games, dances, studying—those things just leave me hollow. But I know Sam is there. I know she is.

"Do you still see Greenwood?" Sam asks softly.

"Not like I used to," I say. "There are other things I need to focus on. Remember." I wish I still had the kind of heart to come up with the stories I used to. They were so pure and simple. And because we were making the rules, I always got to be the hero.

But there's no room left for play or pretend in our lives. Even these minutes we've had are being stolen for reality. I need my shell, but I can't lose my focus on the future because I'm letting myself get lost in the sweet glow of the past.

"I think about them all the time," Sam says. "There was this one—Mia was the sorceress and she took over the fort and held you captive. I can't remember why she was pelting me with her stuffed animals, though."

I have to smile. Mia had a flair for the dramatic. She was happiest as a sorceress, an evil queen, or monster—and even happier if Mom let her raid her makeup to complete the look. "She could control the animals of the forest, remember? They were defending her." Including her stuffed Tiger, Ty-Ty, because, of course, why couldn't there be large predator cats in Greenwood?

"And she'd turned you into a beast, too! How could I forget?" Sam's laugh is so faint I think I've imagined it. "Her weakness was water. I broke your Super Soaker."

"But then you realized you could sing her to sleep," I say. "Sammy saved the day again. How did that one go? *I've got the joy, joy, joy, joy down in my heart . . .*"

"*And I'm so happy, so very happy . . .*" Her voice drifts off as she swallows hard. "I missed you. Is this even real? I can't . . . Is this really happening?"

"I'm gonna bet I missed you more," I say with a heat that has nothing to do with what I am, but who I am, who I want to be. "It feels the same." *You never left me.*

Sam sits back, her lips parting, but if she means to say something, I'll never know. The lights overhead suddenly snap on and I rocket to my feet, straightening out. The drug-like daze rips away from my mind and I slam back into reality. Sam scrambles back against the metal bottom of the crate. In the second before she disappears from my line of sight, I see the desperation on her face, and I'm cut in half by the kind of pain that's worse than any baton, any shock, any blade. My ear is buzzing with updates, the Control Tower coming through with a firm *"Power at full capacity, return to schedule."*

I force myself to walk toward the door, back toward the wall of crates, then toward the door again, trying to play off my indecision as pacing. My mind is looping. Olsen said to leave when notified that surveillance was operational—technically I haven't been notified of that, only that the power is on. That's an excuse they'll buy, I think, that I took her words literally. They think our heads are vacant, waiting for them to pour in whatever thoughts or orders they want us to have. I can play dumb forever if it means not having to leave Sam alone. *Shit.*

This is going to be a problem—I'm not going to be able to concentrate on what I came here to do, on playing the part of perfect toy soldier. I'm not going to be able to think of anything but Sammy.

She's humming again, picking up that same song about joy and happiness, and it stops me in my tracks. It settles my mind.

The door swings open behind me, letting in a spray of rain on a strong gust of wind. I set my legs apart in a strong stance, like I could be the wall that keeps it from reaching her. I turn my head around, fumbling for some kind of excuse to give to Olsen for why I'm still here.

But it's not her standing there, filling out the doorframe.

It's Tildon.

THREE

SAM

Something's wrong.

Lucas has stopped pacing, slowing turning himself inside out with each stride, but the agitation that electrifies the air has billowed out to become something far more dangerous. The temperature in the room ramps up, until I'm sure it's not just the heat coming back on through the overhead vents. I strain against the side of the cage, trying to see, fighting the urge to kick and kick and kick until I smash it into pieces. I want *out*.

The door shuts again, muffling the wind's howling.

"Dismissed."

One word. A bolt of dread shoots through my heart. Stops it dead in my chest.

I press my back against the far corner of the crate. There's a lock between us. A cage. *I'm safe in the cage.*

Unless he has a key.

Would they have given him a key?

Could he have taken it from Olsen? Where was she? Why didn't she—

His boots squish as the water leaves them. He takes three

short steps forward, but I still can't see him or Lucas. I press a hand to my face, my back alive with throbbing pain, my head still aching from the White Noise. My throat burns with the things I should have said to him in the few minutes we had.

Don't do it, I think. *Lucas, it's not worth it.*

He has to get out of here. He has to find Mia. I don't know what these Reds are supposed to be, what role they're meant to serve here, but I can guess insubordination is not going to play well with any of the PSFs.

Lucas's heart is too soft for this place. He has the most beautiful mind of anyone I've ever known. I shouldn't have let him . . . I shouldn't have talked to him. The realization is like swallowing boiling water. I got so wrapped up in him and the feeling of having him close again. He's different, in so many ways. His voice is deeper but still has the usual hint of a smile in it, no matter how much it's dimmed. And where he used to be short, skinnier than me, Lucas has shot up to his dad's height and he's filled out. They have shaped him into someone who fills a room just by standing in it.

I don't know how he's doing it, how he's strong enough to bury his heart that deep inside him, the surface never once betraying how he feels. It's only because I knew him—know him—so well that I see the pain that's in his eyes and I can recognize it for what it is. How long has it been since he's been able to even talk about his parents? How did he survive all of these years, locked inside of his own head?

This morning I'd felt the power boiling under his skin, and I'd just assumed that his heart had hardened over the years as much as mine. It's not true at all. He is still good, sweet Lucas. I know how deeply he feels everything, and I can't imagine the inhuman strength it's taken to be able to move on from losing two of the people he loved most in the world when just the *thought* of their loss has actually shattered my heart. When we were kids, he was the crier. Things didn't upset him, they devastated him, and it just made me want to fight every single kid who gave him trouble for it.

He can hide it from them, but he can't hide it from me.

"Dumb or just deaf?" Tildon snorts. *"Get out."*

I hear a step, and then another, lighter step that mirrors it. Something clicks—the baton coming off its hook. I recognize the sound now. It's a bruise on my memory, one that'll never fully heal.

Someone is breathing hard, and it's not me. I don't think it's Lucas, either.

"There are plenty of cages here. Are you looking to join the little princess? You'd probably like that, wouldn't you?"

Lucas says nothing. Tildon does nothing. I can hear him squeezing the baton in his fist, but he doesn't hit Lucas. I try to imagine what he must look like, facing a Red, knowing what he'd done to torment the Reds in the past, knowing that some of them must remember it.

Go, Lucas! My mind is screaming the words. If only I could see his face. He would know it's okay to go. He can't stay here for me. It's not worth it.

Lucas takes a halting step toward the door as Tildon walks around him, careful to keep an arm's length of distance between them. Suddenly it's needles and knives pumping through my veins, not blood. Tildon's boots are the first thing I see, his mud-splattered boots. I can't breathe. I realize it suddenly, the truth sinking deep inside of me. This is never going to be over. This is my life now, until the camp controllers step in and move him again, make him another girl's problem. I hate that the thought actually gives me relief. I hate how selfish I have to be just to survive.

He crouches down, tapping the lock with his baton. I do feel like an animal then. Caught in a trap, waiting for the knife. "Hi, sweetie. We didn't finish our conversation earlier."

I won't look at him. I won't. I can feel his eyes rake over me, the way my wet sweats cling to me, the tangled mess that is my hair. I wish Olsen had just cut it all off before she left. I see what she does, now, the intensity of his gaze as it locks on the place where strands of my hair brush my collarbone.

Tildon tugs on the lock to test it, laughs at the way I cringe as he drags his baton over the front of the crate, up and down, his eyes never once leaving me. I want to crawl out of my skin and disappear in the shadows. I want to dissolve the way Ruby did. I can't be here anymore. I can't.

The entire cage shifts as the baton smashes against it. I'm rattled from the top of my head to my feet so hard I bite my tongue and the taste of blood explodes in my mouth. Tildon laughs again as I cover my face with my arms. The thin metal has warped where he struck it. The gap between the bars has expanded, bent and twisting inward unnaturally. He wedges the baton into the bottom corner of the door and starts to bend that, too, pulling the corner toward him, creating a hole large enough to stick a hand through. I twist around again, tucking my legs up against my chest, my left side against the back of the cage to avoid his touch.

"Sweetie," he calls, "sweetie—*come here!*" He punctuates the last two words with the baton. He can't get to me while I'm in here. I'm safe in the cage—

Tildon stands suddenly and seizes the front of the kennel and hauls it toward him, the center of the small room. The scream that leaves my throat is drowned out by the screech of the metal against the cement, the thunder of the empty cages above it filling in the empty space, crashing to the ground. He drops the weight with a satisfied grunt, a smile that's all teeth. I can't get away from him now. He stands over me, looking down through the bars, considering. I have to force myself not to look at Lucas, still facing away from us in the corner.

He can't help you—you have to get out of this—think, Sam, think—

"This is M27 requesting permission to leave the cages to return to my post," I hear Lucas say. His voice has a halting quality to it now, each word clipped. "Officer Tildon is here to relieve me."

Tildon's breath whistles as it's sucked in between his teeth. He twists around, pinning Lucas with a look of such undisguised malice, I can't imagine how both of them will walk out of here alive.

The instinctive panic smooths out to horrified understanding. He's telling them Tildon is here in a way that makes it seem like he's only asking permission to act. But he doesn't get it. The power is on. The camera is operational. The Control Tower must know he's here. They just don't care.

Don't! I want to scream it. *Don't put a target on yourself. Just get out!*

He tried, though. He *tried*. My throat is thick with the need to cry, I'm so grateful.

Neither of them has moved, and I'm too much of a coward to make a sound and break the tense silence. Tildon is still, frozen, his hand still dangling inches above my head. Someone in the Control Tower must be talking in his ear. For the first time, I wonder if maybe they didn't know—if someone hadn't been watching this room from the moment the power came back on.

Lucas turns around slowly, crossing the short distance to the door. He pops it open and holds it; the room seems to gasp, sucking in the cold air. Doesn't say a word, just waits. His eyes never once leave Tildon.

"You stupid little shit," the PSF seethes. "Don't think I'll forget—"

"Our orders," Lucas says without an ounce of warmth in his voice. *"Sir."*

He is good. It's almost terrifying—like there are two different boys trapped in his body. The last traces of fizzing brightness I'd felt with him fade and die completely.

Tildon looks down at me and, before I can turn away, spits in my face. The smile he gives me is somehow worse than anything else he's done to me here; it's a promise. I duck down, folding myself inside the cramped space to wipe every last trace of him away with my sleeve. The smell of him hangs over me like a cloud of poison, and I feel myself gag again and again until he finally crosses the room and switches off the lights.

The door swings shut and locks behind them.

And when there is nothing and no one but the walls around me to hear, I begin to hum again. I lift the pitch higher and higher until the ache in my throat clears and the wind begins to answer back.

It seems impossible, but I sleep.

It's the shallow kind, one that I dip in and out of until I finally feel more exhausted than I did at the start. The day has cut me open and exposed every last nerve in my body. As night comes, early as always, the leftover haze of light from the storm is stained a deep violet. My back is stiff no matter how I bend and twist around, and I have to imagine my skin is turning the same color as the sky. I grit my teeth and close my eyes, drifting back out of reality.

By the time my eyes open again, the light has gone out of my world completely. The metal grating on the side of the cage digs into my back, groans as I shift again. There's no way for my eyes to adjust, and there's nothing to see save for a prick of red light on the door where the electronic lock is. Instead, every other sense sharpens to fill in the gaps. The smell of wet fur is slowly easing out of the small room, but what replaces it is the stench of soggy dog food. My belly cramps with hunger and my throat is dry, but it won't be unbearable until the morning. How long did they say I have in here? This morning feels like it happened in another life.

Did I imagine Lucas? The fear takes hold of my throat and squeezes tight. It wouldn't have been the first time. He is always there when I need him, waiting for me to pluck him out of my memory box. There are new images now, tucked behind the old ones. I close my eyes and imagine him sitting there again. I remember every curve and dimple so clearly, I think I could paint him into the air, back into existence. I wish I could have trapped the sound of his singing in my head.

I draw in another breath. *Real.* I can't tell if this has all been a dream or a nightmare. It seems so out of line with my life to be given this one small thing. My mind is trying its best to quickly burn the fire out in my heart; it's actually thinking this through, dragging me back down into this reality.

The odds are I will never have the opportunity to speak with him again as long as we're both here. So many different moments of chance had to line up to bring him to this camp, for us to recognize each other, for him to step in, for the power to go out—my hands shake with how frantic I feel at the thought. I didn't appreciate it enough while he was here. If I could go back and live those few minutes again, I'd have paid closer attention to his smell, the details of the scars on the right side of his chin, the way the warmth of his voice shrank and broadened depending on what he was talking about.

He'll go, and you'll stay, and you'll live through that, too.

Will I?

Do I not get a choice in *anything*? He walked back into my heart as a conclusion, not a question. Maybe that's the whole point—life showing me how good it could be, letting me have it just long enough to want it more than I've ever wanted anything else, only to rip it away. When you have nothing for so long, you forget the terror of having something to lose.

The rustling starts like a foot dragging against the concrete. I lift my head up, trying to squint into the darkness. There are all kinds of rodents in this camp. I've had to kill more than one mouse, not to mention an assortment of roaches and spiders, with nothing more than the heel of my flimsy slip-on sneaker. The sacks of dog food must be heaven for them, the easiest pickings for miles around.

But I know what mice sound like as they scrabble against the concrete and through the walls. That is not a mouse.

Someone exhales between their teeth. I don't hear it so much as feel it near my ankle.

"Who's there?" My voice sounds unnaturally loud to my ears,

even at a whisper. How long had I been sleeping? I would have heard someone coming in; the creak of the door alone would have jolted me out of the deepest layer of sleep.

I start to draw my legs back from where I've stretched them out. But that small movement sparks another one—warm, smooth muscle glides along my skin, up my calf with silent intent. And I think, *He's back,* I think, *He's here, he's got the lock off.* I can't see a damn thing, I can't get out of this damn cage, this room, this life; the darkness has taken on weight, and I can't get out from under it. I can't get out. *I am never getting out.*

It's not until after I frantically kick that I can hear my mind whisper, *Snake.*

The hiss sounds like I've tried to throw a bucket of ice water onto a fire, it sounds like my heart, the frantic pulse of it just before it stops completely. My numb, frozen body is alive with feeling, overwhelmingly aware of the weight stretched out along my hip, down my leg. By then, it's too late.

The metal sheet beneath me pops as weight suddenly shifts. I can't go still, limp, anything I know I'm supposed to do, I just want out, I want *out* of here. There's a moment's grace as it coils before the lunge. I feel it spring forward, and, God, do I feel it when its fangs punch through my skin and strike the ankle bone.

I scream in pain and shock and it only—it hurts—

It hurts—

It electrifies my brain. I can see colors and lights that aren't there. I feel the devil in this room as surely as if he'd guided the snake in.

Stop. Moving.

It whips out of the cage so fast, I think it's flying. It leaves the way that it must have come in, through the gap Tildon made trying to pry the door off. I choke on my next breath as its scale-slick body rubs against the first bite the last time. *If it's leaving, it won't bite again. It's as scared of you as you are of it.*

I stay still for as long as I can bear it, until the trembling starts. Reaching down as best as I can, I rub my fingers along the punctures, already swollen and tender. They come away slick and warm—warmer than any other part of my body. I can almost imagine how it happened, how the snake was washed out of its deep hole by this winter's rain and made a shelter of this place, and then a home when he realized how many mice risked running wild to get to the dog food. I wasn't anything more than a heater to it. It stretched out to try soaking in what warmth I had to offer. To—

Waves of nausea churn in my stomach. I was a Girl Scout for all of two years before the change, and they taught us to identify the poisonous ones, how to avoid them on hikes, what to do if you can't. But I can't remember any of it. There's nothing in the box. My mind is scrambling back through the years, but none of it matters because it happened before I went through the change. I can't remember how to tell one snake apart from the other, and, in the end, it doesn't really matter. It's too dark to see anything. The only thing I know is that I don't feel right.

I can't pretend it didn't happen, and, for the first time in years, I don't want to lie here and let luck roll the dice on whether I have to hang around, or if I'm finally getting off this ride. I see now that there's something for me at the end of all of this. When I get out, no matter how many years it may be from now, I know there is someone who'll care. If Lucas can't escape this demented program they've set up for Reds, then he'll need me to find him. I will help him find Mia, and even though I have no idea what to do or where to go from there, none of it matters because we'll be speeding away, the darkness disappearing into the dust the wheels will kick up. I will outrun this place and protect them both from ever feeling the pain of loss again.

I shift onto my knees, mind and leg throbbing with my pulse. I need to get someone's attention—in our cabins, if anything were to happen, we had an emergency button to push. That's how they knew to come and get Ruby. I don't have that luxury, and I haven't understood that it *is* a luxury until this moment when every single part of me is shaking and panic is making it hard to focus on anything. I gasp in a deep breath, feeling my leg again. My fingers don't even brush the bite, but my leg feels waxy to me, and aside from the shooting pain, there's barely any sensation outside of the feeling of sand pouring into my bones.

What I have is a dark room, and one lone camera somewhere on the wall behind me.

I stick my hand through the opening that Tildon created in the metal bars. Each time my mind brings up the image of a snake, I stubbornly turn it back to Lucas's face. *No one is coming* becomes *He'll come, he'll come, he'll come to get me.* I don't want to be a realist. I don't want to pretend like I'm okay living in this gray numbness anymore. I want to get out of here. I want to live. I want to feel every ounce of pain and happiness life can serve up, because it'll mean I've survived. It'll mean I'm alive.

I fit my arm as far through as it'll go and wave it up and down. Minutes tick down, second by second, until I can't ignore the way the metal is cutting into my arm and that nothing has happened. I tug on the lock but my hands are shaking too hard to keep my grip. Shuffling back along the metal bottom of the kennel, I pull off my shirt and expose my skin to the cold. It feels good, actually. There's something boiling just under my skin; I feel it bubbling in my stomach, too, until it starts to cramp. The shirt is pushed out the hole first, and I reach down to grip it, hoping beyond hope that they'll be able to see the color moving in the dark better than my arm. I wave it frantically up and down.

Nothing happens, and no one comes, and the longer it takes for me to realize it, the worse I feel. *It's too dark here.* Unless the cameras can see in the dark, they have no idea anything is wrong. I could try to scoot the crate back, get close enough to the stacked crates to try to send them crashing to the ground, but it wouldn't matter. They wouldn't see it.

I have to get to the lights.

At this point, the punishment I know will come stops mattering and I flip myself around again, scraping my back against the top of the kennel. I can't make out anything in front of my face, it's all feeling fingers and desperate hands. Still, I lay on my back and I *kick*. One leg, the one that feels like it's actually on fire, I can't so much as move. I grit my teeth and use my other to kick against what I think are the crate's hinges—they can break, can't they? Anything can break if you hit it hard enough. Aren't we all proof of that?

I hear a snap; the reverberation of the hit races up my leg. *One more.* Please, just one more—

The door flies off and clatters against the cement. I don't waste a second in twisting myself around so I can use my arms to drag myself out. The contents of my head are swinging around. I can't get a bearing on the ground with my feet under me. It's farther to fall, anyway, than if I go on hands and knees.

I move through the dark, scraping my skin, feeling the loose pieces of concrete dig into my skin. The hand out in front of me bumps the wall and I reach up, feeling along the wall for the switch. My fingers fumble, slick and clumsy. I force myself farther up until I hear a *click*, and the light that floods the room burns tears into my eyes. I shield my face and look to the door. It would lock from the outside, wouldn't it? I could try. *I need to try.*

But that's just it. Strength seeps out of me, beading on my skin as sweat. I'm shaking and I can't stop. My head isn't in control of anything below my mouth.

"Help!" The word tears out of me. I squint up toward the dark blur in the upper corner of the room. *"Help me! Please!"*

I don't want to die. I don't want to die like this.

"Help me! Help—"

It hits me so fast, I barely have time to turn my head before the contents of my stomach come rocketing up and out of me. In between heaves, I can't release a breath, let alone another word. I'm gasping and it doesn't stop. Even when there's nothing left, I'm heaving and cramping and crying because it hurts, *it hurts—*

The dark swallows me up and spits me back out; there's no way to measure how long I drown before my body drags me up from the depths again. My hair clings to my face, my neck, my shoulders as the world goes fizzy and foggy around me. The dreams that emerge from the dark are disjointed and bold, colors like vivid sunsets.

My father's voice trumpets through the night, *Behold, I give unto you power to tread on serpents and scorpions, and over all the power of the enemy; and nothing shall by any means hurt you.* I see him standing at the altar, wings with purple and gold feathers expanding behind him, casting shadows over pews. My mother's perfect, icy face melts off and falls into her lap. Lucas, older Lucas, is above me, climbing up and up and up through the branches of a tree. When he turns to look down, I see a crown of stars around his dark hair. The sparks drift down around me as I reach up for his hand.

I'm on the bus in the pouring rain. The kids around me are silently crying, turning their faces down so the men and women standing in the aisles can't see. It plays in black and white, an old movie my brain has filed away. But in the row ahead on the opposite side, there's a little girl with dark hair. I see her in color—green eyes that flash toward me, blue-and-yellow Batman pajamas. I remember this—the gunshot, the Orange. The blood on the bus windows that the rain resignedly washes away. That girl walks next to me the whole way to the big brick building until we're dripping on the black-and-white checkered tile inside. I hold her hand. I remember holding her hand.

It's Ruby. I know it is. Ruby, who slipped away, Ruby who disappeared. Is this what she felt like? All those nights I used to wonder, *Where did she go?* If there's a Heaven, will they let any of us in? Where do we go? If there's no place for us outside the fences, where do we go when we die?

The girl crumbles into a pile of ash. I try to scoop her up, mold her back into her shape, but she's gone, it's all gone—I hear scratching, a metallic whine, and turn toward the other end of the hallway where a pale blue light glows. The kids around me fade to shadows. A voice like a gunshot cracks through the silence.

"—gency—require—immediate—transportation to—"

The world rocks and rattles, shaking me out of the black and into the blue. I blink against the foggy light around me and try to turn my head to see what dark shape is moving near my feet, but my body is locked up tight. My tongue is swollen and it tastes like bile in my mouth. I can't feel anything anymore. All that's left of my heartbeat is a soft, tentative knocking in my chest. A *Stay awake*, a *Fight harder*, a *You can't go*.

It's too hard to keep my eyes open for long. When I come back, there's a face I don't recognize above me, saying things I can't hear. One of his careful hands is on my throat, the other on my leg. Gone, back, gone—I'm moved, lifted up on something stiff and unbending. The cold air can't touch me, but the smell, the smell of clean air, the last traces of rain, it makes me want to cry. I glide under a sky so blue, so purple, so golden I fight as hard as anything to keep my eyes open, because I want to remember it forever, however long that lasts.

Because I know it'll be the last thing I ever see.

FOUR

LUCAS

WE WAKE UP ABOUT A HALF HOUR BEFORE THE REST
of the camp does, not with the piercing alarms over the loud-
speakers, but the clang of a PSF dragging their baton along the
barred barracks window. When you've trained your body and
mind to rest without ever falling into a real, deep sleep, it's
enough to send you shooting straight up out of your bunk to
kick-start the morning routine of wash up—pull on uniform—
make bed—stand at attention—wait for instructions. I seem to
do all five in one quick motion.

The barracks are silent save for the shuffle of feet and the
running of water. The building is old but well heated and decently
maintained. We have windows and tiled floors and painted walls,
which makes the whole thing almost seem homey in comparison to what I saw of the cabins yesterday. And where they kept
Sammy overnight.

Up until last week, it housed PSFs about to hit the end of
their mandatory service. We only had to slide neatly into their
vacated place, set our uniforms and toiletries in the small chests

at the end of the bunks that used to house theirs. There were no decorations on the wall, but they do have a few sun-faded posters up—one with the camp's posted schedule, which apparently hasn't changed in seven years, others with charts of the color classifications. The angry slash of red at the top of the chart is labeled FIRE, HIGHLY DANGEROUS.

My breath comes out as a harsh snort.

F13 falls into place beside me, smoothing a braid back over her shoulder. In my head, I've always called her Rose, because of the color of her hair. I've imagined a whole fake life for her, for all of them, always something silly to counteract the harsh reality. For Rose, I pretend that her parents are zookeepers, and growing up she had a pet armadillo named Fernando and monkeys that hung out in her backyard. I pretend her voice sounds as soft as falling petals, because I've only ever heard her scream. The Trainers stripped these kids down to a letter and a number, sapped every feeling and thought that belonged to them. I want to see them as humans. I will dream for them, if I have to.

She's finished wrapping the sheets over her bed with the pointless military precision drilled into us, and takes a moment to straighten out her uniform and make sure that her shirt is properly tucked in. I do the same, smoothing out a wrinkle that's not there; I'm bursting with the need to move, to rock back and forth on my heels until it's time to head out and start the day.

Instead, I picture someone pouring plaster under my skin, letting it dry, keeping me trapped in that same stiff pose. It helps. A little. But I've been waiting hours to check on Sam. I kept looking toward Olsen during the dinner rotations, ready to be sent to bring her food, to check on her, to be posted there overnight. I tried to do the math in my head of how long I could disappear from my post and go out around back of the building before anyone would notice.

But Olsen never said a word to me, and neither did the camp controller who dismissed us for the night and sent us back here. I didn't exactly expect them to, but I wanted some kind of hint that she'd at least been brought a blanket or water. What happens when she has to go to the bathroom? Do they let her get up and move around for a few minutes at any point during the night? The questions kept my brain from shutting down. I couldn't escape them, and a part of me felt like I didn't deserve to.

The only thing I'd been able to do was watch Tildon to make sure he didn't disappear at any point, but after the dinner rotations? There was no way to know for sure. He could have gone back, slipping out when he should have been returning to his own barracks.

I close my eyes and take a deep breath to steady myself against the flood of violence and flame that filters through my mind.

The door at the far end of the room swings open, and a camp controller strides in, her gaze sweeping over us. I straighten as a PSF moves between the beds, inspecting the cotton for wrinkles and untucked corners. Satisfied, he nods toward her.

"Your assignments for the day are as follows," the camp controller begins. I listen only long enough to hear that I'm the medical escort, not assigned to Sammy's cabin block. A lick of defeat hits me right at my center. I'm babysitting a whole bunch of kids who aren't her, and, worse, they haven't rotated me to any of the Blue cabin blocks to confirm for myself that Mia isn't here.

We follow the camp controller out of the barracks, heading our separate ways. The world around us is still damp and dripping, with the promise of another storm. I'm handed a clipboard with a single sheet of paper listing the names, locations, and times to pick the kids up and walk them over to the Infirmary. At the end of my day, I have an allotted two hours to "assist medical staff" before dinner rotations.

Whatever that means for them, it means something else entirely for me. There are computers in the Infirmary. If I can find one, it's just a matter of finding a room not under camera surveillance to run a simple search in their system—I'll know, for better or worse, exactly where Mia is.

I let that thought carry me forward to the Mess Hall for first meal, arms swinging in time with the others'. I feel in control of myself now, enough not to fly off into a rage when I see Tildon smirking from where he's posted at the door, holding it open for the kids who are filing inside.

My feet carry me over to our small table as my eyes scan the room again. Sam's cabin is included in the first meal rotation, and there—I can see them across the way, over hundreds of heads bent over their Styrofoam bowls. The girl with dark, curly hair, the one I saw crying yesterday, looks like she's been dusted with chalk, she's so pale. Her eyes dart to the blank space next to her as the PSF patrolling the aisle behind her leans down and whispers something in her ear. A thick finger runs along the shell-pink curve of her ear and I know, even before he looks up and catches me staring, that it's Tildon.

That empty space is Sam's. My stomach turns to stone and I barely manage to swallow the food already in my mouth. They still have her locked up, then. She is still in that goddamn cage.

The tables vacate one by one, faces and numbers assembling into orderly lines, two by two. We do the same, and I'm surprised to find that I'm actually eager to get moving today. Work means the hours will pass faster, and I'll see Sam when our schedules collide one last time at the final meal rotation. I pick up my clipboard from the table and tuck it under my arm, ignoring the terror on the faces of the Green boys who have assembled to our right.

F14 turns toward them, her eyes as dull and flat as sandstone. If it weren't for the PSF standing nearby, I think the kids still would have scattered like mice. The proximity of us is wearing down their nerves.

The kid listed as 5552 on my list turns out to be a teenage girl, who knows to wait at her table, even after the other girls in her cabin have stood up and shuffled their way out for the day's work. I press the clipboard to my chest as I walk around the rows of long tables to stand behind her. She glances back, then looks again. She remembers herself just as quickly, and her dark eyes fall back to the table. Her body is as rigid as the icicles that have frozen like teeth along the edge of the Mess's roof. Shame sweeps through me when I take her by the arm and haul her to feet. The minute my glove touches her arm, it's like I've stabbed her there. She couldn't have jumped higher if I had been a live wire.

When it's our turn to head to the double doors, I finally notice that Tildon has repositioned himself at the exit, still wearing the look of a cat contentedly grooming itself after a kill. My unease spikes into real, living fear as he catches my arm and holds up the line behind us.

"It's just too bad," he says, tilting his head toward mine. His voice is light and airy. "It's just too damn bad you weren't there this time."

I am three steps away when the words register, dissolving like static in my brain. I start to turn back, but can't—I know I can't. It would confirm it for him. An alarm is screaming in my head and I have to hold my breath to keep from releasing the flame building up inside me. He knows, or at least he thinks he knows, that I care about Sam. Why else would he say it? Calling in to the camp controllers yesterday was a gamble, but I thought it had paid off. The only thing I'd cared about in that moment was getting him away from her.

This asshole—he's a tried and true predator. Whatever he wants out of you, it's in his nature to detect a whisper of weakness, exploit every small crack in your wall. He picks at wounds just as they start to heal, he touches, knowing you can't touch back, he takes from people who aren't in a position to give.

I'd been stupid enough to assume he was too much of a chickenshit to try to turn around and hunt me. I should have known better—I got between him and his chosen prey.

Sam. My heart is like thunder rolling through my ears. I'm convinced that the girl can hear it, too, it's so damn loud. Tildon must be lying—testing me. He wants to see if it'll affect me, slide like pins beneath my fingernails and drive me crazy. I saw the look on his face, how closely he watched me as I passed. He suspects. He must.

And, well, it's working. The dark wood structure behind the Mess has become the center of my universe, and my whole body is so attuned to it, it's the fight of my life to not look back over my shoulder more than once.

I can't stop seeing it, what he could have done to her. How he must have touched her. Disgust turns my blood to acid and the girl cringes as I feel myself go hot—too hot. My left arm jerks hard enough that it knocks her forward a step.

Sorry. The word is so damn worthless. *I'm sorry, I'm sorry—*

He's lying. He couldn't have hurt her. I would have heard it broadcast over the wireless.

Not if you were still sleeping . . .

The words work through me like poison, eating away at my faith.

The Infirmary is the one building I've yet to step inside. The camp controllers didn't have time to include it on their initial walk-through, and, from what I can tell, I didn't miss much. The smell of it is like every dentist's and doctor's office—rubber, antiseptic, fake lemon. The ground floor's checkered tile is half hidden by the stacks of boxes, plastic crates, and piles of what almost look like curtain rods. It's not anything alarming, but the girl beside me stops dead and stiffens as she takes it all in.

They don't know they're leaving here, I think. Of course not. They'll just be woken up in the middle of the night and marched out. They won't even be told they're never coming back, I'll bet. They'll always fear the possibility.

Still, I have orders. I turn toward the staircase as the sheet on my clipboard instructs. She drags her feet at first, pulling back against my grip before she remembers. She's staring up at the second floor, but we're going to the basement and she doesn't ease up on the resistance until she realizes that fact for herself. I look between her and the first few steps leading up, and wonder what the hell is up there to provoke that immediate, unconscious response—to turn her so inside out with dread she'd be willing to challenge a Red, even for a second.

I tug her forward, down the steps, feeling like the uncaring asshole she must think I am. The closer we get to the small landing, the easier my ears can detect the voices whispering there. We take the two of them by surprise—and then I'm caught by the same thing. Olsen is standing in the corner with a younger guy, no more than thirty, decked out in gray scrubs. His ID badge is swinging from where it's pinned on his pocket as he gestures harshly toward the PSF, his face marred with angry lines. "—is not going to make it if you don't help me—"

Olsen holds out her hand, silencing him as we come fully into view. I wait for her permission, a nod, to squeeze past them with the girl, but my ears are straining the whole time, trying to catch her words when she speaks again. "Handle this . . . best you can . . . it'll be okay . . . again . . ."

The basement of the building mirrors the structure of the first level: it's T-shaped, one long hall running horizontally—this one packed with expensive-looking medical machines—the other, with a series of doors, intersecting it. The sheet tells me to bring each kid to office number twelve, which seems to be at the other end of the hall. Small gift. It lets me glance inside the rooms that have been left open, assess what's still left inside. Shelves, filing cabinets, more than one computer.

I bump shoulders with a PSF hauling a stack of boxes in his arms, but he's concentrating too hard on not dropping them to level me with a cutting remark or hit. I draw the girl over to the side to make way for more uniforms and boxes, and we narrowly avoid colliding with two women in gray scrubs. Nurses, I think. They're weaving in and out of all of us, shouting, "Coming through!" with what looks like bags of blood in their hands.

I glance back, alarmed, just as the first door on the right opens and two men step out, allowing the nurses inside the room. One is O'Ryan, rubbing his buzzed hair, the other is in a white coat. We reach office twelve before their words can carry down the echoing hallway, but I feel unsettled as I guide the girl inside and kick the stool over so she can climb up onto the metal examination table. Two sharp, dark thoughts try to connect to one another, and then a third, but I force them out. I need to be focused on finding a way back into the kennel today. I have to make sure she's okay.

I position myself by the door, near the small counter with its jars of cotton balls and ear swabs. I let my hand rest on the flat surface, fingers inching over to the computer's mouse. At the smallest touch, the dark screen erupts with light. *It's on,* I think, but the screen it brings up is locked and the only thing on it is a space for entering a password.

The door swings open behind me and I straighten, shifting to allow the person in. Gray scrubs, reddish-brown hair—it's the guy from the landing, the one who'd been arguing with Olsen. When he turns to shut the door, he takes a moment to collect himself and clear the anger clouding his expression. When he faces the girl again, he's not smiling, but he no longer looks like he wants to rip someone's head off.

The nurse steps past me to get to the computer. My eyes dart down to the keyboard as he types his password: Martino9! I track his progress as he clicks through several different programs and screens to bring up the girl's file. Chelsea. Her name is Chelsea.

"How are you feeling? The cold giving you any trouble?" he asks, and, to my surprise, there's no malice or irony coating the questions. The girl relaxed the moment she saw him and is no longer trying to wring her hands raw. She shakes her head, keeping her eyes on the toes of her shoes.

Right. No eye contact.

The nurse reaches up into the cabinet on the wall and unlocks it. Inside are rows upon rows of bottles and jars. I shift my gaze back to the ceiling as he turns around and fills a paper cup with water from the sink. Chelsea accepts it along with two pills.

He takes a long, thin piece of latex and ties it around the girl's arm. A tourniquet. He's drawing blood. Only, even when he gets a grip on her arm, she's trembling so hard he's struggling to get the needle in.

"You have to stop shaking," he says.

Her gaze slides over to me before jerking back to the nurse's face. Her bottom lip is caught between her teeth, bloodless with how hard she's biting it. A look of understanding breaks across the man's face. The way the girl clutches the examination table makes me feel like I'm wearing a disgusting Halloween mask I can never take off.

Oh, I think.

"Oh," he says. To his credit, it only takes him a second to steel his nerves and turn toward me with that same calm face. For the first time I see the name on his ID tag: R. Dunn. "Step out for a moment."

I don't release the breath I'm holding until I'm in the hall again, and the door is shut behind me. The rumble of his voice starts up again. I press my hands flat against the wall behind me, turning my face away. I don't want to hear it. For some reason, it feels like a rejection—it feels like I've been stung, and I'm swelling with toxic resentment.

The day marches on with half my thoughts on the wooden structure behind the Mess, and the other half on monitoring the Infirmary's hallway. I'm barely listening to a sound track of status updates in my earpiece and nearly miss a request aimed at me.

Sam isn't in the Factory when I go to pull one of the girls there so she can get a hit from her asthma inhaler. She isn't in the Mess during the midday meal. If it hadn't been for Tildon, I would have assumed that they'd just forgotten about her, or stretched her punishment out another night to drive home their point with a wrecking ball instead of a hammer. Has she eaten anything? Did they bring her water, at least? I come up with a thousand different ways I can ask Olsen about her without actually asking, but none of them work. They all make me seem like I have a heart.

Focus. Computer. Then Sam. I just have to be fast.

I bring each kid I go to collect for their treatment down to the nurse in that same room, counting the minutes it takes for him to finish with them. In those minutes, I look for cameras. In the hallway. Through the doors that swing open. In the room directly across from where I'm standing I have seen not one, but two separate pairings of female nurse and male PSF disappear inside of it. I have heard the door lock behind them. And I have pretended not to notice how winded they always seem when they come out again a short time later. Whatever happens in that room is not being monitored, clearly.

I bring the last kid, 2231, a Green boy, in, open the examination room door, and practically push him inside to where the nurse is waiting. I take two seconds to look both ways down the empty hall and duck through the door opposite me. *Fast,* I think, *just be fast.*

My heart slams against my rib cage as I lurch toward the dark computer. The room is a mirror of the one across the hall, with one exception: the PC isn't already on. I waste two full minutes waiting for it to boot up, my ears straining at every muffled sound bleeding in through the walls. Sure enough, the camera in the upper corner has been all but torn off the wall and has been left dangling there by its rainbow wires.

There. Finally. The log-in screen glides into place and, before I can second-guess myself, I'm typing in the username and password I'd seen Dunn use. The system seems to load pixel by pixel, and it seems like each second is being shaved down to fractions of their former selves. I can't explain the rush of power I feel when the database finally loads and a blinking cursor appears in the search field.

I type *Orfeo* and hit Enter.

No results.

I have to look again, because that can't be possible.

No results.

I go hollow at the core. Pure, helpless anguish rushes in to fill the empty space where hope used to be. She's not in the system at all? That means—it's not possible, I won't—Mia—*Mia*—

The door slams open behind me, hits the wall, and slams shut again.

"Dammit, dammit, *dammit*, heartless son of a *bitch!*"

I'm up and on my feet, whirling around, reaching for a weapon I don't have. He's so busy cursing and tearing his hands back through his chestnut hair that he doesn't even notice me until the stool I'd been sitting on rocks back against the counter and clatters to the floor.

There's a second where neither of us moves.

"What—*oh*." It's Nurse Dunn.

I can actually feel my heart stop on the next beat. I know what the others feel now, because my head has gone completely dark. I don't have a thought inside, save for a single word: *shit*.

How is he already done treating the kid I *just* brought in?

He's breathing hard, his pale face flooded with furious color. And just when I need it most, my brain just walks off and abandons me. My body has to rely on instinct to protect it, and instinct is telling it to pick up one of the jars from the counter and—

"Easy—easy—it's okay," Dunn says, balking at the way I raise my arm to reach for the glass jar. He seems to remember what I am suddenly and puts his hands out in front of him. "Pal, it's okay. You just . . . I didn't see you in here. What's—"

His eyes flick between the computer screen and my face. A roar of blood moves between my ears, and I can't speak, I can't think of an excuse fast enough. Why did I come in here without thinking of one? Damn, I'm so *stupid* I didn't even think to try locking the door.

"Did someone tell you to come in here?" he asks. I can't read his expression now. His words sound strained. *He thinks I'll hurt him, kill him, burn him—*

Maybe I'll have to.

No. I can't. Not without setting the room on fire. People with flames racing along their skin don't just stand still and calmly let their bodies be burned to cinder and bone. He'll take the whole place down with him. It's a gruesome thought, one that brings the sickening smell of burnt flesh to mind. My stomach flips over. In what scenario are both of us getting out of this room?

"Okay," Dunn says when I don't answer.

My heart is slamming against my ribs. He doesn't know it wasn't an order for me to come in here. Not yet. Maybe he won't think to radio in and ask someone.

Can I scare him into silence? I think so—I take a step forward and he takes a generous one back. The Trainers taught us to fight with fists as well as fire. They wanted strength in body, not strength in mind. But he would know, wouldn't he? That we aren't supposed to do anything without orders, that my will has supposedly been crippled. Two issues with that: he can't be as scared of me as I think, but when he finds out the rules don't apply to me, he *will* tell someone. There's no way he won't. These adults are all on the same side.

Think, Lucas—Christ, do something, say anything, get the hell out of here—

Killing him won't help me and Sam get out of here. It won't help me find Mia who—a wave of nausea passes through me—might not be findable. I can break the jar, use the shards to cut him deep where the Trainers showed us to, but how long before the Control Tower puts together who did it?

"It's . . . hey," the man says, his voice strained, "everyone needs to take a break, get away, right?" He starts to lower his hands. "It's fine. Go get the kid you brought in and take him—"

His eyes have latched on to the computer screen. He squints at it and my pulse starts beating behind my temple.

"Orfeo?"

The name cuts me like a knife through my spinal cord. *I didn't clear the search field.* I shouldn't have done this, I should have made a plan, a real one, but—*I need to get out of here. I need to get Sam out of here. I need to find Mia.* My uniform is drenched in hot, clammy sweat and the collar of my vest has me like a hand wrapped around my throat.

The nurse steps closer to it, giving me a wary look as he reaches past my arm. I can't speak. And not just because I'm supposed to be playing a role.

"Did you search for this?"

Can't. Breathe.

I want to disappear into my head so badly. The silence that stretches between us is unbearable. I look down. He must take it as a nod.

"There's no one here by that name," he continues, leaning over the desk to move and click the mouse around. Another field appears on the screen, and the whole thing refreshes. "But there's a Natalie Orfeo who's listed as being in Belle Plain. That's in Texas, apparently."

I hadn't searched right? I catch myself before I can spin toward him. *He's baiting you. He wants to catch you. He'll turn you back over to the Trainers.*

But . . . if I hadn't searched right, that meant that there were listings I didn't see. It meant—

"No? What about a Mia?"

My body reacts before my brain can stop it. My whole body surges toward the computer. Dunn jumps back, both arms up, but I don't care about anything other than what's on the screen. Joy crashes into relief. My knees might give out on me if I don't hold on to the table.

There's a photo of her next to a profile—her hair is longer

than I remember, dark and curling over her shoulder the way Mom's used to. My throat burns. Weight, height—classified as Blue. God. Thank you, God. She's alive. She's not like me. Something brittle in my chest snaps, and I have to keep swallowing back the urge to cry.

Black Rock. That's her camp. Where is it? I keep scrolling, but it doesn't say.

"Is that . . . your sister? A cousin?" Dunn is edging back toward me but stops when I turn and pin him with a glare.

They're all the same. The Trainers, the PSFs, even these nurses. They are not on our side and they'll never be. He is going to take so much pleasure in taking me down for this. Was this worth it? I know she's alive and where she is, but I'm done. Done. I won't even get to say good-bye to Sam, or somehow tell her that they're taking me out, back to the Facility, back to be worked over again and again until they figure out a way to turn my head into an empty husk. The thought of the building with its bleach-white walls makes me feel almost manically desperate.

Mia is alive. She's *alive.* Any happiness at the thought is smashed into pieces under the weight of knowing that, yeah, she's alive, but she's in a place like this. I'll never be assigned there once the Trainers are told about this. They'll keep me for months, trying to break me. Would they hurt her in order to hurt me? That would work. God—oh my God. There would be no place safe for that kind of pain.

Dunn leans against the counter, his arms crossed over his chest. "They would never ask any of you to look something up in the system, so I have to believe that this was important enough to you to risk getting caught. I'd ask whose log-in you used, but it doesn't matter. I admire your balls, but if you're going to try this again, you have to be more careful. Anyone could have walked in."

I rise to my full height, clenching a fist and drawing it up in front of me like I'm about to . . . do something. I have enough control over the fire to spark a flame with a small snap.

Dunn flinches. His voice goes tight and high as he waves his hands in front of him, saying, "Wait—*wait.*"

For some reason, I do. I wait as he turns back to the computer to type something else into the program. When he's finished, he turns the screen toward me so I can see the profile he's brought up.

The photo attached to it is a young boy with reddish-brown hair like Dunn's and a wide, round face. He's staring at the camera dead-on, with a look of open hatred.

"This is Martin," Dunn says. "He's the reason I'm here, and if you really think I'm going to turn around and report you for caring about someone enough to risk your neck then . . . you can tell the camp controllers that. We're forbidden from serving anywhere we have a family relation."

I don't move. My brain has disconnected from the rest of my body.

"The draft caught up to me just as I was coming out of college and applying for medical schools. I served my four years at a camp in the Midwest, but I re-enlisted. You know why? Because this posting opened, and I'd been able to search our network and see they'd brought my brother here. I also knew that he'd gone into the system with our stepfather's last name, and I'd kept our father's—so I applied and, sure enough, they didn't catch it. I wanted to be a good brother . . . I thought, if I can't get him out, I can at least watch over him. It turns out I'm just as powerless now to help him as I am to help everyone else here."

"Why?" The word is out before I can swallow it back down my throat.

The lines on Dunn's face ease, but the shadows in his eyes are still there. "I'm limited in what I can do to help the kids. We can't give them crutches when they sprain an ankle because they could be turned into *weapons*. We don't allow them to stay overnight for treatment unless there's a real chance they might die without being monitored. I can barely keep the medicine I need stocked. And the doctor doesn't care. He won't even come in to check on this poor girl we're treating for a snakebite until the end of the week. *Family time*." He makes a sound of disgust. "It's all been for nothing. Martin isn't here. Someone managed to break him out."

I can't keep shock from breaking through. "How?"

"Ironically, it was two nurses. Or, I guess, they weren't real nurses after all. They put him in one of the large bio-waste bins we use to dispose medical trash. Just loaded it in their car and drove away. Business as usual, just going to dump it with all the rest. I have no idea where he is, but I'm stuck here, twiddling my thumbs, waiting my term out to start looking."

Something sour rises in my throat. I swallow hard and shake my head to hide how desperate I am to find out more. It can happen. I can get myself out of here—more importantly, I can get Sam out, too. The way he described won't work. They would have immediately changed that protocol. It's more that it's proof that this place isn't necessarily the maximum-security prison they want the kids to think it is. The equipment and buildings are run-down and practically painted with rust, patched over too many times. The PSFs and camp controllers are spread too thin, and because of it, they've let the blade dull in their hands. There have to be other gaps we can slip through.

"What's your name?" Dunn asks.

"M27."

"Your real name," he says. "You're not a number. Don't let them make you think that."

I think of all those kids I brought in with me today. How they spent the whole walk over to the Infirmary all knotted up with fear and anxiety. They didn't relax until they were with him. He called them by names, not by numbers. I want to believe—I want to believe there's no game here.

And, anyway, it's in my file. I might not show up in the computer system, but I'm sure he'd have access to the information if he asked. "Lucas."

"Lucas. I'm Pat." The nurse's smile is weak, uncertain, like there's a thundercloud hanging over us about to burst. "I think we both have to get back to work."

We do. My ten minutes were up two minutes ago. Dunn steps out into the hall first, which gives me a minute to wrap the shell of stony detachment back around me. It's only the small, dark, curly-haired nurse waiting for us, rubbing her hands up and down her arms. The miserable look on her face is so at odds with the calm, sweet expression she'd been wearing with the kids.

"Sorry," Dunn is saying, "I had to borrow him—"

"It's fine. I sent the boy back to his cabin with one of the PSFs," Nurse Kore says quickly, "but you need to come now. The swelling's gotten worse and the fever's back."

Nurse Dunn goes rigid, his skin pulling back as he grimaces. He pushes past us both, all but running down the hall. The floor has emptied out almost entirely, but I see one PSF stick his head out of an office he's packing up. Kore waves the soldier off, right on Dunn's heels as he enters the first room—the one I'd seen O'Ryan and the doctor come out of earlier.

I follow them down the hallway, at a slight loss as to what to do. After taking the last kid back, I was supposed to return here and assist the staff until the last meal rotations began. I want to keep an eye on Dunn, though, see if he shows any inclination on going back on his word.

Nurse Kore is blocking the doorway as I pass, but I can see well enough over her head that Dunn is throwing open cabinets and drawers. He fires off a series of questions. "What did you give her last? When did the symptoms begin? Shit—she's wheezing— we need epinephrine. Where is it? Can you look next door?"

It's only then, when Kore brushes past me to burst through the door of the next examination room, that I see the kid on the table.

Pieces of the room start to disappear. The wires. The bandages. The beeping machines. The IV drips. The adults. What I see is a pale face, tense with pain, dirty, limp blond hair fanned out around it. Something wet tracks down her cheeks, but I can't tell if it's sweat or tears.

No. The word pierces through me like a flaming bullet.

It's just too damn bad you weren't there this time.

What the hell—what the *hell* is wrong with this world? The temperature under my skin rises like the desert sun. This girl apparently can't suffer enough. There's no limit to what she'll be subjected to here. Sammy is good and *this* happens. *This.*

And what? We're supposed to take comfort in the fact that one day she'll be rewarded for her struggle? I can still hear her father preaching eternal life, how the meek will inherit. The singsong Sunday school lessons. *He's got the whole world in His hands . . .*

My feet carry me into the room as Dunn leans over her, adjusting an oxygen mask. I see the leg they've pulled over the thin blanket for the first time. It's swollen to twice the size of the other and there's a bubble of purple and black skin right around her ankle. My gag reflex makes me choke on the next breath.

People die from snakebites. How long was it before anyone found her? How long was she alone in the darkness?

I should have gone. I should have figured out a way. I shouldn't have left.

What choice did I have? What choice do any of us have?

Kore jostles me as she comes in, holding out a syringe to Dunn. "Was it the antivenom we tried? The only other thing I gave her was morphine for the pain."

I jerk out of my daze. "She's allergic to morphine."

They give her the shot. I'm not sure either of them heard me. So I repeat myself. I have to. They cannot give her morphine. The last time they tried was when she broke her arm and she was stuck in the hospital for an extra two days, she had such a bad reaction.

Dunn and Kore finally look up, turning first toward each other, then toward me.

"It's the morphine," I say again. I've already damned us both, haven't I? But they have to know so they don't make the mistake again. They have to help her.

"Lucas . . ."

My vision tunnels. For a second, I think I heard her voice in my head, but Nurse Kore is talking now, she's telling Dunn, "She's been saying the name all day. I've only been able to get a few other words out of her."

"Samantha," Dunn says. "Samantha, can you hear me? I need you to open your eyes. It's Nurse Dunn. I need to check to make sure you're all right."

She's not all right. Sammy is not all right. She's never going to be, not ever again. I can't—I can't—

". . . door is . . . Lucas . . . the door . . . dark . . . *Lucas* . . ."

My armor doesn't crack. It shatters. It falls to ash. My vision blurs and fear wrings every bit of caution and worry out of my head. The last thing I see is Nurse Dunn turning toward me, saying something. Static pours into my ears. I press my hands over my face to try to hide it, but it's too late. I'm crying.

I'm weeping like the kid who was pelted with rocks walking home every day from school by older kids. I'm weeping like the kid told he has to leave his best and only friend behind. I'm weeping like the kid who watched both parents bleed out in front of him, who watched the men in uniforms break his sister's hand because she wouldn't let go of his.

I sink against the wall until I feel the cold tile under me. I'm breathing so hard I can't catch my breath. I understand now. I can't help anyone. I can't even help myself.

"What's—?"

"Get the door," Nurse Dunn says sharply. There's movement at my left as the door clicks shut.

"You—" I can barely get the words out. "You have to sing to her. She'll wake up if you sing, she loves music—she can't—she can't die like this—the silence—"

"Lucas. Do you know Samantha?" Dunn's voice has a strained quality to it. I force myself to look up, eyes and throat aching.

Dunn is kneeling in front of me now. Kore is pressed flat against the door, looking up at the ceiling, shaking her head.

"*Sam,*" I say, correcting him. "Best friend. *Sammy.*"

The curse that follows blisters my ears. I breathe deep, trying to suck enough air into my chest to keep the crushing feeling out.

"How is he . . . ?" Kore starts to ask, then actually looks at me. "You remember things? They said you all wouldn't. They made us think—"

"It doesn't matter," Dunn says, cutting her off. "Her condition is very, very serious, but she's alive. Do you remember what I was saying before, though, about how things work here?"

I nod.

"I don't think it was a timber rattlesnake, otherwise she wouldn't still be here . . . maybe a copperhead. The problem is, we have no stock of antivenom left, and the camp controllers won't grant my request to leave camp premises to acquire more. They think it's a security breach. But by the time it's ordered and delivered through the military transport . . ."

"She's going to die," I finish.

"Lucas, listen to me. A lot of people aren't treated with the antivenom and survive. We're worried, though, because her symptoms haven't gotten any better and there's always the risk of infection. I just don't have enough experience with snakebites to tell you anything with certainty."

Sammy is a fighter, I want to say, but who can fight this? Who survives this? "Her leg?"

"We cut away the necrotic . . . the dead tissue. There might be nerve damage—a limp. I can't lie to you, she might not be able to walk normally again if she doesn't get proper medical treatment."

"She won't be able to run."

"No one can run here," Kore says, pressing a hand to her forehead.

"From *him*." I spit the words out. "Tildon."

Kore and Dunn exchange looks that are easy enough to read.

"What did he do to the other girls?" I ask. "The other kids?"

"I've only heard rumors," Dunn says slowly. "The doctor always treats them. I saw one of the boys once, though, and he . . ." He shakes his head. "Are you saying that Tildon has something to do with this?"

I somehow manage to tell them what happened yesterday without giving into the compulsion to run out, find the man, and watch him burn from the shoes up. I'm angry all over again; I don't even care that my arm is spasming. It doesn't matter that he didn't put the snake in the building with her. She never should have been there in the first place.

I can't stop seeing it. I can't stop seeing Sam alone in that cage. I left her in the dark.

"Jesus . . ." Kore breathes out. She turns to the other nurse. "They won't do anything about it until he escalates. That's been the case for all of the others, right?"

"I asked one of the camp controllers after I saw the boy. They need physical evidence of abuse and improper behavior," Dunn says, rubbing his face, "before they can transfer him to another cabin block. They don't take preventative action. They only respond."

"What about discharging him?" I demand. "How many strikes does this guy get?"

They seem unnerved by the heat coating the words. It takes Dunn a moment to say, "There are so few PSFs willing to re-up their service and stay. He's one of them. With the camp closing and the kids being sent to other camps, they . . . I have a feeling they're just going to let it fall between the cracks. They have bigger messes to clean up."

"We have to . . ." Kore can't seem to figure out what she wants to say, so she starts pacing instead, working out her thoughts that way. "We have to try talking to O'Ryan again. Make him understand how serious this is. I can't let her die. *We* can't let her die. Dammit, it's a *snakebite*. It should be treatable. This shouldn't be happening."

"O'Ryan won't do anything. It's easier to explain away a dead kid than bring her to a hospital that can actually treat her. Too many questions. Too much attention."

"Why do they have to wait for the military to bring in the medicine?" Desperation stains my voice, makes it sound different to my own ears. "Won't it be faster coming from a civilian supply?"

"It'll 'compromise the camp's secure location' to bring someone in," he says with no short supply of bitterness. "Even if we could get someone past the gate, they won't have enough time to treat her before someone notices. The only way to help her is to take her out."

"Stop!" This is clearly a conversation they've had before, because Kore knows exactly where it's headed. "*Dammit*, Pat, stop!"

"Do you really want this on your conscience?" he asks, on his feet now. "We'll walk out of here in a few weeks, but what about her? Say she pulls through fine—great, we've just saved Tildon's latest victim. Do you really want this shadowing you your whole life? Lissa . . . we promised we'd do whatever it'd take to help these kids. I have a plan. I just need to adapt it to her."

Oh my God. I can't stop looking between them. Seconds stretch into minutes, punctuated by the steady *beep beep beep* of one of the machines.

"You think I don't know that?" Her voice cracks as it drops to a whisper. "You heard what they did to the woman they caught. She only helped and they did *that.* They called it treason. If you get caught, there's no coming back from it."

"I'll do it," I hear myself saying. "Whatever you were planning, I'll do it."

It has to be me. I will take care of Sam, and I will find Mia. I can't do it from within the camp, and I can't ask the only two people in this camp who seem to give a shit about the kids to leave.

"You're upset," Kore says. "You don't know what you're saying."

"How would you do it?" I ask, refusing to be dismissed.

"The plan was originally meant for my brother and involved getting him out with the materials leaving the Factory. I just need to tweak it. We'll take advantage of the move," Dunn explains. "Get her into one of the crates we've been using to pack the machines. They're moving a bunch out today, while the kids are in the Mess for the first dinner rotation. You'll be in there with her. They'll move both of you out without realizing it. I'll find you a crowbar to get the top off. Do you think you can time two hours in your head? I'd wait that long before getting out. Off the truck. You'll have to fight. There's going to be an escort of PSFs with it."

"I can take care of it," I say. If they try to stop me, they won't have a chance.

"This is crazy," Kore hisses. "Listen to yourself!"

Crazy is only crazy until it works.

"I'm going to give you a cell phone that has one number pro-grammed into it—my Uncle Jeff. He's the one who helped me figure this out. I'll give him a heads-up, so he knows to expect you. He'll bring you back to Ohio with him. Aunt Carol is a doctor. She'll be able to treat her. You'll be safe there until she recovers."

"How do you expect him to get out of the locked truck?" Kore demands.

"I can melt the latch," I say, ignoring her startled look. That's going to be one of the least complicated parts of this.

"It has to be soon—before your last two-hour shift here is up. You can't be missing for more than fifteen minutes without someone realizing you're gone. I'll cover for you as long as I can."

"Understood."

"Lissa—" Dunn draws her into the corner of the room and lowers his head so I can't hear what they're saying. Kore looks like she has one toe over the edge of hysterics and needs just one nudge to fall into it. I'm not used to seeing adults look like that—like they have something to lose. Everything to lose.

I move toward the bed for the first time, keeping my eyes on Sam's face. Someone cared enough to clean the grime and mud off it, but even clean, there are shadows. Her cheeks are sunken, and with her eyes shut, I can't help thinking, *She looks like she's already gone.* I run a knuckle along the curve of her nose, the way Dad used to do to Mom and, before I can question it, I lean over to kiss her cheek. A part of me feels like it'll be the greatest act of rebellion I ever do. Because I let myself feel how soft her skin is, I imagine taking her face between my hands, and it feels like I've set off a firework inside of my chest. No wonder they turn us hollow. I've always thought the danger in experiencing these emotions lay solely in being caught, but living them makes *me* danger itself. There is nothing I will not do to get her out of here.

I kneel down near her head, tucking a loose strand of hair behind her ear, studying the familiar shape of it. It makes me think of all the summers in the tree fort, when the wet heat hung low from the sky and we didn't have the energy to do anything other than just lie under the canopy. I can't bring myself to sing. It hurts too damn bad. So I hum, low enough that I think it'll be for her ears only. *You are my sunshine, my only sunshine . . .*

Sam shifts suddenly, her head rolling toward mine. I have the vague sense that the nurses have stopped talking and they are staring, but it doesn't really matter. I don't have anything to be embarrassed or ashamed about. I keep humming.

"Lucas . . . ?" Her voice is a faint rasp. It sounds like some part of her is still asleep, but I hear the tinge of annoyance. "Hate . . . that song."

A faint laugh bubbles up inside of me as I reach down and take her hand. She gives a light squeeze back. "I know, Sammy. But how else was I supposed to get your attention?"

Someone gasps at the sound of her voice. When I look up, I see that Kore has pressed both hands to her mouth.

"Sparks . . ."

Her voice draws me back to her, the way it always does. "The sparklers from the Fourth of July? You remember those? I bet that would have gotten your attention."

She gives a tight nod, her jaw clenched. "Hurts . . . Lucas . . ."

"I know, I know—I'm going to get you out of here, okay? Get you real medicine. You'll be back on your feet in no time."

"Mia . . . medicine . . ."

"No, medicine, then Mia. You have to get back on your feet first."

"Mia, medicine," she says, with a bit more heat this time. Her eyes flutter open against the bright lights. I recognize the look she gives me.

"We'll have to agree to disagree," I say. Looking up again, I see Dunn rubbing the top of his head, a far-off expression on his face. He turns to Kore, who's been staring at our linked hands the whole time. I don't breathe easy again until, finally, she nods.

"All right . . . okay," Dunn says, suddenly pale at the abstract idea becoming actual reality. My own heart is speeding out of control, and I have to look at Sam again to calm down.

Don't do anything stupid, her expression says.

Too late.

FIVE

SAM

I HEAR THE SONG LIKE THE BIRDS HIGH UP IN THE branches of our tree in Greenwood. I turn toward the sound, trying to imagine it's a cool blanket, one that'll put out the simmering heat trapped inside my head and leg. I'm not surprised, not in the least, when I open my eyes and see Lucas.

Just . . . muddled.

I think I'm in the Infirmary. I know these are nurses, I recognize their calm, kind voices, but it doesn't—it doesn't make sense, the things he's saying. They're all talking so fast. *Medicine, Mia, sparks, out* . . . I try to watch his lips move, read the expression on his face, but he's wearing that mask again. The Lucas I know disappears behind it as I lose my grip on his hand and he rises to his feet, shucking off his crimson vest, his uniform. The female nurse hands him a pair of gray scrubs as the man starts unhooking the machines. Fever and pain have turned my vision glassy at the edges, and the things hanging near me, things that have only been blurs up until now, are set on my stomach. I have to strain my ears, fight the black water rushing over me, to stay at the surface and listen to their low conversation.

"—bring one of the crates over—"

"—be fast—"

Footsteps, doors opening, doors shutting, doors opening, problems—

"—too small, can't do both of you—"

Lucas sounds the strongest, the calmest. "Then I need a PSF uniform. I'll pose as one of the escorts. It might even be easier that way."

"They don't have those just lying around!"

"I can get one," Lucas says. "Do you have any zip ties? I'll need one of you to lock an office after I'm done . . ."

They go away long enough that I drift back down into the haze of pain and don't surface again until I feel hands on me.

"No, this isn't—stop . . ." I try to get my lips around the words but they come out sounding slurred, blending together. When I open my eyes again, I see a black uniform, red Psi stitched over the heart, and try to twist away.

"It's me." It's Lucas above me, blocking out the lights over-head. I can't see his face. I want to see his face. "You're okay, Sammy."

He eases his arms under my shoulders and legs. He's so warm that I forget. I can't think of what this means until he says, quietly, "We're getting out."

No.

NO.

He doesn't know. He hasn't been here long enough to have seen it—they kill kids who escape. They shoot them. I remember every single shot, the way the single crack of thunder would roll through an otherwise silent camp and we would all just *know.*

"No—Lucas—"

No matter how gently he lowers me into . . . the crate, I think, it still jars my leg and sends a stabbing pain racing up through it. "Sorry, sorry, I'm sorry, Sammy." He's breathing the words out, carefully arranging me so I'm flat on my back, my entire right side throbbing. I don't want to think it, let alone say it, but it's shaped long and shallow, like a coffin. They've put down some kind of padding, but the wood is cheap and I can feel it splintering as it rubs against my back. The sawdust smell makes me think of old, gone things. The town fair. The horse stables Lucas and I walked by every day to get to school.

Before he can pull away, I force myself to reach up and grab the front of his uniform coat. I want to shake him, but I can barely tighten my fingers enough to pull him in closer. Lucas's horrible blank mask cracks enough for a small smile to come through. He leans over and takes my face between his big, warm hands. I barely feel the tremble in them as he presses his lips softly against mine.

"You can hit me later, okay?"

"Again," I demand, turning my face up. I feel dizzy. A good dizzy. My headache evaporates.

"Later," he promises. "Love you, Sammy. Don't be scared. I'll be with you the whole time."

His words stay in my ears, even as the lid is lowered and snapped into place.

The male nurse is still nearby. I hear him say something to Lucas, and Lucas's low, rumbling response. "Whatever happens, keep walking out. Look like you know what you're doing. You might get separated, but don't try to hover over the crate. Don't turn back."

"Thank you . . ."

"Just . . . be careful . . . okay? Wait inside the office until the PSFs are down to pick it up."

And that's it. That's all there is left for us—waiting. I close my eyes, focusing on making the sound of my breathing as quiet as I can manage, but it still sounds like a wet windstorm in my ears. It's dark, so dark and tight and cold. And without anything else to focus on, there's only the raw, blistering pain left in my leg.

The boots the PSFs wear are heavy enough that you can always hear them coming. They're the sound of strength; they trample over everything. I crane my neck back, peering through a crack in the wood joints.

A door creaks open as the black boots come closer, closer, closer.

"Is this one going out?" comes a gruff voice.

"Yeah. It needs to be on the truck with the MRI." It's Lucas's voice, sounding as easygoing and natural as I've ever heard it. "The nurses said it's delicate."

"Yeah, yeah . . . You one of the drivers?"

"Yes." That's how he'll try to get away with this insanity. He knew they wouldn't recognize his face. All of the PSFs here have been working together for years.

I hold in a yelp of surprise as the crate is heaved up and off the floor with twin grunts. It rocks wildly—one of them is either stronger, or has a better grip. I feel myself sliding back, my head connecting with the side of the crate.

"Careful!" Lucas growls.

One of the PSFs mutters something filthy under his breath,

and the whole crate sways again with their first few steps until they work out their rhythm. When I look through the split in the wood again, I see Lucas's broad shoulders, the scrubs stretched out over them. He's walking stiffly, keeping ahead of us as we start up the stairs. The moment the crate tips up, I slide again, this time toward the base of it. My right leg already feels raw and shattered; having it rub against the side of the crate makes white spots flash in my eyes. I shove my fist up against my mouth to keep from crying. I try to imagine that I'm a spark, rising up through the dark. Up, and up, and up, out of the cold, black stillness.

Please, God, please lead us out of this, please don't abandon us, give me the strength to be delivered from this fear—they're fragments of prayers I can't fully remember. My throat aches with the need to speak the words out loud.

"—shitty weather, make the drive out to New York rough, but it should be okay once we're in Jersey—"

"—can't believe we got stuck with this shit. Our luck, right?"

"Here, here, careful, last step up—"

The crate evens out again, and I have to twist around more fully to see through the crack again. Lucas is still there, still with his back to me. I recognize the first floor of the Infirmary, even without the beds and curtains hung up. There are more black-uniformed soldiers moving around us with boxes and crates of their own. It sends a trill of panic through me when Lucas disappears again and again, forced to weave through them to get to the door.

Please help us, please let this work, I'll never ask for anything else again . . . please, God. I know He doesn't grant wishes, I know that's not His role, but just once, just this once, I want to believe that I was right, and not my father. I want to believe that He will be there like a guiding hand. I squeeze my eyes shut again, trying to clear the haze that's crowding in on my line of sight. My head is feeling too light; I know this. I'm disconnecting again. There are hands at my back, trying to drag me back under, back . . .

When my eyes open again, it's to faint pattering on the lid of the crate. The sudden cold is a shock to the system, like I've jumped into a freezing pond, and every muscle in my body contracts, pulling in to protect what little warmth is left. Water drips through the gaps in the wood, landing on my face, my chest, my feet.

Lucas's rain poncho is plastered to him, his ink-black hair flat against his skull. He keeps his head down, looking at the mud. In front of him, no more than a hundred yards away, is the gate. It's wide open, and a semitruck, the kind I used to see all the time when people moved in and out of our neighborhood, is parked there. Crates are being walked up the platform, but it seems like the PSFs are struggling with the thick black mud sucking at their feet. I see several in ponchos that look like little more than trash bags with holes cut for the arms. They're like shadows moving against a dreamy gray mist.

The PSFs grunt as they lower me down onto something. The crate goes sailing back, bumps against something, and rocks forward again. Someone voices the cuss word that screams through my head as my leg is jarred. My breath comes out in small, uneven bursts. Then, the crate is tilted again and we're moving— it's rolling smoothly. I peer through the crack again, searching for Lucas's form. He is walking away, around to the front of the truck.

Please, I think. *Please let him get on without any problems . . .* Let the driver think he's someone from Thurmond. Let the Thurmond PSFs think he came with the driver.

There's a horrible creak as the crate is lifted and dumped off the roller. My teeth catch the inside of my lip and I can't keep the hiss of pain from slipping between them. The truck rumbles to life and the door clatters as it's pulled down like a shade, cutting the soft steel-toned light to a sliver. It's secured with a deafening bang that rattles around inside of my head. After a minute, the driving rain drowns it out.

It's several terrified heartbeats later that I realize the truck is moving.

Slowly.

Rolling.

Working.

I close my eyes, drawing my hands up to my face. The engine revs as the truck picks up speed. We must be through the gate, or getting close. I wish I could see it. I want to know what the camp looks like as it disappears into the horizon like a fading memory. It's like Greenwood in that way, I think. A secret place that exists outside of the world's reality.

The progress is halting. The truck jerks now and then, and I hear the engine rev again as we rock forward, then back. There's a horrible metallic roar as it lurches forward, rocks violently from side to side. I think, for a second, that something's slammed into us from behind. The force of the movement sends me crashing forward. There's banging, the sound of wood splintering—something smashes onto the lid of my crate and cracks it down the middle. I scream, bringing my hands up in front of my face. The spray of splinters. Sawdust in my lungs.

The truck doesn't move.

I hear the engine rev again.

Voices—shouts of alarm. Slamming doors. The sound is almost lost to the storm.

The back door rolls open like it's in a rage.

"—busted up everything!"

"Christ, what a mess—"

"—have to dig the tires out—"

We're stuck, then. The truck is trapped in the same mud that's constantly trying to suck us down. With the light, I can peer up through the crack in the lid of my crate. See the damage of every-thing that's been knocked loose. Rain pours down the open door like a sheet. Like the waterfall Lucas dreamt up for Greenwood. It hides something valuable. Something waiting to be found.

It's like I can feel him before I see him. A dark shape appears, passing through the rain as he hauls himself up. Lucas stumbles as he comes closer. He's lost his hat. Dark hair is plastered to his pale, panic-stricken face. His eyes meet mine and he gulps down a shuddering breath. His whole body sags with relief as he pulls off the crate that's crashed onto mine.

What are you doing? I want to scream. *Why didn't you stay in the truck? You weren't supposed to turn around.*

Someone yells. I can't make out her words, but Lucas does—he goes rigid again, whirling back. I see his fist clench at his side. The smell of smoke fills my nose, and, for a second, I think I can see it rising off him.

What are you doing?

His eyes are blazing. He still thinks he can get us out of here.

What are you doing?

"No—" I choke out.

"*Stop!*" A woman screams the word. "Red—*M27!*"

I see him make the decision. I see how fast fear turns to fury as he raises both hands. *Lucas, no, Lucas, please, just*—He can't run, he can't do anything, they'll kill him, *they're going to kill him for this.*

Fire coats his hands, races up his arms. I'm caught in its glow. I bang on the crate in horror. Why did he get out? Why did he—"*Lucas!*"

I am still screaming, still beating on the crate's lid, trying to break out, when the tint of the sky warms to a horrifying red-gold, and the panicked outrage outside turns deadly.

"*No!*" It was working—it was *working*—we were getting out—the mud—the rain—

If it had been clear skies—

There are never clear skies here.

The world explodes with White Noise. It spikes into my temple like a ratchet, and for the first time, I'm able to ignore the pain in my leg because everywhere else hurts that much worse. There are shadows closing over me. I can't keep my eyes open. I turn my face against the crate as the monsters in black rip the lid off the crate and iron hands clench my arms, dragging me out. Freezing rain slaps my skin, my eyes burn with tears at the intensity of the White Noise and the overcast light. I smell burnt skin. There are PSFs on the ground, screaming, rolling in the mud. There are more pouring out of the gate—the gate—God, we were almost through, the rear of the truck only needed to move a foot more, and we would have been past it. The truck sits low in the mud, half the wheels hidden by the black, grasping earth.

I'm dropped into the watery earth like a bundle of dead limbs. I force my eyes open, searching, but my vision is splitting in too many ways.

"Sam!" The sound of his voice tears at my heart. It's ragged, lanced with the same desperation that's pumping through me. *"Sammy!"* At first I think there are ten PSFs surrounding Lucas, but they seem to duplicate the longer I search for him.

I have to get him out of here. I have to save Lucas. He can't die here. He can't die for me.

He's on the ground at their feet, his hands pressed against his skull as though they're the only things to keep it from splitting in two. I recognize one of the PSFs—the woman who must have recognized him, shouted for him. She's the one that put me in the cage. Who hit me over and over again in the Factory, in front of everyone. *Cut my hair. Don't act like I want it.* There's a White Noise device in her hands, pointing down toward Lucas, and of everything she's done or said until now, nothing makes me hate her more.

"Sam!" He is still calling for me, still fighting against the sound blistering his mind, even as they drag him away.

This can't be it. This can't be the last time I see him. Hear his voice. *Not Lucas, please, God, not him.*

I try to push myself up out of the mud. Water is collecting in the deep wells feet have left behind. I'm going to drown in an inch of water. I try to reach for him, but it's too far, he's too far away, and everything, every last hope burns out inside of me.

Under the carriage of the truck, I can see the road we would have taken, the wild, open road ahead of us, I can see Lucas smiling as he takes my hand, and all of these things, all of these precious pieces of dreams become as insubstantial and cold as the air I'm trying to grasp in my palm.

SIX

LUCAS

THERE IS NO GUNSHOT.

There are no hands around my throat.

There are restraints that cut deep into my wrists and ankles.

There is darkness. Sleep. Nightmares. Blood, hot blood, a pale face—Sam.

There are four white walls where there once were electric fences and trees and cabins.

There are printouts of my parents' old IDs, the names blacked out. Who are they? The answer becomes razor and agony.

There are the hands that throw me down, the hands that haul me up, the hands that strike—strike-strike-strike—

There are lights that never go out, voices that never stop, screaming *obedience is the key, you are wrong, tell me you are wrong so we can fix you*—I try to slip away, wrap myself in layers of memories and stories and songs, but every time I try to go, the Trainer is there, and he cuts at each one with his blade. He drags me out. He digs into my skin. I feel electricity snapping between my teeth. Drills screech. It does not stop hurting until I stop trying. Until I can't remember where I was going to begin with.

There is hunger—

Thirst—

Pain—

The door opens, but it is not the man in black who comes in. It is a piece of bread. They show me photos, a smiling man, smiling woman, but I can't remember their names and it hurts too bad to think. Another piece of bread. *Yes, they are no one.* A warm cup of water. *You are no one.*

I am a shadow. I am weak. They will fix me.

There is a girl with sunshine hair who turns my world to shreds. She burns my eyes, breaks my thoughts to pieces. There is a glow around her like the sky at noon, but it narrows, the image, it shrinks, and the pain eases its grip into numb nothing. It shrinks and shrinks again until it becomes a pinprick of light in the dark.

A spark that fades to nothing at all.

SEVEN

SAM

AFTER WEEKS OF RAIN AND DARKNESS, HE'S THERE AT the edge of the Garden one morning.

Just . . . *there.*

The morning fog curls around his crimson vest as he stands as still as a statue, like he has always only ever been there. The color is gone from his skin, his face shaded by shadows and new scars. My memory of him alters sharply, a new snapshot to add to the box, another one I can't touch in case one day it cuts too deep and takes me to a place I can't recover from. Every part of me is shaking as I limp forward through the white fence.

I have been in the Infirmary for weeks, my fingers curled around the edge of a cliff I know we only fall over once, unwilling to let go. They knew the real punishment would be living. That's the only reason I could think of why they gave the female nurse the medicine, even after they made the male one disappear. The harder I tried to give up, the tighter they strapped me down to this place. They fed me with tubes when I would not eat. They made me sleep. My leg will never be the same; they treated it, I'm sure, because they know it will hurt me the rest of my life. It will be a reminder of *what happens* when you try to run.

And this is *what happens* to boys who dream.

There's a fist around my throat. I know I shouldn't look, but I can't help it, I have to see if it's like before. Even with his mask on, I saw the soul beneath the stone.

He turns as I slow.

He looks at me. Through me. There is nothing, not even a flicker of life in his face. My knees buckle and I'm falling forward, stumbling through the gate into the black, soft dirt. The wind carries the last traces of mist away as Lucas turns back toward the camp spreading open in front of him. And I know.

He has gone to a place I cannot find him.

I cannot sing him home.

BEYOND THE NIGHT

YOU HAVE TO REMEMBER.

I know you will, if you'd just try. Can't you see it when you close your eyes? It's tucked behind the stern-faced houses and neatly groomed lawns left to brown and die. It's a wild place of half-told stories and overgrown dreams.

Come on. You know the way. You have to remember.

Can you hear me?

There are three keys, three secrets, three paths.

Place your steps inside the footprints left behind by the giants.

Don't drink the water, the sorceress poisoned the well.

Don't trust the animals. They are always hungry.

Walk toward the place where the sunlight turns the leaves to green glass.

Don't listen to the voices, the ones that try to tell you to *shut up, don't say a word, can't you move faster, freak—* work, sleep, work, sleep, hurt. Try to catch the sweet song calling to you. It's the only map you'll need.

Can you see me?

There are shadows you cannot come back from.

Don't look. Hold your breath as you pass them.

Walk until you feel the damp earth start to seep through the thin soles of your shoes, the holes in your socks, your skin. The air will go as silent and soft as a feather when you see it—the heart of the forest, the castle built inside the unbreakable bones of our tree.

I'm here.

It's a place far away from here. I'm not supposed to remember, but I can escape. I catch a glimpse of it in cracks and splinters, and it catches me in return. It drags me out from under the humming electric wires, the sharp kiss of a blade against skin, the *nothing no one nothing no one.* I can scratch at the darkness.

I'm here.

It's a place that has to be guarded. Protected. Otherwise they'll take that, too.

I'll burn it down to the ground before I let them have it.

Please.

You know the way back.

You know where to find me.

Find me.

ONE

MIA

ONCE UPON A TIME, THERE WAS A GIRL NAMED MIA Orfeo.

She lived in a sweet little house surrounded by a family who loved her. They played games every Friday and she cheated ruthlessly whenever it seemed like her brother was going to beat her. He always let her. She ate three meals a day, one of them usually burnt, because her mom would start reading a book halfway through baking it and would forget to check the timer. Her parents let her repaint the walls of her room hot pink on her seventh birthday when she claimed that the current color, peach, was too "bromidic" and "dispiriting." She liked looking up big words in the dictionary and saving them for the perfect moment.

After wasting hours at school that she could have used to write her next work of dramatic genius, or to experiment with her mom's makeup while she was downstairs trying to placate their cantankerous cats, you could more often than not find her outside, trailing behind her brother and his best friend, the girl next door with hair like gold thread. And there, in the vast backyard of the aforementioned sweet little house in a small town in Virginia, among the overgrown barberry bushes, was a secret place; a happy place. They called it Greenwood, and it belonged to them and no one else.

The girl, Mia, found out that she could slip into any skin her moods and whims demanded—bear, princess, sorceress, mermaid, tiger. Sometimes she just wanted to be Mia. Mia of the untamable curly black hair. Mia of the woods. Mia bored-with-real-life.

Mia Orfeo.

Now there is no girl; just a *thing*. And the thing goes by the number that is spray-painted on the back of its thin blue uniform: 6575. The thing does not have a house; it has a room inside of an enormous concrete building that is slowly sinking into the mud. The thing does not have a family; it has twenty-nine other things stacked into bunks around it. It works. It sleeps. It eats. From its top bunk, it can see the colors of the sky changing pink, orange, sapphire, violet, all melting into one another. It does not get to go outside.

But it remembers.

I know the smell of smoke, and I know the smell of blood.

There's a memory attached to both that I don't like to touch. It's hidden beneath years of overcast skies and black-and-white monotony, compressed, smashed into slivers and splinters. But every now and then, it sneaks out. It tiptoes up while I'm sleeping and spreads itself over my chest, the way Luc and I used to dog-pile on Dad in sneak attacks.

Everything was a game to us back then.

It stuns me, each time I feel that weight settle over me again. A girl doesn't get over something like that. She doesn't move past the flash of a bullet streaking out of a gun. She doesn't get to purge the sound of her mom's screams. Her hand—the one the men in black uniforms broke, to get her away from her brother—still hurts whenever the camp's electricity goes out on winter nights and there's no heat. It's easier to be the *it*, the little monster that they think I am.

Monsters can devour nightmares.

Monsters aren't ashamed if uniformed soldiers are afraid of them. Monsters think their fear is delicious.

Monsters shred, with their razor claws, daydreams of being a princess locked away in a castle, waiting for rescue.

Monsters save themselves.

Tonight it's different, though, and the moment I open my eyes to the low ceiling inches above my face, I know why. The smoke isn't trapped in my head, staining the ugliness of that day in the parking garage. It's burning my nostrils, curling down my throat and into my lungs.

I can't move, I can't get out of bed without one of the eight black-eyed cameras seeing it. The coughs rip out of me as I turn onto my side. My eyes water and burn in the darkness; girls slam into awareness around me, their voices bubbling with panic and fear.

Trepidation, I think. That's a better word than simple "fear" and plain "panic."

"What's happening—?"

"—that smoke?"

"Fire!"

The long fluorescent lights snap on, burning white-hot. Some of the other girls scream, but most are staggering to their feet, trying to shield their eyes and then their ears as the alarm above the door goes off. It sounds like metal piercing metal. It cuts up the inside of my skull, makes me feel slow, stupid, even as the first touch of panic lances through me. I'm watching the alarm's flashing light, the red, the blue, the red, the blue, as it whirls around. Red, blue, red, blue, Red, Blue . . .

Lucas, me.

A dark hand reaches up through the silvery white smoke and clamps around my ankle, hard enough for the nails to break the skin.

"*Mia!*"

It's Elise, all tear-streaked and fluttery. She's out of breath, like the fear has ripped it out of her.

"Mia, come on!"

I climb down from my top bunk stiffly. It's been my tiny slice of space since I moved out of the Blank Rooms five years ago, when the monster in me finally decided to grow teeth, and sent one of the Camp Controllers shooting across the room with its abilities a week after my tenth birthday. I was sorted into the last space left in this room. Bare walls, bunk beds built into the walls, girls who still occasionally wet the bed despite being fourteen, fifteen, sixteen: my consolation for surviving the change. If I'd known what it was like over here, I would have tried harder to turn my two years in the Blank Rooms into three or four—shocker, I didn't have a lot of foresight at eight years old. I didn't even appreciate how good and quiet and calm it was over there. They played us *music*. Now the only songs I get to hear are Elise snoring in the middle bunk, and Alice sniveling in the bottom bunk.

Here is all you need to know about Alice: she is currently in the middle of what little space we have at the very center of the room, curled up into a ball, hands clasped over her head like the building is about to drop down on top of her.

The sprinklers burst open with a *whoosh*, and there are shrieks as we're drenched with ice water. I can't shield my eyes; there's a sharp metallic tang to the water when it gets into my nose and mouth. There's got to be a real problem, something must be genuinely wrong, if they're letting us do this; if the girls can cling to each other, talk to each other, get out of their beds, without them sending in one of the PSFs to leash us again.

Is this some kind of sick trick? Force a reaction to teach us some kind of lesson with baton strikes or Calm Control? I wouldn't put it past them—mind games are second nature to these people. But . . . my mind is folding over and over on itself, trying to sort out the possibilities. That wouldn't make sense. They've never needed an excuse to punish us, to pick a little lamb to roast so the rest of the flock learns not to stray. My jaw clenches to keep my teeth from chattering. Elise is shouting something to me, and I don't hear her. Some of the girls start to line up, shifting into alphabetical order out of habit. I'm tugged in front of Alice, who leans forward and cries into the back of my uniform.

My whole world narrows to the solid metal door in front of me; it's like I can feel something shift, some charge running through it. I straighten up, the muscles in my lower back aching, cracking the bones and joints that have been bunched up for too long.

Open sesame, I think.

The door pops open.

Just.

Like.

That.

I don't know why it surprises me. We had one fire drill two years ago, and this is exactly what happened. Well—okay, no, it's not. There weren't any sprinklers or smoke, but the alarm went off, and we assembled in the center of the room. A PSF appeared there and marched us to the end of the hall. I think we all thought they'd take us outside.

They didn't.

But this time, there isn't a PSF standing at attention, clutching a rifle. When the electronic lock releases, the familiar hiss and click is drowned out by the flood of voices carrying down the hall. All of the doors have opened, and the sound of the alarm is now amplified by a hundred. It pours down through the ceiling from the floors above us. It seeps up from the floors below. If I didn't know better, if it wasn't totally contrary to every single thing they've done up to this point, I'd say they were trying to smoke us out. Like exterminators do with pests.

None of us move. I wonder if there's something racing in the pit of everyone's stomach, like there is in mine—if they feel like their hearts are simply going to tear themselves into pieces. The sprinklers sputter and belch out buckets of water, which rises up to our bare ankles, and still none of us move.

And then two kids race by the doorway. The Green girls, their ponytails streaming out behind them, are weaving in and out of smoke that looks as thick and solid as cream.

Even as all signs point to our world burning down around us, only two kids—two out of the two hundred on our floor—are following their instincts. The rest of us are all standing here stupidly, waiting for an announcement to tell us what to do. We would rather risk being burned alive than tempt the Camp Controllers into action. We know what will happen.

But the monster *also* knows what it should be doing, what *we* should be doing. I feel the snarl curl my lips, the lick of anger curdling my blood. I like that word: *curdling.*

I take the back of Elise's shirt in one hand and Alice's arm in the other, and I drag them forward.

"Let's *go!*" I shout, when it's clear no one else will. I glance back over my shoulder at the pale faces, dripping with sprinkler water and tears. "I'm not waiting here to suffocate!"

"No!" Alice is crying, trying to yank herself free—and I almost let her go. I can feel my fingers slipping against her slick warm skin, and the monster bares its teeth and thinks, *survival is a choice you have to be strong enough to make.* But I can be strong enough for the whole room if I have to be.

"There's no one coming!" I say, coughing around the words. "Don't stay here and wait until there's no air left to breathe! *Go! Move!*"

In some ways, life is easier when you surrender control to someone else. It doesn't surprise me that half of them don't move until I bark at them, until I turn it into orders. The PSFs made our shells too tough to let any of us feel a soft touch. We only respond to hard, sharp, vicious.

The temperature under my skin reaches a thousand degrees as I step out into the hall. Elise and Alice follow, and I wait half a heartbeat to see if the rest of the girls will, too. They do; it's a slow spill of blue uniforms. We cough our way down the white tiled path to the staircase at the very end. Faces pop into the cloud of smoke around us, kids peering out of the doorways. I don't need to try to wave the cloud of steely gray away to know that every room looks exactly like ours. The Camp Controllers never tried to give this facility a sweet complexion, hide its ugly metal joints and cement bones.

More girls stumble into the hallway behind us, shouting to be heard over the screeching alarms. I don't realize we've reached the stairwell until someone nearly pulls the door open in my face. Again, no locks.

No PSFs.

Unease begins to fizz in my blood. The stairwell is small, packed with kids descending from the facility's six upper levels. The smoke rises up, curling around their shock-stiff faces, scorching my throat dry. Boys, girls, Greens, Blues. I manage to squeeze my way inside, blindly feeling for the nearest step with my foot, using the girl next to me for balance as I risk a look back at the other girls from my room. A flare of pain rips through me as someone steps on my foot.

Flipping shoes, I think. Of course, I'm the idiot who forgot to put on her shoes.

There's no way back up now. The crush of bodies has practically lifted me off the ground, and I'm being carried forward by the urgent flow. Fear feels like a second layer of smoke, and none of us can escape it.

One floor down, two—how are we still moving so slowly? How many flipping kids are in this facility—

The lights flicker. There's a clanking groan, something grinding to a stop. A *clang, clang, clang* . . . and then, nothing at all. The overhead lights, the whirling colors of the alarms mounted on the stairwell landings, blink out as one.

The screeching sirens choke off.

In all the years I've been in this nameless place, I have never felt a moment slant around me like this. It feels like the air has evaporated, and every last trace of sound has gone with it. Hot wet breath licks at my skin, clinging to the back of my neck and shoulders.

And then the screaming starts, and it doesn't matter where the fire is, or how it started. Panic incinerates us.

Elbows, feet, knees bunching and driving and shoving—I swear something snaps in my chest just as Elise's skull is shoved toward me, cracking against my cheekbone.

"Stop—!" I shout. The crushing dark—it's a black tide and it's rolled over all of us—no air—forward—*forward*—

Mia is going to be crushed.

The monster is going to roar.

I can feel the itch, the need, racing up and down my arms like I've wrapped them in thorns. I can get these kids out of the way, I can *push* them without ever touching them, clear a path for my girls—

But someone else has the same wicked idea and we, all of us on this set of stairs, seem to explode forward. We're flung against the cinderblock wall with all the gentleness of speeding cars hitting a cement barrier. *Pain—slap—crunch—screams—*

I manage to lift my head out from under someone's leg in time to make out the form scurrying over us like a little rat. It's *Alice*. I-puked-when-a-PSF-looked-at-me-funny Alice.

The little monster finally grew some claws, and is climbing over us without missing one flipping beat.

I'm one of the lucky ones—I've landed on top, my hands are pressing down on someone's neck, cheek, as I struggle to stand, to get off the boy who's wailing under me. The sound—it's the crying that tears at me, tears *me* in two, three, four, not his hands as he scratches up at my arms and legs. All those times I called us little monsters, somehow I never thought we'd be capable of this. It's like the others don't even see us on the landing. Their feet stamp us back down every time we manage to get up.

They don't care.

I know how fear can blank your mind, bleach out every last thought. But this reaction is more than just instinct; it has to be. All these years they've been teaching us to keep each other at a distance, even as we've basically been sleeping on top of one another, constantly shuffling by each other in blurs of color to the cafeteria, to the Wash Rooms, to the sleeping rooms. They've taught us not to *see* each other, cursed us into becoming monsters who will eat each other to survive.

This isn't what I want—this isn't who I want to be—

You can't be a monster, I think. *Stop listening to the monster!*

They don't stop coming. The air thickens, and all I can taste is my own sweat, bile, the charred ash spinning through the smoke. My vision starts to dip into black. It hurts—I shake my head, trying to clear it, to pull back away from the memories tailing it, crowding in—

Dad in the front seat, saying, *We have money, let me get it, pal, just stay calm—*

The man with the jitters, the one with a face like a warty toad—the black gun—

Mom looking back at us as she reaches for the glove box, the money spilling out of the paper towels it's wrapped in.

Lucas covering me—the toad turning glassy red eyes on us— the idea reflected there.

The gunshot—

Dad twists. Mom screams.

The gunshot—

Lucas, no, Lucas don't—

Fire.

The second man; the knife.

The black uniforms.

Why didn't I die? Why didn't I die with them?

"Stop!" a voice bellows. It catches me at the edge of conscious-ness and drags me back. "*Stop where you are!* Slowly! Careful! *Slowly!* Calm down!"

Someone is giving orders behind us—another Blue boy is standing on the last step before the landing, his arms linked with three others'. My eyes have adjusted to the darkness enough to see that they've created a wall, damming up the swell of straining bodies behind them. With a little more biting, we'd have a zombie movie on our hands.

I feel hands scooping under my arms, hauling me up.

"—you okay? Hey! You okay?"

Another Blue, head and shoulders taller than me, has me back on my feet and keeps me upright until my knees stop buck-ling. My knight in grimy soot.

The Blue boys give me and the others enough time to help each other up. The monster wants to tear the rest of the way down the stairs before it happens again. *Save yourself, everyone saves themselves.* For the first time, I don't listen. I feel so bad about accidentally mauling the face of the boy under me, I make sure he goes first.

There's not a single inch of me that doesn't hurt as I stagger—*lurch*—down through the last few feet of darkness. Cold air reaches out for me, and I feel myself strain toward its waiting arms.

I'm shoved through the open access door and into the dead of night, stumbling awkwardly onto my knees and into the nearest patch of brown snow.

Outside, outside, my fingers are curling in the mud, I'm *out*. . . .

The kids keep spilling through the doorway behind me, collapsing onto the sopping wet ground. It's like we're going to have to fight through a swamp as one last trial, I think. A test of strength—no, *fortitude*.

My cough rocks my whole body. I feel like I'm trying to purge poison from my blood. The air is sharp with the bitter cold, but sweet on my tongue, soothing to my scorched throat.

Glass explodes down around me, shaking the ground and sending us scattering forward again. We're in some kind of cement courtyard or driveway. The facility sits like an enormous U behind us, but the gate in front of us is so tall and black it's camouflaged by the night sky. I duck down and cover my head as a wave of heat rolls out over us, rising. When I think it's safe, I look back, trying to confirm my suspicions.

I'm right. All of the first-floor windows are blown out. Fire and smoke are pouring up over the empty frames, licking, slithering, almost like liquid. It's most intense right at the center of the building, where we've always thought the control room for the camp was—the hive mind of machines and misery.

I crawl toward where I see Elise's dark shape. To the right is—oh my God. The other buildings are burning, too. The Blank Rooms, and the smaller version of the facility specially designed to house the Yellows.

Their yellow uniform shirts are moving through the night

like wandering stars, rushing through the blisteringly cold air. I wrap my arms around my center, frozen in place, as several of the older Yellow and Blue kids emerge, carrying or holding the hands of other, smaller ones in white uniforms—the kids who haven't "changed" yet. The Blanks.

An engine revs, roaring from behind the Blanks' building. A Hummer bursts through a pile of snow as tall as me, forcing several Greens to dive to the ground to avoid being hit. I turn back to the gate just in time to see the last of the PSFs' trucks drive away, dragging the metal doors shut behind it.

It's five hours before our rescuers come, their silver coach buses streaking up through the rose-glow of the sunrise. We can see them coming over the head of tangled barbed wire that sits on top of the fence none of us have been brave enough to try climbing over. The PSFs bolted the locks from the outside before they blazed off—I guess so we couldn't wander away? They—the Camp Controllers—smoked us out of the building, set fire to the one room that would have kept things running after they abandoned it. Why? To leave us out *here* to slowly freeze to death?

To . . . let us go?

Kids toss out theories, volleying them back and forth between chattering teeth. And all I can think is, *this feels like a prologue for another story.*

One that might have an even worse ending.

Forbidden words buzz around us in a swarm of hope. *Mom. Dad. Family. Leave. Home.*

There is no more home.

There is no Mom and Dad.

And Lucas . . .

"Bull," Elise says as the bus engines shut off. "They're just moving us to another camp."

And when the soldiers come into view, I realize she's right.

Different uniforms. Different soldiers. Same story.

I watch them watching us, their careful—*ginger*—approach, like we're animals who have escaped our cages at the zoo and need to be guided back to them. Their rifles are up and pointing at us like long black snouts, sweeping us back as their boots squelch against the soggy ground.

We don't come when they call. None of us step onto their buses, not even when a man gets on the megaphone and starts trying to redefine the word *safe*.

"We're taking you to your families," he says, the machine in his hand crackling and popping, clipping his voice. "The camp program is over. We are here to help you and escort you away from Black Rock."

Black Rock. They keep using those two words like they mean something, and I can see on the faces of the girls around me, the boys who've kept to their side of our makeshift pen, that they've come to the same conclusion I have: Black Rock is the name of our facility. It has a *name* and in addition to being a burnt-out husk of its former self, it will never be repaired, never reopened.

We will never have to go back inside.

The words burst inside me, exploding into a shower of white-hot hope. I think I am wearing it all on my face, that the color is drawn on my cheeks in wide strokes, the way I used to apply Mom's makeup. Elise tells me I'm an idiot and if I go along with them, then I deserve whatever I get. I know she's scared and she doesn't mean it, not really—her nails are biting into my wrists,

232

holding me, and I can see the desperation in her face like it's sweat coating her skin.

But . . . these soldiers don't shoot at us when we disobey them. They don't use Calm Control. They give us water bottles and ask to see our burns, they give some of the kids oxygen masks to use. I wonder what they see when they look at us—if we look as haunted as we all must feel. It feels like standing on top of a fence post, waiting for the moment they decide to knock us off it.

They don't.

They want to know where the PSFs and Camp Controllers are, and one of the older Yellow girls explains exactly what happened. She is tall and brave, like a queen. We let her speak for us.

"They set fires to all of the buildings, unlocked the doors, and left."

Fled, I think. They didn't leave. They *fled.*

When Colonel Megaphone sees the charred remains of the control room, he swears so viciously that the kids around him recoil from the heat. All six feet of him stalks back to the soldiers who are hanging back by the gate, their light camo fatigues darkened by a drizzle of rain and the wet snow.

"They did it again!" he snarls. "They shouldn't have gone public with the first camp. It's all scorched earth—the cowards! It's going to be a fucking nightmare to prove accountability!"

That's when I believe him, all of them. That's when the arc of the story clicks, aligning all these little clues in my hands.

The camp *is* closed. Over.

The PSFs burnt their records, digital and print. They knew to feel ashamed. They *knew* what they did to us was wrong.

And then they ran, knowing these soldiers were coming— that they'd have to answer questions with uncomfortable answers.

I feel the burn of tears starting at the back of my throat. If this has happened before, it means other camps are closing, too. Which means . . .

"Lucas," I whisper, my hands twisting the mud-splattered fabric of my pants. It feels like my chest is too full, like I'm about to burst all my seams. Who cares? *Who cares?* I'd go out on this feeling. It's been years since I let myself catch it and hold—*cling*—to it.

My brother is going to come get me. He promised. What are the chances that he's already out and waiting for me? Good, I know. This is Lucas, after all.

Elise hisses between her teeth when they call for volunteers to take the first bus to a place they call Pierre. Colonel Megaphone finally figures out that we aren't just going to take his word and ride off into the sunrise, no matter how warm those buses look. I hear him working on some of the older kids, telling them to *set a good example,* pulling out some kind of handheld device to say, *this is where we're going—look, there are already parents waiting there.*

In some ways, it feels like we've spent endless days wandering lost through a forest, only to be met with a stranger dangling a sweet, ripe apple in front of us. Another test. It's a risk, sure—if the thing's poisoned, we're all dead. But if we stay here, we're dead anyway.

And I want to see Lucas. I want that more than anything.

Elise's gaze rakes down my back as I step forward, following the first few kids heading through the gate. The monster doesn't care. The monster wants what it wants, and feels strong enough now to push back on anyone who's stupid enough to get between it and the only thing it has left. I feel like I'm shedding an old skin, one weighed down by scaly ash, as I pass through the entryway and move toward the first bus, up the stairs that lead into the enormous beast's belly.

There's a soft-faced woman at the wheel who gives me this little nod of encouragement when my feet slow to a stop so I can look around. I don't need it. My toes curve like claws against the ground as I square my shoulders and follow the Blue boy in front of me to the back of the bus. The heat kicks on and pierces my frozen skin like a thousand small cuts. It feels so much better than the *nothing* that gulped me up the minute the PSFs drove me through the gate. If they are taking us to another camp, if the plan is to kill—*dispose*—of us somehow, then at least we get a few minutes to thaw out after being trapped in the facility's cold arms.

But I'm going to hope. I'm going to believe.

I'm going to see Lucas.

I pick a window seat on the side opposite the camp. I don't want to see it ever again. My pulse is kicking so hard as the engine starts for real, and one by one heads appear, coming up the stairs, filling the empty seats. There's a crackle and pop, drawing my eyes down to where my hands have twisted and crushed the empty water bottle.

A laugh swells up inside me, chased by another, and another, and I can't figure out why. None of this is funny, but others are doing it too. Some are still crying, and I have no idea where that energy is coming from because they've been going at it for hours now.

The bus jerks forward, finds a dirt road running through a field where nothing grows. The land around us is achingly empty, and we seem to fill only a fraction of it, one small sliver moving up its spine. And as we pass low rolling mountains pockmarked with black stone, as we drive through empty towns, that same buzz of hope I felt at the start of the journey begins to fade, settles into a monstrous little growl. Because no matter how far we go, it's never far enough.

I can still see the camp's trail of black smoke rising into the clear blue sky.

TWO

SAM

UNCLAIMED.

I think it is the worst word I've ever heard. The worst label they've tried to give us, at least. Call us freaks any day of the week, we're all so used to it that the sting barely registers. But this . . . it confirms the one fear so many of us have carried around like a blister on our hearts.

Part of me wishes the news and officials would just be honest about it; "unclaimed" is the polite whisper for *unwanted.* "Unclaimed" means a loose end, something that could change any minute, any day. It's something that gets lost, or left behind, and is only waiting for the owner to return and retrieve it. It's only a matter of time. . . .

"Unwanted" is a statement of fact. It is something to come to terms with and move past. Wherever my parents are, whatever they're doing, they are never coming back for me. And that's by choice.

How many times did Ruby and I talk about exactly this? *When this is over,* I told her, *no one is going to be waiting. No one*

237

will want us. She'd nodded in that quiet, sad way of hers. It was the same for both of us. We were the only girls in our cabin who would admit it.

I swallow the bile in my throat as I finally pry the piece of plywood away from the doorframe. I've been carrying around this screwdriver for the past few weeks; I don't know how to use a gun, and I'm not sure where I'd find a knife, but this is more than enough to hurt anyone who tries to hurt me.

This is the first time I've had to use it, and it's not even in self-defense, but a break-in. I'm already a thief; why not add "trespassing" to my score?

I found this emergency exit after a full day of slowly circling the towering hotel. Someone, or something, has smashed in the central glass pane, and if I'm right . . . I *am* right. There's a turning lock on the other side. I grip it with stiff, half-frozen hands, turn my wrist until I hear the metal *click* as it unlocks, and slowly ease the door open.

My shoes are coated with so much mud and snow I have to take some time to wipe them off against a nearby patch of carpet, to keep them from squeaking and alerting everyone to my presence.

This is an in-and-out type of thing. I need to see if she's still here, or confirm that someone's already come to get her, and then I'll be able to go. But if they catch me, identify me . . . well, they'll have another "unclaimed" to add to their list.

I sidle up along the far wall, keeping to the edge of the open space. There are a few soldiers in uniform milling around, but most of them are sipping cups of coffee to stay awake. Some are finally breaking down the tables lining the opposite end of the room, along with the signs above them, where the families were supposed to line up to claim the kids by last name: A-D, E-H, I-L . . . Highlighted rosters, the names crossed off, are being dumped into the overflowing trash cans.

The concierge desk is empty, dark. I wait there in a crouch, hanging back. My hair is stuffed into a knit cap, my oversized parka zipped up all the way, half-masking my face. I picked them up out of a charity bin somewhere in Kentucky, thinking *These jeans, this sweater, these sneakers, this coat—they'll give me the confidence I can't fake.* All they've done in the end is make me feel like I'm ten all over again, wearing a costume pieced together from Mrs. Orfeo's closet.

Someone's already come for her, I think, hoping I'll believe it this time. *You can go in a second. . . .*

The hotel's lobby has been left in shambles by the media. Empty, half-crushed soda cans are scattered alongside empty food wrappers. There's a protest sign, highlighter-yellow, that somehow found its way inside. A soldier bends down to pick it up, angling it so the other man can see. WOULD YOU FREE CRIMINALS FROM PRISON? They laugh.

I almost can't believe how filthy the world is—in every sense of that word. Thurmond might have been falling down around us, the grounds covered in enough mud to make walking a challenge, but we kept the buildings spotless. Not a crumb left behind in the Mess Hall. Everything stowed neatly in the Factory. The Wash Rooms scrubbed on hands and knees.

But trash is the media's footprint, its calling card, and that's exactly what they've been producing each night on the TV and each morning in the papers. I've had to wait all day for them to leave. The news—the channels that have been turned back on—love this. They serve everyone the sweet stuff, try to make them feel better about what they did to us by shoving image after image of family, tears, hugs, in front of them.

What are they trying to prove? That it's *all good now?* All better? All anyone has to do is look out the window and see the peacekeeping forces on their patrols, implementing the new curfews, distributing meager foreign rations of imported food and water. Because, of course, even our crops have been watered with Agent Ambrosia.

Business as usual, the Washington types keep saying. *We'll get there soon.*

Yeah. Right.

I count about a dozen kids left—not bad for a camp this big. The radio report said there were upwards of twelve hundred kids at Black Rock—a little less than half the size of Thurmond, but it's like comparing a leopard to a lion; size is relative when a camp has you between its teeth.

They've been reporting on camp closures for the last three weeks. The peacekeeping force is clearly working its way down some secret list. Most of the shock and novelty of seeing the kids and the camps has worn off, but Black Rock sent a ripple back through the calming waters. It's one of only two camps that took kids *before* they changed, whether their families volunteered them or not. To study them, or . . . I don't know.

Mia would know. They grabbed her before her switch was flipped: death or freak? Lucas didn't even know if she had survived the change after they were separated.

I squeeze my eyes shut, grateful to whatever stone is lodged at the base of my throat. It's the only thing that keeps me from screaming.

Because . . . she's here.

She's still here.

I recognize Mia right away, sitting on the far side of the lobby. This place must have been expensive, a real jewel, before the economy sputtered to a stop. The furniture curves around the sitting area in a smooth arc, facing the large television screen. Someone's started a fire in the hearth on the far wall, which makes the dark coils of her hair gleam. Wide, dark eyes like Lucas, rimmed with thick lashes. Small for fifteen—too thin, but I can fix that.

She's still here. I press my hands to my face, trying to get control of my breathing again. I've become so used to the feeling of terror these past two weeks, I don't even bother trying to stop it as it grips my lungs and shakes me until the world blurs.

Every small clatter or groan of a sound makes me jump. No matter where I go, it feels like someone is constantly two steps behind me, trailing after my shadow. I can't sleep. I can't close my eyes. Fear and I have long conversations in my head, and I tell it to stop being ridiculous, to leave me alone, but it never does. And when it hits me, I just have to wait for it to pass, hating myself the whole time, wondering what happened to the Sam who could look a PSF in the eye and risk getting a beating for it.

I think I left her behind at Thurmond.

The kids around Mia are fixated on the same news report about the progress they're making to strip Agent Ambrosia out of the water supply. It's the same story they've run a thousand times at this point.

Unlike the others, she has her standard-issue supply pack given to her by the government at her feet, all packed up and ready to go, ready to leave at any moment.

Like she hasn't spent the last week sitting here, waiting, watching a thousand kids get escorted back to their former lives. Waiting, waiting, waiting . . .

The papers added her to the "unclaimed" column a few days ago. It's the only reason I knew to come. If her grandparents were still alive, they would have been here days ago, no matter what. I tried to get here faster, I did. It's just . . . things got really complicated.

And now the only one left to get her is me.

I need to get her attention somehow, lead her away from the others, or follow her up to her room when it's time to call it a night—and I need to do it before the soldiers wrap up what they're doing and actually start paying attention. One goes outside to light up a smoke, and I have to grit my teeth to keep from snarling at her. If *I've* heard the reports of snatchers after their next big pay day, abductors selling kids on something the news has taken to calling the "freak market," then they have, too. They need to have eyes on these kids at all times.

I crawl forward, toward the roster of names posted on the wall next to the concierge desk, considering my options.

The sliding doors behind me glide open, sending me scuttling back behind the desk. It's no shield against the freezing air that blasts the back of my neck, raking icicles down my spine. My whole body clenches as I ease back, just a bit, to see who's come in. I absorb the most important details: adult man, suit a little too tight, an outline of a holster under his jacket. The tightness in my shoulders doesn't ease until he holds up some kind of ID badge, and the soldiers give a distracted wave in greeting.

The man's focused on the kids. His shoes click a quick path toward them. They've been sucked into the void of the TV screen after years of separation, and nothing can break them out of it until the man reaches down to turn it off.

"Hey!" protests a kid in a plaid shirt, maybe fourteen at the most. They've given them all street clothes, and something about it looks unnatural to me—I wish I didn't expect to see uniforms, I wish I'd never had to wear mine, but I don't know how to mentally sort these kids without them wearing who they are and what they can do.

"I know," the man says, his voice soothing; like he's speaking to toddlers, not teenagers. "But I have something important I need to talk to you all about."

I ease back a step, around the corner, toward the dark set of elevators behind me. A soldier passes by, bringing a box of supplies outside. *Packing up, heading out.* I can already see the direction this conversation is moving, and it cracks what's left of my heart in half. Because the kids *don't.*

"It might . . ." The man looks up to the ceiling for a moment, gathering his thoughts—or cursing his bad luck. His hands burrow deep into his pants pockets and he rocks back on his heels once, clearing his throat. "We're hitting the road today. The hotel owners have plans to reopen, and it's time to get you ready for the next phase of your lives."

Next phase. Something in me coils so tight, I can't breathe.

"Where are we going?" the girl sitting beside Mia asks.

Mia hasn't so much as looked in the man's direction; although she's physically present, her mind is clearly skating a million miles away.

"We're going to Chicago," the man continues. "You'll be given the procedure by a very skilled doctor there, and then safely re-homed."

He seems relieved to have it out, the whole of it. The longer I stare in disbelief, the more it feels like the floor is knocking up against the soles of my shoes, trying to move me forward. To take all of these kids and *run*.

The procedure? The "miracle cure"? Do these kids even know what it involves—that they'd be letting this doctor drill into their skulls and implant some kind of device that might change who they are, or might one day stop working, or might not even work for them at all?

"I thought we had a choice?" one of them asks, the words trembling only a little. It's another boy, all bony limbs and untidy hair, his knees drawn up to his chest. This one is even younger than the first. I'd put him at twelve. "That's what the lady said."

The man looks up at the ceiling again and taps his fingers against his leg, one at a time. I know what he's doing now— counting to ten—to, what? Steady his temper? He's *annoyed* with these kids? I bristle, feeling my hackles rise. My ribs ache from how hard I've wrapped my arms around them.

"There's no law on the books saying that yet," the man continues, his voice strained by the effort it's clearly taking to sound patient and compassionate. "It's hard to understand, I know—"

No. Nothing about this is hard to understand.

"But you're our responsibility—you're officially wards of the transitional government until otherwise notified, and it's been decided that our wards will proceed with the instructions we were given."

Unclaimed. Unwanted. And now, everything that they are . . . undone.

If he'd tried to use the argument that the procedure would make the kids less appealing as targets to snatchers, more appealing to prospective parents fostering and adopting them, I would have understood; I maybe even would have supported the idea just a little bit. But he doesn't say that. There's no other reason than *because we said so*, and I'm so tired of that attitude, that no-explanation explanation.

The man kneels down beside one of the younger girls. She can't be more than thirteen, and I can see the tears filling her eyes from here. "Don't you want a home? To live with a kind family?"

So many parents lost their kids to IAAN. I have to imagine that there are some kind ones out there that want to fill that hole in their family again. But I also have to imagine there are plenty who have dollar signs in their eyes over the promised "support packages" from the government for each child taken in.

"I have a family," she says, her voice trembling.

The man doesn't touch her, the way you'd normally comfort a kid who's clearly on the verge of a full-blown panic attack. I can tell by the set of his shoulders that he didn't expect this. There's no strategy. The expectation was clearly that they would just nod and follow him out like a line of ducklings.

"Sweetheart," he begins, looking around. "You don't. I've spent the better part of the last two weeks trying to track down your families. They've either moved and disappeared, they've passed on, or they—"

Say it, I think. Finish that thought. *Or they said they didn't want you back.*

Then, a new voice: "My brother is coming for me. I'm staying."

I'm sure I make a sound, but I can't hear it over the growing buzz in my ears. If someone wedged a dull knife into the back of my skull, it wouldn't hurt half as bad as this.

I was right.

In all the hours and days that I spent wrestling with myself over whether or not to come, one fact kept slipping under the chains of my resolve: Lucas wanted, more than anything, more than his own life even, to find his sister. Enough of his mind was intact after the training the Reds were subjected to that he actually volunteered to serve at Thurmond to search for her there, knowing full well that he could be caught. Instead, he'd found me.

Why did you turn around?

Why did you hesitate?

Lucas, why didn't you leave me?

We were going to find her. He was going to get us both out of the camp, and we were going to look for Mia together. As much as the scars from that day still burn, and as many times as I've relived the moment they caught him, the emptiness in his face when he was brought back to duty at Thurmond, fully broken . . . it's nothing compared to the way this image is scorching my heart. Mia has been waiting weeks for a brother who will never come for her.

I'm here, I'm here, I'm here.

She's not alone. For the first time in weeks, I muster up enough anger to pull against the chains that apprehension has thrown over me. Anger—beautiful, dark, sweltering anger—burns out all my trembling uncertainty. Adrenaline hums through my blood, and I wish I were any other color but Green. I'd throw this man and all of these soldiers across the room, as far away as I could get them. I'd blow out the electricity and drag her away in the darkness. I'd burn this place and its lies to rubble.

Mia turns slowly. Her eyes are sharp, dark, with none of the distant dreaminess that softened them before.

"Your brother?" the man repeats. "I searched for him in the system, but there's no record of him at all."

"That's bull—" Mia manages to catch herself before the curse can slip out. "He's a Red! They knew what he was when they took him. And if the other camps are closed, then he's coming to get me."

"Mia . . ." the man begins. The other kids go stiff at that word: *Red*. It's a single syllable that carries nightmares in its back pocket. Mia doesn't know to be afraid. She knew the Lucas who was in control of his abilities, the fire simmering beneath too many layers of soft sweetness to be frightening. She hasn't seen what they made him. How they cut, and cut, and *cut* to make sure he'd never bloom again.

"I'm *staying*," she says. "If that's still a problem, then you need to check your equation and solve it."

The man's back on his feet, looming over her, his arms crossed. "I need you to be a good girl and listen to me."

Mia's features pull back in a snarl. "I'm not a *good girl*. I'm waiting for my brother."

"Even if he—" The man shakes his head. "Even if he were to come, he would be in the same position as you. He'll be a ward of the government."

"No he won't, he's eighteen now. He can be my guardian."

Mia is so clearly proud that she's figured this out. She has no idea that the usual rules don't apply to us—we're Psi, not human. The classification doesn't overlap, not as far as the rest of the world is concerned. We can't be our own guardians. That's a direct quote, courtesy of the radio station I listened to on my drive through Nowhere, South Dakota to get here. We don't have enough education and we lack a basic understanding of how life works, according to them.

And maybe . . . maybe that's true. I hate that idea, that we can't take care of ourselves, but . . . we had our world in the camp, we had our rules, and now we've been pushed back into this one. None of it makes sense. Everything changes out here so quickly, I can't keep up.

The man exhales loudly through his nose. "If he isn't in the system, he never was—"

"My sister is eighteen . . ." one begins.

"I have a cousin—he's nineteen, he should be able to—"

"I searched for every name you gave me," the man snaps, whirling back toward the other kids. "Either they never made it into the system and are out there, lost to the world, or they died before they ever made it far enough to be sorted into a camp!"

So much for patience, I think, biting my lip.

His temper blows his lid off. The words crash down around them, blasting whatever is left of their world into a storm of flaming wreckage. One of the kids bursts into tears, shattering the shocked silence that follows.

"They took him! I saw them!" Mia protests, jumping to her feet. "I was right there!"

"You're my ward, and you'll do what I say," the man says, bending down so he's eye level with Mia. "Understood?"

Mia's face hardens, transforms right in front of my eyes into something so much harsher than all of the sorceresses she used to play in the make-believe world of Greenwood. I'm barely keeping myself still, and it only gets more difficult when I recognize her posture, the way she shifts and her hands tremble at her side. This is the Mia who used to put the forest at her mercy, control the animals, take hostages up in her tower.

Only now her power is real, and I don't know what the punishment is going to be for her shoving or striking this man, only that it'll come. All I need to see is the outline of the man's holster, and any final reservations I have about this melt away like the last of the early spring snow.

"Look, it's just the way it is," he says, and I can hear the regret adding weight to those words. He might not have meant for the truth to come out like a punch, but he still has the gall to clap his hands and say, "Come on, quick-quick. I'll wait here while you go get your things. . . ."

Most stand, casting quick glances at each other as they move to the elevators. The soldiers trail behind them like reluctant babysitters.

Mia slumps back into her seat, resting her elbows against her knees and her face against her hands.

"Sorry," she mutters from under a veil of dark hair.

"It's fine, kid," the man says. "This isn't easy for any of us."

Oh really? I think savagely. *I can tell how difficult this is for you.*

"Are you going to be okay waiting here for a sec?" he says. "I need to make a call."

Mia nods, says nothing more.

"Good girl. Thanks." The man hesitates for a beat, then steps out of my line of sight, toward the main elevator bank. I can just barely make out his reflection in the darkening windows behind Mia as I creep back around the corner, and I say a small, tiny little prayer that they can't see my likeness there, too.

I have a plan. It's just a matter of getting her attention now, and in the right way. Because if I get caught, then I'm in the same situation as the rest of these kids. And there's so much more than just my and Mia's lives riding on this.

Carefully, I peel one of the sheets of the camp roster off the wall. There's a pen buried somewhere deep in my backpack, and it has one last gasp of ink left to write a single word. I start the S's curve, only to change my mind halfway through—there are so many Sams in this world, who's to say she'll be able to put together that I'm the girl who used to live next door to her? I'm too far out of context.

So instead I write a different name, making the letters as large and bold as the pen's thin tip will let me—a secret we kept between the three of us.

Greenwood.

I glance toward the windows again. The man has shifted away from Mia, turning to lean his shoulder against the wall. His voice is a low murmur of sound, almost indistinguishable from the heat snapping and hissing out of the vents around us.

Mia's eyes are fixed on the ground, like she's trying to find the scattered pieces of herself there. I wave my arms, hoping the movement is big enough for her to see it out of the corner of her eye.

It is.

Her face goes blank with surprise in the second before I see her start to gasp. I hold up my makeshift sign, hands shaking. *Please, God, please let this work, please, please let me get her out of here, away from them. . . .* Mia's forehead wrinkles, and I know the exact moment she realizes who I am. Her eyes are electrified, her mouth starts to form my name. My pulse is hammering, and

I barely manage to get a finger up to my lips in time to shush her and wave her forward.

She's confused. Glances over to where the man is still on the phone. I shake my head.

And then she gets it.

Mia rises slowly, silently, her eyes fixed on the man's back. Her movements are as light as a mouse's as she weaves through the curving furniture, and her sneakers barely register a sound as she starts toward me. I turn, already prepared to spring forward as she reaches my side.

"Sam?" she whispers, and it's the best thing I've heard in weeks. I take her hand and drag her forward, past the clean, empty surfaces of the bar. Her backpack's strap catches one of the chairs and sends it spinning. Whatever is inside rattles, too loud, too loud—

We are halfway down the hall, the side exit in sight, when a loud *"Hey!"* cracks through the air.

I swallow the burning as it rises in my throat; my lungs suck in more air. Mia and I both look back over our shoulders in time to see the man rush out the front, and bark something at the soldier still smoking there. I am so high on fear and exhilaration at pulling this off that I'm worried I'll rip the door off its hinges when I finally reach it and fling it open.

"Stop!" the man shouts. *"Mia!"*

Will they kill me for this? Will they hurt her? Did I just destroy what little chance we had for a good life? I can't predict the response—I don't know their minds the way I knew the PSFs'—

The emergency exit opens up on one side of the parking lot.

There aren't any cars or trash containers to duck behind, nothing for cover when the man shouts, "I'll shoot!"

"Sam!" Mia gasps, feet slipping against the black ice. I'm already slowing us down with my limp. Pain lances up it, spiking each time I swing my leg forward. *"Sam!"*

"Keep going!" I choke out. Across the street is a line of store-fronts, and behind them, the car. "Don't stop!"

The gunshot tears through the dusk, echoing back to us a thousand times over. The bullet pings against one of the streetlights—he's shot wide, a warning.

Don't stop, don't stop, don't stop. My thoughts keep pace with my tortured gait. *Lucas, Lucas, Lucas—*

Mia whirls around, dropping my hand. I skid forward against the ice, my breath a harsh white cloud around me. "No!"

But she's not turning back. She throws her arm out at the same moment the guy takes aim, and she sweeps it sharply to the right. I stop, stunned, as the man goes sailing right back into the hotel's brick wall, and he folds, as limp as any of the trash blowing by our feet. The papers didn't list what ability each unclaimed kid has—Mia, then, is Blue.

"I . . . never tried that . . . before. . . ." Mia's teeth are chattering, and I can't tell if it's from the shock or the cold.

I take her arm. "Come on, it's just a little farther."

"W-where are w-we going?" she asks. "W-what are you doing here?"

I don't stop, not until we've crossed the deserted street and bolted straight through the ravaged storefront directly in front of us. The racks and overturned shelves are totally bare, but if you take a deep enough breath, you can still smell polish and leather.

The back door swings open as I barrel my shoulder into it. Mia stumbles, her toe catching on the frame. "Wait—Sam, *wait!*"

I spin back, my breath wet in my chest. I cough, trying to get my wild, tumbling thoughts back in some kind of order. It's not until the panicked haze clears from my vision that I look at her face—*really* look at it.

Mia is frightened.

I've scared her worse than the man back there ever did.

Of course you did! I press the back of my hand against my forehead, surprised to feel sweat there. *You didn't even ask her if she wanted to come with you! You took her—you took her just like one of the snatchers would!*

"I'm sorry." My lips are numb. It's barely a mumble. "I just . . . do you want to go back? Do you want . . . do you want the procedure? Tell me you don't . . . *please*, whatever they've told you . . ."

"I just want to know where we're going!" she pants out. "Is that your car?"

There's only one back here, and it's parked at a diagonal across three spaces. A tan Honda sedan that was left unlocked in front of a shopping center not unlike this one. It was harder to teach myself how to shift gears, which pedal was stop and which was go, and the rough mechanics of parking, than it was to find the car itself.

"I'm taking you wherever you want to go," I say, climbing into the driver's seat. My hip is so stiff by the time I finally sit, my calf muscle strung so tight, I have to bite the inside of my mouth to keep my gasp in as I floor the gas pedal and send us sailing backward in reverse.

"*Whoa!*" Mia scrambles for her seat belt—why didn't I warn

her to put it on? I should have warned her before ever getting into this car. I got her out of that mess, but now I'm going to get her killed because I don't really know how to drive, and I don't know how soon that man and those soldiers are going to come for us, and why did I do this? Why did I do this?

Lucas.

I whip the car out of the parking lot, and it turns on what feels like two wheels as we find the road. I painstakingly charted my drive out here on a map, but I know the way back by sight. Mostly. Was it right at this tree? No—*left*. The car flies forward into the intersection, cutting across the traffic lanes as I make the turn too sharply.

How long have I been gone for? How long will it take to get back? I glance over at Mia and catch her watching me with dark eyes, and I'm scalded all over again. Those are Lucas's eyes. Those are their father's eyes. And for a second, it's like they're both watching me—they're both judging me for taking a mess and dropping a bomb into it.

"Breathe, Sam," Mia says. "It looks like you're going to rip the steering wheel off the dashboard."

My hands *are* choking the wheel, chapped and red from weeks of being exposed to the cold. But what Mia doesn't see, or maybe she does see and just doesn't really understand, is that there's so much ice on the road that the wheels feel like they're trying to slip out from under us. It's like being on the bare back of a horse that suddenly bursts into a gallop. You have to bury your fingers into its mane and hold on for dear life.

"I'm . . . not very good at this yet," I admit, too scared to take my eyes off the road again, much less look in the rearview mirror to make sure we aren't being followed. Most of the buildings we pass have the same look as the rest of the country: battered and empty, boards where there should be windows, yellow police tape whipping around in the breeze.

Before I went to Thurmond, I had a sense that things were bad; the only reason we were able to stay in our house, while the Orfeos had to move, was because our house was paid for by the church my father served. But I was so focused on what was happening to me inside of the camp's electric fences, I barely spared a thought for what kind of world we'd find outside of it. Imagine my surprise to find that it's only slightly less welcoming to us than it is to everyone else.

Mia shifts next to me, turning in her seat to face me more fully.

"Can you teach me?" she asks, the words singing with excitement. "I want to learn how to drive!"

It's some kind of bizarre reflex—some conditioning ingrained too deep to rub out—that makes me say, "Not until you're sixteen."

"Oh, because *you* took lessons and you're all official with a license?" Mia snorts. "Give me a break."

Good to know Mia's attitude survived Black Rock. For one sickening second I'm almost jealous of her—that she hasn't seen enough of the world beyond her camp's gates to know to be scared of it. She hasn't seen that nothing is in our control, that there aren't a set of rules to follow to ensure our survival. I miss rules. I miss stability. I miss feeling brave.

I start to respond to that, but rain—sleet—suddenly patters down on the windshield, which is already fogging up from our combined heat. I fumble for the windshield wiper and only manage to turn on the left blinker, which lets off a taunting little *click*

click click until I turn it off again. I push every button under the glowing clock on the dash—triangle means four flashing lights, good to know—until the right heat vents kick on, and my view of the world is no longer masked by a cloudy gray.

But figuring it out doesn't settle me, not the way it should. It feels like my stomach is rolling itself up, and I'm half a second away from bursting into tears or puking. I'm not a crier, and I'm not a puker, but right now I don't feel like myself. Actually, I feel like I'm sitting in the seat behind mine, watching a girl who looks like me. Eyeing the crack that's forming along the ridge of her spine as it widens, spreads out into a thousand thin veins. She's barely holding herself together.

Why did I think I could do this? Why did I think I could take care of this girl when I'm barely keeping myself alive?

"Where are we going?" Mia asks again.

I bite my lip. I know she doesn't have any other family, and I don't know if any of their parents' friends would take her in. I didn't really think this through, beyond getting her away from them—the government. My gut wants me to take her back to the house, but—my whole body clenches as fear slips through me like a knife. It's so dangerous—it's too dangerous. But what's the alternative? Bring her back to have her skull cut open, to be dropped into the lap of a foster family that might not treat her right?

"Why did you even come?" Mia asks, brows raised. "You're barely talking to me. It's been like . . . what, six years? Seven? Why would you even think to look for me?"

"You . . ." I feel the icy burn of her gaze on the side of my face. I came because of Lucas, but I can't tell her that; I can't. *Not yet; please.* . . .

"What are you not telling me?" she demands.

"I'm just here for you. I didn't want to leave you there, with those people, alone—"

"Well, I want to look for Luc. Can we do that?"

Several seconds of silence pass. Too long to play this off. I have the heat turned down to try to preserve what little gas we have, but sweat dampens the hair on the back of my neck, and I have to tug my knit cap off. The steering wheel is suddenly too slick to hold. *Not yet, please don't make me tell you. . . .*

Mia's too perceptive to let this drop. I should have known.

"You know something!" Her voice rises and rises, spiking through my sluggish thoughts. "That's how you knew to get me, isn't it?"

I can't get the words to my mouth fast enough. My lips, my face, are numb with panic. This is my new normal—I can't remember how to get back to the anger, to the unbending strength. Take a girl out of her camp, tip her world over, and she has to figure herself out all over again.

"Sam!" Mia grabs my arm too hard and the car swings wildly to the right. I try to slam my foot down on the brakes, but we've hit a patch of black ice, and the locked wheels simply spin and spin and spin to the right.

I can't tell our screams apart. The steering wheel jumps out of my hands as it corrects itself. The curb checks us hard enough to finally stop us before we can go plowing through the front of the nearest drugstore.

This time I do throw up. I barely get the door open fast enough to lean out. The emptiness in my stomach is only compounded by the gaping hole left behind from unleashing all of that terror in those few seconds. I'm so tired and rattled that I'm shaking as I look over at my passenger.

"Are you okay?" I rasp out.

Mia is leaning her forehead against the glove compartment, breathing like she's just made a run for her life. Her rich, warm complexion has gone as white as milk. As white as the patches of snow melting on the sidewalk beside us.

We can't sit here, not with what's happened, but I can't bring myself to move.

"Sam . . ." Mia's voice drifts over, sounding as small and scared as I've ever heard it. "Just tell me . . . is he . . . is Lucas dead?"

I lean back against my seat, squeezing my eyes shut. *Not yet, not yet, not yet . . .*

But then, when? If our seats were reversed and Mia was the one in control, I wouldn't stop, I would fight the information out of her. It's not fair for me to keep it from her, even if I can justify it by thinking I'm protecting her from the pain. It's no different than all the secrets the government kept about us, it's no different than the parents who left their kids at their schools on Collection days without telling them what was happening. Like my father did.

"No," I say finally, watching the last bit of sunset play out across the sky. "It's so much worse than that."

The truth is, I don't even remember making the decision to do it.

I woke up that last morning in Thurmond with a head stuffed full of thoughts and memories that had . . . been blocked, I guess. I'd asked Ruby to undo whatever she'd done, fill the empty spaces she'd left behind, and she did. And then some. Each memory rolled through my mind like bursts of static shock. A thousand little bridges grew between all of the disconnected hazy images and feelings. Like eating a full, satisfying meal when you didn't even realize you were hungry in the first place.

Not Green. Never Green. *Hiding.* For years, hiding.

Dangerous one. Ruby was one of the dangerous ones. . . . Orange. If she could play with my thoughts that way, then she was Orange. And it was so strange, because the second that this realization sank through me, the traces of trembling anger I felt toward her evaporated. It made sense why she had been the way she was: as much my scared little shadow as my friend. All of those times she shrank back, stayed silent, left me to deal with the PSFs, were cast in a new light. We all knew what happened to the dangerous ones at Thurmond.

I spent my last day at camp beside a girl who didn't look anything like my memories. She didn't flinch and fold up into herself to try to fight off the cold. Ruby had been so stark when we were younger: black hair, white skin. Thin limbs and sharp joints. The spectrum of her emotions consisted of only *calm* and *terror.* She came back to us in full color. Even Ruby's quietness had a different tone—when I looked at her, I could see thoughts moving behind her hard eyes, not fear. It was unnerving, actually, the way Ruby wore such a serene expression. Most of the girls were so caught up in her miraculous return from the dead, the fact that she had seen the *outside* and had lived there for months and months, that they didn't see the charge building in her, like a thundercloud forming beneath her skin.

I was so distracted sorting through the new set of memories, shuffling them, categorizing them, re-adding them to my mental box, that I didn't realize Ruby had something planned until it was already underway. Until they dragged her away at dinner.

The two Reds assigned to escort us that night, both girls, marched us back through the drizzle of rain to our cabin. For the hundredth time that day, I caught myself looking for Lucas, and saw the back of him as he led the way for another group of Greens. My eyes tracked him until I saw him step up to Cabin 40 and unlock it. Then I went back to looking for Ruby. A PSF had walked her out of the Mess through the kitchen, which was bad news—that was one of their favorite spots to bring us for discipline because it wasn't under any kind of camera surveillance.

There was no thud of the electronic lock, just the scrape of the manual one as the Reds shut us in for the night. So . . . the power was out *completely.* No backup generator kicked in; not ten minutes later, not twenty, not a half hour.

Then, without warning, our world exploded.

The bunks actually shook, jittering and shuffling across the floor, the way everything trembles under the force of an oncoming train. The roar of the explosion shredded the quiet murmur of the storm. I was on my feet, stumbling against the nearest wall as the ground shuddered violently, rolling some of the girls out of their beds.

"What the hell?"

"Was that—?"

The questions were choked off by the familiar whip-crack of gunfire. I pushed past Vanessa toward a small window, only to find that, whatever the blast was, it had knocked the thick sheet of plastic out of its frame. We had a clear view of the Red stationed nearby as she took off at a run in the direction of the camp's entry gate, her gun already up and aimed.

Someone's here.

"Everyone—*shut up!*" Ellie had been the one to take charge when Ashley disappeared. She was only beginning to wake up from the shock of that loss now that Ruby was back—there was just the smallest possibility that Ashley was out there, too. "Come here, *come here!*"

I wanted to stay by the window, but Vanessa dragged me with her toward the center of the room.

"Circle up, come on—whatever it is, it'll be over soon," Ellie said.

And what if it isn't? I thought. *What if we need to protect ourselves, not curl up into little balls?*

The shots got louder, splitting the air, making it impossible not to flinch with each one, until they finally knocked against our door.

And nearly blew it off its hinges.

It swung in, still smoking, as two figures dressed in head-to-toe black rushed in. The taller of the two tugged up his mask—and the face there was young, so much younger than I was expecting. His blue eyes scanned our faces frantically as the girl beside him lifted her mask and reached for her radio.

"Negative on Twenty-Seven," she said, voice harsh. There was a static response I couldn't hear over the drumming in my head. Her hair was tucked up into the ski mask, but a single vivid purple strand escaped as she unleashed a torrent of cussing.

"Ruby?" The boy was Southern, his words curling in a familiar way that made something inside me ache. His movements were jerky, frantic, and he seemed to forget he still had a gun in his hands. "Where's Ruby?"

They're here for her? Amazement stole through me. People

had broken *into* the camp. And if they were here for her, did that also mean they were here . . . for the rest of us?

These were *kids*. They were like us. And they were . . . they were . . .

"She—they took her out of the Mess Hall. Out back." Ellie barely managed to get the words out. "It's the big building to the right of the camp's entrance."

The girl raised a dark brow at the boy. "Go ahead. I got them."

The boy threw us one last look over his shoulder before rushing back out into the rain.

"All right, ladies, listen up because I still have ten more cabins to clear and do not have one more goddamn second to waste. Pull on your big girl panties, grab your shoes, a coat, whatever, and follow me." The girl was already at the door before she realized none of us had moved. "Why the fuck are you all staring at me like that? You want to stay in this shithole and get flushed with the PSFs?"

"We're . . . leaving?" Ellie managed. "For real?"

"For-fucking-real, girl," she confirmed. "We're taking you *out* of here to your families. But we aren't going anywhere if you keep staring at me like this place fried your brains. I'm not going to let anything happen to *any* of you. You're Ruby's girls, and she'd straight-up murder me."

That, at least, got us rushing back to our bunks for our shoes and sweatshirts, assembling into the usual line. The girl gave us a look of disbelief, shaking her head as she waved us forward—outside.

I was the first one out the door, grabbing the front of her bulletproof vest. The girl's eyes narrowed as she wrenched herself out of my hands.

"You're going to kill the PSFs?" I demanded. "What about the Reds?"

"Nothing would give me more pleasure—"

I didn't hear the rest of what she said. Kids were pouring out of the cabins around us now, flowing toward the main gate, assembling in a long line of blue and green shirts. But in front of me, still guarding Cabin 40, his gun's sight raised to his eyes, was Lucas.

Aiming at us.

At my sharp *"No!"* the girl spun around, throwing out a hand. Blue. She was Blue. I launched into an uneven, limping run just as Lucas flew back, skidding across the mud, the gun in his hands knocked free.

"Hey!" the girl called after me. "Get back here, dumbass!"

"Sam!" Ellie. "Come back! *Sam!*"

"Go!" I called. "I'll catch up!"

"What are you doing?"

I shook the last of their voices out of my head, didn't turn back to watch them leave me behind.

"Lucas, Lucas—don't—" I fumbled for the words as he jumped up onto his feet. Smoke filtered through the air. I'd seen it coasting over the tops of the cabins, but I had no idea where it was coming from, the Reds or the firefight. "Lucas! Listen to me!"

I wondered if he could hear me at all. His beautiful face was set in a grim mask of violence, spattered with blood. Pale with anger. There was a buzzing coming from somewhere nearby, like an insect, and I realized almost a second too late that the earpiece he was wearing over his right ear was still active. He was still getting orders.

"Lucas!" The name ripped out of my throat as he raised a

hand. The air heated, jumping twenty, thirty degrees around me. *"Stop!"*

I tackled him hard enough to nearly bite my own tongue off. Lucas went wild under me, bucking and thrashing to get me off, but it wasn't going to happen, not until I ripped that piece of plastic out of his ear and sent it sailing into the wall of Cabin 40.

They'll take him, they'll kill him, they won't let the Reds live, I will never see him again, can't have him, can't take him—my thoughts spun out as Lucas stared at me. As his eyes *fixed* on me. There wasn't a whisper of emotion in his expression, but, for a second . . . for a second there was *something*.

Doubt.

Confusion.

And all at once, I understood. There was no one barking commands in his ear. He didn't know what to do if someone hadn't directly ordered it. They must have—conditioned them? Was that the right word? They must have done something to get them to listen to the Camp Controllers and PSFs. Lucas hadn't wanted to talk about his training. I scrambled to remember if he'd said *anything* that I could use now.

Mud stuck to the back of my legs and side, and the rain, it didn't stop. I reached toward him, brushing his red vest. *Need to get him out of here, need to save Lucas, need to hide him*—he had fought so hard to get us out, it was my turn now.

My fingers brushed him and he snarled.

I held my hands up. "We need to get you out of your uniform! They'll take you!"

He didn't move, and when I tried to grab him again, it felt like his skin was going to blister my palm. His own hand convulsed violently at his side.

Why had he stopped before, but not now? What had I said, done, beyond telling him to stop?

You didn't tell him. You ordered him, I thought. *Commanded him.*

The Reds responded to commands, the way trained dogs would. Not requests.

"You listen to me now. *I'm* in charge." God—would he hate me for this later? I sucked in a deep breath. There wasn't time for this. The girl who had come to my cabin was working her way down toward us, clearing each cabin as someone else in black did the same from the other direction. They were about to cut us off before we even had the chance to run. *They'll take him, you have to get him out of here.*

"Take off your vest!" I shouted, the words hard and clipped. I couldn't look at the number spray-painted there: M27.

Lucas stripped off the blood-red vest, the whole of his attention focused on me. My throat squeezed so tight, I couldn't breathe.

"Drop it!"

He did.

"Stay beside me! Run!"

He did—into the open door of the cabin in the next, outer ring. It housed the Green boys we'd passed on the way to the Mess Hall. In their scramble to leave, to fall into the line flowing *out* through the open gate, they'd left behind their spare summer uniforms. Shorts and a t-shirt would be brutal in the freezing rain, but so much better than his uniform.

"Change into this!" I barked, closing off the part of me that felt agonized about this. "Hurry up!"

I turned my back, drifting toward the door, and watched the shockingly calm progress of the kids being ushered forward by

265

men and women in ski masks. The firing had stopped, but here and there you could still pick up the crack of one-off shots. When I turned back, Lucas was in the green uniform, shoeless.

I looked for a pair of the camp-issued slip-ons, I really did, but if the choice was between him going barefoot and someone noticing his black boots, I would risk the boots. He pulled them on, silent and efficient, so machine-like. I knelt down, searching his face, trying to find some hint of what he was thinking or feeling—Lucas was someone who registered pain on such a deep level, who let himself live in feelings of soul-lifting joy, and this . . . Lucas in front of me had all the working parts, but not the electricity to spark them.

"Follow me, stay close beside me, don't say anything, don't look at anyone—"

Lucas let out a sharp yelp, his hands digging into his hair like he was trying to crush his skull. It was only then that I realized how close I was to the edge of breaking down completely.

I made the mistake of trying to touch him again, and this time he threw me off hard enough to send me slamming to the ground.

Suddenly, Lucas curled down, moaning as his hands slid down, pressing over his ears. Blood dripped down his chin from where he'd bitten his lip. I'd only ever seen kids react this way for one thing, and one thing alone: White Noise. But I couldn't hear anything, only a metallic grinding sound coming through squeaky, sputtering speakers. It wasn't anything like what they used to blast us; it didn't cut, it didn't split me open.

No time, no time, no time . . . I dug through his uniform, still warm from his skin. My hands fumbled with the pockets and pouches on his belt until they found the earplugs I had seen them use when the Camp Controllers turned on the White Noise for us.

"Put. These. In. *Now!*" I bit out, knowing better than to try to do it myself. "Follow me. Say nothing. Do *nothing* but follow me. Understood?"

Lucas didn't even blink.

"Understood, Luc—M27?"

He let out a sharp breath. Nodded. I dropped the earplugs onto the ground in front of him, and another little piece of me broke off into numbness as he scrambled for them, jabbing them deep into his ears with a heaving sigh.

This will work. This has to work.

"What the hell are you still doing here?"

The deep voice rocketed me out of the moment, slamming me back into full-on panic. I whirled, finding an older man, his face stained with soot, gun at the ready. "These cabins are supposed to be cleared! Get going, or you'll be left behind! *Go!*"

I didn't need to be told twice, and neither did Lucas. It was back out into the rain. Back on the sopping wet, muddy trail between the cabin that would lead to the main path out. I felt him a step behind me, a walking radiator against my back as we fell in line with the rest of the stragglers being waved forward, forward, forward by another set of kids, their ski masks up around their faces.

Do they know Ruby, too? That boy—I hoped he found her, that she was already clear of the fence. I knew there was something crucial I was missing here, some obvious connection between her return and *this*, but my thoughts were as scattered as the PSFs were across the grounds of the camp. Some lay on their backs and stomachs, unmoving. Others were bound hand and foot.

Several of the older soldiers had bullhorns in their hands—the source of the White Noise that only Lucas and the other Reds could hear?

Lucas jerked at my back. I turned, strangely hopeful that I'd find some kind of feeling reflected on his face. Instead his dark eyes were hooded, fixed on the spots of crimson a few hundred feet away. Two men were dragging a limp Red forward, easing her down in line with the others. More men in black masks were working quickly, snapping cuffs around their hands and feet, linking them together so they were bound like animals, like they used to back when Thurmond had Red cabins.

My feet slowed. Something dull and silver flashed in their hands—needles? It must have been. They jabbed them into the exposed skin on each Red's neck, leaving the kids to slouch back into the mud, boneless.

Dead?

God, would they kill them?

Don't think, just go, don't think, just go—

Maybe I should have looked back, taken in the sight of the few smoldering cabins left behind by either Reds or explosions. Maybe I should have taken more pleasure in seeing the PSFs trapped in the mud, kicked down again and again. Maybe the moment should have felt bigger than it did—maybe it would, later. After all, I never forget anything.

But what mattered was right behind me, that I was finishing what he'd started.

We slowed our pace, drifting back farther and farther from the thousands of kids in front of us spreading out among the trees, edging farther and farther to the right until I could barely make out the trail of lights they cast, and a booming voice telling them to stop where they were.

I didn't need to go with them. I was with my family.

I got us out of there. He was with me. That should have been enough.

But just because you want something, it doesn't mean you'll get it.

Just because I wanted to save Lucas, it didn't mean I could.

THREE

MIA

THE CAR GLIDES UP INTO THE CARPORT WITH A TINY jolt, the headlights sweeping up over the house. It's a small—*minuscule*—wooden structure. A cottage, almost; the stone walkway leading to the door is overgrown, covered by dead crabgrass and pockets of snow. There are a few icicles dripping, dripping, dripping off the edge of the steeply peaked slate roof. A sunshine-yellow paint trim is peeling off the windows and has been dropping into the snow-filled flower boxes.

The car's wheels find the well-worn grooves in the dirt as we coast around the side of the house. Sam brings the car to a hesitant stop, inches from some kind of shed.

Neither of us have said a word since we crossed out of South Dakota and into Iowa. The sign at the city limits proudly declared LE MARS: ICE CREAM CAPITAL OF THE WORLD. And, okay, I guess there are worse things to be known for, but what good is ice cream going to do in our situation?

This place is a people desert, and I'm sure that's why Sam picked it—why she felt safe here leaving him behind. *Alone.* We haven't seen a single person out, even when we were blazing down its main street.

Sam slips the keys out of the ignition and sits back. I can't tell which has exhausted her more: the drive, or the story she just unloaded on me.

"Remember what I said. . . ."

"I remember!" I snap. God, like I could forget with her repeating it a thousand times. I don't need her rules or her warnings. If I want to hug my brother, I will. He was *looking* for me. He was coming to find *me*.

And he would have been there at the hotel if he hadn't tried to save her, too. He wouldn't have left me feeling humiliated, like a stupid overeager kid who was one of the first to board the buses, only to end up being one of the last to leave.

Am I supposed to be grateful that she came to get me at the very last second, out of guilt? Sam can say whatever she wants, throw a million denials my way, but Lucas will know me. You don't forget family. And when we leave, it won't be with her.

I slam out of the car, running—*bounding*—up the stairs. But of course, Sam makes me wait for her to limp up and unlock it, and then pockets the key. I see the little stone hedgehog she found it under by my feet.

"Move," I growl, shouldering her out of the way when she doesn't.

"Mia, remember—"

Slow, use a quiet voice, don't touch him—she wants me to treat Luc like he's some kind of rabid dog, foaming at the mouth, and I won't. I refuse to. Screw all her stupid rules.

"Lucas?" I call the second I'm through the door. "Luc?"

I wrinkle my nose, trying to breathe through my mouth. It smells like sour milk and weeks-old garbage. I spin around like I'm balanced at the center of a merry-go-round, trying to see everything at once. The décor in here is like . . . cut and pasted together from an old lady's dreams. Ugly—*hideous*—floral wallpaper is curling off the walls, mimicking the shape of the faded green vines. There are flowers sewn—*embroidered*—onto the pillows and samplers. The curtains are yellowed white lace, pooling onto the dusty rose-shaped carpet. A part of me wants to laugh at how ridiculous it is, but the bigger part wants to find Lucas.

I pass through the kitchen, carefully picking my way through the sticky black-and-white checkerboard of tiles, the shards of broken pink plates and glasses all brushed to the side under the lower cabinets. Somewhere a clock is ticking, keeping track of how many seconds I'm wasting.

There's a bundle of blankets on the floor between the white sheet draped over the couch and the ancient TV set, and it's so still, I look right past it at first. It shifts ever so slightly, like it's being ruffled by a soft breeze from the nearby window. The room is dark, the whole house is, and it makes me feel like a shadow as I slip around the furniture and say, "Lucas?"

It would be wrong to say that his face is set in a blank expression—it's not set at all, but soft, almost waxy, like it's waiting for the right hands to carve a smile there. He is so still, it makes my insides bob up and down in my chest. Next to him is a bottle of water and a plate with a sandwich, both untouched. He's wrapped the blankets around himself so many times, I don't even know how to begin untangling him from them.

"Luc?"

His gaze is fixed on the floor, near the glow of a lantern

flashlight. My brother doesn't even look up as my feet pound across the floor and carpets. "Lucas?"

He must not recognize me—he's probably so tired after everything he went through, and he just doesn't—

"It's me," I manage to choke out, dropping to my knees in front of him. "Lucas . . . Luc, it's Mia. It's *me*."

Nothing. A swift, jagged claw seems to cut me, neck to toes. He won't look up, it's like he doesn't hear or see me, but that can't be right. That can't be. I'm right in front of him. It's been years, and he needs to know that this is real.

"It's me, Mia," I say again, the words high, brittle. *Don't cry, you can't cry.* "Do you remember me?"

I think I hear Sam say my name, high and sharp, like she's trying to slice through the air. But I'm already reaching toward him.

There are so many stories, you know, sweet little tales about princes and princesses who are turned to living stone, cast into eternal sleep. They breathe, they live, but their eyes never open. Until someone comes and breaks the curse.

Some stupid part of me thinks I've done it when his head jerks up the moment before I touch him. I don't stop to think about the way his eyes harden as they fix on my face, like he's taking aim.

I just hug him.

And I pay for it.

"Mia!"

Lucas throws me off him, knocking me back with the full force of his weight. The breath explodes out of me as sharp pain rips up my tailbone. He's struggling to get his arms free from under the blankets—to, oh my God, hit me again? To hurt me worse than this? I scramble back. "Lucas! Lucas, stop!"

Sam limps over, coming to stand between us just as Lucas climbs up onto his knees and I catch the first hint of smoke coating the air.

"Stop!" she snaps. "M27, sit down!"

He fixes that same look of hatred on her, and I see her hands shake in the instant before she presses them flat against her baggy jeans. And apparently it is possible to hate her more than I do, because he listens. She treats him like he's a dog, an animal, and he *listens*, settling back into his previous position.

Sam's voice is thick as she says. "You didn't eat. I told you to eat! Do you understand? Eat that. Drink that!"

"Shut up!" I yell. "Shut up, shut up, shut up! He's not your pet! Don't talk to him that way!"

"Mia—listen—"

I can't. I won't. Lucas has picked up his food and is eating it slowly, mechanically, just as she asked. I back up and even though Mia knows it's a rotten thing to do, the monster shoves Sam with every ounce of strength in her, knowing it'll be harder for her to get up and follow me with her ruined leg.

She goes down hard, with a gasp, and I ignore it, starting back toward the kitchen, only to change my mind at the last second and turn—*veer*—left, where I see another door. I don't want to leave Lucas. I want to stay close, but I don't want to deal with *her*.

It's a bedroom. I slam the door shut behind me and lock it, trying to block out Sam's voice as she calls after me. I feel a fire burning under my skin as I thread my hands through my hair and start pacing that slice of space between the bed's stripped mattress and the busted dresser. My fingers snare in the curls, but I don't care. I want anything, anything, to distract me from the throbbing pain in my back. I can't stop shaking.

She did this to him.

This is her fault.

I hate her, I hate her, I hate her—

I'm crying so hard I have to sit down, and I hate myself for it. I haven't let myself cry in years. It was so bad at first, right when they brought me to the Blank Rooms, because I couldn't stop seeing Mom and Dad, and the pain in my hand—the one the PSFs broke dragging me away from Lucas—kept me up all night. I cried until I thought I would drown in myself. The only way to pull myself up and out was to remember that I'd be out of there eventually. I knew Lucas would find me, and we'd figure out what to do, what happened to Mom and Dad . . . their bodies, if they were given a funeral, where they were buried.

There's a sound I don't recognize—it's one I haven't ever heard before from her. I turn toward the door, straining my ears to hear if she really is crying, too. But when she speaks, Sam sounds so calm it's infuriating. "The people who did this to him . . . Lucas called them Trainers. I don't know what they did to him and the others, but this is the only way he'll respond. I've been trying to get through to him in other ways, but I haven't had any luck."

Of course, because she got to be with the real Lucas in her camp before they did . . . *this* to him.

No. I don't want to think about her being in her camp for years. I don't want to picture her parents just ditching her at school. I don't care that she got that snake bite, that it almost killed her. I don't want to feel sorry for her.

I stand up, my hands closing around the old brass handle of one of the dresser drawers, and just *pull.* There's so much fury powering the movement that the heavy wood comes flying out and I stumble back. I let it fall, kicking it until one of the sides breaks. The drawer liner is covered with daisies, and a shower of brittle receipts and a few buttons scatter across the floor.

I reach for the next drawer and do it again, again, again, and there's something here, there's something good in wrecking this the way that I'm wrecked. I don't stop until I run out of drawers, and then it's only to see what I can smash next.

"I'm sorry . . . Mia, I know it's my fault, I'm sorry," Sam is saying. I think she's been talking this whole time, and I just haven't heard her over the thunder pumping through my ears. "I tried to get him to leave—"

"Not hard enough! You should have made him go!"

"I know," she says, "I tried, he wouldn't—"

"You should have tried harder! You should have done *everything* you could! And now he's—he's—"

Gone. He's here, but a thousand miles away. He isn't just disappearing into himself, the way he used to when he got tangled up in one of his daydreams. They've erased him, drained him of every piece of kindness and love that added up to who he is. They *hurt* him, and I couldn't do anything about it.

"Don't shut me out," Sam pleads. "He'll never forgive me if he knows you saw him like this . . . that he did that to you. I think he's still there, I think he's in there, and we just have to—" The Sam I grew up with would have shouted me right back down. This one just sounds like she's been dragged off a cliff by her hair and left there to dangle. Exhaustion is grinding her words to dust, and I can feel them drifting down between us like sand in an hourglass.

"Stay with me, please—" Her voice catches so sharply it makes my own throat hurt to hear it. "I need your help. If anyone can figure out how to reach him, it's you."

I swallow the bitter words before I can throw them back at her, but they don't go down easy. The truth is, if anyone can figure out how to help him, if there's anyone he'd want help from, it's her.

Sam and Lucas. I remember looking for a word to describe them. *Inseparable.* So close you'd say their names in one breath. *SamandLucas.* They spoke in a language the rest of us couldn't even hear, let alone understand. I was just the annoying sister Mom forced them to hang out with, the one that was always pathetically desperate for them to notice her and like her and *want* to play with her. I followed them everywhere.

She was like the sister I never asked for. Mom and Dad called her Sunshine, even though they were the ones trying to brighten up her life, while her parents kept trying to lock her up in a tower and guard her like jealous dragons or something. I know what Mom told me once is true—that love multiplies love and there's no limit on it, and that just because they loved her too, it didn't mean they somehow loved me less. I know at fifteen that I shouldn't still get that little ache at the thought that I've somehow been left behind again, but I do. I can't help it, and I hate it.

"Are you hungry? There's some food. . . ."

What appetite I had is gone. "Just leave me alone."

"Okay," she says quietly. "Let me know if you change your mind." The floorboards creak as Sam steps away, but not before she adds, in a tone that makes it sound like she doesn't even believe herself, "It's going to be okay. Everything will be better. We can do this."

Her footsteps carry her farther away, until I can only hear the murmur of her voice as she says something to Lucas. The room is in pieces around me and when I bend down to start picking up the panels and fragments of the drawers, I get this twinge of pain in my tailbone, the spot I landed on when Lucas . . .

Threw me off him like I was covered in poison. Like he had no idea who I was.

I can't hold it in a second longer. I press my hands to my face, trying to quiet—*stifle*—the horrible raw sound that comes from somewhere deep in my chest, the way I used to see the girls do in my room at the facility when they didn't want the PSFs to hear them and come in to shut them up.

I climb up onto the bare mattress, curling my legs up around my heaving stomach, the hole at my center that can't seem to fill itself. The tears are boiling hot against the freezing air trapped in this room; they spill out over my fingers, into my mouth, down my chin, into the fabric.

I want to go back—I want to go back to the facility, to Black Rock, to the routines and the rooms. I would give up being outside again, I would give up everything, to still be able to live inside the hope that Lucas was okay and that he was coming to find me.

There's a part of me that wishes for sleep; I want proof that I'm not in a nightmare, someone else's story. I just want to pass out and not think about any of this anymore, because if I keep letting these thoughts spin around me, they're going to circle round my neck like a rope and choke me.

Calm down—I want to be the monster, not Mia. The monster doesn't get hurt. Nothing can touch it. Not fear, not anger, not misery.

Not even guilt.

It sneaks up on me in the silent hour that follows, thickens the air until I have to sit up to suck in a deep breath. There's a thought I've been pushing down—kicking down, really.

She didn't do this to him. She didn't ask him to help her.

But blaming Sam is easier than blaming Lucas.

The thing is, I know my brother, and I know the kind of person he is. He wouldn't have left Sam, no matter what she said or did. It would have broken his heart. It wasn't a choice between saving her or saving me, not to Lucas. He was always all ideas—he could imagine anything into reality—but Sam and I were the ones that used to have to figure out a way to make his Greenwood schemes actually *work*.

Sam didn't have to risk getting Lucas out of the camp, knowing he was like this.

Sam didn't have to risk getting me away from that hotel, knowing she could just as easily have been caught.

But if she hadn't, where would Lucas be? Where would *I* be?

The bed creaks as I push myself off it. I'm a step away from the door when I realize the soft sound I'm hearing isn't the old house shifting its bones, it isn't the wind rushing around its rotting skin. There's a rhythm to it. A melody.

". . . little light of mine, I'm gonna let it shine . . ."

It's Sam.

Sam is singing.

It's that one from all those years ago. We had this game, you know, in Greenwood—our own version of Marco Polo. Lucas would get himself lost in the woods, or he'd pretend to be a prince and I'd be the witch who captured him, and Sam would sing and he would call back and they would meet each other halfway. It was all pretend, but . . .

I unlock the door and step out into the hall, moving toward her voice. A feather-soft hope rustles inside my chest. Is this how she gets him back to himself? Did she figure something out?

". . . all around the neighborhood, I'm gonna let it shine . . ."

The house is dark, save for that single flashlight. Sam has moved it toward the couch. There's a dark shape stretched across it, big feet dangling off the edge; Lucas, of course. He's impossibly still, his face turned up toward the ceiling.

And just like that the hope dissolves, and I wish with all my heart that I could just disappear with it.

She's in a chair she's positioned near his head, her knees drawn up, her arms wrapped around them. In the instant before the floorboard creaks under me and she looks up, the flashlight perfectly lights—*illuminates*—her face.

Sadness.

Devastation, I think.

"Sorry—I just—" Sam jumps to her feet, but can't seem to figure out what she wants to do with her hands. She smooths her pale hair down before lacing them behind her back, like I've called her to attention.

"Why did you stop?" I ask.

Sam flinches, but I see the stiffness in her shoulders ease just a tiny bit as she sits back down. "It's pointless . . . I don't think it helps."

I don't either. His eyes are open, almost unblinking, and he doesn't stir or look in our direction. I come around closer to her, hating the rapid strike of my heart, the way my feet seem to unconsciously take a wide path around the couch to reach her.

For a second, I just *look* at him. Luc was so bundled up before, came at me so fast, I didn't even have a moment to really study him and try to sort through the changes. His face is almost the same as I remember it, though it's not as round or soft as it used to be. Always tall, it looks like he's grown a solid foot, maybe more, and the process has left him stretched and way too thin. He reminds me a lot of Dad, the shape of his nose, his ears, though we both got Mom's coloring. I don't know why I like that—why it makes me feel better to see evidence of people who are gone. The reminders should hurt more than they do.

"Is he . . . always like this?" I ask, my voice low.

Sam glances up at my face before turning back to Luc. Her shoulders rise on her next deep breath in. I already know I won't like her answer. She bites her lip so hard, it makes the scar from her cleft palate bright red.

"No . . . in the beginning, right after I left Thurmond with him, he was . . . he responded a lot more. Faster, too. He would take care of himself—things like, he'd know that he was hungry and that he should eat when I put food in front of him, and now I have to beg him. His eyes were still blank then, but there was something moving behind them."

"What happened?" I ask. "What changed?"

Sam rubs at her forehead. "I don't know. I can feel him just . . . drifting away, no matter how hard I try to pull him back in. The only way to get him to acknowledge you, just *look* at you, is if you try to touch him. He *hates* that."

He smells a little like unwashed clothes. It's not horrible, but I see what she means about him not caring for himself. I imagine it is hard to bathe someone who doesn't want you to touch him.

"What else sets him off?"

"For a while, right at the beginning, I tried to talk to him about your family. I told him about your parents and he just . . . he lost it. Maybe that was it? Maybe I shouldn't have pushed so hard to try to get him to remember. Whatever they did, they made him break from that." Sam swallows roughly. "Mia . . . I think they really hurt him. He has these scars, all up and down his arms, like they cut him bit by bit."

My view of him blurs. I take a second to push back against the tears. I don't want to cry. Lucas is right in front of me. We haven't lost him totally. We can figure this out, how to help him, but it doesn't involve throwing another temper tantrum like I'm five, not fifteen.

"I'm sorry . . ." I say. "I'm real sorry, Sam. I was just . . ."

She holds up a hand. "Everything you said was true."

"No—it wasn't," I say. "I was upset and just kind of freaked out on you, and it wasn't fair."

Sam can't look at me, or won't. It takes me a minute to work up the courage to touch her, to put a hand on her shoulder. I'm scared I messed this up, and if she pushes me away, then I really will have no one—

She doesn't. Sam puts her hand over mine.

"He's getting worse," she says. "Every day. I keep thinking, did I make the right choice? Should I have let him go with the other Reds? Someone must be taking care of them . . . right? Helping them?"

"No!" I say sharply. "I mean—I mean *yes*, you should have gotten him out. You don't know what they're doing to the other Reds. If they did this to them—hurt them so bad—then who knows what they'll do to them now? I wouldn't put it past them— the PSFs, the government, whoever—to just try to . . ."

The unfinished thought sends me into a kind of tailspin— the smoke, the fire, the stairwell, being crushed, being knocked down, and down, and down . . .

I don't realize I'm shivering until Sam stands up and wraps

a blanket around my shoulders, forcing me down into her still-warm seat.

"Try to what?" she asks, crouching down beside me.

When I can, I form the words on my numb lips. "Destroy the evidence. They . . . the people in charge of my facility, Black Rock . . . they burnt the control room to try to destroy all of their records. The military guy who came for us made it sound like they'd been doing that to all of the camps since yours was closed."

Sam's lips part, and her face goes as gray as a thundercloud. She starts to shake her head, like she can shake the idea loose before it can get its claws in.

"You know they would do it," I say, "you know it's a possibility. . . ."

"I don't know anything anymore, apparently," she says bitterly.

I'm not sure where she's going with that, and I'm not sure Sam does either. She seems relieved just to be talking to someone other than herself.

"Lucas beat this before," I tell her, and it's good to remind myself of that, too. "He can do it again. He just needs our help."

"I don't think it's going to be that simple," Sam says, turning her eyes back on him. "He doesn't even really sleep, Mia. He just gets to the point of being so exhausted he passes out. I'm afraid one of these days he just won't wake up."

"We'll figure it out," I insist. "We have to. We have everything we need right here."

She releases a shaky breath, taking my hand when I offer it. Her skin is freezing.

We will get through to him by persevering, by not giving up on him, by showing him love when everyone else only showed him fear and pain. And if Sam can't have faith, then I'll believe enough for the both of us.

Sam shakes me out of unconsciousness before the sun is even up.

"Hey," she whispers, "sorry . . ."

I roll onto my back on the mattress, tugging the scratchy gray blanket down from where I've pulled it up over my head. It takes a second for my eyes to focus on her.

And then I remember where we are.

What happened.

Lucas.

"What's wrong?" I ask, sitting straight up.

Sam holds up her hands. "Nothing—nothing, I promise. I just need to take the car out and find an open gas station and some food. I didn't want to leave without telling you."

I nod, rubbing the sleep from my eyes. There's a sour taste in my mouth I recognize as hunger. "How are you going to do that?"

"I have vouchers for the gas. We're good for at least a few more tanks. . . . Food will be harder."

"Vouchers?"

Sam stands up for a moment, tugging something out of her back pocket. It's a small wad of silver paper with black type on it. She's angled it just enough that I can read the words GASOLINE VOUCHER and a barcode with numbers filling the space beneath it. Printed over everything is a kind of iridescent ink with the words UNITED NATIONS printed over and over again, the way you sometimes see images and words printed on money.

"How'd you get this?" I have a hard time imagining they'd just give it to a kid, especially one who's just out wandering around, not getting the procedure, not under the thumb of any adult.

For a second I just stare at her, watch her look away and stuff the vouchers into her pocket again. I can feel the guilt coming off her in waves. She'd told me before, toward the end of her story about getting Lucas out of Thurmond, that she didn't want to go back to her parents—she didn't even want to think about them. But I can see in her face that she's doing exactly that now. She's dueling with one of their Sunday school lessons.

"How do you think?" she gets out between gritted teeth. "I stole them. I took them out of someone's pocket. They left their jacket on the back of a chair, and I just . . ."

Survival is a choice, the monster whispers.

"Whatever," I say, "we need them more. That person is an idiot for leaving them."

The monster is right about this one. It would be one thing if the usual rules still applied, but there's nothing usual about life now. We have a temporary government that's been appointed, not elected, that serves governments from a half dozen other countries and their combined militaries. They've chopped up the country into four zones to try to manage it. No one wants to drink from our poisoned wells. Everyone is on some kind of journey—trying to get home, trying to find their families, trying to get to that place where they can start again. We are all trying. But sometimes you have to cheat to get there. Just a little.

Sam shakes her head. "Everyone is having a hard time right now, not just us."

"Whatever you say." I shrug. "How long are you going to be gone?"

I don't love the idea of her going out by herself, but this will give me a chance to study Lucas, try to find some kind of hidden seam I can use to crack him open.

"It might be a while," she admits. "There's still some canned soup left for dinner, and Lucas will probably sleep most of today—"

"I'll be okay," I promise.

She starts to rise, but reaches down at the last second, ruffling my already insane hair. My curls always spring out in every direction, like they're trying to escape my head. "Go back to sleep."

I do. I crash back down into the Never Never Land of sleep with ease, and the next time I open my eyes, the sun is coming through the bedroom's lace curtains, warming the blanket. I throw it back, straining my ears to catch Sam's voice. Nothing. She's still not back.

Of course not, stupid. She said she probably wouldn't be back until it was time for dinner.

I'm not scared of the quiet, and I'm not scared of my brother; it's just so strange to feel so alone when there's someone else here with me.

Lucas is still on the couch, turned onto his side. I can't tell what he's looking at as I pass him—the painting of the flowery meadow above the bricked-over fireplace, maybe? I head out through the door in the kitchen, hugging my arms against my chest, trying to firm up my armor against the cold. Sam warned me about the lack of running water—that if I needed to go, I had to find a place outside in that tiny pocket of trees—but the actual thing is even worse than I imagined it being. At least we had functioning *toilets* at Black Rock.

I give up on trying to scrape the frozen mud off the bottoms of my shoes, and bring it inside with me.

Good ol' Sam has left the can of soup out for me, along with two water bottles. There's a note, too, on the back of a grocery store receipt dated three years ago: *If something happens, take Lucas and go. I'll find you. xx S*

It chills something inside me, giving it real, tangible weight. What does she think is going to happen? She'd looked reluctant to go this morning, but I'd thought it was just because she didn't want to leave me to take care of Lucas. . . .

I find the can opener in a nearby drawer, and a pot to heat the soup with—but there's no gas, apparently, to light the stove. So, cold soup it is.

My stomach feels like it's eating itself, I'm so hungry. I don't bother with a spoon, just tip the contents back into my mouth and drink it down before I can think about how weird it tastes without the usual warmth. I need a second to force a smile on my face before I walk back into the small living room. I don't know what he can hear, if he can understand what's happening, but I want him to know that I'm not scared, and that I love him no matter what.

"Hey, Luc," I say, making sure to keep my voice even and quiet. I claim Sam's seat, my toe brushing against another uneaten sandwich half. "You gonna finish that?"

He stares over my head, chest slowly rising and falling.

"You should, you know," I add. "Sam's going to worry, and you have to make sure you keep your strength up."

Inhale, exhale.

I don't want to do it, but . . . "Eat. *Eat.*"

I get nothing, even from that order. Just a flutter of the fingers on his left hand, the one half trapped under him.

Is it possible to be too tired and hungry to find—*muster*—the energy to move? I lean forward slowly, carefully picking up the sandwich. Lucas might be still, but leaning in close to him actually makes his whole body go *stiff*, like he's . . .

Like he's bracing for some kind of a hit.

I bring the peanut butter sandwich up to his lips. Press it there. He turns his head into the pillowed armrest.

It's not what I want, but it's *something*. It's a reaction. Sam said he doesn't have many of those, not anymore.

"Come *on*, Lucas," I say, pressing it against his lips again. His leg straightens, but his lips are pressed in a hard, tight line. My brother is doing the exact opposite thing I want him to be doing, but at least he is *fighting back*—in this small way, he's pushing back against what I want him to do. I try to focus on that, not the idea that he's willfully starving himself in the process.

"Okay, then we'll talk instead." I sit back down, putting his sandwich on a plate in my lap. If he's pulling away from us, I need to find some kind of hook to lure him back out. The more I roll this plan over, tossing it around inside of my mind, the more it feels like *he* is the only one that can really break this spell that they cast on him. Lucas has to be his own hero.

"After . . . after they took me away, they brought me to a facility in—I didn't know it at the time, but it was in South Dakota. We're in Iowa now, if you didn't know. Never thought I'd ever go to Iowa, but I also never thought I'd have real powers, so . . ." I clear my throat. Ten seconds in, already rambling. "Because I hadn't gone through the change yet, they couldn't classify me. They had a whole bunch of other kids like me. A lot of them were orphans. Some said they were taken from their parents while they were out shopping or at parks—how sick is that? Anyway, it was almost like going to preschool. There weren't soldiers watching us, just these women who used to be teachers. I'm a Blue, did you know that?"

Lucas blinks. Keeps staring at that painting

"Do you remember Mom and Dad? Anything about them? I wish I had pictures of them. . . . I wish that more than anything. Sometimes it takes me longer than it should to remember what they looked like—what they sounded like. Melissa and Peter Orfeo—do you remember, Lucas?"

He does *not* like those names. He does *not* like the words "mom" and "dad" and he lets me know the only way he knows how. Lucas manages to get his left arm free from under him and reaches out, pushing me farther back into my seat. It feels like his blood is boiling under his skin, and his right hand does this little twitch—I don't know what it means, but I know it means *something* by the knife-sharp expression on his face.

I stand up and step farther back out of his reach, waiting to see if he'll get up and follow. I don't care if he hurts me, I just want to know what's driving this inner . . . no, *instinctive* need to protect himself against those particular words.

Sam is right. Isn't this proof? Isn't the fact that some part of him *recognizes* those names proof that he's still Lucas somewhere in there? Whoever did this to him, they turned the good things in his life to pain—*agony*. He doesn't attack, he just recoils, drawing his legs up tight against his chest. He's not a monster, not like me. He's just . . . hurting.

I realize I'm crying and have to turn around to scrub the tears away. Not that he's even looking—not that he'd even understand.

Would he?

"We don't have to talk about them yet." My voice is strained as I take the seat again. He's shifted his eyes down to the floor; his arms are locked around his knees.

I feel so restless, like my bones could jump up out of my skin and start pacing the room, but I stay where I am, just breathing in and out. The only way I can deal with this Lucas is to focus on the Lucas he was. The time he cried about the bird's nest that fell out of a tree. How he would come home with bruises from the other boys in his class and refuse to talk about it. On the nights I had nightmares about the little shadow creatures that lived under my bed, he would come into my room and sleep on the floor to protect me from them. He'd tell me stories until I fell asleep.

Hours pass. I don't need to look at the clock to know this. The sunlight shifts, gliding over the walls and floor.

There's this one thing . . . there's this thing I used to do to comfort myself. One glimpse of Greenwood I let in on the days that felt too hard to get through at the facility. If it brings him even a fraction of comfort, then it's worth trying.

"We were in the car in the parking garage—it was a few weeks before they separated us. You told me this story . . . what was happening to Greenwood while we were gone. Sir Sammy was still there to protect it, but because she didn't have the other two keys—*our* keys—she couldn't get inside. The forest, all of the trees—their branches grew together, weaving and lengthening until they made one big knot. The bushes stretched up and up, their thorns popping out like spikes. The animals trapped behind the wall drifted off into a magical enchanted sleep. Everything was just suspended. Time stopped. No one grew old, no one ever got sick, but no one was happy, either; no one got to play and have fun."

I lean against the chair's winged back, closing my eyes. I like that idea—that everything will be the same when we finally go back.

"Then one day, Sir Sammy came to find us. She set out on a quest across roads, through forests, even over rivers and swamps. She brought just enough gold to trade with the trolls who guarded the bridges. She tricked the ghosts into turning her invisible to pass the roadblocks and checkpoints. . . . I think you said she even had to run through a burning castle? But she found us eventually, and we all went home together."

I don't know if I've ever studied anyone as closely as I'm watching Lucas now. It's the only reason I notice that his legs aren't tucked as tightly against his chest as they were before, that he's starting to stretch out again. His breathing is slow, easy.

Better, I think. That's better than before. He's calm enough that sleep is at least a possibility. The story didn't upset him—interesting.

I keep going. I tell him the story of how Greenwood came to be—the same story that *he* wrote in that ratty green notebook with the dirt-stained cover. He had hundreds of these little tales, and we must have acted all of them out at some point, but it's so hard to reach back through the years and retrieve the memories when I fought so hard to get them out in the first place. When you have nothing, you don't exactly want to be reminded of the time you had everything.

It gets easier, though. The words start to roll into sentences, and sentences into scenes, until it doesn't matter that I don't remember exactly what he wrote for us because I have enough blooming inside my head to fill in the cracks and blanks. Greenwood is a garden where everything grows, even ideas, even us.

I talk until my throat hurts, closing my eyes to picture the stories that much better. The clock *tick-tick-ticks*, matching my pace. I don't stop, though, not when I go to get the last water bottle, not when it starts getting so dark that I have to turn on the flashlight lantern. My stomach rumbles, and I laugh, turning it into sound effects for the story of a huge storm that swept in one day and nearly washed the three of us away.

But I do run out of steam eventually; the tickle in my throat turns into scratchiness, and I can't ignore the way my stomach is tight with hunger. It's getting late—where's Sam?

"You must think I'm crazy—"

I look over at Lucas and the words catch in my throat.

He's looking back.

He is looking *right at me.*

His throat is moving, like he's working himself up to speak.

"Luc?" I say. "Lucas?"

There's something in his eyes—something bright that flickers there and is gone. But I saw it, I know it was there, I know *he* is there—

I can't help it, my hands reach out for him before I can stop myself. And, just like that, whatever spell I managed to cast is shattered. He pulls away, pressing himself against the firm back of the couch, and looks ready to snap at me if I bring my fingers too close. Message received.

I step back from the couch, showing him I won't follow through, no matter how much I want to. It's such a small thing, that one look, but I swear, he saw me. *He recognized me.*

Recognized what I was saying?

If these people, the ones who trained him to hate and dread Mom and Dad so much—even the *idea* of them—who did their best to stain his old life, turn it so ugly he can't even stand to think about it . . . My mind races, trying to assemble the pieces before I drop them again. They would have had access to information about our family. The house where we lived, the names of families, even pictures, the schools he went to . . . but they wouldn't ever know about Greenwood, would they? They wouldn't know to turn that place into a kingdom of thorns.

This is our way in, I think, letting my feet carry me back and forth across the floor, behind the couch. I look at the kitchen door again; I'm waiting to pounce on Sam when she comes through, waiting to tell her what I discovered. We can try it again together, see if we can draw Lucas out and get him to say whatever it was he was trying to before. I feel as light as dust, like I'm about to scatter and float to the ceiling.

I know where we have to go.

But Sam still isn't home.

I listen for the car engine, wait for the lights to flash through lace curtains in the front windows. The hours stretch on into the night and my patience is about to stretch into fear when I hear the jangle and scratch of keys in the door.

Sam is barely inside, locking the door behind her, when I launch myself at her.

"You said you'd be home by dinnertime!" I hate the way my words come out like a whine. Sam startles violently; the plastic bag bursts as it hits the floor, and cans go rolling in every direction. She actually clutches at her chest, like she has to catch her heart before it goes leaping out of her.

"I know, I'm sorry," she breathes out. We both bend to scoop up the food. She's found soup, mostly, and beans, and a jar of peanut butter. All of which sound a thousand times better than the nothing I've had to eat since this morning.

Sam cringes as she steps forward to put everything down on the counter.

"Are you okay? What happened?" I ask. Her limp is worse—it looks like it hurts her just to stand.

"I told you I might be late," she says, with an edge to her voice. "I had to drive halfway across the state to find a filling station."

"Sorry, I didn't mean it like that—I was just worried," I say. "I've been waiting for you. Something *really* incredible happened!"

Sam looks like she's physically bracing herself for whatever is about to come out of my mouth. It pricks at my nerves, but I don't let it deflate the flutter of excitement that's still trapped under my skin.

"I know where we have to go," I say, grinning. "We have to go back to Bedford. To the old house."

"Bedford," she repeats slowly, carefully, like she hasn't said the word for years. "Why?"

"Because earlier, I was talking to Lucas—trying to see if there was anything he remembered, or if I could just . . . find him, you know? And he reacted. I told him one of his old stories and it calmed him down. And I kept going and going and by the time I was finished, he was *looking* at me, Sam. He was *watching* me."

I don't understand why she isn't smiling, too. Why she isn't running over to test this out for herself. This is so simple: we just need to take him back to the place that meant so much to him, one that doesn't bring him any pain.

"By Bedford, what you really mean is Greenwood, right?" Sam leans back against the counter, crossing her arms over her chest.

"Well, yeah."

Her brows draw together sharply. "So your solution for help-ing him is to bring him back to a place where we played as kids and, what, expect him to be magically fixed? He'll suddenly remember everything?"

"Why are you acting like this?" I demand, getting angry myself now. "It's not a stupid idea!" It isn't! And even if it is, it's not like she's offering any other solutions.

"Because this isn't some fairy tale, Mia!" she says, throwing her hands up. "This isn't make-believe. He can't even hear your parents' names without lashing out—how is he going to handle seeing your house?"

"I don't know! And neither do you!" I say, my voice cracking. "That's the whole point! We have to at least try. Maybe they haven't ruined that place for him. Why are you shaking your head? Why are you acting like this?"

Sam sucks in a few deep breaths, rubbing at her forehead. When she finally speaks again, the words are strained to the point of breaking. "Because I *have* thought about it . . . all day, every day, for weeks. It's *all* I think about! I've had to watch him get worse and worse, and then, yesterday . . . I thought maybe *you* would be the thing to bring him around. He didn't react to your name the way he did to your parents', so I hoped that seeing you would be enough. I really did. But it did *nothing.*"

That stings, more than I can put into words.

"What are you saying, then?" I demand. "You . . . what? You want to just let him go?" No—it hits me then. Her words add up to a horrifying truth. "You want to give him back to the people who made him this way?"

"No!" She presses her hands to her face. "I don't know! I don't . . . he wouldn't want to be like this."

"They're going to *kill* him!" I yell. "You're sending him back to be killed! You're giving up on him!"

"You don't know that!" Sam shouts. "What if the only people who can fix him are the ones who made him like this? There's no need for the program anymore, right? Maybe they . . ."

"I will take him and run if you even *think* about it," I warn her. "If you want out of this, then just go. We don't need you. We never have."

I'm aiming to hurt with that one, to make her feel that same jagged pain that's got me in its grip. But instead of responding, she tilts her head back toward the kitchen door, brows drawn together. Not listening to me.

I hear it a second later—a car engine. It clatters and moans and only gets louder before it cuts off completely.

Doors open.

Slam shut.

"*No*—" Sam's whole body tenses as she closes her eyes. "Get in the bedroom. Lock the door."

She pushes past me, limping into the living room. She turns off the flashlight and throws my gray blanket over Lucas's still form before I can even move.

"Mia! *Now!*" Sam throws an arm out, pointing toward the hall. "Don't come out—no matter what. Promise me!"

"What's going on?" Why won't she tell me? Why is she so pale?

"*Go!*"

I'm mad at myself—*furious*—that I listen to her. I don't want to leave Lucas, but if I stay I think Sam will drag me to the bedroom by my hair. Whatever she has planned, I don't factor into it.

Someone's here. . . .

Someone's here for us?

I go into the bedroom and twist the lock behind me. It has to be someone from the government—Officer McClintock, maybe. The guy is a pain, but he's not stupid. He could have followed us here, and now he's going to take me back. He's going to bring me to Chicago and cut into my brain—

I don't realize how hard my heart is flipping—*careening*—around my chest until it's all I can hear. I wipe my slick palms against my jeans and climb over the mattress to the crevice between the bed frame and the wall.

Coward, coward, coward, coward!

"—around front—take the back—"

I have to press my hands against my mouth to muffle my sound of surprise. The man sounds like he's right on top of me.

He is.

I'm right below the window—out of sight to someone looking through the curtains into the room. A single beam of light sweeps in, flicking over the wall and door.

"Car's parked three blocks over—"

There are two of them?

My pulse is fluttering like a moth's wings.

"Yeah, but one set of fresh tracks leading here. Tricky little bitch tried to cover 'em."

"Better pan out—wasted gas—auction—" The second voice fades, breaks up into a trail of mumbled crumbs that I can't follow for much longer.

My breath is too hot—*scalding*—to hold. It comes out like a silent scream.

They aren't just here for me, are they? Soldiers would have blasted their way in by now to grab me. I only went to school for a few years, but I can put two and two together here. Sam was spotted by these men, and despite her shapeless clothes, despite her tricks, they figured out what she was and followed her back here.

The *bang* sends me shooting straight up off the floor, flying over the mattress.

"There you are, pet!"

Inside, they're inside—

"I don't know who you are—I don't care, but—y-you can take the food, you can take it!" Sam is clearly struggling to sound calm, and it's not working, not really. "I have bottled water, too. It's clean."

The men laugh. I press my ear against the door hard enough to hurt, my hand is curled like a claw around the knob. This doesn't make sense to me. Sam is a fighter. She's the one who won't take an insult, who always got a second punishment for reacting to her first punishment. She's not fighting them.

She won't fight them.

She's going to go with them so they don't come farther into the house.

She's distracting them.

She's not fighting them because she's protecting *us*.

They are going to hurt my friend.

"Take the water?" This is a new voice—a woman's. "I think we will. You can carry it out for us. That's right, nice and easy. You don't want my finger to slip, do you? We don't need you unhurt, just alive. Remember that."

"There's been some kind of mistake—"

"Aw, pet, don't cry about it. We ran your li'l face through our system. Samantha Dahl. That's your name, ain't it?"

System? How could they know her name?

"You've got the wrong person—"

"You're just a Green, but, lucky girl, there's plenty of people willing to pay to get a look inside that brain of yours," the man continues. "Nothing to be ashamed of. We all know that you got nothing to hit us back with. Now come on, pet. . . ."

I'm going to be sick.

There aren't skip tracers anymore, not according to the news. There are just snatchers and a whole new illegal market for people to buy and sell freaks—turn them into personal weapons. Study them.

They're going to take her.

The floor creaks as I shift my weight, a quiet sound, but it blows the conversation in the kitchen out like a candle.

"Someone else here, pet?" that same man asks. "You go check—I got this one—"

"Come on, girlie, you don't really want us to hurt you—that's it, grab her, Bill—grab her!"

No, no, no, no, no, no—what am I *doing*? They're taking Sam and any second they're going to find *Lucas* and I'm in here *letting it happen*—

"Stop! *Please!*" Sam is yelling, her voice hoarse. "I'm not her! I'm not! I'll come with you, but you—"

There's a heavy *thud*, and I hear her ragged gasp.

"Don't make me do it again!" the man grunts out.

I reach down, unlocking the door.

Heavy footsteps.

Harsh breathing.

Hate.

It boils the air like a spell, thickening the darkness around me.

Now, Mia.

The look on the woman's face as I fling the door into her is almost funny. She looks like she could be someone's grandma—a halo of rough, choppy silver hair, eyes set deep with wrinkles, sweatpants. She looks like she should be going to the grocery store, not staging a kidnapping. "You—"

I don't let her finish.

I wasn't lying to Sam before. When I pushed Officer McClintock, it was the first time I'd ever tried to hurt someone with what I could do. When I was in the Blank Room, trying to hide that I'd changed, I'd accidentally move things around. I'd want the glass of water from across the table, and suddenly it'd be zipping toward my hands. There's a learning curve, I guess, for controlling the intensity of it, but no one has to tell you how to do it. I look at something, I want it to happen, and somehow it does. The answer is in the ask.

I want to hurt this woman; so I do.

I fling both hands out and she shoots back into the hallway with a scream, against the wall. The impact cracks the plaster, leaves her limp. I jump over her legs and run the short distance to the living room. Lucas is still there, moving beneath the blanket, but they've already dragged Sam out through the kitchen door. They kicked it in so hard, it broke off its hinges.

"Sam!" I scream. *"Sam!"*

They've pulled a hood on over her head, bound her hands in front of her like she's some kind of criminal. I feel the last of my calm burst into ash. She's struggling, not making it easy for them, but not fighting—not until she hears my voice.

The two men are built like football players—one with dark skin, the other light, one with no hair, one with a ponytail, both in the same camo jackets you see some hunters wear. I take in all these details in the span of a blink. The only thing that really matters is that they both have guns; one has a small one pointed at Sam's head. The other has a shotgun pointed at me.

"What do we have here—?"

I don't let the man holding Sam finish.

"Don't—! *Run!*" she chokes out, trying to turn back toward the house. My hand is out again and the night air tackles the man holding her, drags him back toward the trees. It's panic, or it's an accident, I don't know, but the gunshot cracks the second before I knock the gun out of his hand.

I'm not fast enough with the other man. I should have hit them both at once. Sam is screaming, trying to get her hood off, calling my name over and over again, and I barely have a second to dive back into the house before he fires the shotgun in my direction.

"I'm fine only taking one of you!" he yells. *"Bitch!"*

He's taken a whole section of the doorframe out—literally— he's blown it into splinters around me. I stare at it, ears ringing, reaching up to touch a warm, wet cut on my cheek. When he fires again, the shot whips through the wall over my head, smash-ing into the cabinets.

I don't even see the old woman come up behind me until she has an arm locked over my throat and is dragging me up.

"I got her—I'm coming out! Stop shooting, you idiot!"

I thrash, twisting, trying to drop low out of her arms as she drags me forward. The broken glass and wood whirls around us. I can't focus on any one thing long enough to use it to defend myself. The man with the shotgun is still aiming it at me, and he doesn't take kindly to being tossed violently to the side. Before I can turn to the man limping back from the trees toward their pickup truck, the old lady is already cutting into my skin with some kind of knife. I can barely move without the edge biting into my throat.

"Be a good girl, now. . . ." The old woman smells like coffee and stale sweat, and the hand she uses to cover my mouth tastes even worse when I bite it.

The knife digs in harder.

"Brat!" she spits. To the men, she says, "Make sure that one's secure. We're going to have to drug this one."

One of them tosses Sam so hard into the truck that the whole thing dips. I hear her scream around her gag as she lands on her bad leg, and my vision flashes red. The closest man must see it in me, because he launches his fist into my face and the world dissolves into black around me.

I can't . . .

. . . think . . .

. . . hurts . . .

Mom . . . I want my mom. . . .

"—come on, let's go—wait—Bill, wait—*look*."

My vision can't seem to focus. The whole right side of my face aches, and it's getting harder to open that eyelid.

"Three! Anyone else want to come out and play?" the old woman says, laughing. "Anyone else hiding in there?"

Three?

There's a fog around my thoughts and a strange rainbow halo around my vision. It makes it harder to focus on reality—on the dark shape standing in the battered doorway of the house.

Lucas.

"Boy, too," says one of the men behind me. "Even better."

"No . . . wait. . . ."

Sam starts screaming in earnest now. I think for a second that she's scared for him, that they'll take him and hurt him, too. The realization crawls up my neck, and I start to shiver.

She's scared for these people.

Lucas stands there, motionless, as he always is. His shirt collar is stretched out, and standing upright it's even more obvious that he's lost too much weight. The bones look like they're popping out of his skin. I'm too far away to read his steely expression, but the tendons in his neck are bulging, and I see that his right hand is jerking at his side.

I see it happen out of the corner of my eye. The man with the shotgun is standing, in one piece, and then he's not. The gun explodes in his hands. Both me and the old woman are rocketed back by the force of it, the spray of blood and embers that follows the man's screams.

The second I'm out of her grip I crawl forward, toward where Sam is rolling herself out of the bed of the pickup truck, hitting the ground *hard*. She doesn't stop, just keeps rolling until the hood is off and she manages to get the cloth gag out of her mouth.

"Lucas!" she shouts. "Stop!"

Crack—

Crack—

Crack—

The other man shoots fast and wild in Lucas's direction, screaming, *"Get 'im! Get 'im!"* to the old woman, who's still on the ground. I swing my arm out in the snatcher's direction, knocking him back against the truck. The second he loses his balance, so do I, and I stumble down again. A hand clamps down on my ankle and rips me back across the dirt and gravel. I hear the sound of barking dogs and sirens, and none of it registers, nothing beyond the fury etched into my brother's face.

The scene comes into focus, and it takes me too long to understand why: the area is lit—*illuminated*—by fire. It circles the man who's still screaming on the ground, cradling the burnt remains of his hands and arms. It's jumped up to the trees, spread like a carpet across the wild grass, caught the other man's pants and jacket sleeves and—

The car.

Smoke is pouring from under the hood, and all I can think of is the facility, how the glass blew out—

If the truck explodes, we're all dead.

He's . . . I've always known who Lucas is, and he didn't try to hide it from us when he changed, but this isn't him. This is a weapon. I don't understand. Is he protecting us? Or is he just lashing out at a threat?

"Lucas! Look at me! *Lucas!*" Sam forgets her rules, all of them, as she stumbles toward him. The doorway is ringed with fire, and smoke pours out of the house behind him as it catches and tears through the wood and old, moldering fabric.

I kick at the woman's head but she's already letting go, her attention on the driveway and her last route out from the fire. I push myself up onto my feet, chest tight from the smoke, just as Sam reaches him—

There's no hesitation.

No fear.

Her hands are still tied together in front of her, but it hardly matters. Sam loops them over his neck and then around his shoulders. She doesn't let go. She holds onto him.

The fire flares white-hot around me, and I have to run forward to avoid being caught in the same wave that's sweeping toward the men and the old lady as they scurry away like the rats they are.

"Sam!" I shout. "Come *on!*"

I'm not stupid enough to think that Lucas will try to hug her, return her touch.

He's going to hurt her—and for Lucas, there's no coming back from that. Even if I can draw him out later, if he does what it looks like he's about to do, he will never forgive himself. He will let the shadows eat him again. And I am too shocked to move.

Already he's bucking and thrashing in the circle of her arms. Sam's lips are moving, but I can't hear what she's saying to him over the crackles and pops of the fire roaring through the trees.

Lucas is yelling now, not words, just—screaming, his hands clenched at his sides, his eyes squeezed shut. There's smoke rising from Sam's coat, but she doesn't let go, even when I would have.

He kicks at her, his ragged fingernails coming up to rake the backs of her arms. She doesn't let go.

He goes limp in her arms and my heart stops dead.

She doesn't let go. Her back bows under his weight, the effort it takes to keep both of them upright. The gravel shoots out from under my feet as I scramble to get to them.

"Are you okay?" The words tumble out of me. "Are you hurt?"

"He's passed out," Sam says, ignoring my questions. "Can you find something to cut my hands with?"

A piece of glass is sharp enough to cut the plastic tie. Sam gasps as her hands are released, and we both stoop to take Lucas's arms, looping them over our shoulders. Lucas is so hot to the touch, I wonder if the fire is moving through his blood, too.

"The car is . . . a few streets over . . . we can make it. . . ." Sam has to stop and adjust her grip on Lucas again before we start down the curve of the driveway. Lucas really is out of it; he's so much taller than both of us that his feet drag and bob against the ground, and there's nothing we can do to stop it. We've just reached the street when a wave of heat and pressure knocks us forward. The truck goes up in a ball of fire, streaking into the night sky.

"This way—" Sam starts to tug us left.

No.

I blink, eyes watering, as the wind finally starts playing games with the thick gray smoke, tugging it down the street. I think I'm imagining it at first—spots in my vision that just need to clear after staring so long at the flames.

A single word forms in my mind: *No.*

I can't squeeze out the rest. My mind is shutting down, turned to ash by shock.

No. Way.

No way out.

No way forward.

The dark spots in my vision take shape, sharpen into something so much worse.

Neighbors, their coats pulled over pajamas, talking to each other in tight circles of concern. Soldiers in their baby blue berets and armbands, guns in their hands, shouting. A fire truck, firemen rushing past us with a hose. I think about the sirens I heard earlier; I stare, hypnotized by the red, blue, red, blue lights, and I don't understand how I have been so stupid to let this happen. To not know what would be waiting for us.

This town isn't empty at all. It's full of people who stare at us like the monsters we are.

It won't matter what we say to defend ourselves. It won't matter now if we try to protect ourselves the only way we can. It doesn't matter that I can't see the snatchers, the ones responsible for all of this.

"Get down, hands behind your backs!"

I look toward Sam in question, but she only shakes her head and starts lowering Lucas to the ground.

There are too many people for me to fight.

Too many chattering radios and guns. Every part of me— every *atom*—screams in protest as I drop onto my stomach on the cracked road, as my cheek is licked by its rough tongue. The plastic zip tie the soldier puts around my wrist eats at my skin and what little control I've got left over my fear.

I twist around as the soldier hauls me up to my feet, trying to see what's happening with Lucas. Another man is carrying him over his shoulder, and all I can think is *Don't let them find out what he is, don't let them hurt him, not again, not again—*

All Sam can say is "I'm sorry," over and over.

She's right.

This isn't a fairy tale.

But we're somehow still the villains.

FOUR

SAM

THE SOLDIERS WHO PROCESS US INTO THEIR CUSTODY use zip ties to secure us, but their hands are careful, and they ask in accents I've never heard before if they're too tight. They watch us out of the corner of their eyes as we sit on the curb, not to make sure we won't run, but because I doubt most of them have seen one of us up close. When they pull out a small handheld device and fumble to turn it on, I know to look straight into it as it takes a photo.

The soldier working it, a young Asian woman, relaxes when my identification file comes up on the screen. Of course. Like the snatchers demonstrated, no one is ever scared of a Green. They don't think we're fighters.

But I'm not . . . am I? I can't claim I'm one, not anymore. I lean forward and press my forehead against my knees, ignoring the way it pulls my shoulders painfully with my hands behind my back. I drove around and around for an extra hour, wasting gas to lead the snatchers off my trail, and I still managed to bring them home with me. I basically surrendered to the snatchers instead of trying to get us all out of there. I didn't try to fight these soldiers.

I wanted to bring Lucas back to the people who made him this way. I am a coward. I'm not a lion, I'm not a knight. Out here, I'm nothing. I hate myself.

I turn, watching as the paramedics take Lucas's vitals and put an oxygen mask on him. I don't know if I should be grateful or terrified that he's still passed out. He was already weak from exhaustion, from not eating nearly enough, and I know the fires must have taken what strength he had out of him, but . . .

What if he doesn't wake up?

What if they do take him away?

What is wrong with you?

It might be the smoke still coating my lungs, the aftershocks of what happened, but my stomach heaves, and I have to close my eyes and swallow hard to keep from throwing up.

He saved us. Lucas . . . he . . . I shake my head. No—there wasn't anything in his expression. He was just reacting to the sound of gunfire. His instincts told him to fight and protect himself.

"—to the hospital!" One of the paramedics has been fighting with the soldier in charge for the last fifteen minutes, since they tried to run Lucas's photo through the system and nothing came up. After hearing the officer in the hotel tell Mia that there was no record of Lucas that he could find, I'm not sure why I'm so surprised by this. I guess I've always thought of the government and military as one big body; I didn't realize that they could wall off sections of themselves when it came to keeping secrets.

It makes me think that Mia is right, though. Maybe there is no record of him because the other Reds have already had their records purged, and the kids have been . . . dealt with.

And you wanted to give up and give him back.

I squeeze my eyes shut harder. *I want him to live. I don't care how. I want him to live, and I can't help him—*

"No, not until he's been positively ID'd." I don't know what the soldier's rank is, but he's lording it over everyone else around him, to the point that even the woman who identified me stops to stare at him. He's broad-shouldered, tall, a huge presence with his red hair. The neighbors actually scrambled back to their homes when he barked at them to stop gawking at us. If I hadn't dealt with his type every day for seven years, I might have been impressed.

Firemen are still fighting the blaze across the street. Mia ignores the woman snapping her photo and watches as the flames devour the small house. She won't look at me, and I can't think of anything to say to her. So neither of us try.

I did this.

The skin on my neck and arms still feels like it's on fire, burning down layer by layer. When I was a little girl, my mother once tried to pretty up my hair with a curling iron before church. I couldn't sit still long enough for her to finish, and the barrel accidentally brushed my neck; all Mom could say was *You did this to yourself.* I feel the same small agony with each burn on my skin now.

It must have happened when I was trying to push myself onto my feet, after I got out of the back of the truck. Holding on to Lucas was like embracing a furnace, but there's no way his skin could have been that hot . . . right?

I don't know what I believe anymore—I can't shake the idea that there is someone out there, a God that created us. My father used the Bible as an instruction manual for how to earn the right to Heaven. He saw everyone's life as split between that destination, and another very different one below. I guess some of his words have burrowed into my heart deeper than I imagined, sinking in like thorns, because there was a moment before I reached him, when Lucas was standing in the middle of a ring of fire, and all I could think was *I've already lost you.*

Hell isn't a place you go; Hell is where we live now. Hell is being helpless to protect the people you care about the most, and save them from themselves.

We will never have that Lucas back, I think. Not the one we grew up with. Even if I can shake him from this, the last thing to heal will be his soul. It will break his heart, and no matter how many times I'm there to help piece it back together, the cracks will always be there, the mends will only harden it. But then again, am I the Sam he grew up with? Is Mia the same sister? How can we fit together, now that this world has snapped and bent our edges?

"Girls!" The word is barked at us from across the street.

I sit up again, bracing myself. The soldier in charge is cutting a path toward us, shouldering aside anyone who stands in his way. The woman who processed us with the device makes a quick, quiet report to him, and both of their eyes shift to Mia, who is glaring back at them from under a mass of curly black hair.

"Girls," he says again, standing over us, hands on his hips, "I need to know who the young man is."

Here is something else that's different: they ask us questions like they expect to believe us. And, well, the PSFs would have already had us rolling in the direction of the nearest camp. I wonder for the first time if the only reason we're still here is that these people literally have no clue what to do with us now, or who should make that call. With the PSFs, at least I knew what to expect. I have no idea what these people are capable of, what they're willing to do, and that's a whole new flavor of fear.

Closing the camps didn't knock the players off the game board. It didn't even rearrange them. It just added unknown rules and elements; now we have to learn how to live all over again, and it's still not even on our own terms.

"He's no one," Mia says.

"Yes, apparently," he says, impatience rushing the words. "There isn't a record of him. No ID, either."

"He's no one," Mia repeats, daring the man to ask her one more time. He senses the challenge in her voice and shifts the full weight of his attention to her. I can barely make out his face in the dark.

I know what Mia is trying to do; if he's no one, then they won't send him wherever they're sending us. But that'll only last as long as he's unconscious. When he wakes up, and he's surrounded by people in a hospital he doesn't recognize, then what?

"He's her brother," I say, and my shoulders hunch at Mia's hiss. At this point, I don't think she could hate me more than she already does. But this might be our only chance to stay *together*. "He's a Green. There's no record because he was never taken into a camp."

"That so?" The soldier glances back at the ambulance, and I think, *Is that a hint of admiration in his tone?* "What happened to him?"

"He tripped as he was coming down the stairs, knocked his head," I say. "We were running to avoid these people . . . they were trying to kidnap us."

He looks like he can't quite believe this.

"Didn't you see them?" I ask. "Two men and an older woman."

The man shakes his head and my fragile little piece of hope starts to splinter. I'm so used to thinking about life in terms of action and reaction, crime and punishment, that I can't take my eyes off his sidearm, or the baton hanging against his thigh. A new thread of worry weaves in and out of the mass already choking me.

"We didn't mean . . . the fire was an accident," I continue, and I can't believe he's let me say this much. "We were just trying to protect ourselves."

"You could have destroyed this whole neighborhood," he says sharply. "You shouldn't be out here running around—this isn't a game!"

I'm so stunned by this—that of all the conclusions he could have drawn, it's that we're out here *for fun*. That they think we would actually choose this for ourselves.

They're going to punish us, I think, fear battering my anger. How do I stop this? What can I say? If I say *I'm* the one that set the fire, me and me alone, then will they let Mia off? I will work the rest of my life to pay off the damage if I have to.

"You're lucky that someone called this in and our patrol was close enough to answer."

Lucky is not the word I would have chosen in this situation, but I nod anyway, feeling my stomach flip.

"There's no family contact listed for either of you," he begins.

How completely unsurprising that my parents have figured out how to legally wash their hands of me. I'm "unclaimed," too.

"But I have a notation that *you*"—the man nods toward

Mia—"at least, are the ward of the government. Officer McClintock has been notified of your whereabouts."

"My parents are dead," Mia says, her voice wooden. "I'm with the only family I have left."

I know she means her and Lucas, but the man seems to lump me into that *family* as well.

Another soldier, a young man, jogs up to us from behind one of the Humvees with a large cell phone in his outstretched hand. "Sir, there's a call for you—"

The man swings around, and I can only imagine the expression on his face, judging from how quickly the blood drains from the young soldier's.

"I'm sorry, sir, but it's from Washington."

I lean forward, trying to catch every one of the man's gruff words as he presses the phone to his ear and strides away, back in the direction of the ambulance. Mia sighs and rests her forehead against her knees, closing her eyes, but my mind is spinning itself sick, churning out one horrible theory after another, each a tiny needle moving through my veins. I can't make out his words, but I can read the language of his body—the way he storms toward the paramedics and begins to gesture between Lucas on the gurney and something else, and they begin to gesture back.

The younger blue beret is standing a few feet away from us, his gaze fixed on that same scene, shifting his weight between his feet. My anxiety deepens to outright dread.

They know.

They know about Lucas. What he is. Where he should be. I don't know how, but they found out, and now they're going to take him away—

314

The man ends his call, gripping the phone in his hand for a moment. When he turns back toward us, it's like Mia can feel the wave of furious heat pouring off him. She sits back up, her spine as rigid as the streetlights around us. She swings around toward me, eyes wide.

The man barks, "Load them!" to the soldier still standing over us. He windmills one arm, and it's the signal that sets the gears around us into motion. The soldiers scatter, stomping out flares, packing up supplies.

"What's going on?" Mia asks. "Hey—*ow!*"

We're hauled up and deposited onto our half-frozen legs. I lean back, trying to see around him, see the ambulance. Doors are slamming, people are shouting; the buzz and crackle of radios electrifies my nerves until I think my blood is humming. The muscles in my right calf are so stiff, they send a lance of pain shooting up my knee, my thigh, my hip. The younger soldier has us both by the arms and all but drags us forward, toward the back of a black van. I try to drag my leg to slow us down, but Mia is the one who's doing most of the work.

"Where are you taking us?" she's shouting. "Where is Lucas? Lucas!"

"You can't separate us, please," I'm begging, "he's a good person, he's not what you think, don't separate us, *please!*"

There are benches running along the sides of the van, cuffs dangling above them, a metal grating separating the two front seats from the back area. Up close, the soldier looks even younger than I thought; there's still a fullness to his face, and his age is never more obvious than when he glances at me, frowning. He hesitates, a flash of pity cutting through the stiff mask of determination.

And I think about it. I do. If he's soft, I can be hard. I can shove him, give Mia a chance to run—

She beats me to it, drives her shoulder into his chest, hard enough to knock me sideways too.

I'm not sure what hurts worse, the first jolt of hitting the street, or the hundred-plus pounds of the soldiers who slam me right back down onto it. My vision blanks to static white as the air explodes out of my lungs all over again.

The soldier snaps at Mia in a language I can't understand, lashes out a booted foot. Words sputter in my throat as he catches Mia around the ankle and trips her before she can take two steps. It's almost impossible to get myself up onto my feet with my hands bound and my whole right side throbbing. I grit my teeth and lurch forward onto one knee, then the other.

"Stop this!" A large hand hauls me up by the scruff of my coat. The head soldier has a voice like a cannon, but I don't catapult back into the thick fear until he holds up a small black device and brings it to within an inch of Mia's panting face.

"Do you know what this is?" he asks, biting out each word.

My body is already trying to curl around my core to prepare for the piercing grind of White Noise. Our hands are still tied, there's no way to even cover our ears. Hate powers through me, pumping like thunder. Because, of course. Of course—they can close the camps, they can disband the PSFs, but they still need a way to control us. As long as there are freaks in the world, there will always be White Noise and the people who get to use it, who will never understand what it feels like to have a noise send razors through your brain.

"I do not want to use this," the man tells her. "Not one of us wants to use this. But we are authorized to do so, and we will. Understood?"

I see now that Mia is braver than I am, because I nod, distracted by what is happening over by the ambulance. She's the one that asks, "Where are you taking us? Which camp?"

His surprise betrays the hardened expression on his face, like he can't quite believe that's our first assumption. All of this, the new government, the international peacekeeping force, happened so fast—these people have been injected into a reality that must feel as upside-down to them as it does to us.

"No more camps." He shakes his head. "You are to be processed, and . . . re-homed."

Re-homed. My lip curls back. Meaning . . . rewired. Released back into civilization with tiny machines implanted in our brains. I wonder if this will be our lives, for however many years we have left—no say, no choice, just orders and changes and handcuffs. I wonder if they think we are even really human.

We are, aren't we?

"My brother—" Mia starts.

"Get in," the soldier cuts her off, jerking his head toward the back of the van. When she doesn't move, Mia is picked up and tossed inside.

"Stop it!" I shout, launching myself at his back. I'm thrown back immediately, lifted up and dropped onto the bench before the dizzying black spots can clear out of my vision.

I try to stand, but the man already has a seat belt whipped out and over my hips, securing me in place. The zip ties are traded for cuffs attached to the seat. Resentment steams under my skin, and my burns feel like they're blistering.

Lucas, I'm sorry. If there's a way to fix this, if it's not too late, I will.

I won't let them change her. Give her to adults who'll mistreat or neglect her. I can find my old self long enough to do that one last thing.

"Where's my brother?" Mia says, and it's the first time she sounds like a kid to me. I think she's hit the point where pride doesn't matter, when desperation isn't a weakness but a last resort. "Please don't take him away, not again—he's all I've got, he's all that's left—don't take him to a place we can't find him—"

"For Christ's sake, kid—you are goddamn relentless!" he cuts her off. He steps back from the doors to allow the two paramedics to get to the van. A stretcher is slung between them, weighed down by Lucas's body. I try to jump up from my seat, even with the belt and cuffs, and Mia does the same, just as another soldier secures her hands to the bench.

He's been strapped down, and bags of clear fluid are resting on his stomach, feeding the IV lines. The paramedics shoot furious looks at the soldier in command as they slide the stretcher into that tiny bit of space at our feet. Mia and I both have to lift our legs up to make room.

"Luc!" Mia says, ignoring the soldier slamming the back doors shut. In the instant before the internal lights shut off, I get a good look at him. They've cleaned the smudges of dirt and soot off his face, bandaged a cut on his upper arm. Aside from the slight rise and fall of his chest, he doesn't seem to be moving at all.

When we first got out of Thurmond, I could never get through a full night of rest. It was like trying to fall asleep while floating on my back in a pool of water—every time I relaxed enough to sink into it, I'd startle myself awake again before I could drown. Every small sound was amplified and stretched by the paranoia that someone was creeping up on whatever house or hole I'd found for us to spend the night in.

Lucas never had that problem. I used to check on him while he slept. Count the measure of his breathing. Watch the way his eyes moved beneath his lids. I heard somewhere once that that only happened when people were deep asleep and dreaming . . . maybe it was Mr. Orfeo who told me? He was so smart, spilling over with the need to explain every mystery to us. Seeing it happen to Lucas was like some small miracle. I remember thinking, *He's still there. He's dreaming.* Something was happening beneath the blanket of his skin and bones. He never thrashed, he never cried out—they weren't nightmares, I don't think. I hope not.

And now he's just . . . still. He breathes, but he doesn't dream. But if there's still a piece of him to save, I'll find it.

We travel by darkness.

Time is broken up by the faint voices of the men talking to each other in the front seats, the scratchy van radio, and the few times we get to use the filthiest rest stops on the face of the earth. There isn't an opportunity to talk to Mia without them listening in or tracking us with their eyes, not even when they uncuff us to give us sandwiches and water. Every word would be dissected, anyway, and I don't want to give them any reason to discipline us or suspect we're planning something.

I try to plan something.

In the early morning light that slips in through the front windshield and the tinted back windows, I study Lucas's face. At the next stop for food or a bathroom break, when they uncuff us, Mia can shove the soldiers back and I'll lunge for one of their guns. If she can't knock them unconscious, then I'll—

"No, Sam."

I look up. Mia watches me, her dark eyes intent. The radio belches out more static, interrupting the song the driver was humming along to.

"But—"

"No," she repeats, glancing down at Lucas. "It's over. You were right." Mia's voice trembles. "You were right. I was just . . . stupid . . ."

"No," I say, "*I* was wrong—"

"Wouldn't it be better . . . for him?" she asks.

Maybe. An unwanted voice whispers the word in my mind. Is it better to let him live like this, force him to eat and drink, when he's clearly determined to drift away? How would Lucas feel about living as a shadow of himself, while we cling to the memory of who he was?

I must have fallen asleep at some point, too, because the next thing I'm aware of is waking up. I'm angry with myself all over again, blinking against the bright interior lights of the car, disoriented by the blast of icy air that charges into the cramped space. What time is it? The engine is off—I can't read the dashboard clock. How many hours have I wasted in sleep?

A soldier with a face I don't recognize is peering down at me, a pale blue helmet secured tightly under his chin.

"Where—?" I rasp out, my throat dry to the point of pain. *Where are we?*

The floor at our feet is empty.

Lucas?

They've already taken him out—God, they did it while we were asleep? Did they stop before now? Did they take him out just a few minutes ago? Mia struggles against her cuffs, straining to see what's happening outside of the doors.

"Where is he?" she shouts. "What did you do to him?"

"What are you doing?" I demand. "Where is Lucas?"

Panic scrambles under my skin like a thousand ants. The soldier's hand clamps down around my wrist hard enough to pin me there while he replaces the van's cuffs with zip ties again. Where is he? Is he all right? Anything could be happening—he might slip away completely, and neither of us would know—

I'm choked by my own helplessness. I have nothing to pour my anger into, and it just feeds itself, until I practically push my escort out of the van, which earns me a stern look and a sharp tongue cluck, like I'm a dog getting my behavior corrected in obedience class. We're under an overcast sky thick with steel-spun clouds, but I have to squint against the pale light. I swallow back the familiar wave of nausea that comes with too many nerves stewing in too little sleep, searching for Lucas.

Then I hear it.

It is a sound that lives inside me, vibrating at the edge of seven years of memory. The low hum turns me inside out in a second, and it happens so fast—my lungs constrict painfully, my vision tunnels on the tangles of barbed wire. The air shivers with electricity. Green trees—even the smell of the air and wet earth is the same. The fog hides the body of the camp, but I know it must be there. The electric fence—

Thurmond.

They brought me back—the electric fence in front of me is quivering with laughter—*thought you were gone, did you, thought you got away*—I recoil hard enough to trip up my escort and nearly bite my tongue off. Blood fills my mouth. Why are they doing this? Why—

I squeeze my eyes shut, open them, squeeze them, repeating it until the throbbing in my temples finally calms.

Not Thurmond.

Mia is talking to me, eyes wide—I don't understand how I'm looking up at her until I see that I'm on my knees, that I've tripped and fallen. It takes two men in uniforms to get me back up.

One of them, his blue helmet gleaming from a light mist of rain, squints at me, his eyes as dark as his skin. "—won't hurt you, won't hurt—"

The drumming in my head gets louder as the darkness at the edge of my vision clears, expanding so I can finally take in the real scene in front of me, not the nightmare my mind decided to terrorize me with.

There *is* an electrified fence. I didn't imagine that, at least. It stretches across the four lanes of empty highway we're standing on, and disappears into the damp, spring-rich forests cushioning either side of it. There are trailers everywhere, but two enormous concrete buildings have already been erected on either side of the road. Construction workers in bright orange vests are building another section that will bridge them together over what looks like it'll be some kind of tollbooth, or security checkpoint. National Guardsmen with blue bandanas tied around their upper arms are overseeing the work, hovering around as if they're unsure what they're supposed to be doing.

The asphalt is cracked and scattered with rotting leaves and tire tracks as we weave through the concrete barriers they've erected to slow down approaching cars. To our right, two soldiers in blue helmets are covering up the WELCOME TO WEST VIRGINIA: WILD AND WONDERFUL sign with one that reads ZONE 1 SECURITY CHECKPOINT HAVE PASSES READY.

Wild and wonderful. I don't know if I should laugh or cry.

I should have paid better attention to the news reports about how the peacekeeping force was dividing the country up into four zones for better management—I do kind of remember hearing that West Virginia would be the western barrier and Virginia the southern barrier for Zone 1. It includes all of New England and the Mid-Atlantic states. Which would make Zone 2 . . . the southern states, including Texas. Zone 3 would be the middle slice of the country, from the Great Lakes through Kansas, and everything west of that would be Zone 4.

They think it will be easier to manage the populations and rations this way, controlling the flow of both, telling us what to do and what's right. But dependence won't outlast desperation. I think they are building dams that will never withstand the hundreds of millions desperate for clean water, food, and work.

"Where is the boy? The one who was with us?"

He shakes his head, leading me through the construction, the deafening whine of drills and jackhammers hidden by work tarps. A shower of sparks falls from where the welders are binding the bones of the structure together over our heads. They strike the ground and disappear before they can catch.

When I dig my heels in, the escort signals to another soldier and they lift me, kicking, up the short stack of stairs into the warm arms of the building. The doors slide shut and seal behind us. A lock beeps.

Every head in the small, cramped entryway swivels in our direction. Mia and I are half walked, half dragged down the length of a door-lined hallway.

I am used to being watched. I am used to knowing that, even when I showered in the Wash Rooms, there was a camera there, keeping its eye on me. I ate under supervision. Worked with the eyes of PSFs drilling into my back. I am used to living like a shadow, a poor imitation of a person, but not invisible.

What I am not used to . . . is being *stared* at. Having men and women lean out of doorways, trail steps after us like we're the circus coming to town. It feels like I'm being passed around, crumpled by their careless hands. These aren't lethal looks. Mostly just plain, ugly curiosity. *Fascination.*

I can see the same realization dawning on Mia. Her shoulders hunch, her fingers curl, and a look like death comes over her face as she stares into each of the faces we pass. She's winding herself up, cranking up her temper. I shake my head, but she ignores me.

We make a sharp turn down another hallway with more doors. But these have glass observation windows, and instead of offices and supply closets, there are cots and four blank walls. These are prison cells.

They don't even cut the zip ties off our hands before they push us inside and let the door slam and lock behind us. Mia surges toward the window, where a crowd of soldiers and men and women in suits are slowing as they pass, or stopping altogether to look in.

"Where's my brother?" she yells. The men and women turn toward each other, whispering, confused. "What are you even *looking at?*"

Mia whirls back to me.

"Don't," I say, reading her expression. She wants me to pick a target for her—I think she wants them to see that glass isn't enough of a barrier to keep her from them. "It'll only make it worse."

It's my turn to address them. "We want to talk to whoever is in charge. *Hey!* Are you even listening?"

We can hear the rumble of their muted voices, but no one actually speaks to us, no one so much as moves, until a short, stocky man pushes his way through the crowd, slides a key card through the door's lock, and lets himself in. Two National Guardsmen trail in behind him, looking decidedly more worried.

The man in the blue beret motions for us to sit, but Mia and I remain on our feet, stepping back to the far side of the small room.

"I am Major Benn." The man's accent is heavy, filling whatever space his physical presence doesn't. None of them are armed with guns, and I wonder if that's a reflection on them, or on us. "You are at the Zone One Processing Center."

"Where's my brother?"

Major Benn waves his hands, shooing the question away. "You'll be kept in this facility until you are collected for . . . re-homing. You understand?"

"Where's my brother?" Mia repeats. "I want to see him!"

"Perhaps you will soon, if you are a good girl, okay?" the man answers, and I know I will hate those words, *good girl*, always. "You are . . . Mia, then? Mia . . ."

"Orfeo," one of the National Guardsmen finishes, shifting uncomfortably. He glances down at a printout in his hand before passing it to the major.

The man's blond brows rise and rise as he reads it over. "Then you are *blau*—Blue?"

325

My whole body tenses. Mia stares at him, her hands clenching where they're bound behind her back. "Yeah. So?"

"You do the trick, please—you show us?"

What?

Major Benn unclips a pen from his shirt's front pocket and lets it drop on the ground. "You pick this up. No touching, right?"

Mia and I exchange a look of disbelief. I think I've misheard him until I see the blood drain from the faces of the National Guardsmen. The muscles in my back tense to the point of pain. He's watching us, brows still raised expectantly.

The pen is a deep blue, rimmed with gold. It's still rolling back and forth, back and forth on the ground.

Maybe he does just want to see her abilities, marvel at them the way he would a magician's trick at a kid's birthday party. But I know for a fact that the group—the one that led to Thurmond being closed—released videos of the kids using their abilities and kids talking about the use of their abilities. So it's not like he hasn't had the chance to see it before.

"Is there a problem?" Major Benn asks, the words sharper now. He is not smiling, and that alone makes me straighten, catch my breath. I ease in front of Mia, just a step. He holds the paper up. "Is this wrong? Is this not what you do?"

"Sir—" one of the National Guardsmen starts to say, only to be silenced with a look.

At Thurmond, using your abilities—using them accidentally or willingly—was a punishable offense that involved lost meals and being forced to sit outside and let the elements prey on you. If not that, then . . . my leg throbs at the thought of stacked dog cages, remembering the snake, how it felt to be curled up and locked inside.

This isn't fair—we don't know the rules now! We don't know if they've changed, if Mia will be hauled off for doing this, or applauded for putting on a good show. Could he claim that she was trying to use the pen as a weapon? That he *had* to kill us to subdue us?

"She's not—" I start to say, but it's already too late. Mia doesn't have to lift a hand. She looks at the pen, looks at the faces peering in at us like we're animals at the zoo, and she sends them on a collision course.

The glass doesn't shatter, even with the force of the tip driving through it, but the cracks radiate out in a web that reaches the edge of its frame. There's a collective gasp as the men and women standing there scatter, but it's nothing compared to the click and swish of the National Guardsmen pulling out their White Noise machines.

What is she doing? Does Mia really think they'll let us see Lucas now?

"It was an accident," she says, all sweetness, and if I could reach back to strangle her without them tackling me for moving, I would. "You said you wanted to see me move it. I guess my control isn't very good."

Every last trace of humor is gone from Benn's face as he crosses the room in silence and slides the pen out of the window slowly, carefully, like one wrong move could bring the whole thing crashing down.

The person who slams the sheet of paper up against the glass behind him has absolutely none of these concerns. I don't see her until Benn takes a surprised step back, and then it's the electric purple hair that draws my eyes first, even before her fury-tight face.

"Show's over, assholes!"

Every voice but hers seems to have been sucked out of the world. My stomach lurches, starts to flutter again.

It's so strange to me that I remember this girl's voice and can connect the right memory before I can do the same with her face. Or . . . not so strange. She'd been wearing a ski mask when she burst into our cabin.

This is the girl from Thurmond. One of the team that came to open up the camp. The window distorts her face, breaks it up into pieces, but what I see are dark eyes, rich skin, high cheekbones, full lips, and a glare like venom. The few stragglers in the hallway duck away into nearby offices; I don't blame them. She's shaking like she's about to detonate and bring the whole building down.

Benn signals to one of the National Guardsmen to open the door, and the girl fills the doorway. She's too smart to step inside, where they could trap her, too—actually, on second thought, I'm not so sure anything could cage her. She's a full head shorter than all three men, and looks about ten times as lethal. Gun holstered at her side. Knife peeking out of the top of her combat boots. Plus whatever else she's hiding under her oversized green army jacket.

"Transfer order," the girl says, handing the paper over. "Signed, sealed, delivered—what the fuck are you squinting at? Get a fucking pair of glasses if you need a better view!" The National Guardsman who's been staring at her immediately turns back toward Benn, who is reading and rereading the piece of paper.

"What—?" I give a sharp shake of my head at Mia, silencing her. I don't know how she's even speaking. My throat is so tight I can barely breathe.

"This is signed by . . ." he begins.

"Interim President Cruz," the girl finishes.

"Where is—you are—" Benn releases the next few words in

German. "You are not an officer of the law, armed forces, United Nations—"

She holds up what looks like a small identification card. I can't read what it says, but it looks official. Mia watches the girl with wide, wondering eyes.

Benn is still holding the card when she snatches it back and gestures toward us. "Get moving, girls."

I don't need to be told twice. The door slams shut behind us, and I don't risk looking back at the wreckage we've left.

"What's going on?" I whisper. "How did you get us out?"

She narrows her eyes and slides them over to us. "Someone called in a favor on your behalf, so don't jack this up, hear me?"

Someone? Who?

The girl doesn't cut our hands free, and keeping up with her long, steady strides means jogging on a leg that's hurting badly enough for me to want to cut it off myself.

"What about my brother? Where is he? Are you getting him?" Mia asks the second we reach the door, when the spell of silence from the hallway finally wears off. The blast of damp air and gray skies is so at odds with the dry, white glare of the new building, it's staggering. I have to limp slowly down the steps to keep from falling.

"Treating you like you're fucking animals, the assholes, *God*— come here," she says, tugging Mia over to her. I'm right, that *is* a knife poking out of her boot. The girl makes quick work of the zip ties around Mia's wrists, then mine. By the time she's finished, the door to the other building hisses open and a tall, lanky teen appears, his silver-framed glasses fogging up from the sudden change in temperature. He's wearing something my dad would have worn—nice slacks and a dark fleece to keep out the cold.

I recognize him, too. This is the one who was at the press conference. The kid that spoke up.

The numbing hit of confusion takes away all of my words. I fumble for them, for the question screaming across my mind, and come up with nothing but a gasp.

He looks at the girl and shakes his head. "It's like we thought. They already moved him out."

"Lucas?" Mia asks. "Are you talking about Lucas?"

The girl throws a quick glance around to the soldiers moving between the construction site and the building. "Shit, girl, can you try a voice level under *screeching*? Let's *go*."

"I'm not leaving without my brother!" Mia leans back, digging in, nearly red with the effort to keep from either screaming or crying, I'm not sure which.

"You want to stay here?" the girl challenges, squaring her shoulders. "You want back in that jail cell?"

"Vi"—the boy tries to step between them—"we don't have time for this."

Mia raises her hand, and my mind blanks again.

The girl only arches her brow. "Try it. I'll break both of your fucking legs and you walking out of here won't be a goddamn question, will it?"

I feel like she's reached in and ripped away my shock. My hackles rise, and no one is more surprised than me to hear a sound like a growl come tearing out of my mouth. If she so much as touches Mia—

"Look, we're running out of time," the boy says. "I checked the other building. Wherever your brother is, he isn't here—but none of us are going to find him if we don't get moving."

Mia is breathing so hard it steams the air. She looks to me for an answer, and I hope I'm not making the biggest mistake of my life when I nod.

"Follow the road out—see that SUV? That's our ride." The girl jerks her thumb toward the car parked across the lanes, about a half mile down the road. "We'll be right behind you. But for the love of God, *hustle*."

It's raining in earnest now; the clouds pelt us with cold, fat drops that do more to clear the haze of exhaustion than the growing disbelief that we're out, that we're with other kids, that this is happening.

"Who are these people?" Mia whispers. "How does she know who you are?"

"They're friends . . . I think," I say.

And I know I'm right a second later, when the back door to the car opens and a small figure climbs down, awkwardly trying to swing a heavy walking cast out without slipping. I don't realize I'm moving faster, hobbling forward on my own bum leg, until suddenly I can see the worry fade from her face and relief settle in. I laugh at how pitiful we must look with our limps, but somehow it's perfect. Despite all of our differences, Ruby and I have always been a pair.

She was always so careful and reserved with her touch and words, I'm shocked all over again as she throws her arms around my shoulders. Her clothes breathe out the heat of the car, and I let myself sag against her, too close to sobbing to say anything.

I knew she was okay. I read everything about her the papers published, including the fact that one of the Camp Controllers had broken her leg when she shut down the camp's power. I saw the news reports speculating what was "to be done" with her, because of what her abilities are, every minute spliced with shots of a thousand exploding camera flashes as she left the hotel in West Virginia to go home with her parents. But I didn't realize how badly I wanted and needed to see her until this moment.

"Are you okay?" Ruby asks, voice breaking. "Did they hurt you? We got here as fast as we could—"

Something about the way she cries finally triggers my own tears. They collect in my lashes, disappear in her long, dark hair. Another door opens and shuts; the driver comes around the front of the car. I recognize him, too. There's a bit of scruff on his face, and he's wearing a plaid shirt and leather jacket instead of black fatigues, but he's the one who came rushing into our cabin with the purple-haired girl looking for Ruby. Now he hangs back, watching us with a wary expression, his hands shoved deep into the pockets of his jeans.

"How?" I manage to get out as I pull back. *How did you know? How did you find us?*

"I had a friend flag your profile in the system so it would alert me if someone searched for you," Ruby says, green eyes bright. "I hope that's okay. I was so worried when I realized you weren't at the hotel, and your parents never checked in. I've been looking for you for *weeks*."

She turns to Mia, who hangs back, arms crossed, clutching at her elbows. Ruby brings a small, encouraging smile to her face. I haven't seen one like it from her in years, maybe ever. Something about her steadiness must speak to the part of Mia that craves it, because she takes Ruby's hand when she offers it, shakes it all proper and civilized.

"I'm Ruby Dal—"

"—I know who you are," Mia blurts out. "I mean . . . the news . . . they let us watch at our hotel."

332

Ruby's smile falters, just for a moment. "I'm guessing you're the mysterious Mia?"

Called in her favor. Isn't that what Vida had said? It makes more and more sense as I weave the thought through what I know. Ruby was part of the group of people who freed the camps, she worked directly with Senator Cruz—maybe the government felt like she was owed something?

And . . . I made her blow it on us.

"We need to go," the boy says, the driver. The words are gentle but firm, as is the way he cups her elbow.

"I'm sorry," I say. I don't know why I'm apologizing, exactly— that she could have gotten something amazing from them, that I've somehow shuffled my mess into her lap, that she's been through her own hell and now I'm forcing her to walk into mine.

"Don't say that. I owe you everything." She startles, as if just realizing something. "Where's the boy who was with you? I thought he might be the one from Thurmond . . . the Red?"

I swallow. Nod. "They separated us."

Ruby doesn't react the way I expect her to—the way anyone would, who saw what the original Reds at Thurmond were like. She doesn't even tense. "They didn't have any details about him in the report that was filed in Iowa, other than that he wasn't . . . responsive."

"He's not himself," Mia says.

We are all dancing around the real, straight truth: Lucas is broken. He can't or won't take care of himself.

He will likely slip away and die.

He has already started to go.

He could die before we ever find him.

Someone could hurt him again.

I might never find him again.

The breath burns in my chest and fear becomes a wasp nest in the pit of my stomach. "It's . . . bad, Ruby."

I made a mistake.

Her lips compress, but her eyes are still soft, understanding, as the others finally reach us. The girl with the crazy hair shakes her head.

"It's okay, we'll figure it out, I promise." She turns to Mia, reaches back for the door. "In you go."

Mia glances back at me. "Are you sure he's not here?"

There is sheer agony in not knowing—if we leave and he is here, if he's only hidden, I don't think I could recover from that. Knowing we left him here to die alone would kill me. It would.

"Positive," says the boy in the fleece; then, after being elbowed by the driver, adds, "I'm sorry. He's not here."

"Look," the other girl says to Ruby, who is now also hesitating—who, with a single glance, tells me that she won't leave if I don't want us to—"we'll call Nico on the way. I know you don't need me to remind you about how fucking close we're cutting this—"

"Agreed," the driver says. "Let's roll and figure it out as we go—just like old times."

"Yay," the other boy says, without a hint of enthusiasm. "Because *that* always went so well."

With a steadying breath, I climb into the way-back seat, trying to ignore how badly I'm shaking, how cold I feel at my core, despite the heat coming through the vents. Mia is right behind me. The others quickly fall into place—Ruby in the front passenger seat, our rescuers in the two middle seats, and—

"Sam, Mia, this is Liam," Ruby says as Liam buckles up and

starts the engine. He makes a wide arc and sends us sailing down the open highway. "You already met Vida and Chu—Charlie."

"Hi," Mia says, which is good, because I can't seem to get whatever is stuck in my throat out. "Where the hell are we going?"

Vida actually snorts. "My thoughts exactly."

Liam glances up at us in the rearview mirror. "Where do you want to go?"

"What he means to say," Vida says, "is what the hell were you planning on doing with that Red?"

"That Red is my *brother*," Mia growls. Vida turns fully around in her seat now, brows raised, assessing.

"She didn't mean it like that," Ruby interrupts.

"Of course she did," Charlie says, rolling his eyes. "And, by the way, it's a valid question."

"Still need a direction to drive, here," Liam says.

The way these kids talk to each other, the way they look at each other, it's so . . . comfortable. I bring my arms around my center, hugging myself.

Ruby told me once that her parents died, way back when we were first processed into Thurmond. Though I know that's not true now, she's clearly found a new family all the same. A part of me wonders if it's not what she went through that has shaped her into something so solid and strong, but the people who went through it with her.

I'm not jealous . . . not exactly. I feel a longing that surprises me, though, to capture this easy warmth with Lucas and Mia again. I want to stay inside this warm bubble of Ruby and her friends, and start believing in the possibility of finding steady ground to stand on again.

I can tell Mia is still, despite Vida's bluntness, a little star-struck by everyone in the car. Save for Vida, these are all faces that have appeared in the press, people who've had their stories told—they're the ones who have been speaking up on our behalf. These kids got to *fight* for the rest of us. If you had asked me seven years ago who I thought would be at the helm of the ship torpedoing the camps, I would have reached into the box of memories in my mind and pulled out some senator's name, or a general's. I would not have offered up Ruby's.

But here she is, so much more than I ever thought. So much braver than I ever gave her credit for.

"We want to find Lucas," I say finally. "We appreciate you . . . we're so thankful you got us out of there, but we can . . . we can do it on our own. We've already been enough trouble."

"Luckily for you, this particular group specializes in trouble," Ruby says, pulling what looks like a small cell phone out of the cupholder. She starts to tap out a message as she continues, "Did you guys hear anything about where they might be taking him? Anything at all? Damn—I thought we fixed this stupid battery. It just died again."

Ruby turns to Vida, who's already reaching into her jacket pocket for something.

"No. *No*," Charlie says. "Bad enough we're out here, but using a phone they can listen in on?"

Vida already has the device in her hand and is dialing. Her other hand covers his mouth as she flashes him a look of utter exasperation that he returns tenfold. Charlie peels it off, but instead of dropping her hand, he wraps his long, narrow fingers around hers and holds on. And she lets him. The tension that had seemed to ricochet through her softens.

"Hey, Zuzu—yeah, everything's good here, what about you? You keeping Cate on her toes? Ah, that's my girl." She gives the others a little thumbs-up. "We'll be back soon. I know, I'm sorry—"

"She's a friend," Charlie explains in a low voice. "They have her enrolled in a school pilot program in D.C. We couldn't take her with us without raising some red flags, and she was *not happy*."

"My ears are still blistered," Liam complains. "The sass. *The sass!* Too much time with Vi."

To Vida, who is now smirking, Charlie adds, "Tell her to do her homework!"

"She's been sassy all along," Ruby says, rolling her eyes. "You and Chubs just treated her like she was a little angel—"

"Excuse you," Charlie—do they seriously call this string bean of a boy *Chubs*?—says, outraged. "She *is* an angel."

"Exactly. She wasn't born, she was found at the end of a rainbow," Liam agrees.

"Why do you always have to take it to such a weird place?" Charlie complains.

I can't keep up with this back-and-forth.

Vida hushes them with a wave of her hand. "Yeah, the chatter died," she says into the phone. "We'll try to recharge—did you find the present I left for you?"

"Was this present a knife?" Liam asks, sounding legitimately nervous.

"An angel that is now fascinated by weaponry," Charlie amends, glaring at Vida.

Vida ignores them both. "Can you get Nico for me? Hey, Nico—yeah, no, everything"—her voice pitches several degrees louder—"*everything is fine.* Are you near a computer—yeah, okay, stupid question. Slow *down*, Turbo—"

Mia leans forward, trying to catch whatever hints she can from the voice on the other end of the line. I'm gripping the seat cushion so hard, pieces of the upholstery are gathering under my nails. A green blur of trees slips by us, and it feels like we are being fast-forwarded through this; I can't keep up with my hope and confusion.

"Can you check to see if a kid was transferred out of the Zone One station—what other station would I be talking about? Yeah, it'd be deep network—these asshole bureaucrats can't take a shit without someone filling out a form in triplicate, of course there's got to be some kind of a record—I don't know, whatever key-words they use as code for Reds? Oh my God, I swear—"

"Put him on speaker, Vi," Ruby says, interrupting whatever is about to explode out of the girl's mouth. She does as she's asked. "Hey, Nico, it's me. You might find something if you look for a medical alert or incident flag."

"I'll try that." The voice that comes tumbling out of the phone sounds as young as any of us, and that catches me off guard. But . . . of course. Of course they would trust another kid with this, over an adult. *"But Ruby, aren't you supposed to be heading back now?"*

Another reference to some silent clock that's ticking down without any sort of explanation as to why. Everyone's eyes in the car swing over to her, even Liam's. I've been watching his expression grow harder and harder in the rearview mirror, until now it seems set in deep unhappiness.

"Plenty of time," Ruby says calmly. "Anything?"

"Well . . . actually, yeah. There's a request for a medic at a safe house in Ashland, Ohio—urgent, prefer one with PSF training." As he talks, my heart begins to throb painfully in my chest; it's so

real, I can barely feel Mia's broken nails clawing into my arm as she grips it.

"Ashland? Why Ashland?" she's asking.

"Ohio?" It's the first word we've gotten out of Liam in a while. He breaks his gaze on the road again and shoots Ruby a pleading look that she acknowledges by brushing her fingers against his cheek. I realize I'm staring, and force my eyes back on the forest sailing by us.

"Ohio's on the way to Indiana," Nico points out. *"And—yeah, another requisition just came in for a unit to meet them at the safe house with Grade Five restraints."*

Grade Five restraints. I can't let myself imagine what those look like, but Mia clearly is. Her breathing grows harsh, uneven.

"Then they do know what he is," Ruby says, confirming my fear. "Dammit. Is there any kind of address listed for the safe house?"

"I'll find it and text it to you, but—I don't think you'll make it back in time, not if you go to Ohio. It's a six-hour, twenty-eight-minute drive between there and Salem, and that's a direct route, without having to figure out how to get back through the zone blocks—"

Salem. Ruby has to be home in time for something, and while she clearly doesn't seem worried about it, the others *are*.

"No," Charlie and Liam thunder together, the second she clicks off the call. Even Ruby looks taken aback by the force of the words. Vida straightens, leaning away from Charlie, with a look of calm, cool murder on her face that makes *me* wince. She likes them trying to make a decision for Ruby about as much as I do.

"Neither of you have to be involved—" Ruby starts.

"Do not pull that with us," Charlie says. "Don't act like we'd ever choose to separate. Look—" He turns back to us. "I'm really sorry about your brother. I am. If you want to try to go find him, you should know you're dealing with armed soldiers who will happily take you back into custody and put you through the procedure. You'll be back where you started. But you are not dragging us any further into this than we already are. It's too big of a risk."

I think I'm going to be sick. My guts have knotted themselves so tightly, I can barely breathe.

"We don't need your help," Mia spits back. "You can pull over right here. Go ahead. Let us out. If you think my brother is a *risk*, then you won't want to spend another second with *me*."

"It's not that," Ruby says quickly. "We—*I*—want to help."

"Same," Vida says, to my surprise. "All I've done these past few weeks is listen to old white people talk about what to do with us. I could use a good fight—and no, Charlie Boy, you *don't* get to decide that for me."

"Ruby, I know . . . I get it, all right?" Liam says, dividing his attention between her and the road. "But it's too dangerous. You *know* that. Think about yourself for once."

"Why do you get to decide whose life is more important?" Mia demands. "It's because he's a Red, isn't it? You have no idea who he is, or what he's like. He's the kindest—" Her voice cracks. "He's the best person in the world, and you'd leave him there for them to kill. You'd let them take him back in and break him more than they already have, break him until there's nothing of him left!"

There's one of those old-fashioned rest stops up ahead, the kind that are meant to look like brick ranch houses, I guess. Without another word, Liam pulls us off the highway, turning into its empty parking lot. Throwing the brake on, he unbuckles his seat belt and twists around in his seat, clearly struggling to keep his voice and expression in check.

"You don't have one damn idea what you're talking about," he says, his voice low.

"Liam—" Ruby tries, clearly reading his temperature on this. "She just wants us to help her brother. *I* want to help. I know why you're against it, but *you* also know why it's important to me."

He glances at her, takes in an unsteady breath, and gives a curt nod.

"Girlfriend has the power to melt brains and underwent extensive combat training," Vida says, as if she's reminded him of this a hundred times.

Extensive combat training? Ruby?

She won't look at me, acknowledge this.

"And if I'm there, you know we'll get in and out quickly," Vida continues, as if it's simply the truth, and not arrogance. And maybe it is, because the others don't exactly contradict her. "You need to stop with this stupid, smothering, protective bullshit—"

"Oh, *I'm* sorry!" Charlie says, raising his voice. "But if you'd been *this close* to getting killed and there was nothing I could do to stop it, if you were getting buried under death threats, if *you* had a multimillion-dollar bounty on your head, then, yeah, I'd be a *little mistrustful* of the world, too! I'd shoot anyone who gave you a wrong look and then destroy their bodies with lime!"

The blood drains from my head at that rush of information—*killed, death threats, bounty*—Ruby came for us in spite of all of that?

Vida smiles. "Please. Like you could hide bodies without my help. Besides, acid works faster."

"True," he concedes. "And you'd probably be the one to shoot them."

The silence that follows is somehow louder than his ranting. Mia's breath catches as she turns to look at me. I hear myself ask, "Ruby, is that true?"

"Yes, but—" she starts to say, only to be cut off by Charlie.

"She's been expressly forbidden by President Cruz and the interim government to leave Virginia, never mind Zone One," he explains. "It's bad enough that we already crossed state lines!"

"And you agree with her?" Ruby says, her voice sharper than I've ever heard it. "You agree with all of them that I need to be *monitored*, that I need to be *contained*, that I can't be *trusted*?"

"No, it's not that," Charlie says, flustered. "You know that's not what I meant! And, once again for the record, it's not about them seeing you as a threat, it's about you being an asset to them, and them wanting to protect you from the people who are *literally hunting you!*"

"It's about what happens when you get caught missing your check-in tomorrow," Liam presses. "We don't know. We have no idea what they'll do if you provoke them, and darlin', *that's* what we're scared of, even if you aren't. This is bad enough—do you really want to make it worse?"

I don't know what to say. My loyalty is with Ruby, always, but I understand Liam's side, too. If Lucas or Mia had a target painted so prominently on their backs, I would find an underground bunker and lock them inside of it until the trouble blew over.

I feel horrible for being comforted by the fact that they seem just as lost, as at sea about everything, as I am; if these kids, the ones who played a huge role in the turnover of the government and the end of the camps, don't even really know what our future looks like, how are the rest of us supposed to paint a picture?

Ruby has remained silent through both boys' outbursts, waiting for her turn to speak. The strain on her face makes her exhaustion that much more obvious, but she doesn't let it dampen her words. "What's the point of everything we did if we can't help kids who need it? We let them take the Reds, we let them put them back in a facility, and *nothing* is being done to help them. Can't we help this one?"

"Facility?" Mia repeats.

"Is this really about proving Cruz wrong?" Liam asks. "Showing her you should be allowed to try to treat them? Why not give them time to at least try to do it themselves?"

"Luc isn't—wasn't—like the others!" Mia insists. "He did this thing, when we were little . . . he retreated into his head a lot. Sort of lived there, you know? The first time he went through the Red training, he avoided being controlled by them. When he got to Thurmond, he told Sam that's how he got through it all—escaping into his memories. Isn't that right, Sam?"

I nod.

"Can people lock themselves up—*retreat*—into their own heads and just go too far?" Mia asks Ruby. "He's still in there, I know he is—he just needs help, more time. Please don't let them have him, *please*. We were figuring it out, we were drawing him back up to the surface, and it was working . . . it was going to work."

I lean my cheek against the back of the seat in front of me. "We don't know that."

"*You* don't know that," Mia counters, "but *I* do! He's in there, but they'll destroy any part of him that's left if they take him back in!"

"Look, I'm sorry—" Liam starts.

"You're not!" she snaps. "You're *not* sorry, so give me a break and stop pretending like you are! You have no idea what it feels like! You get to keep all the people you care about safe—he is the only family I have left!"

I can feel it, even if Mia can't or won't—the dead weight that seems to settle over the car in the silence that follows, underscored only by the hiss of the warm air coming through the vents. Liam's jaw is a sharp line, jutting out slightly as he works it back and forth. He can't stop blinking as he stares out at the rest stop. Charlie looks like he wants to climb back and strangle her; he opens his mouth, eyes shining with anger, but someone else speaks first.

"We owe it to him to finish what he started."

Vida and Charlie exchange a look of raised brows with each other before turning to look out their respective windows, but Ruby holds Liam's gaze until he releases his breath in a long sigh. She hasn't just played a winning hand with that, she's wiped every other card off the table. I'm not sure I totally understand the dynamic of this group, beyond what Charlie said about them not wanting to separate—why is it so important that we convince *Liam* to do this?

He leans forward and rests his forehead against the steering wheel. Ruby puts a familiar hand on the back of his neck, stroking the skin there. And I know, if I know nothing else, that the *he* they're talking about isn't Lucas, and that Mia is wrong—that he does know what she's feeling. Maybe better than the rest of us.

"Ruby, when do you have to be back for the check-in?" I ask.

"The government agent usually comes by in the morning," she admits. "They randomly pick a time to make sure I'm where I'm supposed to be—usually around eight o'clock."

"And that was the compromise," Liam says, "to avoid her having to wear an electronic monitoring device."

That sends a shudder through me.

"But I talked to my dad before we left," Ruby charges on, "and he can stall them until at least noon."

"How?" Chubs demands.

"By saying he sent me off so he could talk to them privately about *safety concerns*," she explains. I have to imagine that her parents are terrified of her leaving, but, at this point, are willing to do just about anything out of their lingering guilt for letting her be taken to a camp.

"Fine," Liam breathes out, "but promise me that if it looks like it's going to take us an extra day to get there, we turn around. Promise me."

Mia tenses again, and I think she's about to call him out on being selfish for choosing her over Lucas, but I grip her wrist and give a sharp shake of my head.

Ruby doesn't look like she's about to cut that deal until Liam adds, "That's *also* what he would want."

Finally she nods.

Charlie throws his hands up into the air before settling back against his seat, arms crossed. Vida gives him an affectionate pat on his knee, and it turns into a surprisingly sweet, quick kiss on the cheek when Ruby and Liam turn and face forward. I'm almost embarrassed I get caught watching.

It's decided.

We're going to find Lucas.

I'm surprised at the small scream I feel welling up inside my chest, ballooning out until I'm sure I'll burst at my seams. I don't want this—I do, but I *don't*. If something happens to Ruby while we get him, it will be trading one of my people for another, and I don't have any spares, I don't have a single person I can lose now. I've handed out all the keys to my heart, and losing either of them—or, God, *both*—will lock it forever.

The phone vibrates. Ruby looks down and then back over at Liam.

He sits up, reaching for the small screen on the car's console, bringing up a menu. "All right, darlin', read me the address. When you're done, you'd best ask him where we can still cross the zone border undetected."

Mia looks like she's about to jump out of her seat and punch the air—and, actually, so does Vida. But I keep my hand on Mia's, pinning it to the seat. We can't celebrate yet—my mind is already churning out all of the reasons why we can't. He could be gone by the time we get there. Too far gone to save, or already removed from the safe house, brought to the . . . my mind stretches the word, turns it into a hiss. *Facility.*

The same one he was in before?

I bite the inside of my lip hard enough to tear it, draw blood.

We are not safe yet, either. When this is all over, we will not have our own safe house to return to. This will be our life now. Cars, moving, guessing, fighting, hoping.

I'm so grateful Ruby has found her courage, but I wish she could carve off a piece of it and pass it back to me. How strange that we've managed to trade places, that I'm the shadow now. Maybe that's okay. Maybe I get to rest, just for a little while.

No. It's not okay.

Liam pulls back onto the highway after Ruby reads off some instructions from Nico about where to cross the zone lines, as well as a reluctantly delivered estimate of the new driving time factoring in traffic patterns and roadblocks.

Ruby reaches over and turns on the radio, searching until the static is pierced by a man's wailing voice as he rocks out about heartbreak and fury. My mind can't make sense of it against the sight of Liam kissing the palm of her hand and holding on to it, fingers interlaced.

"Okay," she says. "We have a few hours to kill. Why don't you start from the beginning—what happened when you left Thurmond? We'll see if there's some clue about how to help him. . . ."

The burn of tears is real at the back of my throat, choking me up all over again, leaving a confused Mia to explain.

Ruby has found her strength—she's escaped the cocoon of fear that kept her too terrified to even meet anyone's gaze directly.

I can do this, I think. I can do this, for him. I can't let Ruby risk herself for me, not when she's already sacrificed so much. I feel my hollow heart swell with it, the determination.

If anyone is going to risk their life getting Lucas out, it should be me.

It's right there in the name, *safe house,* but some part of me still doesn't expect them to keep him in an actual house. It's an indication of how dire it is, I think, this whole situation, that they haven't brought him to a more secure location, some kind of a bunker or prison to try to contain his abilities. As it stands, this house looks like it could belong in any town; it's as perfectly

American, with its white trim, blue paint, and swing on the front porch, as the Fourth of July; and I resent the hell out of it because I know what a mask it is, what its sweet face is hiding. It reminds me of a story Lucas told us once, about a witch that lured kids in by decorating her house with candy and sweets, only to try and eat *them*.

We park two streets over and walk between the rows of foreclosed houses and their neglected backyards until we reach the house directly across the street from the one we're trying to get to. Vida leads us, and forces us to wait as she crawls forward to make sure that this house is empty, too. That no one is watching the safe house from across the street. The boys go next, then Ruby, and finally me and Mia. We crouch down like the others and keep low, using the house's brick fencing out front as cover.

"All right," Vida says, voice low. She checks her gun's clip with a kind of practiced ease that's unnerving if I think about it too hard. "Liam, Charlie, and I will do a quick sweep of the streets and houses—"

"I want to go," Mia interrupts.

If I think Vida will laugh off the suggestion, I'm so wrong. She seems to take a moment to size up Mia. "You're with me, then. And you do *everything* I say, understood?"

Mia nods eagerly, and I want to protest this, to keep her here beside me where we can both keep an eye on the house, but I can't bring myself to clip her wings. Despite what little sleep she's gotten, she's vibrating with energy, ready to spring into whatever Vida wants her to do.

"Okay, she and I will take nine o'clock, you take three o'clock," she tells the boys, before giving me and Ruby a loaded look and adding, "And *you* keep your asses planted right there until we get back."

"I want to go in," I tell her. "To get him."

"One step at a time, boo," Vida says. "We'll get you in, no problem, but only after assessing the threat."

Assessing the threat. There's a handgun casually tucked into the back of Ruby's jeans, like it belongs there, and I realize that *assessing the threat* has been her life, probably from the moment she got out of Thurmond. I need to ask her about that night, about all the new scars I see and feel in her, the grim days spread out between when they took her away and when they brought her back into my life.

I ease back a bit, settling more firmly on the ground. My mind is flinging thoughts at me too fast to take apart. As much as I want to storm across the way, push Ruby back to safety, I trust this system they have. I've already messed up so badly in losing him in the first place. I can't make another misstep. I will wait.

For now.

As Liam crawls by her, Ruby grips his hand and pulls him back around, stealing a quick kiss. It leeches some of the tension from his face, but doesn't erase it completely.

"Be careful," she whispers.

"Who? Me?" The smile he sends her actually makes my stomach do an unexpected swoop, too. He's no Lucas, but he's what Mrs. Orfeo would call "easy on the eyes." I wonder if this Liam, the one with the bright eyes and sly smiles, is the Liam the others know and recognize—not the distant, defensive one with his back up against the wall.

The others have been gone for less than a minute when Ruby

turns to me and says softly, "I'm sorry about all that in the car. The truth is, he does want to help—it kills him to know what's going on with the Reds. He's just . . . fighting his way back from fear."

"I know how that is." The words are barely a whisper, but she catches them. Ruby nods, turning back to watch the safe house. There is something instantly validating, something that fills the cracks in me, about how her immediate response isn't, *You?* or even a look of surprise. I find that I can finally breathe again.

"You know, the most poisonous thing about the camps wasn't really our time there," she begins slowly, "it's how they tricked us into being afraid of the world outside of them."

"The world *is* kind of rotten, as far as I can tell," I argue.

"It is and it isn't, but it's always been that way, even before all this. We just were conditioned into a routine, so everything else feels overwhelming in comparison." Ruby shifts so her weight is off her walking cast. "When I got out of Thurmond, I could barely stand to be around the others: Liam, Chubs—sorry, *Charlie*—our friend Zu. I couldn't stand their attention, or to be touched."

"No problem there anymore," I note.

She gives a little smile, lifts one shoulder into a shrug, as if to ask, *Do you blame me?* "Part of it was being trapped in the fear of what I could do, but when I think about it now, I realize it was an issue of control. I couldn't control my abilities, I couldn't control the way the world reacted to me, I couldn't even control whether or not I lost the people I cared about. The thing is, there's plenty about life none of us will *ever* be able to control. You have to let uncertainty become your normal. And that just takes time. You have to give yourself permission to let it take time, without beating yourself up about it."

"I don't *have* time," I remind her.

"You will, but I get it." Ruby glances over. "When I was having a hard time, when I didn't think I was ever going to find solid ground, the only thing that helped was focusing on the people around me, instead of whatever fears were chasing each other in my head. If I couldn't find the courage to protect myself, I could find it for *them*, protect them the way you protected me, the way you protected all the girls in our cabin."

I barely remember that Sam.

"You want to know the real reason they never let us touch or talk to each other if they could help it? It made us strong. If you have people who love you, you can fall back on them when you're afraid."

She reaches over, takes my hand, waits until I'm looking at her before she says, "It may feel like you're alone, but we're here with you now. We will always be here for you. *That* is a certainty."

The promise hollows me out at my center; isn't the fact that she's here now, that she had someone watching for my name to appear in a system, that she came without being called, proof enough? It takes away whatever weight has had my stomach in its grip for the past few weeks, and leaves room for something else to come rushing in. "Ruby—"

The sound of a rattling engine cuts me off and sharpens Ruby's attention on the world around us. She motions for me to get down, and—walking cast and all—crawls over to the edge of the fence, where it meets the open driveway at the house's garage.

I try to stay as low as I can without losing my own view of the white van as it comes down the road, its brakes screeching to a stop just outside of the safe house. There's a single beat of stillness before the front door opens, and an older soldier tromps across the porch, down the steps. His National Guard fatigues are rumpled in a way that hints at how often he's had to sleep in them, and he can't seem to stop his hands jittering at his sides. There's a jumpy swing to his steps as he comes toward the van, gun drawn, and that sets my panic trilling.

Two more men, both dressed in beat-up black clothes, step out of the van and shut the doors quietly behind them. The driver stays where he is at the wheel, obscured by the window's dark tint.

They aren't PSFs despite the colors they wear, and they aren't UN—so who are they? The medics?

That innocent, rosy little guess is stomped out when I see Ruby's face, the fury carved into it. She recognizes them—or at least what they are.

"You're late—Christ, we've been waiting *hours*."

"Traffic," deadpans one of the men wearing black. "It's a bitch. Where is it?"

"Give me what I asked for first—I need to count it before I let you in."

The one who spoke before, his hair buzzed short and his whole body stiff with obvious impatience, shoves the small duffel bag in his hand at the soldier's chest. I take a closer look at the other, what he's swinging around in his hands. It looks like a plastic mask, only it's attached to chains and handcuffs.

Grade Five restraints. The words bloom a bloody red inside my mind.

I know those restraints.

I saw them at Thurmond.

I saw the Reds shuffle around in them through the mud, in the months before they disappeared.

"Medic did what he could. Hope you packed ice to transport

352

the body," the soldier says, unzipping the duffel bag, rummaging through it.

The body.

Mr. Orfeo explained to me once that the light we see from distant stars travels years and years and years to reach us, and that, after that time, some of them may no longer be burning. He said that when certain kinds of stars die, they burn themselves through, collapse under their own gravity, shrink to a core that explodes into a blinding supernova. And what's left, when all of that energy, that stardust, is gone, is nothing but a sucking void.

I know that feeling. I am alive with it; the pain as my ribs seem to contract in around my heart is staggering. But it's the power of my fury that pushes me up over that fence, even as it feels like the world is collapsing in on me. I am halfway across the damp, empty street before the men on the porch register me, before any of them go for their guns.

I don't care.

What was the point? I want to scream, beat my fists against the ground until I split it open and fall through the crack. I don't care what happens to me now, if Lucas is gone then—

No one else will be there for Mia.

The thought brings me up short, almost stops me dead, but I'm too far into this to pull back, to run. I don't stop, not even as shots ring out behind me, and the soldier and one of the men in black fall, clutching wounds that are pulsing out more blood than I've ever seen in my life. A car revs and peels away, shrieking. More shots explode from the street, as if chasing it.

One day I will think about this, that my friend has just sent two men to their deaths without a second thought, but that day is a long way off from this one.

"What the fuck—" the last man snarls, aiming his gun at my head. I don't care, I don't care what he'll do to me now—there's nothing that can be worse than this. I see my hand outstretched, my fingers curled like claws, and I think, *I will tear you apart, I don't care, I don't care, I don't care anymore*—

He goes rigid, straightening up like a kite that's suddenly caught the wind. I turn, only to find Ruby is right behind me, her chest hauling in breath after breath, face flushed, her cold focus on the man's face. It's like she's released a valve in him; his expression drains away from his face, leaving slack, roughened skin.

She tilts her head to the side. A small movement. Tiny. But it sends him running, his gun clattering onto the porch as he disappears into the sunset at the far end of the street.

"Stop where you are!"

There are soldiers on the other side of the screen door, rifles trained on us through its fine silvery netting. Three in all, eyes wide and dark like beetles. The one in front risks a glance down at the duffel bag that exchanged hands. A stack of green bills has spilled out into the pool of blood collecting at my feet.

It's more money than I thought existed in the world, and it damns them all, not just in my eyes, but Ruby's.

I have never been afraid of Ruby, never once in all of the years I've known her. But now I see that I should be; that, if she was anyone other than my friend, I should be following after that man, running as fast and hard as my lungs would let me without bursting.

She might not have had control before, but she does now. It takes a single look from her, and the soldiers, all three, step back as one, set their weapons down, and then move again, pressing their backs to the hallway walls.

There's yelling, voices behind us.

"Ruby! *Ruby!*"

"Sam!"

I shove my way inside, grateful beyond words that it is the two of us alone right now, and Ruby turns and tells Vida, "Keep her outside!"

"Sam!" I hear Mia yell again.

The body.

The body.

The body.

Mia can't see this—I'm sobbing so hard, the rooms in front of me disappear into blotches of color and light as I move through them, searching, and I'm calling for him, I'm calling, even though I know he can't call back.

The kitchen is littered with clear, empty IV bags. There's still one hanging from a thin, silver stand beside where they've stretched out his dark form on the wood table. And my first thought, the one that rises above all the others as I catch myself in the doorway, is that it looks exactly like the one we ate on hundreds of times in the Orfeo kitchen.

"Sam," Ruby says from behind me, "Do you want me to . . . ?"

Do you want me to see? Do you want me to tell you for sure?

I love her for this, I do, but it has to be me. It should be me. I can be strong enough to do this, to force my legs to solidify under me, to wipe my face. I don't want anyone else's hands to touch him.

Liam's voice carries down the hall, through the house, followed by heavy steps on the porch.

"Here," Ruby calls back. "We're . . . we're all right."

I am not all right.

Lucas is so, so still on the table, his normally rich skin a sickly gray ash. His too-long dark hair has fallen across his forehead and I start to reach out, to brush it away, but I catch myself. I have to . . . I have to know for sure, but I can't . . .

The body.

It's the kind of touch I'd use to brush away a stray eyelash on his cheek: light, quick. His skin is still warm.

Somewhere inside he is still burning.

I lower my head down, and in that instant before I give in, close my eyes and scream, I see the slightest movement of his chest rising. I hold my breath, too terrified to move and disturb the moment—but there it is again. There it is.

He is breathing.

I choke out a gasp, a laugh, a sob, all rolled into one. When I look up, it's Charlie pushing into the kitchen, picking up Lucas's wrist, feeling for his pulse.

I want to cover him so they can't see him like this, so weak, so gaunt, not when my Lucas is as bursting with life and light as the first morning of summer. Liam looks as stricken as I feel, and Ruby has her eyes shut. When she opens them, I see the relief there. I know we three have confirmed it in our own ways.

"Lucas?" Mia's panicked voice breaks through the breathtaking relief that swamps me. It pushes everyone into action. I catch a glimpse of Vida's bright hair as Mia slips past Ruby and Liam and rushes over to grab her brother's other hand.

"We need to make a pass through the house, grab any of the camera feeds' hard drives," Liam says. "They can't know we were here."

"The exterior cameras were already switched off, so no

worries there," Vida says. "They must be knee-deep in something sketch to risk that."

A deal. An under-the-table deal to sell Lucas to snatchers.

"I'll have the soldiers deal with the . . ." Ruby trails off before she says *bodies*. God—she's broken all of the rules they set for her, for *me*, and now she's killed *soldiers*.

"It's okay," Ruby says, seeing the terror pull down my face. "It's taken care of. I'll give them a story to explain it. Chubs, can we move him?"

The boy rubs his forehead. "Yes, but he—"

"Good enough for me," Vida says, looking at Liam. "You take his legs. We'll carry him out—and someone grab one of the AK-47s for me, yeah? Cate took mine away."

"I wonder why," Chubs mutters, unhooking the IV bag from the stand and tucking it into the front of Lucas's shirt for now. He turns and grabs the red bag on a nearby counter, the one with the white cross printed on it, and peers inside. "Ooh! Coagulant!"

"Chubs!" Liam grunts, adjusting his grip on Lucas. "Focus!"

"Right, okay, sorry."

The soldiers are gone. So are the bodies. We trample through the blood like it's a puddle of sun-warmed rain, moving at a pace that's slower than a run but faster than a walk and it is agonizing, every second of it, not just for my stupid limp, but because we have him out in the open for anyone to see. All of us are moving targets.

"Get in the back," Liam tells Mia and me when we finally reach the car. "We'll get him laid out between the middle seats."

If he wasn't so thin, there's no way Lucas would ever fit, but he is, and we are running out of time. I keep my hand on him at all times, just to monitor the tiniest movement of his breathing. The car rocks as Liam helps Ruby into the front seat and climbs into the driver's. He doesn't wait until we're buckled up before he speeds us out of there. Mia flies against my side and I have to fight to keep us both upright.

"Way to fuck up my plan, boo," Vida says, reaching forward to punch Ruby's shoulder. "Want to enlighten the rest of us about what the hell just happened?"

Me. I happened. Old Sam came back, as brave and stupid and reckless as always. Ruby was right. I couldn't do it for myself, but I could do it for him.

"Plan changed," Ruby says, looking back to meet my gaze. My heart is still thundering hard enough that I swear I can feel the echo of my pulse in my teeth. Did we get him out—did this really work?

"Who were those men? The ones in the van?" Mia asks. "What were they doing there?"

No one seems to want to tackle that one, so I venture a guess. "Snatchers?"

"Looks like it," Ruby says bitterly. "The reports about the freak market have been all over the press. They must have realized what a gold mine they were babysitting. I'm sure they had the story all figured out for the report on what happened to him."

Liam shakes his head, running a hand back through his hair. "This is turning into a goddamn epidemic."

"Preaching to the fucking choir," Vida says. "Anyone get a plate number off that van?"

"Vi's group is trying to figure out a strategy for the snatchers," Ruby explains. "The Greens are trying to track down all of the different digital copies of the old skip tracer network they've made—that's what they're working from, unfortunately. There seems to be a large, central one that's gone out internationally to bidders."

"They're actually smuggling kids out of the country?" Mia asks, but I can see the real question in her face: *They would have taken us out, too?*

"Yeah, and once they're gone, they're in the wind," Vida says. "And of fucking course, retrieving them isn't priority number one when half of the countries buying them to study or use are the ones involved with the peacekeeper force."

The SUV goes quiet again.

I don't let myself picture it this time. I don't let myself play through what would have happened to Lucas if we hadn't come for him. All that matters right now is that he's safe. That I got him out of that lion's den.

"I need you to explain something me to me, if you can," Ruby says. "I saw something in his mind while we were in the house—I don't want to get your hopes up, but . . ."

"What was it?" Mia asks.

"His mind is . . . it's . . . everyone's mind looks a little different to me, but his is layered. At the top are the memories I'd expect to find, like his training. Thurmond. But there was this one thing— this one image. A tree. A tree house with a line of wildflowers leading up to it. There was something there—a kind of monster?"

Lucas had woven any number of stories with monstrous hearts at the center of them. I'm too scared to breathe. To move. I'm too close to exploding with the hope that unleashes inside me. Mia . . . Mia was right all along?

"Do you remember what it looked like?" I ask.

Charlie and Vida turn back toward Ruby, intrigued, as she

says, "It stood on two legs . . . very hairy, horns on either side of its head, like this—" She demonstrates, cupping her hands over her ears and letting the fingers curl away from her skull. "A nose like a hound's?"

I press my hand against my chest, trying to pin my heart in place. I know what monster she's talking about.

"That's an old one," Mia says quickly. "I don't really remember it, though. Do you?"

I let out a small, harsh little laugh. I have a perfect memory, but only since I've been a Green. My box of memories, all perfectly organized and formed, waiting to be recalled at any given moment, only extends as far back as when my ability manifested. And that was after the Orfeos had moved. After Lucas had told it to me.

"I tried to follow the image through since it was so different than all the others, but I got shut out completely from that part of his memory when I tried to push past it." Ruby raises her brows. "That's not something that happens very often. Almost never. There's a lock on whatever it is, and he's protecting it with everything he has left."

Mia and I look at each other. I see the victory crashing across her face, the tears that she has to cover her eyes to hide.

"It's . . . there's a tree house in their old backyard we used to play in," I say, and it's almost painful to distill what Greenwood is to us into such simple terms. "When we were little. He'd make up stories for us to act out."

"He responded before—yesterday, just a little," Mia says, choking on the words, "when I told him a story about it."

"But you can't remember that specific one?" Ruby asks.

"What are you thinking, darlin'?" Liam asks, uneasy. His eyes dart over to her again. "I see the wheels turning, but they need to be turning in the direction of *home*. I'm pretty sure that we're going to have a hard time explaining him if we just roll up to your house."

"So you want to dump him off somewhere?" Mia challenges. "Wash your hands of him?"

"I'm trying hard as I can to not add to the tally of things they'll hold against her if we get caught," he fires back.

Her jaw juts out. "Then don't get caught."

Vida actually laughs, but she's the only one.

"I'm not sure if this is a good idea or a terrible one, but I really think it could work. Not just on him, but the other Reds, too," Ruby says slowly. "From what I saw of the Reds' training, the Trainers cut into their memories and detached emotions from them by associating certain images and names and places with intense pain and deprivation. I wonder if everything is just so deeply repressed in their minds that they can't function when they're removed from their environment of orders, except to retreat further."

It's confirmation of what both Mia and I have figured out, but the knowledge only drains a little bit more of my hope away.

"No shit?" Vida breathes out. *"Damn."*

"That image, that monster, felt like a path in," Ruby says. "A key that could fit into a lock. If he retreated there because it was a safe place, he might not know how to get himself back out."

"And you think hearing that story again will call it to the front of his mind, and you can access the other memories he's suppressing through it?" Charlie ventures. "Kind of like what you did with Lillian?"

It sounds to me like she's talking about some kind of mental

Trojan horse, that there are paths inside his mind that she can wander down.

"Can we try an experiment?" Ruby asks us. "Can you tell him about Greenwood? Tell a story you do remember?"

I exchange a look with Mia. This is her theory. I want her to be the one to try.

"Hey, Luc," she begins, "do you remember that time we got trapped up in the tree during that freak thunderstorm? The way the whole backyard turned into a swamp . . ."

Her words take flight, weaving in and out and around our silence, as it becomes the story of a sinking ship and of us getting stranded on an island. She talks for an hour, at least, before her voice gets dry and thin, and she finally looks up at Ruby.

She opens her eyes. And, after a moment, shakes her head. "Nothing. He's listening. What you're saying is getting through—it's like little fizzles of images here and there. I can't hold onto any one of them long enough to chase it."

"What are you saying?" Charlie asks.

He's fading, he's too far gone, he's slipping away—

"Do you think he needs that one story?" I ask, finally. It feels too much like a fairy tale for me to really invest much hope into it. Instead of the right prince coming along to wake a sleeping beauty with a kiss, we have a boy who needs the right recipe of words and ideas and images.

"You guys really don't remember it?" she asks. "Is there anyone else who might?"

So it all hangs on this: the one memory I can't touch. Of course.

"My parents, but they're gone," Mia says. "He wrote the stories down, but he—"

I sit straight up. "He wrote them down. He wrote all of the stories down."

"Yeah, and?" Mia asks. "Mom probably threw out all of his journals with the rest of our stuff before we moved—"

"No, she didn't," I interrupt. "Lucas gave them to *me* before you left."

Her dark eyebrows shoot up. "And you seriously think that your parents kept them? That they're still in the old house, and they'll be happy to have you come up and knock on the door?"

I know she doesn't mean that last part to be cruel; it's the truth and we both know it, but it goes down burning like unflavored cough syrup.

"I didn't leave them in my house," I say. "I hid them in the tree house."

Silence sweeps through the car as everyone absorbs this.

"Ruby," Charlie says, taking his glasses off to rub at his forehead, "don't tell me we're going to push back your check-in in the hope that a bunch of notebooks haven't been moved or ruined."

"We are going to push back my check-in in the hope that a bunch of notebooks haven't been moved or ruined," Ruby says.

"Really?" Mia asks, clinging to that thought with every ounce of desperation I feel. I know what Ruby did to me, the way she stowed away my memories of her and retrieved them with all the ease of someone pulling old, dusty file boxes off a shelf. I knew this, but somehow I never once considered that she could help *Lucas*.

I reach down, brush the hair off his face. I reach into his shirt for the IV bag and hang it from one of the car's plastic hooks, watching the liquid drain down the long, thin tube again. It sways each time the SUV hits a rough patch on the road.

"Not to be the proverbial rain on this proverbial parade, but please, God, tell me this house is somewhere in the great commonwealth of Virginia," Liam says. "We're cutting it close as it is."

He's right—I've been the picture of selfishness in going after Lucas, in focusing on him and him alone, when, according to Nico, we have an almost seven-hour drive through the darkening evening ahead of us.

"Bedford's about forty-five minutes from Salem," Ruby tells Liam, and it strikes me all over again how strange it is that despite how close our old towns are, we never would have met in another world.

She looks back, catching my eyes in the rearview mirror. We communicated like this at Thurmond, all stolen glances and raised brows, we had to—no speaking, no touching, nothing. I thought, with all the time we'd been apart, this connection between us would feel brittle, splintered, now that we're back together. But what connects my life and hers is a thread that knots itself back together each time it begins to break. There is a Sam that exists only with Ruby, and when she's gone, that piece of me will disappear.

Are you sure? she's asking.

I hope my message comes through just as strongly. *Yes, please, do everything you can.*

Liam gives her one of those easy smiles, but it doesn't diminish the tightness in his face. "Okay, copilot, you're up."

I don't know if this will work. I have no idea what Ruby is planning to do, exactly, but I accept that things can't always be in our control. The same way you can never get back the connections that were lost, the security you had, the innocence of being a dumb little kid in a world that caters to your every need. So you adjust. Uncertainty never becomes comfortable, but it becomes normal; we learn to deal with it the best we can.

It's not enough for me to learn the rules; I want to be in a position to *make* them. Ruby is right—I feel stronger knowing I have kids to protect. Not just the ones in front of me, but everywhere. The unclaimed ones. The ones being wheeled in against their will to have the procedure done. The ones still out there, running wild, hiding.

I think there is some truth in the idea that gifts come hidden inside burdens. It is so easy for all of us to get caught in the net of wishing for things that were denied to us, to replay over and over the hurt and pain caused by words and hands and weapons. We have lived for too long inside a question the world has posed: if we're even allowed to think of ourselves as human. We have asked ourselves this, and we have doubted. Every single one of us has doubted.

But we are stronger for what's happened to us. *I* am stronger, even if I couldn't see it at first. We have been given the gift of understanding that we can come through struggle and pain. We have built new families in place of the ones that cast us out. We have learned that life is one journey, and the purpose is not to reach some treasure at the end of it, but to find the courage to decide which paths to take, who to travel with, and to let things fall into place as they should and will.

I don't know if this is faith, but I believe that I would never have found Lucas and Mia again if not for everything that happened. That I would never be in the position to help them now if I hadn't taken Ruby's hand all those years ago, when we were just little girls, and she was so scared. There are tests, but there are also small mercies. Life tossed us up into the air, scattered us, and we all somehow found our way back. And we will do it again.

And again.

And again.

A calming sense of gratitude washes over me as I sit back and look out at the approaching night. It stays with me, a warm glow in my veins, until Liam finally breaks the comfortable silence.

"We have company."

There's no one on the highway in front of us, and I doubt there will be for miles yet. But when I turn, I see exactly what he means. A white van, driving without its headlights, is tailing us about three car lengths back. The windows are tinted, too dark to see anyone or anything inside, but I know.

It's the van from the safe house.

"Who wants this one?"

Vida smiles like she's finally caught a fish after spending hours out on a lake. She cracks her neck, then her knuckles, and gestures for Mia and me to scoot aside so she can carefully climb over Lucas to sit between us for a better look.

"Oh, buddy," Liam says, "you picked the *wrong* car."

The van lets out a monstrous groan, a metallic whine as it's lifted off its wheels and flipped onto its nose, its windows exploding out with the force of it. Liam floors the gas pedal and sends us lurching forward.

When I risk a look back, we're far enough away that all I can see are the sparks from the van still smoldering on the road, but even those are swallowed by the light that seems to rain down from the curtain of stars spread across the sky.

FIVE

MIA

THE HOUSE SITS LIKE AN ABANDONED CASTLE AT THE end of Greenwood Lane, slowly drooping into mulch and mud. The early morning light casts it in a soft glow of colors, but I'm too tired and cranky to appreciate the effect. The others took turns driving and napping, but Sam and I didn't sleep at all. I'm too anxious about running out of time—I don't know how long this will take, only that Ruby is risking her freedom for us. She says we have until noon, five hours, but what if this takes longer? What if she has to leave before the job is finished?

What if she can't come back because she's displeased the government?

One side of the house is covered in the overgrown vines that Dad spent years heroically trying to cut down and rip out, only to have them return each spring with a vengeance. The trees have grown so close together that their limbs seem locked in an embrace, and what's left of Mom's carefully—*meticulously*—cultivated flowerbeds have scattered into the lawn, mingling with the bright heads of wild milkweed and thistle, the white, frothy patches of Queen Anne's lace.

If the missing strips of wood siding and the busted-in door aren't enough of a sign that the place is empty—*vacant*—the fact that the sign, the one I hated so much, is still there at the end of the driveway is proof enough for me: FORECLOSURE: FOR SALE BY BANK.

Sam's memory is perfect. She knew exactly which streets to take to find our old neighborhood, and then our street. I let all of that information bleed out of my head when we drove away that last time because I never thought we'd come back.

I never told Lucas that. He believed Mom when she promised we would; he was still crying a little about having to leave Sam behind. Luc could be blind to things, and I think he honestly thought he could will that happy ending into existence, if he only wished hard enough.

Here we are, though, at a house that isn't a home. The upstairs windows are broken, the garage door is half-collapsed, and the old red mailbox has disappeared completely. I used to lie in my bunk and close my eyes, strain to remember exactly what this place looked like, try to catch that last image I had of it looking back through the rear window as we drove away. It's been frozen in time inside of my head, like the cursed sleeping kingdom in Lucas's story about Greenwood. Seeing it now in this state pries my chest open. We have aged, and so has the house. We grew up without each other.

"How are we looking, Vi?" Liam asks, killing the car's engine.

"All clear, as far as I can tell," she says. "I'm going to take a few laps around the block, just to be sure."

"I know it's pointless to say this to you," Charlie says as she opens her door, "but if you see trouble, at least entertain the thought of running away from it."

I cannot figure these two out, and her response—blowing him a kiss and then immediately giving him the finger—does nothing to help me there. It feels like watching a hawk snuggle up to an owl.

"Hey—hey, darlin', we're here." Liam reaches over and brushes Ruby's hair behind her ear. She doesn't stir or yawn; I see her eyes open in the rearview mirror and realize that she hasn't been sleeping at all. If anything, she looks even more exhausted than before.

"Anything?" she asks, turning back to us hopefully.

Sam grabbed Lucas's hand the moment we crossed into Virginia, and she hasn't let go since. She shakes her head. "The same."

"Okay," she says, straightening up in her seat. "We'll find the notebook, then."

So Ruby has been . . . *working*, I guess? No one came right out and said it—almost like that word, *Orange*, has a power to it that no one wants to summon—*invoke*—but I've got enough pieces to fit the puzzle together. This whole drive, she's been inside of Lucas's head.

"Chubs and I will have a look around the house, make sure no one is poking around or squatting," Liam tells her, reaching into the glove compartment for something—oh. A gun.

They have this system down to an art. These kids, they came stocked with food and water, extra canisters of gas so we wouldn't need to stop at one of the overcrowded stations. They know which roads to take to avoid unwanted eyes, someone always watches to make sure they aren't being tailed, and, honestly, they don't seem to feel a fraction of the fear that's rocking every last one of my nerves. I'm jealous—I'm so jealous of what they have, and how surviving seems to come so easy to them when Sam and I failed so miserably at it.

I don't like Liam, but I like the way he looks at Ruby, the way they seem to be able to hold conversations without words. I like that he kisses her hand sometimes, the way knights do in the old legends, or heroes do in Mom's favorite movies.

But he's not happy about helping us—helping *Lucas*—so I'm not happy with *him*.

"Which one was yours?" Ruby asks Sam.

"That one, right there." Sam nods at the stumpy brick house on the next lot over. It gives me a little evil swell of satisfaction to see their perfect—*manicured*—lawn looking just as feral as ours. To see Mrs. Dahl's perfect white fence in pieces on the wild grass. I'll never forget the way the witch grabbed my right ear and gave it a yank, sharp enough to turn it red for hours, after I accidentally knocked into the fence with a soccer ball. After that, and the screaming terror Mom unleashed on the cold woman, I made sure to have loads more "accidents."

"I barely recognize it." Sam rubs her thumb over the curve of Lucas's hand absently.

"I tried to find them after the press conference, to see if they'd picked you up without anyone noting it," Ruby says carefully. "I couldn't find a record of address for them."

There isn't a FOR SALE sign out like every other house on this street, but all the windows are boarded up and the carport is empty.

Sam shrugs. "It's . . . whatever."

I wish I could think of something to say, but I'm not so sure that Sam really needs to be comforted. I get it now; this is what I needed to see to slam the point home. She's as much of an orphan as Lucas and I are—but our parents didn't *want* to leave us. They didn't have a choice. Hers did.

And I threatened to leave her, too. The idea makes my stomach go sour.

"It's sort of sick," Sam says, "but Thurmond felt like more of a home than this place."

"That's because home isn't four walls," Ruby says, "it's the people you're with."

Sam lets out a soft laugh. "I guess so. Are the other girls okay? Did they ever find out what happened to Ashley?"

Ruby smooths her dark hair back, a shadow passing over her bright green eyes. "The girls are all fine. Everyone's just been worried about you. I'll tell you about Ash later—after we get Lucas on his feet, okay?"

"That bad?" Sam says, shaking her head.

It's late afternoon now, and the warm light almost tricks my eyes into thinking some color is back in Lucas's face.

"Does he have to remember?" Sam asks suddenly. "When all of this is over and he comes out of this, does he have to remember what the Trainers did to him?"

Why wouldn't he? Unless Ruby . . . my suspicion solidifies into a real answer. Ruby *can* affect someone's memory. Vida and I were too far away from the house to really see what was going on, but we did pass one of the men as he ran away. Vida didn't seem worried about it—no one seemed worried about the blank faces of the soldiers, or how they would explain the dead bodies.

Because Ruby gave them a memory they didn't have?

"I'm worried about . . . the feelings," Sam continues. "Even if the images are gone, will he still feel that pain?"

Ruby gives her this small, heartbreaking smile I don't

understand. "I'm better than I used to be. When he comes out of this, I can suppress everything—if that's what he wants."

"Can't you just do it right away? Before he remembers it?" I ask.

"Sometimes protecting yourself from the pain only makes it harder to face in the long run," Ruby says. "He'll be the one to make the choice."

I look to Sam, trying to get her read on this. She lets out a soft, tired breath, but nods. Outside of the SUV, Liam appears at the front door, Chubs trailing behind him.

"Are you sure you can do it?" Sam asks.

"I can sure as hell try," Ruby says. "It'll just take time."

Which, judging by the empty IV bags Sam unhooks, and by the way Luc's skin has shrunk around his bones, we might not have much of after all.

I can't stand to be in the house.

I step through the front door, and it's like a portal into some strange mirror world where things are the same, but horribly— *hideously*—different. My skin itches, tightening over my skull. The air in my lungs is full of mildew and damp air, but there's a trace of us still clinging to it. Mom took so much pride in our home that seeing it like this turns my fingers to claws again. It is filthy. The outdoors has come trampling in, leaving muddy stains on the walls and floors. A tree branch has broken through the living room window, spreading glass all over the sunny yellow armchairs and the empty space where a piano used to be.

It's the holes that I see first: the pictures that Mom and Dad took off the walls to bring with us, the pots and pans hanging over the kitchen island, little porcelain trinkets here and there.

When we left, we only took what we could fit in the car. A lot of stuff was tossed out, but the rest belonged to the house, which now belonged to the bank, which would then pass it on to whoever could afford it. The house didn't sell, obviously, and no one cared enough to come in and cover the furniture. The heirlooms and electronics have been picked over, stolen, and whoever took them left the back door wide open.

Both Ruby and Sam watch me move through the kitchen, then the living room, like they're waiting for me to blow my last fuse. I walk over to the back door to slide it shut, only to find the glass pane is missing entirely from it.

I'm sorry, I think, squeezing my eyes shut. *I'm sorry. . . .* For the first time in my life, I am grateful that my parents aren't alive to see what's left of our lives.

Home isn't four walls, it's the people you're with. I repeat Ruby's words over and over until I can feel the truth of them working under my skin.

"Where should we put him?" Liam asks. He and Chubs have followed us in, Lucas between them. "I maybe wouldn't recommend upstairs. We found a family of raccoons that were not particularly happy to see us—whoa—!"

Lucas dips dangerously to the ground as the boys both seem to jump slightly back, fighting the instinct to drop their hands and let him fall. Ruby and Sam both rush over.

His eyes are open, seeing everything and nothing.

There is a second of silence; we're all stunned stupid, I think. But then his expression contorts—contracts into an ugly snarl, and whatever strength is left in his too-thin limbs flares. He thrashes at them weakly, trying to twist out of their grip—or trying to attack them?

The air blows out of my lungs. My chest closes up. The world shrinks to the wall that he's facing, the one lone picture that we somehow missed in our last sweep of the house. The little family portrait hangs crookedly, all of our dusty smiles slanting down to the floor.

"Help—*a little help, please!*" Charlie says to Ruby, his voice high and thin with the effort of holding onto Lucas. "Turn him off!"

The picture bursts into flame.

The fire spills across the wall and, with nothing to stop it, catches the thin, brittle fabric of the ragged curtains. Liam swears loudly as he and Chubs both drop Lucas to the floor and begin to shake out their hands, which look blistered red. He tries to catch Ruby's arm to pull her back, but she kneels down and puts a calming hand on Lucas's chest, even as he tries to knock a fist into the side of her head.

"Oh, *hell* no!" The front door slams behind Vida. She sprints through the smoke and stoops to pick up a pillow from the couch, tossing one to a frantic Sam and taking the other for herself. She and Sam start beating the flames with them, trying to keep the fire from spreading to the carpet.

And me, I . . .

They did poison this place for him.

Our home.

They made him hate us.

I can't stand here—I can't stare at the evidence of my world crumbling to ash. I am the biggest fool in the world. I'm an *idiot.* He's never going to snap out of this. We never should have brought him back here. All we've done is upset him, cause him even more pain than he's already in.

I just need . . .

I need air that's cooler.

I need . . .

I push past Sam and Vida, ignoring their voices as they call after me. I *run*, and I don't know where I'm going, only that it's not back into the house, not yet, maybe not ever again.

The backyard is worse than the front. It's a maze of hedges and trees, and for a moment, I feel too overwhelmed by the unfamiliar sight to move.

And then I hear Lucas's voice; I hear it in the wind that moves through the chimes he and I made out of cans and old silverware for Mom's birthday when we didn't have money for anything else. The smell of sap and damp earth and green life curls on it, drawing me forward like a beckoning finger. I want to fight it, but I can't.

Place your steps inside the footprints left behind by the giants. . . .

I find the stepping stones Dad laid out, and kick the dirt and dead leaves from them. I used to have to hop from one to the next, but now I'm tall enough to walk over them, step by step, until the path curls toward the side of the house.

Don't drink the water, the sorceress poisoned the well. . . .

I cut around the old stone birdbath we inherited from the woman who owned the house before us, stepping carefully through the brambles trying to tug at my jeans.

Walk toward the place where the sunlight turns the leaves to green glass. . . .

The trees grow so tall, so close to one another, that they create a canopy over my head. There's still enough sunlight to warm the leaves, turning them almost clear—*translucent*—until I can see the dark ridges of their spines and the veins that web across them.

But they're nothing compared to our tree.

It seems impossible, but it's still in one piece. The platform that stretches between the old tree's sturdiest limbs, the walls Dad painstakingly measured and cut. Even the thick rope we used to climb up is still hanging, swaying with each faint breeze that rushes up behind me, teasing my hair.

I close my fingers around the rough hemp and give it a tug, testing to see if it'll still hold my weight. I'm not tall by any means, or even that big, but we didn't come all this way for me to fall and break my neck, thank you very much.

It's harder to climb than I remember, even with my feet braced against the rough trunk. The muscles in my arms, shoulders, and back are burning by the time I reach up and grip the lip of the entryway cut into the floor of the tree house and, with one last heave, slip up through it. Two birds scatter, flying out through the small porthole window in a flurry of feathers and wings.

The tree house, the heart of Greenwood, is exactly the same. I know now for sure that Sam took care of it after Lucas and I left, kept everything in its right place. There are old, yellowed books piled up in the far corner, their pages wrinkled and dried stiff after too many rainstorms and water gun fights. The old rug we dragged from the living room is coated in thick dust, but brushing a hand across it is enough to reveal the vivid blues, reds, and gold woven into its pattern.

It feels like I'm in a dollhouse—like Alice trapped in Wonderland after she drinks the potion that makes her grow so big. I can't believe we used to fit in those small chairs. That any of us, least of all Lucas, used to be able to *stand up* in here. I draw my knees up, tucking them against my chest, waiting to feel it, that trace of magic that was scattered over this place like fairy dust.

But I keep thinking of what Ruby said about *home*, that it's not an actual place you leave or return to, and I think I see her point now. All of my memories of this place are colored by the old, perfect magic of imagination, made even brighter by the complete and utter lack of it at our camp in South Dakota. The world outside—the one I dreamt about—was all vivid flowers, streams that curled like slick-scaled serpents, clouds that held idle, happy conversations with each other as they passed by.

The world I see today is bruised with poverty; it is filled with people who are like us, wandering, trying to recapture what they used to have. Maybe they will come back to their old homes now, too. Maybe they will learn what I've learned: you can't. The way that every gentle breeze feels the same, but you can't capture the same one twice.

Greenwood was never the tree house or the woods around us, it was me and it was Sam and it was Lucas. I wanted to come back here for Lucas, but there was another selfish reason, too—I wanted to come back home and find some thread of my parents, the family I had, that I could pick up and knot around my heart. I wanted to find some part of them still here.

But they are gone.

I feel . . . is there a word for this? I look for my dictionary in the corner with the other books, wondering if all of the pages are still flagged the way I liked. And on top of them all sits a stack of spiral-bound notebooks, just where Sam said they'd be. I'm too scared to touch them, to prove that I'm not imagining them there. Is it really possible no one has come back to this place in all the years since we left it? Since Sam, its last guardian, was taken away?

There's a sound, a whistle that comes from below. I lean over the tree house's entrance, and spot the intruder right away.

"This is some set-up you guys had." Liam's hands are stuffed into the pockets of his leather jacket. Some of my irritation disappears when I realize he's not poking fun at me for coming here—he's serious. There's real admiration in his voice.

"My dad built it," I tell him proudly. It took him months, and he almost broke his leg when he fell out of it.

"I always wanted something like this," he says, doing a lap around the trunk. "We didn't have any trees big enough to support the big, strapping Stewart boys, though."

I roll my eyes. "Uh-huh."

"Can I come up? Take some notes on how he put it together?"

I hesitate, catching the instinctive *No! You don't have a key!* before it can pass my lips. "Why? Thinking about building your house in a tree somewhere?"

He shrugs. "I was just thinking I might build one for my kids one day."

That . . . is not what I expected him to say. I lean back, which he takes as permission to climb up. I'm too surprised by how far his vision of the future extends, and too curious about why.

"Whoa," he says as his blond head pops up and gets a glimpse of our old set-up. His blue eyes go wide. *"Cool!"*

"Didn't all those scientists decide the freak mutation would pass itself on?" I blurt out, watching as he runs his hands over the supports holding up the roof and along the walls. He's serious—he really wants to understand how this thing is standing.

"That's what everyone says," he replies. "But with a few notable exceptions, I like us freaks just fine. They won't have to go through half of what we did, and at least they won't have to figure out how to control their abilities alone like we did."

"Unless everyone is forced to get those implants—the procedure," I point out.

"We'll see about *that*," is his only answer.

After he's had his fill of exploring the tiny space and peering out our window, he sits down across from me, crossing his legs. "I'm thinking we maybe got off on the wrong foot. . . . I had a real knot in my tail this morning, and I'm sorry."

It's not okay, so I don't let him off the hook by telling him it is. But I do believe him. The guilt is plain on his face, like it's been gnawing on him.

"Lucas is okay now," he promises. "Ruby got him calmed down again."

I nod, throat thick.

"I think you and Sam are incredible for making it through and protecting him. Keeping each other safe."

I don't know about *incredible*, but I would definitely classify us as strong-willed—*recalcitrant*. "Thanks, but I know why you were upset and I get it. I do."

His brows lift at that. "You do?"

"I like Ruby, and it's dangerous for her to be out in the world right now. But we *really* would have been screwed if you hadn't come and risked it." Lucas especially. He would have been lost to us forever. I am grateful, and I understand better why he wanted her back in Zone 1 as soon as possible. If the snatchers have some kind of "in" with soldiers to cut these deals, the way they did with Lucas, there should be a small army around Ruby at all times to protect her, to keep someone else from stealing her away from the life she deserves.

He scratches at the stubble on his jaw. "It's . . . Christ, it's so bad. The threats are one thing, but the asking price for her on the black market isn't just a million dollars, it's *hundreds* of millions of dollars. She is . . . one of a kind. In every way. And I'm the one that let the world know about it. This is all my fault."

Wow. I didn't realize anyone still had that kind of money. But—not the point, Mia. The point is that I can hear the pain vibrating in his voice, no matter how he tries to brighten it. I can tell he wants to talk about this exactly as much as he doesn't want to, and I make the decision for him.

"What do you mean?"

"I made a huge mistake letting the reporter we worked with do such a huge profile on her," he explains. "Chubs and Vi were both worried, but it felt so important to me. Ruby says it's fine, but it's not. I thought it would show people how brave and amazing she is, but for a lot of people in this country, it's had the opposite effect. If they're not scared of her, they want to hunt her for her skin. We might have been able to keep what she could do a secret from the public—the government could have sealed her records. But it's out there now, and it always will be, and I regret the hell out of it."

"If she says it's fine, you should believe her," I say. It hasn't seemed like she's holding any kind of grudge to me. I'm sure there's a swirl of emotions churning beneath her calm surface, but from what I can tell, she's the calmest—the most *serene*—of all of us. It's easier to feel braver when I see the steady courage in her. "You can't make decisions about her life for her."

"I know, I know—I just want her to think twice before making these calls, really put the danger into context," he explains. "She's made peace with what she can do, but she had to fight *so damn hard* to get there. I know I was the definition of an ass earlier, but I just don't want her to feel like she has a responsibility to help every single person she comes across, or that she owes it to Cruz or whoever to fight for them."

He takes a deep breath, raking his hand back through his shaggy hair, muttering to himself now more than to me. "She's fought enough. We've all lost enough, haven't we?"

I can't argue with him there. If anyone deserves a warm cup of milk, a nap, and a lifetime supply of cookies, it's probably these kids.

"What did you lose?" I ask him, and no sooner are the words out of my mouth than my brain fires, connecting two wandering dots in rapid succession: *newspaper articles, Stewart.*

In the back of my mind, I'd thought he looked familiar. That I'd seen his face *somewhere*, and just chalked it up to the news. But now I have context, and understanding blooms in my heart.

"Was your brother the one that was killed?" I strain back into my memory for the name. "Cole?"

"Ah . . ." Liam swallows hard, rubs his hand over his face. "Yeah. Yeah, he was."

"So we have something in common," I say. "Your brother was like Luc, right?"

He nods, glancing up at the ceiling of the tree house. And now I'm the one who feels like crap, like an idiot, for snarling at him in the car.

"But . . . not like Luc?" I press.

"Not from the sound of it," he says finally. "We didn't really have . . . I guess we didn't really even have a relationship? I don't know. He was never straight with us. He didn't even tell me he was a Red until the day before he was . . . until he . . ."

"Don't say *passed away*," I tell him, drawing from my own

terrible well of experience. "Say he *died*. Death is horrible. We shouldn't give it a pretty name. I only know what was in the paper and on the news, but from the sound of it, it *was* horrible. Those people stole his life."

"*I* stole it." He breathes the words out like a secret he's kept too long. "He died protecting *me*. Covering *me* so I could get out. There's not a day—" Liam sucks in a sharp breath. "I'm sorry, I don't mean to get angry—this isn't the reason I came out here."

"You should be angry!" I tell him, and the monster inside me nods in agreement. "You should be furious!"

"But I'm angry with *him*," he confesses. "That's what's so wrong about it. I *am* furious that he hid what he was and felt shame over it, when our family would never have loved him less for it. And I can't even tell you how unfair it is that I only got ten hours with him—*ten hours*—after I finally found out."

I can't begin to imagine this. The second we found out what Lucas was, what he could do, the only thing that changed in our lives was Mom scraping together money to buy spray to make our blankets in the car more fire-resistant. And Dad saying, in his Dad way, "At least we won't have to learn how to start a campfire by hand!"

"Did your brother have a temper?" he asks. "Sorry, I mean, *does* he have a temper? Does he feel at odds with himself?"

"He might now," I say, "I'm not sure. We didn't have that much time together after he went through the change. But no . . . he really didn't have a temper. He's—he *was* a big softie. I think he was scared of what he could do, though, just a little bit. Was your brother like that?"

"I think he pretty much hated himself," Liam says, voice flat. "He hid it in plain sight and used it to his advantage when he had to, but I'm still not really sure he was ready to admit he was one of us. I guess I shouldn't expect all of the Reds to be the same. Lord knows I'm not like every other Blue on the planet. But I do think there's another layer that comes with being Red—being Orange, too."

"Like the fear that you're not just *wrong*, but you're *extra wrong*?"

He nods. "Which isn't true, but it doesn't invalidate the way they feel."

I wonder if Lucas thought—*thinks*—about himself like that?

"Well, if you're wrong, then I'm wrong, too. I've never admitted this, but . . . sometimes I blame Lucas for not fighting harder. When I'm really angry about it, I even wish he had killed the PSFs that took us."

It feels weirdly good to admit this to someone, like draining an infected wound.

"That's nothing to be ashamed of," he says.

"It is if you know Lucas," I explain. "He's not a fighter or a killer. He doesn't have it in his heart. I'm mad at my parents, too. I'm mad they made us leave this house. Sometimes I'm even mad that I survived. Do you ever feel that way?"

"I used to," Liam says slowly. "At the beginning. Before I was ever in a camp, I was living rough outside—cold, miserable, alone. But you have to weigh that against what you've done with your time, and and what you can do now. Make it count."

"What if you have no idea what you're supposed to do?" I ask. "I want to be useful, I don't want to sit around and wait for things to change. I'm not exactly great at surviving out here, or fighting, but I want to help other kids."

"Well, let's think about this, because there are ways to help beyond what you're saying. And I think the time for fighting—the kind of fighting we were doing, at least—is over for now, and we need to get creative in the way we go after what we want," he says. "Is there something you really love? Something that speaks to you?"

Were we really allowed to think about this now? "I like . . . stories. Words."

"Well, good news, buddy, there are plenty of us terrible at those exact things." Liam lets out a faint laugh. "And if there's one thing these months have taught me, it's how crucial it is to be able to tell our story in our own words, and not let anyone else warp the truth around us. You definitely have a skill for drawing it out of people. Look at how much I've managed to unload on you already—sorry about that, by the way."

It startles me how much I love this idea—how it does feel like striking back against a world that's quickly trying to erase the evidence of what we've been through.

"Are you serious? Do you think kids would want to tell me their stories, and I could help them record it in some way?"

"Definitely," Liam says. "Sometimes people need help putting what they've been through into words. They can't articulate how they feel."

I feel so bright hearing this, like a star has just formed in the center of my ribs and is blasting out for all the world to see; this small idea spirals into a thousand little ones about how I could make this work. My monster will eat the pain of others. It will devour their hurt as it pours out of them.

"Thank you for trying to help my brother," I say. "I'm really sorry about what happened to Cole. . . . I can't . . ." I don't finish my thought, because I *can* imagine how it would feel to lose Lucas. I am right on the edge of that gulf of pain.

"Do you think the memory of someone should dictate how we live going forward?" he asks, threading and unthreading his fingers together.

"It depends," I say. "I think you can probably honor someone's memory, but you can't live for them, because that means living in the past. Does this have to do with Ruby wanting to help the other Reds? She knew your brother too, right?"

He nods. "If Cole couldn't help them, then isn't it my responsibility to finish the job for him, make sure those kids are safe and treated right? But then I start to think . . . isn't it time to let someone else take care of things? Does it always have to be Ruby?" Liam messes up the hair he's just smoothed down. "I know I don't have the right to make the decision for her, but I can't get the thoughts out of my head every time we take a risk. What happens if we go, and something happens to Ruby—God, what happens if I lose her, too? What happens if the government tries to punish her, and I'm not fast enough or strong enough to help her?"

"I don't know," I say. "But what's the alternative? You two run off and go into hiding for the rest of your lives? You have a little herd of kids and build tree houses for them?"

He lets out a choked laugh. "Sounds nice."

"Sounds kind of boring," I say. "But I guess what I mean is, being afraid can't be a reason for us *not* to do something now. It's going to be dangerous anywhere we go, and all those people in Washington are trying to establish rules and laws, and we have to make sure that we're part of shaping that, too."

"Our voice will only get louder the more of us we bring together," Liam agrees.

"So I guess our role now is to do the best we can to make sure we don't lose anyone else," I finish. "No matter what."

"We'll take care of our own." Liam reaches over and puts a hand on top of my head affectionately, the way Lucas used to. "You know, I did come out here to comfort *you*."

"You did," I say, looking over at the entrance to the tree house. Talking to him has helped me clarify what I want. It's made me realize that, no matter what happens to Lucas, I can't be afraid, either.

"Do you really think Ruby can help Lucas?"

His smile is so warm, so genuine, I find myself returning it. "Of course. My girl? She's incredible."

"Mia?" someone calls.

Liam and I both lean over the entrance. Sam is standing below, one hand braced on the old tree's trunk. She looks as amazed as I felt to find it still standing.

"What's wrong?" I ask. "Is Lucas . . . ?"

Sam shakes off whatever feeling had gripped her. "Are the notebooks up there?"

"Yeah," I call back. "I'll bring them down."

"Okay, good," Sam says softly. "Good. Ruby's ready when we are."

"I'm ready now," I tell her, and start the climb down.

It's fully morning now, eight o'clock; the sun has crept up on us, combing its fingers through the last fading traces of night. I can still smell the smoke as I step through the door. The burnt photo is gone, and all that's left is a large smudge of black and a gaping hole in the plaster, where the house's old bones show through. My eyes find Lucas immediately, stretched out across the couch. Ruby is sitting in a chair beside him, one hand over where his hands are resting on his stomach, her eyes closed. Behind me

Liam tenses, takes a step toward her, but stops himself and turns to where Vida and Charlie are pulling food out of a bag I saw earlier in the trunk of their big SUV. He never takes his eyes off her, but he lets her work.

It takes Sam and me a few minutes to find the right story in the right notebook—at least, I hope it's the right story. My blood feels like it's throbbing inside my veins as Sam passes it over to me and says, "Why don't you read it?"

I'm clutching the notebook so tightly, I'm afraid it's going to rip in half. The years have made it delicate, just as they've made me stronger.

I glance back. Liam is leaning back against the kitchen island, his arms crossed over his chest. He gives me another one of his smiles, and nods. "Give it a whirl, buddy. What do you have to lose?"

Our last chance, best chance? Because if this doesn't work . . .

It will work.

I sit down beside Ruby, trying to mimic how relaxed she seems as I lay the notebook across my lap. There is so much here—witches, princes, storms, curses, knights—and it feels like a secret history of our childhood, the real one that no one could steal. I wonder if I'm betraying him by reading it aloud for everyone else to hear.

"It's okay," Sam promises, sitting next to me. Of course she understands.

My chest tightens at the sight of Lucas's messy handwriting. I clear my throat.

"'There once was a prince who loved to roam through his kingdom, even though his parents, the king and queen, warned him of all the dangers that lurked in the woods. But he was brave, and he was curious, and he wanted to know not just what was in the trees, but what lay beyond them. So one morning the prince woke early, packed food and a blanket, and he went to see for himself.'"

I look up, but my hope is stomped out a second later when I see that his eyes are still closed, that he's barely moving at all.

"Keep going," Sam says, putting a hand on my shoulder. "He hears you. Keep going."

"'The prince rode his horse for hours, until he had gone farther than he ever imagined possible. The woods were like a maze, but every now and then a tree would lift its roots from the ground and point them in the direction he was meant to head. The trees would shake down a curtain of leaves if he turned the wrong way. But he soon realized that he should not have listened to them, that they had tricked him, because the path they led him on was treacherous, and at the first shriek of a hawk, his horse threw him. He lay there, hurt, until a woman dressed in robes of white and gold stepped into his path.'"

Still nothing. I don't need to glance at him to know. Sam's breathing becomes harsher, pained.

"'This was no ordinary woman. Her beauty was unearthly, and the trees, the forest, were hers to command. She was the queen of them all, a witch. In revenge for her banishment by the prince's father, she cast a spell on the prince. His hands became claws, his skin fur, his ears horns, his mouth a snout filled with razor-sharp teeth. The witch laughed and laughed, telling him that he'd never be free—that the only way to reverse the spell was to find the one person brave enough to face him.

"'The prince ran back through the forest. Brave hunters saw him and ran away. Villagers screamed as he passed by them on the road. And he knew he could not go home, not as he was; so he returned to the forest, to the trees that rustled their leaves in laughter, to the other animals, who fled at the sight of him. He lived in this place for years, alone.'"

I don't want to cry, but I do. He is not moving. This is not working. I look over at Ruby. Her brows are drawn together, and her hand seems to be shaking. I don't know if it's good or bad, but she is still working. I need to give her more time.

Keep going.

"'One day, his friend the stable girl begged to be allowed to look for the prince. As the years passed, stories of the beast in the woods had spread far and wide. Many believed the prince had been devoured by it; even his parents began to mourn him. They told her she would not survive alone in the thick of the trickster trees, that the witch would find her and turn her into stew. But she did not believe them. She wished only to find her friend. So one morning she packed her own food and blanket, and set out to find him.

"'No sooner had she passed into the woods than she heard the beast's roar. Her courage failed her, and she wanted to run back out onto the road, but she thought of her friend, how much she missed him, and kept going. Soon she realized the beast wasn't angry, and his roars weren't ones of hunger, but of pain. She followed the sound until she saw its hideous body stretched out beside a stream. Its teeth snapped at the air as it whirled toward her, and its roar nearly deafened her. But the girl saw what was wrong. Its foot was caught in an iron trap. *Let me help you,* she said to him, and to herself, *Do not be afraid.*

"'Using all of her strength, she pried open the iron trap and pulled its foot free. The beast did not attack her. It whimpered, its leg bleeding and ruined. So she tore up her blanket into bandages and wrapped it in them. And when the beast still cried, she found herself reaching around it, holding it. And then something extraordinary happened, and at her touch, the beast turned into a lion; but still she did not let go. It became a serpent, but still she did not let go. . . . And at last it became . . .'" I press my hand to my face, my throat too tight to finish. I need a moment. I need just a second to . . . breathe . . . to be brave again. . . .

"'. . . a boy.'"

Sam's fingers dig into my shoulder so hard, it's the only reason I know I didn't imagine the voice. She and I both stand, leaning over him, holding each other up.

"You . . . gotta tell it right, Mia. . . ."

"Luc?" I say, too shocked to move. "Lucas?"

It's a struggle for him to open his eyes, but he does, looking between us. His forehead wrinkles. "Had . . . the strangest dream . . . but you're both . . ." He turns to Sam, terror raining down through his expression. "We didn't make it. . . ."

She takes his hand, presses it against her cheek. "We did. We're okay now."

Ruby slips out of her chair, and in the second before her dark hair falls around her face, I see that her cheeks are wet with tears. Liam is there to meet her, to wrap an arm around her shoulders, kiss her forehead, lead her outside. I can see their outlines, the way their two shapes have become one. I don't know if she is crying for Lucas, if she is as relieved and caught in wonder as we are, or if she's crying for the Red, the one she lost. I think it's all of these things.

"Mia . . . *Mia*." Lucas's voice cracks on my name.

"Let me get you some water—some—" I start to rise, shaking. Every one of my senses is overwhelmed.

His arm comes up, pulls me forward as he struggles to sit up. Sam is there to lift him the rest of the way, and suddenly I'm in his arms, and it's familiar and strange and wonderful and unbelievable. He is here. He's come back.

"I found you," he's saying, over and over, "I found you. . . ."

"We found *you*," I inform him. "Well, actually, Sam found both of us."

"Of course she did." Lucas chuckles, and I think, *That is the best sound.* "Still taking care of us, aren't you, Sunshine?"

Sam closes her eyes, her face pink with the force of holding back her tears. "Always."

But then he stiffens, tensing with a sharp breath. I look back as Charlie comes up behind us, plates of food in his hands. Vida trails behind him a step, arms full of water bottles. They hang back, but I can read the curiosity in their faces.

"They're our friends," I tell him. "And we have a story to tell you."

I sit beside my brother, in a circle of kids who laugh and talk and joke and even sing; we are sharing food between us, making plans, seeing a future that didn't exist before.

And I am not surprised, not in the least, when Lucas says suddenly, "I want to help you. With the others."

The conversation skids into silence. Liam turns to Ruby for her take at the same moment she turns to him. We've propped Lucas up against the back of the couch, and every now and then he has to lean his head back onto the cushion, like it's too heavy to keep upright for long. His features are still sunken, and he has these shadows around his eyes, but I feel the parts of the brother I knew surfacing, bit by bit, as time rolls on around us.

"Lucas," Ruby begins, "are you sure? There's a chance this could explode in our faces—Cruz might not let me have access to the Reds, and even if she does, she might insist that you have to stay at the facility with the others."

I'm grateful she's giving him the truth, but fear still has the power to electrify my every last nerve, until I have to bite my tongue to keep from telling him no.

"Seriously?" Sam asks, looking between them. "Lucas—"

He gives her a weak smile. "I know I'm still a little pathetic to look at, but I'm willing to take that risk, and I will. You don't—well, I guess you *do* understand what they went through," he says to Ruby. "After seeing all of it, you don't think I'd want to be there for them on the other side of this? Help them ease back into the world?"

She looks a little sick at that, but nods all the same. "We would appreciate any help—you wouldn't have to come with us, not if you don't feel up to it."

"What if it's the same facility they kept you in before?" Sam presses. "It could be overwhelming—"

"The difference is, this time I'm myself again," Lucas says softly. "If the Trainers are gone, it won't be so bad. I lived there for almost as long as I lived in this house."

"No," Sam says sharply, "you shouldn't have to live through all of that—you shouldn't have to *see* it again—"

He reaches over, locking his hand over hers, weaving their fingers together. She quiets, but the panic in her face is as obvious as my own heart thundering in my ears. This is too much. He shouldn't have to.

"What can't I face, knowing that in the end, we made it?" Lucas turns back to Ruby, tapping his temple. "Think you can stand poking around in that many minds? It seems like it would be like picking up a thousand splinters of glass."

She seems surprised by this, as do the others, even Liam. I wonder if they haven't understood this one key element—*facet*—of her abilities. That, as powerful as she is, Ruby still is burdened by thoughts and memories and images that don't belong to her. She relives other people's nightmares every time she does this.

"We'll go through it together," she tells him. "And it won't be so bad. Are you sure?"

"Won't he relapse?" Charlie asks. "Go back to his earlier state? No offense, but there is such a thing as post-traumatic stress disorder."

Everything in me grinds to a halt. It never even occurred to me that he *could* go back to the way he was, now that he has come through.

Lucas shrugs. "No offense taken."

Ruby takes a moment to consider this before meeting Lucas's worried gaze. "No, but you have to face any memories of the training head-on. No matter how much they hurt, you can't pull back from them again."

We can all see the scars on his neck, his arms, some still knitting themselves back together. And even I wonder if he's ready for this—if he'll ever really be. The thing about Lucas is, he's never had the kind of obvious, outward strength that all the stories prescribe—the kind that comes to easily to Sam. His touch in life has always been softer. It is a quiet determination, one that wants to believe in the good of things, even as the bad is breathing down his neck. He sets his jaw and nods.

"Can you fill me in on what's happened, though?" he asks. Lucas's right hand jerks. He clasps the wrist hard with his left hand, stilling it. "Is Gray still alive?"

"As far as we know," Liam says. "He's in hiding. Why?"

"The Reds . . . we were made to understand from the beginning that it was *his* program, that we were serving him directly. I just . . . want to make sure that they're far away from him."

"Shit," Vida says. "I didn't even think about that. He could just as easily use that compound as a place to gather up a resistance force, give the peacekeepers a real fight."

I see my own dread reflected on everyone's face, even Ruby's.

But then Chubs says, "Let's operate under the assumption of hope that he's smart enough to know he's been beat. I have to imagine his number one priority at this point is not getting caught. He's probably halfway around the world, hiding in some cave."

Operate under the assumption of *hope*. What a novel idea.

Vida looks at the time on her cell phone, then holds it up for us to read. Eleven o'clock. If it really is a forty-five minute drive to Salem, we're cutting it close. "If we're going to do this, we need to jet back over to Ruby's."

"Drop us off," Liam says. "You and Chubs have to go back to D.C. to check in with Cate and Zu and Nico and let them know what's going on."

"We'll wait until you get there to deal with Cruz." Vida looks over at Lucas. "Would you be willing to make a video we can show her?"

"You won't need to," Lucas says. "I'm going with you. I'll meet her in person."

"Lucas . . ." Sam starts.

"I know, I know," he says, "I promise I won't be a burden. But she needs to see me—*really* see me, to understand that Ruby can help them. I want to be part of this. I think I have to be. It's going to be hard enough for the Reds to understand what's happening to them—they need to see proof they can get to the other side. I couldn't help them before, but if I can now . . ."

My eyes don't find Lucas's, they drift over to Liam's. I'm not surprised to see the rising wave of emotion that crashes through them, over his face, stealing his breath. Because his brother's dream is here, alive. It has survived death and destruction; it hasn't blown away with the ash that settled after his fire was put out. It will go on.

"Then I'm going, too," Sam says, in a voice that shuts down any kind of argument.

"And me, too."

Because where they go, I will always follow.

I REMEMBER.

There is a secret in the woods, on a small street in a small Virginia town. A town, like so many others, that's waking from the spell of a long sleep.

I think of it every time another kid sits down in front of us, or, if they're too weak to stand, we sit beside them. It's like a charm I wear inside of my heart. Knowing it's there, that it's safe, is enough to beat back the darkness that tries to come sliding back into my heart like a shiver. I think of it every time Ruby goes to work caging the monsters instead of them. I want to tell the men and women in suits and uniforms, the ones who watch us from behind the protective mirrored glass, that the monsters inside us may have teeth, may have claws, but when our monsters stick their heads up and begin to scent the air around them, it's not because they're angry, or out for blood. They are lost, trying to find their way home. They are screaming in pain. And when the pain is silent, when they forget what they've lost, or they touch a memory not tainted by the Trainer's

396

razors, it is the fire that speaks to them, whispering, making hushed promises of relief in smoke and ash. There is a burn mark on their hearts that won't heal, not yet.

There are three facilities, and there are a hundred of us left. The others find this number unbelievable, almost amazing. The word Mia uses is *astonishing*. I don't have the heart to tell them about the graves out back, the ones filled with the Reds who burned out during training and were put down. I know it is the same for the other two facilities without needing to be told—there are too many empty cells, missing kids who singed their walls and floors. I do not tell them the Trainers made us dig the graves, pave over them, for no other given reason than we *needed the exercise*. Instead, I burden one of the men in suits with the weight of it; I want the kids found, what's left of them returned to their families. Buried right and proper like the humans they are. The end of their lives should not be a question mark that lingers in the hearts of the people who loved them.

My facility is the last one we visit after months of healing and reconditioning at the other two. They've brought the Thurmond Reds back here, back to their old cradle, to live again with the younger, unfinished Reds, the ones that weren't broken and rebuilt into loaded guns. Pennsylvania. I lived in Pennsylvania for seven years, and I never knew it.

On our second day here, when Ruby needs to rest, to take time alone to swallow the pain and smoke and claws down to wherever it is that she can lock them inside herself, I wander the halls. The freedom of it—to go through the doors that used to be locked, to take a left turn down a hall instead of a right—makes me feel queasy. I push through the feeling and go looking for my old room.

My cell.

It's at the very end of the hall, a heavy metal door with only a small grate to pass food through. It's already open.

Sammy is inside.

She sits, her back as stiff as armor, on my cot. She stares at the wall that was the beginning and end of my everything for seven years. She sees the dents and clawed scratches I left behind, the evidence of cruelty, when I had to pretend to be as damaged and tortured as the others; and then from when I was brought back for reprogramming, when I was sure she was dead and I had killed her. There's a gap in my memory, from when I came back here to when I woke up on the sofa of our old house, and no one seems all that eager to fill it, least of all Mia and Sam.

I hesitate in the door, watching her. She sees the last piece of me I haven't already given her, and she doesn't turn away from it. And it's only then that I feel it: that heady, quick freedom that slices through me to the old pain at my core.

I sit beside her, and it is a small miracle, it is something I will never take for granted, that she leans her head against my shoulder. Her hand finds mine. I let the soft warmth of her skin melt into the fire that burns beneath mine.

"Tell me a story," she whispers.

No more stories. No more fairy tales.

"I love you." It is our beginning, our middle, and one day—please God, a long way away from here—our end. And it is the truth.

I only want the truth.

I want the future.

If I craft words, if I imagine a new world into being, I want it to be the one that we live in—me, Sammy, Mia, our friends.

My sister asks me why *that* story, why the monster? I tell her because no matter what they made me, no matter how far they dragged me away from home, how ugly they made me, some part of me always knew Sam and Mia would find me. I don't know if that's the truth, if we're all just lucky as hell, but I want to believe it is.

There are hundreds, maybe even thousands, of kids who need to be found, too; who need us to rewrite the endings the world tried to give them. We talk about it, me and the others, late at night after our military escorts bring us back to a hotel or safe house to sleep. I think that is our future—how we'll pass our days. We are a unit now. Somehow, impossibly, we three—the ones born in Greenwood—have been absorbed into a group that fiercely protects each other, that closes ranks when the world closes in.

We will hunt the snatchers, search for the kids never sent to camps, track down the runaways who couldn't readjust to life on the outside. If these suits won't give us permission, then we won't ask for it. We will *go*.

We will not let them force us into the procedure.

We will not let them create boundaries, carve out stretches of empty land where they can install more barbed wire fences and designate it as *home.*

My home is here. Mia's laughter and the fireworks of her temper. The laughter of our friends. Sam's thick honey hair falling around us, her warm breath on my neck as I hold her. When we left the house, Dad said something to me that I'm only now understanding, that home is wherever there's love; that as long as we're together, we carry it with us. It will grow as we do.

It will grow as we bring others in, as we bring the lost ones together again, gather up the embers scattered from the same fire. One day, we will ignite and create a blaze that no one can put out, ignore, hurt. We will move forward as one, and in time, rise like sparks beyond the night.

But there is a secret in the woods, a place where old dreams still live.

It's a place that has to be guarded. Protected.

But they will never take it. They can't. It is ours forever.

It is there, waiting for new dreamers to fill its walls with stories; and maybe one day, they will.

But we will always know the way back.

We will always know where to find it.

ACKNOWLEDGMENTS

THANKS FIRST AND FOREMOST TO THE WONDERFUL team at Hyperion, in particular Emily Meehan and Laura Schreiber, who not only helped me shape these stories, but gave me the encouragement I needed to step away from Ruby's point of view and really play in the world. I also would like to thank Seale Ballenger, Stephanie Lurie, Dina Sherman, Marci Senders, Holly Nagel, Elke Villa, Andrew Sansone, and everyone who ever had a hand in helping these stories find their readers—and, of course, for all of the kindness you've shown me over nearly five years of working together.

As per usual, I have to thank Anna Jarzab for her support and feedback on so many early drafts—couldn't do it without you, pal. Thanks for helping me look good!

Merrilee Heifetz is a queen among agents, an actual gem, and I'm so grateful to have both her and Sarah Nagel looking out for me every day.

Mom, Steph, Daniel . . . I hope you don't need me to write it in a book, but thank you for your love and support through thick and thin.

And, finally, to the readers who have been asking me for a print novella bind-up for years (and, well, to readers in general): thank you so much for keeping this story, and these characters, alive in your hearts.

Don't miss a sneak peek at
The Darkest Legacy, the brand-new
novel in the Darkest Minds series.

ZU

The blood wouldn't wash out.

It ran red, red, red, down over my hands, curling around the bruises on my wrists and over the scabs on my knuckles. The water pouring from the faucet, hot enough to steam the mirror, should have diluted the blood to pale pink and then to clear nothing. But it just—wouldn't stop. I watched the dried stains on my skin become fresh again, blooming from a rusted brown to a sickening crimson. Snaking lines of it ran down the basin while the drain struggled to drink it all up.

The darkness of the tight room crept up on me, feathering the edges of my vision. I fixed my eyes on the dried flakes of blood stuck like loose tea leaves to the porcelain.

Hurry up, I ordered myself. *They're waiting on you.*

Blackness burst in my vision as my knees bobbed and the world tilted sharply down. Somehow, I caught the smooth edge of the sink, and had just enough strength left in my arms to stay upright. The caulk that held the fixture to the wall cracked with my added weight, groaning out a warning.

Hurry up, hurry up, hurry—

One by one, I pulled at the spots where the blood had dried my blouse against my skin, choking on the bile rising in my throat, at the sound it made. The pipes hidden in the walls shuddered, keeping time with my pulse.

"Stop it." The whisper disappeared into the steam. I sucked in a shaking breath. Someone had recently left cigarette butts in the trash can at my feet. Their stale smell grew worse the longer I stood there, but it was a welcome change from the perfume of coppery blood I'd been wearing.

One last metallic *clang* reverberated through the sink and up my arms. The porcelain shivered, then stilled. The pipes went silent.

Shit— I looked around, hands searching along the countertop for something to collect the remaining water in.

"No, no, no—come *on*—"

Those timers—those stupid timers measuring out everyone's exact supply of clean water, not leaving a single drop to waste. I needed this. Just this once, I needed them to bend the rules for me. The blood, it was on my tongue and teeth and coating my throat. Every swallow brought the metallic tang deeper into me. I needed to get myself clean—

With one last dull beat from the pipes, the water trickled to a thin stream. I picked up the hand towel, stiff from being bleached too many times, and shoved it under the faucet to let it absorb the last few drops.

I clenched my aching jaw and leaned forward unsteadily, bracing my hip against the sink. After wiping a stroke of the condensation off the mirror, I used the damp towel to dab at the scab on my lower lip, where it had split and swollen.

My eyes slid down the surface of the mirror, fixing on the red crescent moons packed beneath the nails that hadn't torn off completely, showing where the pale, pretty polish had chipped.

I couldn't stand to look at the girl—the creature—in the mirror. But I couldn't look away, either.

Not until the clump of hair landed with a wet slap against the sink.

The cheap fluorescent light fixture buzzed, flaring dangerously bright. It fed the snarling static trapped inside my skull. I couldn't understand what I was seeing. The jagged piece of flesh. The shape of the strands curling against the wet porcelain.

Not long black hair.

Blond. Short.

Not mine.

I opened my mouth, but the sob, the scream, locked in my throat. My whole body heaved as I frantically twisted the faucets on and off, trying to wash away the evidence, the violence.

"Oh my God, oh my God . . ."

I threw the wet towel down into the empty sink, whirling toward the toilet and dropping onto my knees. My stomach churned and my throat ached. Nothing came up, of course. I hadn't eaten in days.

I tucked my legs under me on the cool tile, reaching up to work my shaking hands through my hair, yanking at each sticky knot.

This wasn't working— I needed— I clawed my way up off the ground, reaching for the towel I'd abandoned in the sink. I swiped at my hair, trying to rub it clean, as the bathroom swung around me.

Not again, I thought. I closed my eyes, but all I saw was another place, another burning wave of light and heat. I threw out my hand, catching the empty towel rod and using it as one last anchor.

As I touched the thin metal, a sharp snap of static passed up my arm, prickling each individual hair. By the time it had raced up the back of my neck, a fissure of power had already gathered at the base of my skull. Behind my closed eyelids, the bathroom's light flickered again, and I knew I should let go.

But I didn't.

The electric current moving inside the walls had found me as much as I'd found it. I threaded the power forward, melting the protective covering around the lines, until it reached the towel bar and wove in bright, crackling ribbons around it. My fingers curled tighter.

It had been so long since I'd pulled on this silver thread in my mind, coaxed it across my nerves, fanning the sensation out through the thousands of sparkling nerve pathways in my body. I hadn't dared to try, not with the eyes on me—not until a few days ago. There were consequences to my power. I knew that now.

The blue-white heat, like the heart of a flame, burned away the last of the dark thoughts in my mind. I clung to the feeling of familiarity racing through me like unstoppable lightning. Inside the walls, the wires hummed in acknowledgment.

I can still control this, I thought again. In that moment, I hadn't been frightened, or even angry. I hadn't lost control.

It hadn't been my fault.

The smell of smoldering drywall finally forced me to release my grip on the bar. The charge I'd drawn out from the wiring had left dark scorch marks across the dingy floral wallpaper. I pressed my hand against them, directing the power out of the wires there, cooling the fires before they could fully ignite the insulation.

Beyond the bathroom door, the insensible murmuring of the television cut off, only to snap back on a second later.

I can control this.

"Suzume?"

In the few days I'd known Roman, his quiet, almost unnervingly calm voice had only broken a few times—in anger, in concern, in warning. But there was an edge to it now that I didn't recognize. Almost as if, for once, he'd let fear shape my name.

"You need to come see this," he called. *"Right now."*

I stripped off my ruined blouse and threw it into the trash can, then wiped my face one last time with the soiled towel before tossing that in, too.

My tank top wasn't as tattered or stained, but it did nothing to protect me from the chill of the motel room's window AC unit. I limped forward on my broken heels, well aware that the split up the back seam of my skirt was growing with each step. There hadn't been time to ditch our clothes and find something more suitable for traveling. In a way, it felt right to look as wrecked as I felt.

"What is it?" I croaked out.

Roman stood directly in front of the TV, his dark hair falling across his forehead. His T-shirt was ripped at the collar, exposing an ugly bruise at his shoulder that stretched down over the sliver of chest that was visible through it. Seeing him covered in a caked-on shell of dust and dried blood made me burn hot with embarrassment and regret that I'd wasted the water on myself.

If he noticed the bad state he was in, he'd clearly decided it didn't matter. Instead, Roman was in his usual pose: his hand clenched into a fist, his knuckles resting against his mouth, his brows drawn together in thought.

How weird that after only a few days the sight of him thinking, considering, planning was actually reassuring. One steady thing in this mess, at least.

He didn't answer. Neither did Priyanka from where she sat on the bed, staring at the television screen. She was in far worse shape than either of us, and it only doubled my shame over the wasted water.

In her hand was a bunched-up pillowcase she'd stripped and pressed to the gushing cut she'd reopened over her left eye. Blood soaked into the fabric of her yellow dress, mixing into the older stains of sweat and what had to be gasoline. It could have been where I was standing, or the way her rich brown skin had paled somewhat with blood loss, but for the first time, I saw the faded outline of a star tattoo on the inside of her right wrist.

"Just . . . watch," Roman said tightly, nodding toward the screen.

The newscaster was a middle-aged blond woman wearing a bright pink dress that clashed with her look of severe concern. "Investigators are combing the scene of the incident, and the search is still on for the person responsible for the deaths of seven people. The victims are slowly being identified—"

The victims. The dead.

The static was back, pouring through my ears. Out of the corner of my eye, I saw Roman turn for my reaction, his ice-blue gaze never wavering, even as the screen began to click on and off, matching the pulse beating at my wrists and the base of my throat.

On the screen, my own face stared back at me.

"—though investigators are still searching for a motivation, they believe Suzume Kimura, one of the interim president's most popular surrogates, to have been recently radicalized by the Psion Ring—"

The words wrapped around my lungs, squeezing the air from them.

No . . . *no*. This wasn't right. The words drifting along the bottom of the screen, the angle of the footage they kept playing over and over again—this wasn't right. None of this was right.

The dead.

"I need the burner," I choked out.

I did this.

"My burner?" Priyanka said. "Think again, doll. It's the only one—"

The dead. All those people . . .

Roman turned, stalking over to where the other teen had dumped her stolen goods on the room's desk.

No. I can control it. It wasn't me. "Come on," Priyanka grumbled. "This is ridiculous. You know I could just—"

I can control it, I thought again, curling my hands into fists. Outside of the motel, the power lines whispered back to me, hissing their agreement.

I didn't kill those people. I needed to talk to someone who would believe me—who could fight for me.

"You *won't*," Roman said sharply to her before passing the old flip phone to me. "This better be someone you trust with your life."

I only knew three numbers off the top of my head without the crutch of my cell phone's contacts list, and only one of those was likely to answer on the first ring. My hands shook so badly, I had to enter it twice, squinting at the small black-and-white display, before I hit CALL.

I turned my back on Roman's glare at Priyanka and her furious look in response. Their uncertainty was bad enough; I didn't want them to see mine.

The phone only rang once before it was picked up and a breathless voice said, "Hello, this is Charles—"

The words burst out of me. "It's not true—what they're saying. It didn't happen like that! The video makes it seem like—"

"Suzume?" Chubs interrupted. "Where are you? Are you okay?"

Priyanka made a *cut* motion with her hands. "You called one of your government buddies? Are you really this brainwashed? They're tracking your call!"

"I know," I snapped back at her. There were bugs on all of our work phones. At least this way, there would be an official recording of my side of the story, for whatever good it would do.

The risks were real, but Chubs would have some kind of plan by now about how to handle this. He'd know who I should talk to and what I needed to say. Right then, I could picture him in his office in DC so clearly, flanked by that enormous window and the view of the newly finished Capitol building, the list in front of him.

I could see other things, too. The cameras installed in the ceiling monitoring his every move. The tracking device he wore as a watch. The security detail outside his door.

The years of saying yes, okay, all right, all sped forward, slamming into me now. I almost couldn't breathe from the pressure—the knowing of how quickly every small agreement had added up to this moment.

"Who are you talking to?" he asked sharply. "Where are you?"

A twinge of some ugly feeling planted itself at the base of my skull and took root. The words poured out, and as much as I tried to slow them, they came out nonsensical. "Tell them that I didn't do it. He tried to— Men grabbed me before I could get away—I don't know how. It was an accident—self-defense."

But I remembered Roman's voice, the way he'd spoken so softly in the uncertain darkness they'd kept us in: *For us, there is no such thing as self-defense.*

The truth of it crystallized around me like ice, freezing the explanation in my throat. Legally, I couldn't claim it. No one like us could. Some part of me had recognized the potential problems with that government order last year, when they'd issued it, but it had felt so far away—so reasonable.

As Psi, we could harness our abilities like weapons, drawing out the deadly sides to them. The balance of power between a Psi and an NP, non-Psi, in any given situation would always be unequal. The government had enacted laws to prevent us from being targeted or hunted by anyone. We had special protections. It was only right the others had certain legal protections, too.

After all, hadn't I seen it myself? Not every Psi had good intentions, and the fury at the way we'd been treated in the past was never in short supply.

Every day, we lived at that crumbling edge of cooperation with the interim government. The only choice was to work together, because the other option was no option at all. We couldn't let things spiral into chaos again. That would finally force the government's hand, and the cure would no longer be a choice. That involuntary cure was the marker that things had gone too far—that was the line we had all agreed upon, years ago. It hadn't come to that.

Yet.

My pulse fluttered painfully fast at the silence that followed.

"Hello?" The word ached in my throat. "Are you still there?"

Chubs was so calm, the order so crisp: "You need to drive to the nearest police station or zone checkpoint and turn yourself in. Let them put you in restraints so they know you won't hurt them."

"What?"

He wanted me to . . .

My whole body, my whole soul, recoiled at the thought of turning myself over to be handcuffed and led away. This didn't make sense. He knew what it felt like to be trapped behind barbed wire, at the mercy of guards and soldiers who hated and feared us. He'd promised—they'd all promised—that we would never have to go back to that, no matter what.

The plastic cracked under the force of my grip.

They're not going to take me.

"This is a serious situation," he said, carefully crafting each word. "It's very important that you listen to exactly what I'm telling you—"

They're not going to take me ever again.

"No! What the hell is wrong with you? I want to talk to Vi—where is she? Put her on the phone—call her in, I don't care!"

"She's out on a mission, you know that," Chubs said. "Turn yourself in. That's all you have to do, Suzume. Either stay where you are and tell me where that is, or find the road to a safe place where you can turn yourself in."

My hand was icy as I pressed it against my eyes.

"Did you hear me?" Chubs said, in that measured tone he'd adopted for every council session he was asked to speak at.

That was our lives now, wasn't it? Even. Steady. Accepting. Never allowed to get mad, never allowed to threaten, let alone be perceived as a threat.

For the first time in my life, in all the years I'd known and loved him, I hated Charles Meriwether.

But in the next heartbeat, through the anger buzzing in my head, I heard him. Really heard him.

Find the road.

A small static shock traveled from Roman's fingertips to my shoulder as he brushed it. I glanced back, taking in his apologetic look as he pointed to the phone. Behind him, Priyanka moved her pillowcase over her mouth to stifle her scream of frustration.

"Okay," I said. "All right. I got it."

"You do?" he said, this time with some urgency.

He was right. I didn't know why I hadn't thought of it before now. I wasn't so far away from the place he was hinting at; if I could get past the cameras and drones monitoring the highways, it would only take half a day to get there. Maybe less.

"Yeah. Okay," I told him. "I hear you."

Will you meet me there? The words slipped through my mind, each quieter and smaller than the next. *Do you even care?*

Before either of us could say anything else, I hit END on the call.

Priyanka unfolded her long legs and practically leaped off the bed to take the phone out of my hand. She broke it into little pieces, taking out the battery and SIM card, all the while muttering, "Using my phone to call the damn government. You don't just need help, you need full-on reprogramming. *Deprogramming.*"

"Who was that?" Roman asked, crossing his arms over his chest. "What's 'okay'?"

The last few days had threatened to kill me in a thousand different ways, with a thousand different cuts. But if there was one thing I knew how to do, it was push down the fear and smother it just long enough to keep surviving.

I could wash away the blood. I could prove my innocence and find whoever was responsible for stealing the lives of all those people. This was the first step. The others would fall into place once I was past it.

In darkness, you only needed to see just as far as your headlights extended. As long as you kept going, it was enough.

"I need a car," I told them calmly. I moved toward the motel's windows, pulling back the curtain to survey our options. I couldn't use the one we'd stolen before. It would be reported by now, and, in any case, it was almost out of gas.

"*You* need a car," Priyanka began, arching a brow, "or *we* need a car?"

I turned toward them again, pressing a hand against my collarbone. My fingers traced the jagged edge of a new scab there.

Maybe this was the reason I hadn't let myself consider my options fully, and why I hadn't gone straight there—from the moment everything had exploded, there hadn't been a second I'd been without the two of them. This place was secret for a reason, even from most Psi.

"You aren't involved," I said. "They don't have your faces or your names."

"Yeah, but for how long?" Priyanka towered over me in height, and part of me envied how forceful and confident it made her seem, even when her boisterous voice became a whisper. Even now, looking like she'd been dragged beneath a car.

Which . . .

I grimaced. She basically had.

"These people—whoever did this—clearly know what they're doing." Priyanka gestured toward the television, and, with a look, I overloaded its circuits with power. The bloodied images flashed off with a biting *snap*.

"Okay, yes, that was very dramatic and a waste of a perfectly good TV that we could have sold for gas money, but you do you, girl," Priyanka said. "The problem is, I didn't hear any kind of counterargument."

The fact that she thought I had to argue anything with her was the problem.

"I'll be fine," I insisted. "You're free to get out of here and do what you need to do."

Roman frowned. He raised one hand toward me that fell away before it could touch my shoulder. "Think it through. Just from a reasoning standpoint. I know you don't trust us yet, and that's fine—"

"That's *not* fine," Priyanka said. "We're awesome and we haven't tried to kill you once. What more do you want from us?"

"—but I know you've realized it, too. If a group could plan something like that, if they could take us, it's only a matter of time before they figure out how to track us down. Priya and I escaped with you. They're going to assume we're together no matter what, at least initially, because there's safety in numbers."

"Isn't that all the more reason to scatter?" I pushed back. "To throw them off and force *them* to split up as well?"

Roman opened his mouth, but Priyanka, as always, was faster. "This is a guy who plans his breakfast with ruthless detail and eats it in the most beneficial order to aid digestion," she said. "Don't try to out-logic him."

His ears went red. He gave her a long, meaningful look that Priyanka answered with a sweet, serene smile.

The easiness of the exchange, the way the words flowed between them without needing to be voiced at all, snapped against my heart, stinging.

"You may have a point," Roman said, his low, rumbling voice at odds with the flush that had crept into his cheeks. "But there are benefits to staying together, at least until we figure out what actually happened. Think about it: two more sets of eyes to keep watch. Two more sets of hands to find food."

"Two more mouths to feed," I continued. "Two more opportunities to be spotted."

"As if you know the first thing about roughing it." Priyanka rolled her eyes. "Did you read about it once in your special reports? Have a kid come up onstage during one of your fancy little speeches and tell their sob story? Did you cry a few crocodile tears in front of the cameras to really sell it?"

Every muscle in my body tightened to the point of pain. I could barely get the words out. "I don't need anyone to tell me a damn thing about it. I know what it feels like to be—"

"I wasn't aware government robots could be programmed to have feelings," she cut in.

I sucked in a sharp breath, a pure, unflinching anger gathering at the center of my chest. It was a fire that fed itself. It rose up through my throat, burning my face, until I was sure I could breathe it out and incinerate the room around us faster than any Red.

"*Priya.*" Roman's voice was soft, but like the edge of the sharpest blade, he didn't need power or anger behind the words to cut deep. "Enough."

The mocking twist of her mouth fell away. Her eyes slid to the side, avoiding both of us.

I turned to look the other way, letting that same anger and pain turn to steam. Letting it drift out of me with my next long breath.

"You don't know the first thing about me," I told her, fighting to keep the words even.

The girl took a deep breath of her own, pushing her long hair back over her shoulders.

"Look. I'm *trying* to find a reason to like you—"

My jaw was so tight, I could barely get the words out. "The feeling is mutual."

She narrowed her eyes. "Wow, I was just about to be nice and tell you that despite all of that shit, I thought your shoes were cute before you broke your heel kicking that guy's face in, and that I liked your hair before the other guy tried to rip it out of your scalp—"

"I no longer understand this conversation," Roman interrupted, looking between us. "But we need to wrap this up and head out. Preferably in the next thirty seconds."

I blew out a loud breath through my nose, trying to quickly piece together an argument. But . . . they weren't wrong. When you were being hunted, it was better to stay within the protection of a group, have extra eyes to keep watch, than to try to navigate through danger alone.

I'd learned that the hard way, too.

Priyanka's initial question hadn't really been a question at all, but an offer. *Do you need our help?*

I didn't need it, but I wanted it. As selfish as it was to bring them to that hidden place and risk them exposing its existence, I wanted them to stay where I could make sure, if nothing else, they were safe.

"All right," I told them. "*We* need a car. But I'm driving."

Besides, where we were headed there was someone who could take care of any unwanted memories they might make—or at least guarantee they'd never remember the way back.

ONE

Three Days Ago

THE WHEELS DIDN'T STOP TURNING ON THE ROAD. NOT for gas, not at signs or signals.

A glare of sunlight burst through the window beside me, washing out the words I was pretending to read on my cell phone's screen. A deep grumble from the engine and the renewed stench of gasoline signaled we were slowly picking up speed. The grind of the highway beneath us still wasn't loud enough to drown out the police escorts' sirens or the chanting from the sign-wavers lined up along the highway.

I refused to turn and look at them. The tinted windows cast them all in shadow, one dark haze of hatred in my peripheral vision: the older men with their guns, the women clutching hateful messages between their hands, the clusters of families with bullhorns and their cleverly awful slogans.

The police cars' lights flashed in time with their chants.

"God!"

Red.

"Hates!"

Blue.

"Freaks!"

"Well," Mel said. "No one could ever accuse them of being original."

"Sorry, ladies," Agent Cooper called back from the driver's seat. "It'll just be another ten minutes. I can turn up the music if you want?"

"That's okay," I said, setting my phone down on my lap and folding my hands on top of it. "Really. It's fine."

The machine-gun-fire typing from the seat beside me suddenly stopped. Mel looked up from the laptop balanced on her knees, a deep frown on her face. "Don't these people have anything better to do with their lives? Actually, on second thought, maybe I should send a job recruiter down here and see if we can't flip this around—that would be quite the narrative, wouldn't it? From hater to . . . humbled. No, that's not right—" She reached for where she had left her phone on the seat between us and spoke into it. "Make a note: protester reform program."

As I'd learned—and apparently Agents Cooper and Martinez had, too—it was best just to let Mel talk herself through to a solution rather than try to offer suggestions.

The car snarled and shuddered as it hit a bad patch of highway, jolting the thought out of my head.

Don't be a coward, I told myself. There was nothing any of them could do to me now, not while I was surrounded on all sides by bulletproof glass, FBI agents, and police. If we kept looking away, they would never think we were strong enough to meet them head-on.

With a hard swallow, I turned to gaze out my window. The day's breeze tugged at the construction flags across the divide between the northbound and southbound lanes. They were the same shade of orange as the barriers protecting the workers as they went about the business of pouring new asphalt.

A few of the men and women stopped mid-task and leaned against the concrete median to watch our motorcade pass; some gave big, cheerful waves. My hand rose to return the gesture instinctively, a small smile on my lips. A heartbeat later, just long enough to be embarrassed by it, I remembered they couldn't see me.

Behind the thin barrier of dark glass, I was invisible.

The window was warm as I pressed my fingers to it until the tips turned white, hoping the workers could see them through its tint like five small stars. Eventually, just like everyone else, they blurred away with distance.

Setting America Back on the Right Route! had been one of Mel's first publicity projects for the interim government established and monitored by the United Nations—a way to advertise new infrastructure jobs while also promising that roads would stop buckling under people's wheels, the gas ration would, eventually, be coming to an end, and deadly bridge collapses like the one in Wisconsin wouldn't happen anywhere else—thanks to reinforcements from new American steel. The proof of its success ran on newscasts every night: the unemployment rate was falling as steadily as the birth rate was beginning to rise.

Numbers were simple, real symbols that people could latch on to, holding them up like trophies. But there was no way they could capture the *feeling* of the last few years, that all-encompassing sensation that life was rolling out in front of us again, swelling to fill those empty spaces the lost children had left behind.

The same populations that had shifted to the big cities in desperate search of work were now slowly making their way back to the small towns and suburbs they had abandoned. Restaurants opened. Cars pulled in and out of gas stations on their assigned days. Trucks cruised down the highways that had been patched and knitted together again. People walked around in newly landscaped parks. Movie theaters began to shift away from showing old films to showing new ones. They arrived tentatively, slowly— like the first few people on an otherwise empty dance floor, waiting to see if anyone else would join them in search of fun.

It was *life*.

Just five years ago, driving these same highways, the towns and cities we'd slipped in and out of had practically ached with their emptiness. Parks, homes, businesses, schools, everything had been hollowed out and recast in miserable, dirt-stained gray. Neglected or abandoned like memories left to fade into nothing.

Somehow, we'd managed to shock a pulse back into the country. It fluttered and raced in moments of darkness and frustration, but after everything we'd accomplished over the last five years, it was steady. Mostly.

The truth was, it had less to do with me than it did the others working day in and day out. I hadn't been allowed to do much of anything until I'd finished the new mandatory school requirements. President Cruz had said it was important for other Psi to see me do it, to demonstrate there were no exceptions. But it had been agonizing to wait and wait and wait, doing the homework of simple math problems Chubs had taught me years ago in the back of a beat-up minivan, studying history that felt like it had happened to a completely different country, and memorizing the new Psi laws.

And the whole time, Chubs and Vida had been allowed to work. They'd moved from one closed door to the next, disappearing into meetings and missions, until I was sure I'd lose track of them completely, or be locked out forever.

But it was only a matter of time before I caught up to them. As long as I kept pulling my weight and proving myself useful, traveling where they sent me, saying the words they wanted me to say, I'd keep moving forward, too. And someone had clearly seen my potential, because Mel had been reassigned to me, and we'd been traveling together ever since.

"The problem is that we have to announce road closures days ahead of time," Agent Cooper explained. "They want us to alert the cities to secure the routes, but it's like a signal fire to these folks. It doesn't matter if it's you or someone else from the government. I'm sure their signs all have some variation of *America First, America Only*, or *something-something take back the country!* written on the back in case they need to do a quick change."

He was dead-on. A few people initially had signs that screamed in bold, jagged marker strokes about *They've stolen our country!* and *We stand united in the face of tyranny!* They'd flipped them around to some variation of FREEDOM NOT FREAKDOM when they saw none of the motorcade's cars had United Nations flags to indicate a politician or military personnel. Process of elimination had left just little old me.

I leaned my temple back against the window. As we passed, a woman beat a wooden spoon against a cowbell, leading her section of protestors, six people deep in places, into a stirring rendition of *"Unnatural, unwanted, we remain undaunted!"*

"Oh God," Agent Martinez said, leaning forward to look up through the front window. "What now?"

The banner dropped over the pedestrian bridge ahead of us, unfurling like an old flag. The two grown men holding it, both wearing an all-too-familiar stripe of white stars on a blue bandana tied around their upper arms, sent a chill curling down my spine.

LIFE, LIBERTY, AND THE PURSUIT OF FREAKS FOREVER
IT'S ONLY MURDER IF THEY'RE HUMAN

"Charming," Mel said, rolling her dark eyes as we passed under the bridge.

I rubbed a finger over my top lip, then picked up my phone again, tapping through to the only text thread. I typed, **Are you still coming today?**

I didn't take my gaze away from my phone's screen, waiting for the chat bubble to appear with a response. Out of the corner of my eye, I caught the reflection of Agent Cooper's mirrored sunglasses as they looked up into the rearview mirror, watching me.

Gauging me.

He didn't have to worry. There would be no crying. No emotional mess to mop up. Half the poison they churned out with their signs, their radio shows, their news programs were lies, and the rest of it was nonsensical. *Freak* was an old insult—sometimes you heard a nasty word so often it just completely lost its teeth. That, or I guess your skin eventually could grow too strong, too thick to cut. My heart didn't bruise the way it used to—they were way too late to get in that particular blow.

I swallowed the thickness in my throat, pressing my fingers tight around the phone's case.

If they're human . . .

I cleared my throat again, looking out my window. The group

of protestors was thinner on the ground, but growing again in number as we left the construction zone. "Everyone's entitled to stupidity, but they really abuse the privilege, don't they?"

Mel gave a weak laugh at that, reaching over to smooth back a strand of my hair that had come loose from its elegant twist.

"Still, better call it in," Agent Cooper said, taking his hand off the wheel to nudge Agent Martinez. "These Liberty Watch types are disgusting. We should make an example of them now before they start getting too confident."

"It's not a direct threat," Agent Martinez shot back to the older agent. "There's nothing the agency can do about it."

"We need a record," Agent Cooper insisted. "They need material to build an actual case against them."

"Actually," Mel cut in, reaching back to adjust the pins she'd used to help secure her locs into a topknot, "it's probably best not to give that fire any air. It's what they want—we shut them down and they get to prove their narrative about what tyrants we are by doing away with freedom of speech. *Our* job is to tell the truth about the Psi, and the polls show that we've been hitting that ball out of the park. The people are on *our* side."

That was a small comfort, but it did help. Sometimes it felt like I was talking to everyone and no one at the same time. I never saw the words leaving my mouth reflected on the audience's faces, good or bad. They just absorbed them. Whether or not they processed them was another question.

I glanced down at my phone again.

No response.

"I should tell you before we get to the venue," Mel said, ducking under her seat belt to turn more fully toward me. "I received an e-mail from Interim President Cruz's chief of staff this morning saying that they're going to be sending along some new language for your speech. I'm not sure when it's going to come in, so I might need to add it directly to the teleprompter."

I didn't care if my sigh sounded petulant. They had to realize how annoying it was. "Aren't they done tweaking it yet?"

I never had the time to practice the updated speeches, to get the adjustments straight so that the delivery was smooth and even. "What kind of new language is it anyway?"

Mel slid her laptop back into her satchel. The lustrous leather case tried to spit up a few of the overstuffed folders inside of it to make room. "Just some finessed points from the sound of it. I know you could recite the speech backward and half-asleep at this point, but just keep an eye on the teleprompter."

I'd repeated different versions of the same speech a hundred times, in a hundred places, about the nature of fear, and how the Psi had reentered society with only a few ripples. But the added responsibility was a good sign that they trusted me more and more. Maybe they'd even add dates and use me again in the fall, for the big election.

"All right," I said. "But—"

It was the suddenness of the movement that caught my eye, more than the woman herself. She pulled away from the cluster of sign-wavers and bullhorn-shouters lined up along the shoulder to our left. Long, stringy gray hair, a faded floral shirt, a blue scrap of fabric decorated with white stars tied around her arm. She could have been anyone's grandmother—if it hadn't been for the flaming bottle she clutched in her hand.

I knew we were speeding, that there was no way it could actually be happening, but time has a way of bending around you when it wants you to see something.

The seconds slowed, ticking in time to each of her running steps. Her lips pulled back, deepening the stark lines of her face, as she held the bottle high over her head and flung it toward the SUV. She shouted something I couldn't hear.

I wondered if she could even see me through the shadowed car window.

The small firebomb hit the cement and billowed up with a loud, sucking gasp. It flared as it devoured the traces of oil and chemicals on the highway, blasting my window with enough heat and pressure for it to crack down the middle with a high, suffering whine.

My seat belt locked against my chest as our car swerved sharply to the right. I craned my neck around, watching the road blaze with a wall of red and gold.

"You guys okay?" Agent Cooper bit out, slamming his foot onto the gas. Mel and I were both thrown back against our seats again. I reached out with one hand, gripping the door to steady myself.

Up ahead, one of the cop cars swerved around and blared its sirens. The crowd of protestors scattered into the woods and fields around them like the cowards they were.

"Holy shit" was Mel's only comment.

Fury stormed through me, twisting my at my insides, clawing at them. I shook with useless adrenaline. That woman—she could have hurt another protestor, Mel, the agents, or one of the police officers. *Killed* them.

Writhing heat gathered in a knot at the back of my skull. It crackled there in warning, desperate to follow the length of my veins, down through my arms, and out the tips of my fingers. A sharp chemical smell burned the inside of my nose.

It would be so easy to get out of the car and find that woman. Grab her by the hair, throw her to the ground, pin her there until one of the officers caught up with us. So easy.

The charge from the car's battery seethed nearby, waiting.

You think that's enough to scare me? You think I haven't had people try to kill me before?

Plenty had tried. A few had come close. I wasn't prey anymore, and I wouldn't let anyone turn me into it again, least of all an elderly woman dabbling in a bit of bomb-making with her unpleasant friends.

A single cooling word got through the scorching tangle of thoughts.

Don't.

I forced myself to release my hold on the door. I clenched and unclenched that hand, trying to work out the tension still there. That would be exactly what they wanted. Get a reaction, prove that we're all monsters waiting for our leashes to snap.

She's not worth it. None of them are.

She wouldn't be the last one to try to hurt me. I accepted that, and was grateful for the protection we all had now. There was no room for ghosts in my life now, whether they were living or dead. Ruby used to say that we'd earned our memories, but we didn't owe them anything beyond their keeping. I guess she'd know better than most.

We were moving forward, and the past was best left to its darkness. Its ashes.

"It's all right," I said, when I trusted my voice to be calm. "It's okay."

"That was the definition of *not okay*," Mel said, her tone brittle.

"I think you have your direct threat," Agent Cooper said to his partner, never taking his eyes off the road.

I flipped my phone over from where I had pressed it against my leg, ignoring the pulse pounding at my temple. Even with its rubber case, the screen flickered as a single lance of electricity crawled out of my finger and danced over it. I dropped it back onto my lap, silently praying for the phone to turn itself back on.

Crap. I hadn't done that in such a long time.

Finally, after another agonizing second, the screen flashed back up again. I swallowed against the dryness in my throat, opening the same text thread as before. My message was still there, still waiting for a response.

"About ten minutes now," Agent Cooper said. "We're almost there."

The phone buzzed in my hand, making me jump. Finally—

I glanced down, fingers flying over the screen to input my password. The thread opened.

Couldn't get away. Sorry. Next time?

"Everything okay?" Mel asked.

The smile I plastered onto my face was so wide, it actually ached. "Yeah. Of course. Just a news alert about today's event. Can we . . . can we go through today's schedule? Make sure I have it down?"

"I'm sure you have it down perfectly, as you always do," Mel said, one brow arching. Still, she reached into her bag and pulled out her folder with the day's date and began to run through the outline, matching hours to actions.

I dropped the phone back into my own bag, trying to find something to ward off the pressure building in my chest. It pushed at my ribs like it could split me open and reveal the raw mess inside.

Maybe I should have responded? Or would I have just bothered him more?

"Nine thirty a.m., the dean will introduce you. . . ."

Next time? I was tempted to take the phone back out and reread Chubs's message, just to make sure I hadn't imagined it.

My mind couldn't stop whispering those two words, wouldn't let go of that question mark—that one small symbol that had never existed between any of us before.

"Nine thirty-five a.m., you'll begin your speech. . . ."

That one small symbol that promised nothing, but said everything.

TWO

Once upon a time, I went months without saying a word. About a year, in fact.

It happened by accident at first—or not by accident, exactly. I still struggle to explain it, to justify why I silenced myself. It was as if the barbed wire that surrounded the rehabilitation camp had cut so deeply the night we escaped, all the words in me had just bled out. I'd been so empty under my skin. So cold. Weak enough for shock to spill in and take over.

The truth was, some things go beyond words: The sound of gunshots thundering through the night. Blood staining the backs of thin uniforms. Kids facedown, slowly buried by the soft snow falling from the dark sky. The feeling of being strangled by your own hope in that second before it escaped the fencing and left you behind to die.

The next few days I was just . . . tired. Unsure. Questions would come at me, and I would nod. Shake my head. It took so much energy. I was afraid of picking the wrong words out of the darkness inside my head. Scared to say something the others, the boys who had saved me, wouldn't like.

I saw the possibility in every second we drove around in the van: I would tell them I was hungry or cold or hurt, and they would decide I was a problem, just like my parents once had. They would leave me on my own just as quickly as they'd decided to take me with them on the run.

But they didn't. And, pretty soon after, I realized that they wouldn't. By then, though, it felt more comfortable to pick up that ratty notebook we shared and carefully choose my words.

The world was spinning out around us, ready to crash down on our heads, and I couldn't do anything about it. I could, however, spell out the exact response I wanted, no mistakes. I could choose when I wanted to say something. I could control that.

The problem was that I kept choosing silence. Over and over again, I let myself fall into the safety of its depths. Painful things could stay buried, never needing to be understood or talked through. The past wouldn't come back to hurt me if I never spoke of it. The memory of snow and blood and screams couldn't rise up and bury me in its freezing pressure, its dark. I wouldn't need to admit to being scared or hungry or exhausted and worry the others. My silence became a kind of shield.

Something I could use to protect myself.

Something I could hide behind.

Five years later, I was known to the world for what I had said, not as the silent little girl with the shaved head and oversize gloves. I appeared on television screens and in front of crowds. She became a ghost, abandoned in the memories I no longer wanted to remember.

Words still seemed to sit a little heavier in my mouth than they did for other people. It was all too easy to slip back into those small, comfortable depths inside of me, where there was always quiet. Especially on days like that one, with the last lick of adrenaline making me antsy to move on to the next event.

The two dozen rows of chairs stretched out across the bright grass slowly went out of focus. People became indistinct shapes, faces expressionless smears of color. I knew when they clapped, simply because the mass of them shifted, the applause rippling out through them like a drop of rain falling into a pool.

I couldn't hear the words of Penn State's steely-haired dean of admissions, only the scratching of my carefully manicured pink nails against the fabric of my pencil skirt. I tapped one high heel down, brought the other up, tapped that down, brought the other up, working off the lingering buzz of nerves from the car ride in.

I closed my eyes against the sunlight, and opened them again when the image of the old woman's snarling face flashed behind them.

The air wept with moisture, so heavy with late-summer heat that we were wrapped in a silky haze. My thick hair rebelled, swelling against the hold of the bobby pins, just at the edge of slipping out of its careful style. A drop of sweat rolled down my spine, gluing my blouse to my skin.

Mel gripped my arm, her nails digging into me. I came back to myself all at once, pushing up onto my feet and letting the world open around me again.

The polite applause wasn't even loud enough to echo back off the columns of the large building behind us. Not a good sign when it came to their interest level, but I could win them over. Being a *freak* meant that people were more than willing to stare at you for a while.

I stepped through the shadow cast by Old Main's clock tower. It spilled down to the right of the podium, over the edge of the stairs leading down to the grassy seating area.

Setting my shoulders back, I licked my teeth to make sure there was no lipstick on them, and lifted my hand in a wave. The dean stood back from the simple wood podium at the edge of the top step. He swept his hands toward it as I approached, inviting me forward with an encouraging smile I forced myself to return.

I didn't need encouragement. This was my job.

The meager applause disappeared beneath the music—some sort of fight song, probably—pouring through the speakers. They'd been positioned on either side of the bottom step, their faces turned toward my audience. While I waited for the words to load on the teleprompter, I cast a quick glance around, making sure to avoid looking directly into any of the news cameras and their gleaming eyes.

There were so many reporters, they almost outnumbered the actual attendees.

Talk about overkill, Mel. . . .

"Good afternoon," I said, my hands curling around the lip of the podium. I hated the way my voice sounded as it blasted out of speakers—like a little girl's. "It's an honor to be here with you today. Thank you, Dean Bishop, for giving me the opportunity to address your incredible new class and inviting me to celebrate the reopening of your illustrious university."

I sincerely doubted there had been any invitations involved— Mel pitched all of these events based on population models and where she thought we would get the most media play. She always seemed to know just the right way to threaten someone to get a *No* magically transformed into an enthusiastic *Yes*.

Every speech was carefully altered at its beginning and end to fit the venue. These slight adjustments were the only variations in the routine. My grip on the podium relaxed as I settled into it. I swept my gaze back and forth, reading the crowd for their reaction, measuring their attention. Beyond the cluster of reporters, all scribbling on notepads or half-hidden by the phones they used to snap photos, there was an array of people, spanning almost the full range of ages.

Parents and other family members filled the very back rows. Farther in were the men and women a decade past what you might expect from typical college freshmen. All of them were trying to recover the educations they'd been forced to abandon when the majority of universities had gone bankrupt at the height of the Psi panic.

Then there were those my age, even a little younger. They sat the closest to the front, their thumb-size buttons visible on their shirts, as they were meant to be at all times. I reached up, absently touching the yellow one that I wore just over my heart.

Many green buttons, fewer blues, and even fewer yellow ones like my own. And, scattered between them all, white.

I glanced down at the podium, pausing my speech for a quick breath.

Blank. The word slipped through my mind, as unwelcome as it was ugly. These were the Psi who had elected—or had parents elect for them—to get the "cure" procedure. Specifically, the ones who had received surgical implants to halt and effectively neuter their brain's access to the abilities IAAN had given them.

"We truly are the lucky ones," I continued. "We have survived the trials that the last decade brought our country, and they have united us in ways that no one could have predicted. Of course, we have all made sacrifices. We have struggled. And from that, we have learned much—including how to trust one another again, and how to believe in the future of this nation."

There was a loud, sharp cough from the far left end of the front row. It was just pointed enough to draw my gaze as I took a quick sip from the sweating water glass that had been left for me.

There were two freshmen sitting just behind the speakers to my right. One, a girl with brown skin, glowing brighter than the sun itself in her yellow silk sundress, had stretched her long legs out in front of her. They were crossed at the ankles, just above her strappy sandals. Her head had lolled to the side, her long ponytail spilling over her shoulder. The metallic-rimmed cat's-eye glasses had dipped down the bridge of her nose—but judging by her even breathing and the way her mouth had fallen slightly open, the heat and I had conspired to soothe her into a nice little nap.

Beside her was a boy, also about my age, more or less. His thick, chestnut-colored hair had been cut short, but not short enough to hide the hint of curl. The dark slashes of his brows framed his ice-blue eyes and were the starkest part of his otherwise clean-shaven, pale face. He met my gaze directly, his unreadable expression never wavering, not until the corners of his mouth tipped down.

I straightened, glancing away. "I realize that much has been asked of my fellow Psi, but we must establish limits on those perceived to be limitless. Society can only function with boundaries and rules, and we must continue to work to find a way back into it—to not press so hard against those markers as to disturb the peace."

The girl could get right up and leave if she was so bored with a talk about her future—but I let myself glance back toward them, just for a second, just to check . . .

I had to look again, this time blinking in disbelief.

No buttons.

Idiots. What was the point of pride when the only trophy they'd get for that small act of rebellion was a tracker locked around their ankles for however many years it would take to prove they wouldn't forget their buttons again?

I shifted my full attention back to the speech just as I entered the homestretch. It was my least favorite part: I'd plead with the Psi for patience with those who feared them, and plead with those who feared them to acknowledge the terror that we had lived in every day since IAAN was first recognized. It didn't feel like a fair comparison, but this had come directly from professionals. What did I know, when it really came down to it?

I stumbled, just that tiny bit, as unfamiliar words loaded on to the screen. "And as we enter this new beginning, I think it has become all the more important to acknowledge the past. We must honor the traditional American way."

It was the new language that Mel had mentioned in the car. The teleprompter slowed, accommodating my unfamiliarity.

"That includes," I read, "honoring our original Constitution, the core foundations of faith, and the requirements of citizenship in our democracy—"

The words rolled forward on the screen, even as they halted in my throat.

TODAY, THE INTERIM GOVERNMENT HAS VOTED ON AND APPROVED A BILL THAT STRIKES PSI-BORN, INCLUDING THOSE OF LEGAL AGE, OFF CURRENT STATE VOTE ROLLS IN ORDER TO TAKE THE NECESSARY TIME TO ASSESS WHETHER OR NOT THEIR UNIQUE EXPERIENCES AND TREATMENTS HAVE RENDERED THEM EMOTIONALLY AND MENTALLY UNFIT TO MAKE SUCH CRUCIAL DECISIONS ABOUT THE DIRECTION OF OUR COUNTRY.

THIS IS ONLY A TEMPORARY MEASURE, AND THE MATTER WILL BE REVISITED FOLLOWING THE ELECTION THIS NOVEMBER, AFTER THE NEW, FULL CONGRESS IS SWORN IN.

A tremor worked its way up through my arms, even as my hands clenched the podium's polished wood. As the silence stretched on, punctuated only by the muffled sigh of the breeze catching the microphone, the audience began to shift in their seats.

Adjusting their weight. Glancing at each other. A woman in the second row finally stopped using her program as a fan, leaning forward to give me a curious look.

That couldn't be right. I wanted to look back at Mel, to signal that the wrong text had been loaded in. Whoever thought this was a funny joke deserved a fist to the throat.

The words scrolled back up, repeating. Insistent.

No—this was . . . The Psi already had stricter ID requirements. We had to wait until we were twenty-one before we could get legal licenses. I was three years away from finally getting mine. I'd had a whole speech about how it would be worth the wait, and how exciting it would be to finally be able to turn in the voter registration form with it. I filled mine out years ago, when Chubs and Vida were doing theirs. I hadn't wanted to be left out.

This must have . . . this had to have slipped by him and the other Psi on Interim President Cruz's council. They were probably already pushing back against it.

Except . . . hadn't Mel said the language had come directly from President Cruz's chief of staff?

This time I did glance back over my shoulder. The crowd began to murmur quietly, clearly wondering what was going on. Mel didn't rise out of her chair, didn't take off her sunglasses. She motioned with her hands, pushing them forward, urging me to turn back around. To keep going.

The boy in the front row narrowed his bright eyes, cocking his head to the side slightly. The way his whole body tensed made me wonder if he'd somehow managed to read the words on the teleprompter, or if he could hear my heart hammering inside of my chest.

Just say it, I thought, watching as the words rewound again, then paused. I'd promised them my voice, for whatever they'd need me to say. This was what I had agreed to, the whole point of coming here.

Just say it.

It would only be temporary. They promised. One election. We could sit out *one* election.

My throat burned the instant before my mouth flooded with bile. The podium trembled under my hands, and I couldn't understand why. Why now—why this announcement, and not any of the others?

Just say it.

The girl, the ghost from the past, was back, her small, gloved hands wrapped around my throat.

I can't. Not this time.

Not *this*.

"Thank you for your time," I choked out, "it was an honor to speak to you today, and I wish you the best as you begin a new chapter of your lives—"

The teleprompter's screen blanked out. A second later, a single line of text appeared.

SOMEONE IS HERE TO KILL YOU.

ALSO BY
ALEXANDRA BRACKEN

THE DARKEST MINDS SERIES

THE PASSENGER SERIES

THE PRINCESS, THE SCOUNDREL,
AND THE FARM BOY (STAR WARS: A NEW HOPE)

THE DREADFUL TALE OF PROSPER REDDING